Anonymous

Essays: Educational and historic

X-rays on some important episodes

Anonymous

Essays: Educational and historic
X-rays on some important episodes

ISBN/EAN: 9783337282226

Printed in Europe, USA, Canada, Australia, Japan

Cover: Foto ©Andreas Hilbeck / pixelio.de

More available books at **www.hansebooks.com**

ESSAYS

EDUCATIONAL
and HISTORIC or

X-RAYS

ON SOME
IMPORTANT EPISODES

By a Member of the
ORDER OF MERCY ✠

Author of " Leaves from the Annals of
the Sisters of Mercy"
" Life of Catherine McAuley"
" Life of St. Alphonsus"
" Life of Von Clement M. Hofbauer"
" Glimpses of Pleasant Homes"
" Happy Hours of Childhood"
"Angel Dreams," " By the Seaside," etc.

NEW YORK
O'Shea & Co.
19 BARCLAY ST.
1899

TO THE
REVERED AND BELOVED MEMORY
OF MY
DEARLY LOVED FRIEND
AND SISTER IN RELIGION, REV. MOTHER
M. BAPTIST RUSSELL,
LATE SUPERIOR OF THE SISTERS OF MERCY,
SAN FRANCISCO,
I DEDICATE THIS WORK.

CONTENTS

PREFACE

IN compliance with the wishes of many, the following papers have been republished from the *American Catholic Quarterly Review*, the *Irish Monthly*, and the New Orleans *Daily Item*, proper authorization for that purpose having been received.

CONVENT OF MERCY,
MOBILE, ALA.
Feast of Our Lady ad Nives, 1899.

EDUCATION IN LOUISIANA IN FRENCH
COLONIAL DAYS

I

AST winter the Louisiana Education Society asked for original essays on educational matters, wishing to obtain "the most practical thought and careful thinking in this line."

The desire to receive practical information on this vitally important subject is a hopeful sign. For as soon as people say there is no more for them to learn, progress is at an end; or should any avenues of progress remain open to them, it will be of that species which a humorous native of a certain island, not unknown in song and story, graphically described as "progress to the rear."

Ignorance has been called the foundation of knowledge. An ignorant man has one advantage over an ill-educated man: he has nothing to unlearn. In a similar sense repentance may be the foundation of virtue; there is hope for the evil-doer who admits he has done wrong; while little good is expected of one who argues himself into the belief that wrong is right, and that there is nothing in him susceptible of improvement.

A philosopher of the Middle Ages reproached a conceited brother of the same craft with being unable

9

to say "*nescio.*" The reproach of St. Bernard to Abélard can scarcely be made to the above body, for if its members had seen no room for improvement in the methods employed with their sanction, they would not have sought to obtain "more practical thought in this line."

But none of our contemporary educators appear to have sought any light on early education in Louisiana. Perhaps they deem history a blank as to its educational aspect in Colonial and early American times. The itinerant lecturer, like the schoolmaster, has been "abroad" during the pleasant winters of Louisiana, and the business of this functionary seems to be to tell the rising generation that, despite the statesmanship, military renown, and philanthropy of the past, the light that was in these regions was darkness. Why? Because there were no godless schools. The South was slow to introduce a system which came when Colonial days were over, and which experience has proved to be subversive of religion and morality, as indeed its originators intended it should be. (See Brownson's "Convert," chapters 7 and 8.)

We will endeavor to show some deeds of our predecessors "in this line," which perhaps may awaken in a few a desire to know more of what was undertaken in the distant past, in the face of tremendous obstacles, that in this respect a tardy justice may be done to the "brave days of old." And some who imagine that nothing which *they* cannot remember was ever done for popular education in this State, may be glad to have brought under their notice the earliest, efforts made to educate the youth of "*Notre Chère Louisiane.*"

To elucidate this theme thoroughly, it would be well to give a synopsis of the history of Louisiana, the dynasties that took, but would not keep, for their crowns so fair a jewel, the men of renown who sojourned within her borders, the feats of arms done in her defense by loyal citizens and reclaimed privateers, the Indian wars raging almost without truce, the foreign and civil wars, the stock-jobbing of Law, who was to create wealth, so to say, by the wand of a magician. These remarkable men, and deeds of valor, and banking bubbles, had their influence on education, and it would be a pleasing task to trace it in its various phases through administrative, municipal, religious, and domestic life. But all this will appear sufficiently for our purpose in the tenor of these pages.

II

LA SALLE reached the Mississippi April 6, 1682. On the 9th, he baptized the country which he had explored by the sweet-sounding name *Louisiana*, and his chaplain, in presence of twenty-three French, eighteen Abnaki, ten Indian women, and three children, blessed *Louisiana* and dedicated it to God amid the roaring of cannon, the singing of hymns, and the recital of appropriate prayers. Five years later, La Salle was assassinated. Nothing was done to colonize the immense territory of which he had been viceroy. His grand discovery was almost forgotten, and the Father of Waters disappeared from the navigators' charts. When another famous mariner, Iberville, entered the great river by the gulf, March 2, 1699, not a hut was to be seen. Sea-marsh and virgin forests greeted his eyes; but, as time wore on, mementos of the earlier sailors appeared. A letter, or *speaking bark*, from Tonti, and a breviary in which was written the name of a companion of La Salle, were given to Iberville by an Indian, and Tonti himself came, like a ghost from the past, to tell the mighty deeds of his brave but unfortunate master to the mariners now following up his discoveries.

Chevalier Tonti, La Salle's trusted friend, was known as "the Man of the Copper Hand." The loss of a hand in the wars in Sicily he had repaired by one made of copper.

The premature death of Sauvolle in Biloxi, and of Iberville in the West Indies, left the sole care of Louisiana to their brother Bienville, who became the founder of New Orleans and Mobile.

When Bienville, with unerring sagacity, selected on a bend of the great river the best site for a commercial emporium, he set fifty men (1718) to clear the soil of its rank vegetation and build huts of moss and wattles, roofed with bark and palmetto. In 1722, just as the capital had been transferred to *Nouvelle-Orleans* from the lonely beach of Biloxi, there were one hundred cabins scattered over the highest patches of the morass, and Charlevoix, who visited the embryo city, was touched by the spiritual destitution of the white settlers and the Indians whose camp-fires lit up the river banks and sparkled in the dense forests beyond the flimsy palisade. There was no need of schools. Few children, if any, had come to bless the dismal kraal in which the keen-eyed Charlevoix saw the nucleus of a populous and opulent city. In 1723 the Bishop of Quebec sent Franciscans to the white settlers, and in 1724 Jesuits came to evangelize the Indians. By 1726 many women had joined their husbands, and children were frolicking in the jungle and staring with terror in their wide eyes at the alligators that wriggled in the moat and the frogs that croaked forever in the slime. At that early date the sagacious Bienville was devising ways and means to furnish the Colony with good schools. He was too acute not to perceive that families would not establish permanent homes in the Colony unless educational facilities were provided for their children. A boys' school arose at once beside the warehouse that did duty for a church, and the first teacher that ever instructed the youth of Louisiana was Father Cecil, a Capuchin monk.

So far as I can learn, no picture or memorial of this pioneer of literary and scientific education exists in any college of Louisiana. In the university endowed by Mr. Tulane I saw pictures of several persons supposed to be connected with education in this

State, but not one of them wore the friar's frock. And none of the wandering lecturers, who so frequently come to enlighten Louisiana on her history and educational progress, has begun at the beginning and told his audience of Father Cecil. And yet in giving a history of what rivermen call steamboating, any lecturer would tell of Robert Fulton, and search into his parentage, rightly believing that those who gave him being were glorified by his genius. They might say, like one* of his biographers, that, though born of Irish parents, "his remote ancestors were probably of Scottish origin." Had the educationalists heard of Father Cecil, they might deem it "probable" that his "remote ancestors" were of New England, and himself a priest like Wyclif. But that they completely ignore Father Cecil, shows that they have never heard of him.

Bienville, anxious to root families to the soil, and knowing that civilization depends largely on the careful training of girls, took extraordinary pains to secure capable teachers; and, as the best were to be found in convents,—religious being then the only persons who adopted teaching as a life profession,—he turned to his native Canada for *Sœurs Grises.* But, to his great grief, his project proved impracticable. He consulted Father Beaubois, Superior of the Jesuits, a man of great zeal and energy. Their views were identical, and Beaubois offered to apply to the Ursu-

* Mr. Rennick, who perhaps did not know that the remote Scotch were all Irish.

lines of Rouen. After much negotiation, a treaty was concluded, September 13, 1726, by which these ladies engaged to supply teachers and nurses for New Orleans. It was, then, through the Jesuits that the first school for girls and the first regular hospital were established in the Louisiana of La Salle, which extended from the Great Lakes to the Mexican Gulf, and from the Alleghanies to the Rocky Mountains.

A lady bearing the somewhat singular name of Tranchepain (*slice of bread*) was appointed Superior. Mother Tranchepain, a convert from Calvinism, had taken the veil among the Ursulines in Rouen, in 1699. The contradictions, disappointments, and trials that wait upon all great enterprises were not wanting to this. Bishops who at first approved of their design, afterwards refused to allow nuns of their respective dioceses to leave, and some were obliged to appeal to Cardinal Fleury.* Louis XV., of whom so little good can be said, was a generous patron of this work, as the *brève* or official letter setting forth its objects and conditions testifies. Here is an extract:

"His Majesty, wishing to favor everything that can contribute to the relief of the sick and the education of the young, has approved the treaty made between the Company of the Indies and the Ursuline Religious, the intention of His Majesty being that

---

* Almost all the Ursulines in France were volunteers in the good cause, and those obliged to remain at home had a holy envy of those selected for this perilous mission.

they should enjoy, without interference, all that has been or shall be granted to them by the said Company. His Majesty takes them under his protection and safeguard, and in proof of his good will has commanded the hastening of the present Letters Patent, which he has willed to sign with his own hand.—Fontainebleau, September 18, 1726."

All the nuns for the Louisiana mission assembled in the monastery of Hennebon, in Brittany, to acknowledge as Superior Marie Tranchepain of St. Augustin, January 1, 1727. Their action was confirmed by two letters from the Bishop of Quebec, Monseigneur Delacroix, one to Mother Tranchepain, the other to Father Beaubois. Louisiana was in his diocese, Quebec being under the ecclesiastical jurisdiction of the Archbishop of Rouen. The missionary nuns were twelve. They gave their submission according to their respective ranks, eager to sacrifice themselves for the glory of God and the salvation of their fellow creatures, and filled with a holy enthusiasm which helped them in their sublime vocation. Two, at least, the Mother Superior and the novice, Madeleine Hachard, of Rouen, have left in their "Relations" evidence not only of sincere devotion to God and ardent zeal for souls, which they possessed in common with the rest, but also of liberal scholarship, fine culture, and unusual intellectual ability.

The terms offered by the Indian Company, under whose auspices they were to sail, evinced great interest in the sick and the children. They traveled at the expense of the Company, and each received, before embarking, a gift of 500 livres. Until their plantation should be in full cultivation, each was guaranteed 600 livres a year. A spacious convent, in course of· erection, was given them in perpetuity. Three nuns were to be always at the service of the hospital; one was set aside for the free school, and one to help her in case of overwork. It was expressly stipulated that those in charge of the sick and the free schools must not be disturbed. This shows that New Orleans was scarcely founded when provision of the most liberal and excellent description was made for the education of the "masses." Should the nuns, through want of health, or any other cause, wish to return to France, they were free to go at the expense of the Company. But not one looked back after having put her hand to the plough.

III

ON THE twenty-seventh of January, 1727, the nuns looked their last on Paris, whence they journeyed to L'Orient, delayed by execrable roads and bad weather, but bright and cheerful under all contrarieties. On February 22d, a day since memorable in the history of the United States, they bade adieu to their country, "for the glory of God and the salvation of the poor savages." They sailed in the *Gironde* with the Jesuit Fathers, Tartarin and Doutreleau, and "Frère Crucy," who, with Madeleine Hachard, being the youngest of the party, considered it "their duty to amuse the rest." No words of ours can describe, nor would it be easy to imagine, in these days of rapid travel, Pullman boudoirs, and ocean palaces, the sufferings of those "who went down to the sea in ships" a hundred and sixty years ago. The voyage had its chroniclers; every incident is vividly described in the letters and diaries of Mother Tranchepain and Sister Hachard, which have most unaccountably escaped the researches of all the historians and romancists of Louisiana. These ladies, first teachers of Louisiana, wrote with ease and elegance, and a grace and liveliness which the lecturers who expatiate so perseveringly on the benighted times of old could not, we fear, equal. It would take too long to give details of this seven months' journey from Paris to New Orleans, over the stormy Atlantic, among the West Indian Isles, on the Caribbean Sea and the Gulf of Mexico, and up the Mississippi.* Now they were threatened with a watery grave, again with starvation and thirst; once the ship barely escaped hostile corsairs; later they encountered savages of so peculiarly ferocious a type that they murdered by slow tortures all the whites they captured, and made every victim drink his own blood.

Probably no scene on earth is so bleak and dreary as the entrance from the Gulf to the Mississippi. An

* The Spanish annals add to the trials of their voyage the cruelty of the Captain, but no mention is made of this in the letters of Madeleine Hachard.

interminable waste of waters, a vast morass impassable for man or beast, shoals and sand bars, low strips of coast covered with poplars, prairies of reeds, a wilderness of cane-brakes — the mouths of the river were then strewn with driftwood and half-choked with wrecks. As they ascended, forests that seemed coëval with the creation; here and there a solitary hut for pilots, stretches of green savannah, gaunt trunks of trees stuck fast in the sand, snags, to-day the *crux* of the river-man, gigantic cypress shrouded in funereal moss, half-submerged in the yellow waves. Gloom and magnificence everywhere mingled; fishes disporting themselves ruffled the old-gold surface of the melancholy river; blue cranes like flying skeletons hovered about the masts; swarthy, half-nude natives in pirogues and chaloupes glided among the wondrous waves, shimmering in the mystic charm of the summer sunlight. But dreadful was the navigation of the lower Mississippi in those days. " The trials and fatigues of our five months' sea voyage," writes our novice, " are not to be compared with what we had to endure in our journey from the Gulf to New Orleans, a distance of thirty leagues."

As the Sisters neared their future home, the flat monotony of the landscape was agreeably diversified by masses of dark foliage, sparkling at night with fireflies, which made a gorgeous illumination. Planters' houses squatting among the half-cleared areas,— huge, unwieldy structures, wide halls dividing their whole length,— the river beating against the edge of the miry ground and threatening to submerge it; right joyfully were the travelers welcomed by the *habitans*, "honest people from France or Canada, who will send us their children." "They are enthusiastic over our arrival, because they will not now be obliged to go to France to educate their daughters."

The nuns reached New Orleans on August 7, 1727. An early writer has described the village as a vast sink or sewer. It was surrounded by a deep ditch, and fenced with sharp stakes, wedged closely together. Tall reeds and coarse grasses grew in the streets, and a stone's throw from the rickety church reptiles hissed, and wild beasts and malefactors lurked, protected by impenetrable jungle. Our novice gives a flattering description of the town: " It is very handsome, well-built, and regularly laid out. . . . The streets are wide and straight; the houses wainscoted and latticed, the roofs supported by whitewashed pillars and covered with shingles, that is, thin boards cut to resemble slates, and imitating them to perfection. . . . The colonists sing that our town is as beautiful as Paris. But I find a difference. The songs may persuade those who have never seen the capital of France. But I have seen it, and they fail to persuade me."

The tropical gorgeousness of the vegetation charmed her. The country, save for a small space about the church, was thickly wooded to the water's edge, and the trees were of prodigious height. The streets and squares, laid out by the engineer, La Tour, were still mostly on paper only. The air was on fire with mosquitoes, every one provided with a sting like a fine, red-hot nail. Yet she found the climate balmy and soothing, and readily believed the boast of the Creoles that it was the most salubrious on earth. She remarks that those who had given the nuns a poor idea of the place had not seen its progress for several years. The tremendous hurricane of 1723 had swept away the cabins in which the earliest settlers had found a miserable shelter. And the town was rebuilt on a scale of modest splendor, which surprised and delighted the nuns.

Mother Tranchepain dilates on her joy and consolation on touching the soil of New Orleans: "We set out for Father Beaubois's house, and met him coming towards us, leaning on a staff because of his weakness. He looked pale and weary, but on seeing us brightened up"—he was recovering from a dangerous illness. A crayon sketch, kindly lent the writer by the amiable successor of Mother Tranchepain, gives a lively representation of the "Landing of the Ursulines." The nuns are in procession, wearing the ample garb of their Order. Sister Hachard's fine, strong lineaments are partially concealed by the flowing white veil of a novice. Father Beaubois presents them to the Capuchin pastors of the town, and points out the Indians and negroes, their future charges. A negress, holding a solemn ebony baby, regards the group with awe and wonderment. A beautiful squaw, decked with beads and shells, surrounded by plump papooses, half reclines with natural grace on some logs, and a very large Congo negro has dropped his work and betaken himself to the top of a woodpile to gaze leisurely on the scene. Claude Massy, an Ursuline postulant, carries a cat which she tenderly caresses; another, " Sister Anne," is searching a basket for something. Both wear the high-peaked Normandy cap. Franciscans, heavily bearded, and Jesuits in large cloaks, appear in the distance. Immense trees, which have long since disappeared, overshadow the whole group. The picture is a most interesting and valuable relic, probably the only one in existence which shows *tout ensemble* the first schoolmasters and schoolmistresses of any country, and its earliest preachers of the Gospel of Peace.

The nuns breakfasted with Father Beaubois. Governor Perier, Madame Perier, and all the chief people welcomed them as risen from the dead, for they had been given up as lost. Bienville's country house, the best in the colony, given them provisionally, was a two-story edifice with a flat roof, used as a belvidere or gallery, situated on Bienville street, which runs perpendicularly to the river, between Royal and Chartres streets, which are parallel to it. Six doors gave ingress and egress to the apartments on the ground floor. Large and numerous windows, with sashes covered with fine linen, let in as much light as glass. The garden opened on Bienville street. From the roof the nuns might gaze on a scene of weird and solemn splendor. Swamps and clumps of palmetto and tangled vines; the surrounding wilderness with groups of spreading live oaks (*chéniéres*), cut up by glassy bayous, was the home of reptiles, wild beasts, vultures, herons, and many wondrous specimens of the *fauna* of Louisiana. Here were flocks of the pelican, fabled to feed its young from its bosom, and chosen as a symbol of the teeming soil of Louisiana as it had been chosen from earlier times as a beautiful type of Jesus, *pius pelicanus*, who feeds His children with His own Sacred Body and Blood. Our novice makes the immense trees, which surround the garden, responsible for the terrible atoms she calls *frappes d'abord*, "which sting without mercy and threaten to assassinate us." They came at sunset and, after preying on the nuns all night, returned to the woods at sunrise.

The holy sacrifice of the Mass was offered for the first time in the temporary convent, August 9, 1727, by Father Beaubois, who acted as chaplain to the little community. In accordance with their earnest desire, he placed the Blessed Sacrament in the tabernacle, which their deft fingers had lovingly prepared, October 5th. They were the only consecrated virgins in the vast region now known as the United States, and it would not be easy to imagine their emotion when, bowed down before the Awful Presence, they offered reparation to the Sacred Heart of Jesus for the indifference or sinfulness of the multitude, and besought the Fountain of all mercies to bestow the gift of Faith on the savages they had come so far to reclaim.

23

This, then, was the first girls' school established in Louisiana. It was but a few squares from the venerable hovel on the south of the church, where Father Cecil taught the boys of the town. As to air, light, spaciousness, and picturesqueness, there is not a finer site in Louisiana to-day. It was established primarily as a free school. The receiving of the rich as boarders was an afterthought. "When the Religious find it convenient," says a contemporary document, "they may take paying pupils, if they judge proper." But it was expressly stipulated that the nuns in charge of the free schools and the sick "should not be put to teach in the pension school." So that the free school, instead of being the outgrowth of a new idea due to our northern friends, is contemporaneous with the colonization of Louisiana.

The Sisters at once began to teach the children and extend their cares to the sick, the Indians, and the blacks. Sister Hachard praises the docility of the children, "who can be molded as one pleases." She says it is easy to instruct the negroes once they learn French, but "impossible to baptize the Indians without trembling, on account of their natural propensity to evil, particularly the squaws, who, under an air of modesty, hide the passions of beasts." The Religious were valued throughout the colony as the most precious gift the mother country could bestow. They were loaded with presents. Governor Perier and his amiable wife often visited them. The Intendant, Delachaise, who "commanded for the king in the

absence of the governor," is described as a perfect
gentleman "who refuses nothing we ask of him."
"The marks of protection we receive from the highest
in the land cause us to be respected by the whole
population. This," continues our acute novice,
"would not last long if we did not sustain by our
actions the exalted opinion they have of us."

IV

THE community which thus auspiciously began the
work of education in Louisiana consisted of eight professed members,* one novice, and two candidates.
"Never," says our novice, "was any other community
so well accommodated in the beginning of its existence." The house soon became too small for the
number of pupils, ever increasing. A solid brick convent of ample dimensions was in course of construction
at the other extremity of the town.˙ The Indian
Company promised to have it ready in six months,
which space lengthened out to seven years. The
gentlemen who had begun with so much diligence
grew weary of welldoing.

Neither tears nor solicitations could prevail on
them to supply material and finish the work. The
nuns grew disheartened. They had no pecuniary

---

* 1, Mother M. Augustine Tranchepain; 2, Sisters Marguérite Judde; 3, Marianne Boulanger; 4, Madeleine de Mahieu; 5,
Renée Singuel; 6, Marguérite de Talaon; 7, Cecilia Cavelier; 8,
Marianne Dain; 9, Madeleine Hachard, Claude Massy, and a
candidate styled simply Sister Anne.

means to forward it, and it was with difficulty they contrived to live in a new country where the prices of provisions were enormous. "God, whose designs are impenetrable," writes the annalist, "permitted that several who had worked hardest in this enterprise should die before the accomplishment of their desires." A most efficient member, Sister Madeleine de Mahieu, died July 6, 1728; Mother Marguérite Judde followed, August 14, 1731, and Sister Marguérite Talaon, September 5, 1733. On November 11, 1733, the brave and gentle Superior, Mother Augustine Tranchepain, "submitted to the same penalty, and, like another Moses, expired in sight of the promised land." However ardent her desires of seeing the accomplishment of a work which she had so happily begun, she met death with edifying firmness, and was in a manner angry with those who showed some expectation of her recovery.

Not a stone upon a stone remains of the dwellings consecrated by the joys and sorrows of that heroic band, exiles for Christ,—Bienville's villa, Father Cecil's venerable schoolhouse, the church, the monk's convent and library, and the arsenal and town-hall perished in the dreadful conflagration of Good Friday, 1788, which swept away nearly nine hundred houses, leaving thousands homeless. Tradition asserts that the nuns lived some time on their plantation and points out *Nun* street, a short street flanked with cotton presses and opening on the Levée, as the site of their country house. The nomenclature of the streets that form a network over what is supposed to have been the Ursuline plantation, recalls the holy souls who prayed and taught within its limits, *Religious* street, *Notre Dame* street, *Annunciation* street, *Teresa* street, etc.

The hospital of the Sisters usually had from thirty to forty patients, mostly soldiers. And everything was so well arranged that the officials said it was useless for them to continue their visits — there was nothing for them to do. At first the infirmarian watched the nurses, but ere long she took sole charge. The sick could not say enough in praise of their "mothers," who would even gratify their tastes when it could be done without prejudice to their health. "We bless God for the success of this Christian work," writes the chronicler. "The spirit of our holy institute shows itself in the good our Sisters do for souls while attending to the wants of the body." Like all nuns who serve the sick, they were consoled by many wonderful conversions.

It was on a fair summer evening, the air cool and balmy after days of incessant rain, that the nuns took possession of their new convent, July 13, 1734, the first built on the delta of the Mississippi, and the oldest in the United States by some seventy years. Great progress had been made in the education of the young at this early epoch. Improvements had been introduced everywhere. In the culture of fruits and vegetables, immense advances had been made; figs, grapes, pineapples, melons, oranges, sweet and sour, beans, and potatoes, were quite common. The Jesuits cultivated many rare varieties, and their gardens, hedged with wax myrtle, now the site of the richest quarter in New Orleans, were the wonder and delight of the Colony. Madeleine Hachard speaks of the immense quantities of fruit sent to the convent, which the nuns, aided by their pupils, made into jellies and preserves. As early as April 24, 1728, she tells her father, at Rouen, that Father Beaubois's garden, the finest in the town, is full of orange trees. During Holy Week, the nuns and their pupils gave evidence of progress in music: "We had exhortations attended by nearly two hundred persons. The *Tenebræ* and the *Miserere* were sung; at Easter we had the whole Mass set to music, with quartets admirably executed. The convents in France, with all their brilliancy, seldom do as much." The nuns had twenty boarders, three parlor-boarders, three orphans, and seven slave-boarders, "whom we instruct and prepare for Baptism and First Communion," a large number of day scholars, besides "many black and Indian women, *who attend our school every day for two hours.*" It was usual for girls to marry at thirteen or fourteen, but henceforth no girl was allowed to marry without first being instructed by the nuns.

They received under their protection the orphans of the Frenchmen recently massacred at Natchez, and some *Filles à la cassette* (girls with a trunk or casket), sent hither by the king as wives for respectable colonists and soldiers. These poor girls had scarcely tasted their hospitality when they were claimed by men in need of helpmates. The marriages made on so short an acquaintance usually turned out well. Even girls from French Houses of Correction became excellent wives and mothers, perhaps because they were instructed by the Sisters previous to receiving the seventh sacrament. Father Beaubois expected that the Ursulines would establish religion throughout the Colony by their good example and instructions.

Their removal to their new monastery was the occasion of one of the most elegant pageants ever devised in the city of pageants, one which shows conclusively that the Louisianians had taken, as it were naturally, such culture as the Ursulines were able to give. To-day, after all that has been said about the decorative in art and the æsthetic everywhere, we doubt if anything more chaste, yet stirring and showy, could be devised, great though our resources be. From July 2d, the nuns had been looking in vain for favorable weather. A downpour, lasting three days, began on the ninth, flooding gardens and making roads impassable. On Saturday, the thirteenth, just as they had resolved to postpone their departure indefinitely, the sun burst from the cloudy heavens, and in his brilliant light and tropical heat the waters soon subsided. The sudden clearing of the sky they took as a good omen, and at 5 P. M. all their bells rang out to announce their intended departure. Bienville, whose third term (1733–1743) had recently begun, soon appeared in the convent chapel, where the nuns knelt for the last time. Fathers Beaubois and Petit, and Brother Parisel, Jesuits; Fathers Philip and Pierre, Capuchins, and the most distinguished people of the place surrounded the brilliantly lighted altar, and the troops, half French, half Swiss, drew up on either side of the old convent.*

V

FATHER PHILIP gave benediction, assisted by Fathers Beaubois and Petit. All left the chapel processionally, the citizens opening the march. Then came the children of the orphanage and the day-school, followed by forty of the principal ladies of the city, bearing torches; next twenty young girls robed and veiled in the purest white, and twelve others, representing St. Ursula and her 11,000 companions. The boarders, orphans, and day pupils carried wax tapers. The young lady who personated St. Ursula wore a costly robe and a regal mantle of tissue of silver. Her crown glittered with pearls and diamonds, and a veil of the richest lace fell about her in graceful folds. She bore in her hand a heart pierced with arrows made with wondrous skill. Fair children arrayed as angels surrounded her, and all waved palm branches emblematic of the glorious victory won by the heroic virgin-martyrs whom they had the honor to represent.

* From the old convent, the villa of Bienville, to the new, the distance is less than a mile, along Chartres street. The southern part of Chartres street, on which the new monastery, now a very old one, is situated, was then Condé street.

Lastly came the Religious with lighted candles, and the clergy carrying a rich canopy, under which the Most Blessed Sacrament was borne in triumph. Bienville and his staff, the Intendant, Mons. Salmon, and the whole population formed their escort. The soldiers moved in single file on each side, about four feet from the procession. Hymns were sung by all, the accompaniment of fifes and drums making pleasing harmony; Brother Parisel, in surplice, acted as master of ceremonies, and perfect order and decorum prevailed. This moving panorama of light, color, and beauty halted between the church and the *Place d'Armes*, and defiled gracefully into the aisles, the troops kneeling and presenting arms to do honor to the Blessed Sacrament. The nuns knelt within the sanctuary. Father Philip placed the *Veiled Savior* on the altar, and the clergy knelt in lowly adoration. Soldiers robed as acolytes were swinging censers, whose delicate perfumes filled the church. The congregation remained prostrate till Father Petit, S. J., the orator of the occasion, arose to address them. In a sermon described as most eloquent by the nun whose facile pen has embalmed these precious details, he set forth the necessity and advantages of giving young persons a solid Christian education. In glowing words he congratulated the nuns on their labors to this great end, so conducive to the glory of God and the welfare of the Colony. At the close of this touching address, the soldiers sang hymns to the Blessed Sacrament and St. Ursula. They then fell down before their hidden Lord

with such demonstrations of reverence that a spectator, not given to mild views, feared their interior dis-
positions did not correspond with all this exterior
respect.

The torches and tapers were not superfluous when
the procession wound out of the church; the sun was
setting, but the afterglow remained for a while, bur-
nishing the lofty trees and turning the mighty river into
molten gold. It drew up before the *Place d'Armes*,*
and the bells of the new monastery rang out their
merriest peals as it moved slowly in the deepening
twilight, not ceasing till all had entered the sacred
edifice, a few squares distant. "Thus did we enter
our new abode," writes the chronicler, "amid the
chiming of bells, the music of fifes and drums, and the
singing of praise and thanksgiving to our heavenly
Father whose loving Providence has lavished on us so
many favors." Benediction was given a third time.
As it was late and "insufferably warm," the *Te Deum*
was deferred to the next day, Sunday. "The people
withdrew, apparently pleased and edified, and we were
delighted to find ourselves once more secluded from
the world and all it loves and esteems."

The first day our good Religious spent in their
new home, the Blessed Sacrament was exposed and a
solemn *Te Deum* sung. In the evening there was
benediction and "we sang a motet that won the admiration of the distinguished. people who assisted

* *Place d'Armes*, a field before the church, called, in Spanish
colonial times, the *plaza*, now Jackson Square.

at these ceremonies. We were really charmed with our new house," continued our anonymous chronicler; "much is yet to be done, but the joy of being separated from the world outweighs all inconveniences." '

Father Dagobert, who came to New Orleans in 1723, lived to witness a more stirring and pompous procession. Thirty-five years later, August 18, 1769, he watched the superb battalions and *fusileros* of Don Alexandro O'Reilly crossing the *plaza* to the military Mass and *Te Deum*, which were to celebrate the transfer of Louisiana to Spain. The hoarse roaring of cannon mingled with the mellow tones of all the bells in the town as they rang out a joyous welcome to the hero of the day. O'Reilly, who worthily represented the potent majesty of Spain, attended by a staff of gorgeously accoutred men, preceded by officers bearing massive silver maces, moved forward to the music of hundreds of instruments. When they halted to be officially welcomed by the representatives of the Church, the prolonged shouts which rent the air, *Viva el Rey*, were heard in the cloisters of St. Ursula. The Friar received His Excellency at the church-door, welcomed him with every demonstration of respect, and with utmost enthusiasm promised fidelity to the crown of Spain for his brethren and the people. He then blessed the Spanish colors, which ascended the flag-staff when the white banner was lowered When that redoubtable chieftain bent his pale intellectual countenance, radiant with devotion, and knelt with

3

33

forehead to the earth at the *Te ergo quæsumus*, perhaps he thought no scene could be grander or more
thrilling than that of which he formed the central
figure. Or, it may be, that, like another warrior of the
same race, his triumphs had a tinge of bitterness
because they were not for the land of his birth
and his love. But I fancy Father Dagobert's mind
reverted to the procession of 1734, and that, however thrilled and overawed by the warlike grandees
of Spain and the princely Irishman who commanded
them, his heart preferred the earlier and lovelier
pageant.

The whole scene of July 13, 1734, intensely dramatic as it was, passes before our mind's eye in its
quaint and gorgeous beauty. Civilians in the graceful
costume of that era, officials in their showy robes of
office, matrons in grand toilets of the rich gold-
striped stuffs that surprised Madeleine Hachard on
her first introduction to the women of the Colony —
soldiers in gaudy uniforms, veterans wearing medals of
gallantry won on many a field in Europe; dignitaries
with black servants in bright liveries; Bienville attended by a splendid staff; children in purest white
strewing flowers before the Blessed Sacrament; young
girls richly appareled; "St. Ursula" in sparkling
diadem and royal robes waving the graceful palmetto
of the country. Dark-robed nuns, in flowing veils and
mantles, led by Sister Hachard, whose clever pen has
left such vivid pictures of early colonial days —
acolytes in bright cassocks and snow-white surplices,

swinging silver thuribles — bearded Franciscans in the brown habits of their Order, Jesuits in simple soutanes, the officiating clergy in glittering vestments — the rich canopy borne aloft, soldiers in Indian file, keeping step as a guard of honor, between whose lines passed the hidden God. The rich, sonorous voices of the men, the clear, sweet treble of the women and children, the martial music of the soldiery; the eager-eyed blacks and the swarthy Indians who see in this old-world grandeur a picture of heaven, and the warm beams of the sun gilding the whole; the giant trees whose branches bend low as if in adoration of the *Veiled Presence* beneath the canopy, the red sunbeams glittering through the foliage and forming halos over St. Ursula and her Virgin Companions; the cardinal birds like tufts of fire in the trees, the mocking birds making sweet melody in their hiding places; the clouds of incense ascending heavenward — all this must have equaled in beauty and variety any other religious display ever devised, and speaks volumes for the culture of Louisiana in French Colonial days.

VI

THE Ursulines seem to have been particularly successful in developing and cultivating the musical tastes of their pupils. The women, the children, and the soldiers could, as we have seen, unite with the clergy and the Sisters in singing and moving forward to the accompaniment of military music; and it is always trying to sing while marching, however slowly. It would be interesting to see the scores from which they sang and to which they marched. Perhaps they lie unnoticed in some secret drawer of the Ursuline library. This display shows that congregational singing is not an innovation in New Orleans; it evidently entered largely into the worship of the early settlers.

The nuns were able to afford increased educational facilities to their pupils in their new home. The good wrought by them increased every day, and parents were influenced through their pupils. The blacks, then very few, and the Indians, who came and went at will, were tenderly cherished. Mother Melotte, who succeeded Mother Tranchepain, was a woman of great energy and did much to improve and beautify the monastery, and fit it for its many purposes. Laundry, storeroom, bakery, a small parlor, and a room for the *tourrière*, still standing,were added in quick succession. The day scholars increasing, new school-rooms followed. The convent was built to stand sieges — attacks from the Indians or the English were almost always expected. And, as it was incongruous that such a structure should be surrounded by a fence of stakes, the good Mother, at a cost of 6,000 francs, built a brick wall around the whole enclosure, part of which still stands. All this was done at the expense of the nuns, who were surprised that the sum charged to the building accounts, 100,000 francs, did not supply all the offices and include a hospital. Those who know the old monastery will be interested to hear that the ground-floor had a small chapel, two parlors, a room for the Mother Superior, refectories for the sisters and the boarders, community rooms, kitchen, scullery, and pantry. On the next floor (first in English, second in French) were dormitory, infirmary, sacristy, linen room, wardrobe. The orphans occupied part of the upper story; the rest was used as an instruction room for the colored women. " We succeeded in persuading the gentlemen of the Indian Company," writes one of the nuns, " to erect a separate building for the sick." To this the patients were removed, August 20, 1734. It was behind the convent, facing Arsenal street, which immediately changed its name to Hospital street. The first infirmarian, Sister M. Xavier, before assuming the charge, wished to see how the lay nurses managed the sick. " But her apprenticeship was short, for charity compelled her to take sole charge of them." Heretofore, only patients in danger of death had been received, but the new building was spacious enough to accommodate all the sick. Such were the humble beginnings of the splendid Charity Hospital, which is not the least of the glories of New Orleans.

VII

THE educational advantages given by the Ursu-lines to girls of every class may perhaps be the cause why the Creole women of Louisiana have been re-garded by many as morally, religiously, and even intellectually superior to the Creole men. But it was not Bienville's fault that there was no high school or university for boys. Rich parents sent their sons to Europe, and the benefits of such a course were not always commensurate with its risks and expenses. The truly enlightened founder of the city sought the best teachers for the boys, as he had done for the girls. He wrote to the French Government, in 1742:

" It is long since the inhabitants of Louisiana made representations on the necessity of having a college for the education of their sons. Convinced of the advantages of such an institution, they wished the Jesuits to undertake its creation and management. It is essential that there be one at least for the study of classics, geometry, geography, pilotage, etc. It is too evidently demonstrated to parents how utterly worthless children turn out who are reared in idleness and luxury, and how ruinously expensive it is to send children to France to be educated. Moreover, it is to be feared that Creoles educated abroad will imbibe a dislike for their native country and come back only to receive and convert into cash the property left by their parents."

The Intendant, Salmon, made this petition jointly with the Governor, but it was set aside as premature. Bienville left the Colony for France, May 10, 1743, never to return. As he had always labored for the profit of Louisiana, it may well be believed that he

used his influence in Paris to advance the project he
had so much at heart. But the times were unfavor-
able, and every year increased the difficulties of its
execution.

The sun of St. Ignatius was already beginning to
set. The suppression of his children throughout the
French dominions loomed up in the distance, and
years of anxiety and persecution were preparing minds
for that final issue. So far from being able to found
another establishment in New Orleans, they were soon
to be driven from a Colony in which they had labored
with signal success from its earliest days. The Jesuit
College, for which Governor Bienville asked, was not
founded till the next century. The formal order for
the suppression of the Jesuits was issued by the
French Government in 1764, and their brethren in
Spain and Naples shared the same fate. The plantation which their labors had wrung from marsh and
swamp and changed into a Garden of Eden was confiscated by an ungrateful government to which their
property in Louisiana brought $180,000, an enor-
mous sum for the time. They had introduced
sugar-cane, which later became a fruitful source * of
wealth to Louisiana, " the sugar-bowl of the United
States." By the lamentable exodus of so many zealous priests, the nuns lost their directors and best

---

* In 1882 the Louisiana sugar-crop netted 340,000,000 pounds.
In that year 70,000,000 pounds were lost by the overflow of the
Mississippi. The largest recorded sugar-crop before the war was
(in 1858) 500,000,000 pounds, and 30,000,000 gallons of molasses.

friends, and education in Louisiana its most influential and cultured patrons. Madeleine Hachard was
spared this great sorrow. She died in 1762, after
having faithfully taught the youth of the Colony
for thirty-five years. The letters of this accomplished
woman show her to have been full of high and generous sentiments, and ardently devoted to her holy
vocation.

The administration of the generous and hospitable
successor of Bienville, the Marquis de Vaudreuil, the
Grand Marquis, as he was styled, was a period of unusual brilliancy (1743–1753), though not without its
disturbances. He was succeeded by Kerlerec, a captain in the French Navy. D'Abbadie, who followed,
died in office in 1765. This year was signalized by the
arrival of 650 Acadians, who, after being hospitably received in New Orleans, were sent to Opelousas and
Attakapas, where their descendants remain to this
day. By a secret Treaty of Cession, Louisiana was
given over to Spain, February 10, 1762. But Aubry,
the last French governor, remained in the Colony till
he delivered it officially to O'Reilly, in 1769.

The despatches of the later French governors and
other officials prove the Colony to have been in a
desperate condition. De Bassac tells the home government that "drunkenness,* brawls, and duels,
destroyed half the population." And D'Abbadie
complains that the " facility offered by the country to

* The drunkenness resulted from the immoderate use of *tafia*,
a kind of bad whisky made from the sugar-cane.

live on its natural productions has created habits of laziness," that the "whole population is stupefied by the vice of drunkenness," and that "Louisiana is a chaos of iniquity and disorder." Kerlerec, from his cell in the Bastile, "from the bottom of his heart pities" the Spanish Governor, Ulloa, for being sent to such a country. All this had a baleful influence on education. Those devoted to education, above all others, require peace of mind if they would make their work a success. The Ursuline Religious were always treated with great deference in the old colonial days. But it was difficult for teachers or pupils to attend well to school duties while the City Fathers were holding conventions, sending out deputations, and heading the armed squads that paraded the streets. Spain, having already too many colonies, was slow to take possession of the gift thrust upon her by the degenerate Louis XV., through his infidel minister, Choiseul, who had already lost Canada to France. The most excited condition of public feeling prevailed. Official reports state that anarchy was becoming almost universal. The people besought the king not to separate them from France. The aged Bienville made the same petition with tears, and, it is said, died of grief when Choiseul refused to grant it. The disturbances of the quasi-interregnum affected the cause of education most unfavorably. From 1760 to 1770 was a period of bitter agitation and controversy. The antecedents and consequents of the transfer to Spain disturbed the country socially and religiously as well as politically, and nowhere was the change more keenly felt than within the walls of the Ursuline Convent. The nuns, mostly French by birth and attached to their country and her language, were given to understand that Spanish was to be henceforth the chief language of their schools. The Spanish domination * brought them Spanish subjects, for whom they seem to have had about as much welcome as the French Friars for their Spanish brethern. Even the Indians complained of being "handed from one white chief to another like so many head of cattle."

Difficulties between clergy of different orders, and between French and Spanish clergy of the same order, and later, between clergy and their bishops, had a deleterious effect on education. The first Spanish Governor, Don Antonio Ulloa, a scholar of European reputation, would doubtless have done much for education, had the people allowed him. But they arose in arms against him, and forced him to leave the country. "It is well known," wrote the Spanish Minister, Grimaldi, regarding Ulloa's expulsion, "that the loss of great interest is looked upon in Spain with indifference, but not so as regards insults or contumelies." Charles III. decided to punish the insult offered to the Spanish crown, and enforce his authority. On August 18, 1769, Don Alexandro O'Reilly, an officer of the highest rank in the armies

---

* Four Spanish ladies from Havana took the veil in the Ursuline Convent, New Orleans, 1772. A church was built for the nuns at the expense of the King of Spain about the same time

of Spain, honored with the royal friendship and confidence, appeared before the town with twenty-four
sail and 2,600 picked men, the flower of the Spanish
troops. The mere sight of this armament, or rather
the news of its approach, quelled the insurrection.
Twelve ring-leaders were tried for high treason and
found guilty. Their defense was that Ulloa, whom
they had driven out, had not shown his credentials;
that they had not taken the oath of allegiance; and
that Spain had not formally taken possession. But it
was proved that the Spanish flag had for years been
floating at every post from the Balize to Illinois; that
some of the accused had held their commissions from
the King of Spain, and drew salaries from him while
exciting revolt against him. Six were sentenced to
death, one of whom died in prison, and six were banished.

Though O'Reilly* has been blamed by a few for
suffering the law to take its course, yet, at the time,
he was judged extremely merciful. His power was
absolute; yet only a few of the leaders were punished,
and a full, unconditional pardon was granted to the
rest, *i. e.*, almost all the men in the colony. " I have
the honor," wrote Aubry to the French Prime Minister, " of sending a list of the small number whom the

---

* France gave Louisiana to Spain lest the English should
seize it. Had an English governor come under the same circumstances as O'Reilly, what a butchery there would have been of the
insurrectionists!

General (O'Reilly) was indispensably obliged to have arrested. This proves his generosity and kindness of heart, considering there are many others whose criminal conduct would have justified their being treated in the same manner." Elsewhere he expresses astonishment that "the mere presence of one individual should have restored good order and tranquillity." And the Council of the Indies unanimously declared that "all the official acts of Count O'Reilly merited their most decided approbation, and were striking proofs of his extraordinary genius." With great liberality and profound policy, O'Reilly placed men of French birth or descent in all the chief offices of the State, * and sustained the French clergy in their charges.

It was at 3 P. M. on October 25, 1769, that the five men who were to die were brought to the place of execution. Their sentence was read to them in Spanish, and repeated in French by John Kelly and John Garic, who had acted as interpreters at the trial. The firing of a platoon of grenadiers, distinctly heard by the terror-stricken Ursulines, ended their lives in a moment. It is a great pity that so humane a ruler as

---

* A course diametrically opposite has always been pursued by the English in Ireland. Hence, while the Louisianians became thoroughly reconciled to the Spanish Domination, which was really a despotism very mildly administered, and for years after the American ascendancy would gladly have brought back the golden days of Spanish Colonial rule, the Irish have never been satisfied with the English Government.

O'Reilly should have felt himself unable to restore
order and at the same time spare the lives of these
men to whom the law had decreed death. The widow*
of the condemned who died in prison, Villeré, was the
granddaughter of Delachaise, the early benefactor of
the nuns. When peace was restored, education flourished once more. O'Reilly soon brought order out of
chaos. His romantic story and his wise and vigorous
administration place him high among the small number born to rule. A ripe scholar, versed in the literature of many nations, he warmly patronized the
existing schools, especially those of the Ursulines.
New schools were established and some of the most
learned professors of the universities of Spain came to
New Orleans to preside over them. O'Reilly, who
could have traveled from his native Meath to Moscow
without an interpreter, pleased the people by addressing them in French, though he preferred the stately
Castilian, which he spoke and wrote with classic purity
of diction.† The officers associated with him in the

* Madame Villeré's brother, M. Delachaise, and the chief Creoles and Frenchmen of the colony immediately took office under
O'Reilly, which would seem to show that they regarded the execution of the convicted men as a regrettable act of justice, and that
O'Reilly's instructions from the king left him no choice in the
matter. When O'Reilly wished to raise in the colony " The Regi-
ment of Louisiana," the number of applicants exceeded the number to which he limited this corps.

† Hon. Charles Gayarré, great-grandson of O'Reilly's *contador*,
showed the writer several autograph letters of this celebrated
Irishman.

government were all scholars of distinction, Gayarré, Navarro, and Loyola. The last claimed kindred with St. Ignatius, and was, like him, a model of knightly courtesy, a poet, and a valiant soldier of the cross. Don Joseph Loyola died in New Orleans in 1770.

Perhaps in succoring the Ursulines, to whom he was a generous benefactor, the poetic mind of O'Reilly and his truly Catholic heart wandered to a beauteous green isle, framed in sea-foam and draped with clouds, in which the song of cloistered virgins then seemed hushed forever. His entrance into New Orleans was a poem in itself, which must have recalled to his Celtic imagination the bare-armed Feni, the Ossianic heroes who haunt the shadowy past, and his ancestors in prehistoric Erin — dark-haired warriors wielding ponderous battle-axes, and white-robed bards harping upon their harps of burnished gold. For this princely ruler was almost the last high priest of vanishing chivalry. In the oath of office he administered to his subordinates is a promise to defend the Immaculate Conception of Our Lady, and never to take any fee from the poor.*

---

* Here is another of O'Reilly's regulations: "The governor, with the Alcaldes, the Alguazil Mayor, and the *escribano*, shall yearly, on the eves of Christmas, Easter, and Whitsunday, make a general visitation of the prisons. . . . They shall release those who have been arrested for criminal causes of small importance, or for debts, when such debtors are known to be insolvent,

Although the wants of the Ursulines were fully supplied, the king of Spain, perhaps on the representa‧tion of His Excellency, Governor O'Reilly, insisted on paying the convent a pension for the support of two of the nuns, probably those who taught the free school. Meanwhile the English language, universal in Louisi‧ana to‧day, was slowly creeping in; it was largely spoken in Mobile, Pensacola, and Baton Rouge. From the earliest days the English had traded with the set‧tlers on both sides of the river. They kept up the slave trade, and supplied planters with Africans of every tribe. Bienville himself had met them on the Mississippi when the village of Tchoutchouma occu‧pied the site of New Orleans, and they were among the earliest palefaces the red men saw. Aubry, the last French governor, corresponded in English with the governors of other provinces. In 1769 O'Reilly wrote: "I drove off all the English traders and other individuals of that nation, whom I found in the town (New Orleans), and I shall admit none of their vessels." But despite the Spanish ascendancy and the gradual introduction of English, French continued to be the favorite language of the Ursuline nuns, and was taught to all their pupils, even after the city became *Nueva-Orleans*.

It does not fall within the scope of this article to follow the early teachers of Louisiana through the old

or shall allow them a sufficient term for the payment of their creditors."

Spanish colonial times or the first years of American domination. We will, therefore, conclude with a glance at the FIRST GIRLS' SCHOOL erected in Louisiana, still, battered and decayed as it is, one of the largest and strongest houses in the State. The devouring tooth of time has eaten into the blue-gray stucco which once covered its massive walls, but not a vestige of its old aspect has departed. Dozens of windows, with small panes of greenish glass, look out on its cool gardens. A queer shrine flanks the end of the centre walk. A patch of sugar cane, a few flowers that seem to have been blooming since the last century, and some antiquated fruit trees, bring the past vividly before the spectator. Once this garden stretched to the Mississippi, but now huge rows of ugly houses shut out the river view. Tradition points out where the nuns were buried; but all were removed to the new monastery grounds in 1824. The colored servants who were interred in front of the convent were never disturbed. One would not like to eat the fruit of these gardens. For students have told their friends in mysterious whispers of a nun who sleeps beneath a certain cherry tree — she would not leave her ancient haunts; and of a supernatural spectre, "a ghost all in white," who roams about the grassy walks, and wails in the gloomy corridors, on certain high festivals. Nor would it surprise one who rambles through this old place to meet some spirit-nun on the broad, creaking staircase, with the thin iron balustrades, or in the large

deserted rooms that once resounded with sweet children's voices, and the hymns that charmed the simple
Creoles of old colonial days.

We ascended the top story, once used as an instruction room for blacks. Imagination peoples it in a
moment. There is the desk at which sat the brave
and gentle teachers who had crossed the seas to bring
these poor creatures to God. Dusky maidens and
matrons come hither in crowds for advice, instruction,
and consolation; their faces tell their tribe, — the
comely Yoloff, the treacherous Congo, the fierce Man-
dingo, the quarrelsome Banbarra, the intelligent
Foulah,—all wearing the picturesque turbans of their
full dress. And hither, too, crowd the Indian women,
with a world of sorrow in their long, dark eyes. We
descend; look through the various offices and people
them with the gentle Sisters we know so well. We
gaze on the clumsy gate with its small *grille* and
quaint iron knocker, and think of some who passed
through these faded portals. The early Jesuits and
Franciscans, old Father Bienville, honest Perier and
his pious wife. See how they crowd up from the
dreamy past, not shadowy creatures from the twilight
regions of romance, but beings real and human. The
grand Marquis de Vaudreuil in gilded casque and
heron plume, the pensive *Filles à la cassette*, the weeping Acadians, the chivalrous descendant of MacCarthy
More, the scholarly Ulloa — the austere countenance
of the princely O'Reilly, the dashing Galvez, the

4   49

lordly O'Farrell, the intellectual face and piercing black eyes of Peñalvert,— that group of princes in the centre of which is the pear-shaped head* of Louis Philippe — the spare physiognomy of Andrew Jackson, lean and haggard from midnight vigils, but illumined and glorified by his eagle eye — how they all crowd upon the memory in this hallowed spot, so full of holy and historic associations. The prelates of New Orleans, except Bishop Peñalvert, have always been guests of the Ursulines, who have given them free use of this ancient mansion. But we, for one, could not carry inside these old walls the habits and sentiments of the last quarter of the nineteenth century. The energy necessary to live and go forward to-day would ooze out through our finger-tips. We should be forever wandering in the shadowy past, dreaming dreams and seeing visions. The spirits conjured up by imagination would be more pleasant to us than the stern realities of everyday life. Years would seem but as days when spent in sweet dalliance with many a fair wraith ascending from the old graves under the quivering trees, eluding our grasp and melting, in the calm sweet hours of even, into the dreamy moonlight. And, verily, to a poetic temperament, loving to revel in historic lore, the spectre-nun of the past wailing in the forsaken halls of the ancient monastery, yea, even the "ghost all in white," rising from her green couch

* The future King of the French and his two brothers were in New Orleans in 1798.

under the cherry tree, would be a more pleasing companion than the tiresome votary of fashion, or the
soulless worshiper of wealth, in which our age is so
fertile.

VIII

ON THE tenth of February, 1763, Louisiana, by
a Treaty of Cession, passed under the rule of Spain —
on paper. Spain, already overburdened with colonies, was not eager to invade her new possessions,
and Louisiana was far from being anxious to deliver herself up to her new master. In October,
1764, the first official announcement of the transfer
came to New Orleans in a letter from Louis XV. to
Governor Abbadie. But to the inhabitants, the royal
message was but a diplomatic figure of speech. At
first they did not notice it. When certain signs told
them it was a serious business, they met in convention and appealed to the king not to separate them
from the mother-country. Spain gave them ample
time to ingratiate themselves into the favor of *Louis
le bien aimé*. They dispatched the richest merchant
in the colony to lay their petitions at the feet of the
" well-beloved " monarch. Bienville, then in his
eighty-sixth year, threw his influence, which should
have been great, into the scale in their favor. But
their passionate pleadings fell upon dull, cold ears,
and Louis, through his infidel minister, Choiseul, refused to keep Louisiana.

Meanwhile, Spain appeared to have forgotten all
about her new acquisition. For almost a year no

governor was appointed. "Never do to-day what you can safely put off till to-morrow," is a Spanish proverb which relieves from all danger of impetuosity the wise, slow people who put it into practice. When Don Antonio Ulloa, was commissioned as governor, he loitered in Havana for nearly another year. The people believed the cession a sham instrument. They were looking for counter-orders, when, lo! Spain, after being for years apathetic in the one-sided quarrel, determined to settle it. On the fifth of March the dilatory Ulloa appeared in the streets of the city with two companies of infantry. Needless to say, he was coldly received. Ulloa, then in his fifty-first year, was one of the finest scholars in the world. He was most desirous of conciliating the new subjects of Spain; but as they would not be conciliated, he left them to get over their ill-temper as best they could, and pitched his tent among the reed prairies at the mouth of the river. Here, in a crazy palace of shaking piles, he received the beautiful Marchioness d'Abrado, who came from Peru to become his bride, the parties having engaged themselves when Don Antonio traveled in South America in the interest of science. In March, 1767, when the banks were at the height of their beauty, the trees robed in pale green, and many of them starred with orange blossoms, the newly-wedded pair came up the river to New Orleans. Ulloa threw open his *salons* to the Creoles. His wife devoted herself to her guests. But her fascinations were unheeded; her beauty found no favor in their eyes; her accomplishments did not dazzle them. Everything the young Señora did displeased them. Trifles* were distorted into charges against the luckless couple. Aubry, the French governor, remarked that the colony scarcely knew whether it was French or Spanish. Ulloa turned for consolation to his books, allowing Aubry to govern for him — a service for which the Spanish government liberally rewarded him. The high-born lady who had come so far to preside over the festivities of Government House, having exerted herself in vain to please the people, in future treated them with indifference.

Towards the end of October the malcontents broke into open insurrection, and patrolled the streets as masters of the town. The women and children fled within doors. Aubry successfully exerted himself to save the life of Ulloa, and hurried him on board a Spanish frigate. On the twenty-ninth of October, 1768, the Governor was officially informed of his dismissal from the colony by the insurgents. On the thirty-first he embarked with his family, and next morning, while the captain was waiting for a fair wind, a band of insurrectionists endangered the lives of all aboard by cutting the cables which held the vessel to her moorings and sending her adrift. On the evening of that day Ulloa left forever the country so persist-

* Madame Ulloa made pets of several Indian girls, she sent to Cuba for a nurse for her infant, and, with a humanity that does her credit, she would not allow refractory slaves to be beaten. Worse than all, she laughed heartily when told these things gave offense.

ently antagonistic to him. Aubry denounced to his government the doings of the "rebels" led by a "dozen firebrands whom it was absolutely necessary to punish."

Whether Señor or Señora Ulloa did anything for education in New Orleans beyond showing the example of a most cultured and scholarly pair, we have been unable to learn. It is almost certain, however, that they did not. The colonists were from first to last bitterly opposed to them. Even the exquisite musical talent which the Marchioness exerted for their pleasure failed to please. They could not forgive her for being the wife of the man they so cordially detested. It is probable that the Ulloas were frequent visitors at the Ursuline Convent, situated but a few squares from their official abode. Within its walls they could find congenial spirits, and persons of culture may be expected to fraternize wherever they meet. But the fact that the nuns continued intensely French through all changes of government, may have had the effect of lessening the warmth of the friendship between the Ursulines and the scholarly people of Government House. When the news of the revolution reached Madrid, that court resolved that Spain should keep her new acquisition, and that the insult to the Spanish crown must be punished. The most distinguished officer then in the service of Spain, Don Alexander O'Reilly, was commissioned to effect this.

O'Reilly was one of that large and illustrious band of Irishmen, who, being disabled by their religion from serving their country as soldiers at home, earned honor, glory, fame, and sometimes fortune, under other banners, and supplied the regiments of several continental nations with their most efficient leaders. Their deeds of heroism were recounted by the Suir and the Shannon, under the shadow of the Galtees and by the cottier's winter fire. And the people persecuted at home were consoled to hear of the renown their brothers and sons were winning under the lilies of France and the sombre-hued banner of Austria and the flaming colors of Spain. In the latter half of the eighteenth century there was no braver or more virtuous Irishman in foreign military service than Alexander O'Reilly of Meath.

On the eighteenth of August, 1769, this renowned general made his triumphal entry into New Orleans with 2,600 men, the choicest of the armies of Spain, picked by himself. Artillery, light infantry, mounted riflemen, and cavalry paraded the *plaza* like practised veterans, as they were. The twenty-four sail which formed the fleet were bright with colors, their rigging being alive with sailors in holiday garb. Shouts of *Viva el Rey* rent the air. The bells of the town pealed merrily, discharges from hundreds of guns shrouded the streets in smoke, and fire flashing along the lines made a grim illumination. Drums and all manner of musical instruments gave out their best, while O'Reilly, preceded by splendidly accoutred men bearing heavy silver maces, moved slowly towards the church. This superb pageant concluded with a *Te Deum*.

The very next day O'Reilly, who was a most energetic and untiring worker, caused the case of the authors of the late insurrection to be investigated.
Within two months twelve were found guilty, of whom
one died in prison, six were banished, and five were
shot at Fort St. Charles, behind the Ursuline Convent
to the south, where the Mint now stands. The case
had been appealed from the Governor's head to his
heart; fair ladies besought him with burning words to
suspend the execution of the sentence of the court;
even his colleagues in office entreated him to assume
this responsibility. But, while treating all these sup-
plicants with "the most exquisite politeness," he was
inflexible. Though but thirty-four years old, he resisted the pleadings of men and the tears of women,
and while his words of refusal were mild and conde-
scending, and he listened to all that could be advanced
with extreme gentleness and patience, his mobile features assumed the stony, impassive expression of an
Egyptian sphynx, as he announced that the decision
of the court was final. In refusing the boon he would
gladly have granted, O'Reilly pleaded the orders of
the king. Peace reigned once more, and the nuns and
their pupils were able to devote themselves without
distraction to the improvement of the mind. Among
the pages in O'Reilly's retinue was a princely youth
of eighteen, Sebastian O'Farrell, who subsequently
became governor of Louisiana, and figured conspicu-
ously as the Marquis Casacalvo. He was distantly
related to O'Reilly, whose son and heir married the

niece of O'Farrell. The younger *Conde* O'Reilly settled in Cuba, where his descendants still live. Casacalvo also founded a distinguished family in the same
island.

The wise and enlightened administration of
O'Reilly in Louisiana was most favorable to education,
and His Excellency did not fail to patronize the existing schools, especially those of the Ursulines. About
this time it became fashionable for high officials to
visit and patronize convents. The Princess Louise,
youngest daughter of Louis XV., had entered the
monastery of St. Denis, near Paris — an event which
her royal father considered of sufficient importance to
be communicated officially to every court in Europe,
and, oddly enough, it fell to the infidel minister, Duc
de Choiseul, to make the announcement, which was
couched in the following terms:

"The deep and enduring piety of Madame Louise,
the king's daughter, has inspired her with the project
of joining the Carmelites. She tested her vocation,
and having obtained the king's consent, she yesterday
entered a monastery of that order at St. Denis, where
she proposes to make her profession as a simple Religious, leaving absolutely whatever appertains to the
world or its dignities. The king desires me to announce this exemplary and touching event to you."
This document is dated April 12, 1770.

O'Reilly had several friends and near relatives
in the royal Abbey of St. Denis. The Prioress
who received the Princess Louise, "Julienne de Mac-

Mahon," was an Irishwoman, and most of the nuns were, like herself, exiles from Erin, Irish by birth or extraction. "I have an Irish guard among the Carmelites," said Louis XV.

The successors of O'Reilly adopted his policy, interfering as little as possible with established customs, and filling the offices for the most part with men of French descent. The nine Spanish governors were less masters than fathers; they were all, though in different degrees, men of marked intellectual power and superior attainments. They made themselves one with the people. Many of the governors and other high officials allied themselves in marriage with the families of the soil. The New Orleans girl who married Count Galvez fulfilled a brilliant destiny as vice-queen of Mexico.

This same Galvez, in conjunction with Count Arthur O'Neill (1781), recovered Pensacola from the English. He had previously scaled the heights of Baton Rouge and driven them from that and other forts. These victories brought Louisiana a large accession of English-speaking subjects, to minister to whom the king of Spain sent from the University of Salamanca "four Irish priests of recognized zeal, virtue, and cultivation." These gentlemen, Fathers McKenna, Savage, Lamport, and White, were, so far as we can ascertain, the first secular clergymen who exercised the ministry in Louisiana.*

*One of these priests officiated at Natchez. In 1844 Bishop Chanche petitioned Congress to restore to that city the property

Meanwhile, great attention was paid to education. Governor Miro, whose wife, a McCarthy, had been a pupil of the Ursulines, mentions eight schools in successful operation in 1788, frequented by 400 French-speaking scholars. These do not include the Ursuline schools, always largely attended, or the Spanish schools, for which professors of the first universities had come from Spain. In 1785 the population of New Orleans was 4,900, including blacks and Indians. The population of the whole colony was 31,433. Owing to the preference of the people for the French language, the Spanish schools, established at the expense of the Crown,* were not largely attended till towards the close of the Spanish domination. Bishop Peñalvert, who came to New Orleans in 1795, and wrote unfavorably of the state of morals and religion in that city, admits that " the Spanish schools have been kept as

given to the Church by the Spanish Government. Natchez stands chiefly on church property. The Bishop found the necessary documents in Havana, and was allowed to copy them by the Captain-General of Cuba, Señor O'Donnell. But his application came too late. The lands had already been sold to private parties by the U. S. Government.

*In 1772 there came from Spain Don Andreas Lopez De Armestro, a priest, Director of the Schools, Don Pedro Aragon, *maestro de Syntaxis*, Don Manuel Diaz de Lura, professor of Latin, and Don Francisco de la Celena, *maestro de primeras lettras*. And four Spanish ladies took the veil among the Ursulines. " This," says Martin, " was the only encouragement given to learning during the whole period of Spanish Government." And it was more than enough, considering that *Nueva-Orleans* was already well supplied with schools.

59

they ought to have been." The manners of the young were refined and elegant. They were obedient and affectionate to their parents, to whom they showed great respect. And we think it would not be impossible to show that, in all the essentials of a good education, the people of New Orleans were, comparatively speaking, as well educated a century ago as they are now — perhaps better.

Since the memorable eighteenth of August, 1769, when the terrible vision of O'Reilly's hussars prancing and curveting amid the blare of trumpets, the glitter of brass, and the flash of steel, had cowed the people into completest subjection, there had been no political disturbance. Spiritually, the country had fallen to the ordinary of Havana. He sent hither Spanish Franciscans, who reported unfavorably of their French brethren and of church matters in general. One of the new friars, Father Cyrilo, subsequently became his coadjutor, with special charge of Louisiana. Cyrilo is the only ecclesiastic who wrote a word of censure of the nuns, but he refers merely to lack of strictness of cloister. He mentions their director, Father Prosper, " who is seventy-two years old, strong and robust, and capable of directing them." Cyrilo urges upon masters the obligation of watching over the morals of their slaves, and mentions among the good deeds of O'Reilly that he had got forty persons of this class, who had previously lived in sin, married *coram facie Ecclesiæ.* Indeed, that governor, to his honor be it recorded, always took sides with the weaker races.

He declared it to be "contrary to the mild and beneficent laws of Spain that Indians should be held in bondage," and commanded families who used them as slaves to emancipate them.

From the following, which occurs in a State paper written by Baron Carondelet to his government, April 27, 1793, it would appear that Cirilo was in *Nueva-Orleans* as Bishop: "When I arrived in New Orleans I found it divided into two factions — the one headed by Governor Miro and backed by the Bishop, etc." In 1794 Louisiana was finally detached from Havana, and New Orleans has since been a distinct see.

The Ursulines prospered greatly under the Spanish rule, for which they had at first so little welcome. Mother Landelle, who was Superior when the revolutionary troubles were at their height, in 1768, wrote to France for subjects, but the three who answered her appeal were not allowed to become members of her community until leave was granted by the Court of Madrid. In 1795 Bishop Peñalvert complains that "the nuns are so intensely French that they refuse to receive Spanish subjects ignorant of French, and shed tears for being obliged to make their spiritual exercises in Spanish books." In the early years of the Spanish ascendancy, the nuns gave up the service of the sick,* partly because their number had grown alarmingly small, and partly because of the dislike of the Spaniards of that day to nuns undertaking work outside their enclosure.

* They were empowered to do this by a brief from the Pope.

Many Spanish ladies joined the Ursulines, the most distinguished of whom was Monica de Ramos, who entered the Chartres street monastery in 1770, at the age of nineteeen. Monica was born in Havana. The *Señorita*, as she was called, seemed destined from childhood to some great and holy end. While a parlor-boarder in the Convent of Santa Clara, her soul was filled with a strong desire to devote herself to God and the salvation of souls in some special manner, and this impelled her to cross the seas and enter the cloisters of St. Ursula. Her companion, Sister Antonia del Castillo, who was professed with her, afterwards founded the Ursuline schools of Puerto Principe. Mother Ramos was several years mistress of novices, and in this office showed great zeal and charity, being the first to labor and the last to seek repose. So gentle and amiable were her manners that the Religious were wont to style her their "kind mother," and seculars "the noble lady always devoted to duty." One of her daughters thus apostrophized her in an elegy written in Spanish after her death: "O Monica! admirable even among the perfect, thy kind heart gained all."

Mother Ramos became Superior in 1785, and remained such during the incumbency of Governor Miro. Like most of the Spanish governors, Miro was an excellent English scholar, and with his wife, Señora MacCarthy Miro, was very popular. The piety and charity of this illustrious pair were lauded throughout the colony. They built a hospital* for the unfortu-

* On *La Terre des Lépreux*, in the rear of the city.

nate creatures afflicted with leprosy, a loathsome disease, supposed to have been brought hither from
Africa, and which has not yet wholly disappeared
in Louisiana. As Miro made stringent regulations
for the religious observance of Sundays and holy days,
the colored people were not allowed to begin their
Sunday evening dances till after Vespers. All the
governors were most friendly to the nuns. Their
schools and hospitals were frequently visited by these
high officials, who lived but a few squares from the
monastery. On November 1, 1795, Mother Farjon
being Superior, Bishop Peñalvert wrote: " Excellent
results are obtained from the convent, in which a good
many girls are educated. . . . This is a nursery of
future matrons who will inculcate on their children
the principles they imbibe here."

The Bishop's experience in New Orleans was not
cheering. Immigrants imbued with the atheistical
sentiments — we cannot say doctrines — of the so-
called philosophers of Europe, and many of the wild
and lawless from all parts of America made sad havoc
in New Orleans during the last decade of the Spanish
domination. In 1799 he deplores that " adventurers
who have no religion and no God have deteriorated
the morals of the people." " It is true," he proceeds,
" that resistance to religion has always shown itself
here, but never with such scandal as now prevails."
By a secret treaty Spain returned Louisiana to France
October 1, 1800; but three years elapsed before France
openly accepted the gift.

To the Spanish schools succeeded the famous College of Orleans, the first educational institution incorporated by the Legislature of Louisiana, situated on the corner of Hospital and St. Claude streets. During the first quarter of the present century the forest primeval came to its very gates. Every spring the thorny arms of the blackberry bush, spangled with white blossoms, made a tangled labyrinth of undergrowth, and as the flowers grew into green, red, and black berries, the small boys of the city invaded the forest's edge to seek the luscious fruit. The pupils of this college were celebrated for their classical attainments and courteous manners. Here Charles Gayarré, the historian * of Louisiana, received his education in English, French, Spanish, classics, and mathematics. This venerable gentleman still walks among us, though past fourscore, and, as a scholar and an author, Louisiana cannot show his superior. (He died 1896.)

An apostate priest, Joseph Lakanal who voted in the National Convention for the death of Louis XVI., and against whom other grave charges were made, was appointed principal of the College of Orleans about 1816. The people on learning his history, indignantly withdrew their sons, and the regicide fled. Nor could most of them ever be induced to

* F. X. Martin also wrote a History of Louisiana, but there is about as much heart and style in Martin's work as in a railway time-table. Besides, Martin never had access to State papers in Spain bearing on the history of the colony.

send them back. The institution declined from day
to day, and was finally closed. A church was erected
on its site in 1841, perhaps in a spirit of reparation.
To this church, St. Augustine's, is attached a thoroughly Catholic school.

It is worthy of note that Hon. Charles Gayarré
learned English so well in New Orleans as to be mistaken for an Englishman when he traveled in England
early in the present century. Daniel Clark, a wealthy
Irishman who lived in the colony during the greater
part of the Spanish ascendancy, was U. S. Consul
in New Orleans under the later Spanish governors.
Señor Gayoso, the only Spanish governor who died
in office (1799), was educated in England, and to the
convivial habits there contracted his countrymen
attributed his death at the early age of forty-eight.
From all this and from other sources it may be
gathered that English was always largely spoken in
Louisiana, though not universally, as it has been for
many years.

The closing decade of Spanish rule, like that extending from 1760 to 1770, was a period of turmoil
and anxiety. Red Republicanism and Jacobinism
sought admission; the French Revolution had its influence on the whites, and the success of the San Domingo revolution excited the blacks to form a
conspiracy for the ruin of the whites, which, however,
was discovered in time to be frustrated. To those
who could read the signs of the times it was evident
that Louisiana would, happily, through force of circum-

stances, soon cease to be an appanage of any European power, and enter as a Territory, and later as a sovereign State, the recently formed Union.

Rumors that the mild rule of Spain was to be exchanged for the French revolutionary government naturally raised a tempest in the Ursuline cloisters. The excitement and terror of the nuns, who feared a repetition of the horrors that had disgraced France, were such that Mother Ramos, on the fourth of October, 1802, made a formal petition to the king of Spain, Charles IV., to allow her community to withdraw to Havana or Mexico, or some other city in his dominions. The Spanish annals say that the peace which had reigned under Spanish rule passed away with it, that the revolutionary government showed a bitter hatred of Spain, and that, as many of the nuns were Spanish, they came in for their share of persecution. Heretofore, the fullest religious liberty had been enjoyed in Louisiana. Under the "unenlightened" sway of Catholic France and Spain, not a hair of any one's head was ever touched from religious motives. The old Creoles would shrug their shoulders when they heard that witches were burned, Quakers hanged, and Catholics tortured in New England by a people who claimed liberty of conscience for themselves. Now it was confidently expected that French rule would inaugurate religious persecution, and it seemed only discretion, that better part of valor, to retire before the storm burst upon them. The priests were allowed to depart, but all parties were anxious to keep the Ursulines. Their schools had been a blessing and a boon to the colony from its earliest days. The French colonial prefect, Laussat, besought them not to think of forsaking the city ; the chief citizens knelt to them, but in vain.

It was not a Spaniard, however, but a Frenchwoman, that reproached Laussat with the hideous crimes the Revolution had perpetrated (1789–1803) against religion and humanity, and denounced the French Republic as impious and sacrilegious : "Your promises of protection," said she, "are lies. You know well that Louisiana has been sold to the United States, whose President is not particularly friendly to Spain." The other Religious were terrified at the vehemence of these denunciations, but no guillotine was set up in Louisiana, and Laussat gallantly excused the lady on account of her great age. We may add that Sister Margaret died in Cuba in 1811, in her eighty-second year. The Havana annals note that the surviving Sisters were scarcely able to chant the office at her obsequies, "by reason of their great weeping for this beloved mother."

Mother Ramos consulted the Vicar-General, Hasset, Governor Salcedo, and the late Governor O'Farrell, Marquis Casacalvo, a superb soldier, born like herself in 1751, and allied by blood to Count O'Reilly, under whom he had served as a cadet in Louisiana, in 1769, and who consequently knew the country from the earliest days of Spanish rule. It was unanimously agreed that the safest course for the nuns to adopt under the present critical circumstances was to retire to the dominions of the king of Spain.

It is customary for the Ursulines to make a retreat immediately before Whitsunday, and renew their vows on that solemn day. Greatly did the New Orleans nuns need the strength and grace to be derived from such pious exercises on the feast of Pentecost, May 29, 1803. On the night of that day sixteen nuns, without waiting for the answer of the Catholic king, left the Chartres street monastery forever. With their faces and forms concealed by their ample robes, they issued slowly by the chapel gate into Ursuline street, accompanied to the inclosure limits by the few who remained behind, and whom they were never again to meet. Those who left lauded the courage of those who stayed : "Great was their heroism to stay in New Orleans fighting for God, never heeding the dangers that surrounded them, offering all their pains with loving gratitude to God. The priests had already left, scarcely any remaining, owing to the critical condition of Louisiana. Bishop Peñalvert had been translated to Guatemala in 1802. Dr. Porro, second Bishop of New Orleans, died in Rome the same year, on the eve of his intended departure for his episcopal city. By the transfer of Louisiana to the United States, New Orleans fell under the jurisdiction of Bishop Carroll, and for twelve years Bishop Porro had no successor.

Under the shadow of the convent chapel on that bright May evening (1803), a sadly beautiful tableau was dimly visible in the glare of the oil-lamps, recently swung across the streets by the energetic Baron Carondelet,* and the flickering of the torches and lanterns borne by the slaves who headed the procession. The nuns were accompanied by Vicar-General Hasset on the part of the Church, and, on the part of the king, by O'Farrell, Marquis of Casacalvo, and the aged Salcedo, Governor of Louisiana, both richly uniformed and surrounded by attendants in gaudy liveries. The boarders and orphans formed a sorrowing group about their beloved teachers, and the slaves who worked in the quaint gardens came out to look their last on their kind mistresses. Outside the throng were *gens d'armes* in brilliant uniforms faced with gold, Indians in picturesque feathers and blankets, and *serenos* (watchmen) calling out the hour. Among the old friends who came to see the Religious off, one might note the powdered head, the gold and velvet coat, the frilled and jeweled shirt front, the red-heeled shoe and silver buckle — the shining gown of stiff brocade, the lace head-dress set over high-combed hair, which we see imprisoned in the sweet family portraits of a bygone age treasured in many a Louisiana home.

Slowly over the sedgy *banquettes* (sidewalks), made passable here and there by the gunwales of flat-boats, moved these dark-robed, sorrowing women. They

* One of the principal streets in New Orleans perpetuates the name of Carondelet — Baronne street is called after his wife, *La Baronne.*

were leaving the convent in which some had lived from childhood, in which all had hoped to die, to seek a home they knew not where, and carve out for themselves a destiny they knew not how. No preparations had been made for the journey. They carried away only some documents* which ought to have been left behind, and a few ornaments for the altar which their Sisters forced upon them as precious souvenirs of their beloved old monastery. A negro and his son, a boy of fifteen, formed their only escort. They embarked in a small vessel which had scarcely left her moorings when she was becalmed. For three days they awaited a favorable wind. Their Sisters sent them refreshments, and, "though far away in body, were with them in spirit," as the charming notes that passed between the parties testified. "All were united in the bonds of charity, and tried to act in this difficult situation with the greatest purity of intention."

Our nuns and their black servants had ample leisure to study the little Franco-Spanish city they were leaving forever. It made a pretty picture in the summer sunlight. What forms the French quarter to-day, and is, save in its antiquarian and historic aspect, the least important part of New Orleans, was then the whole city. It extended from the river to the ramparts (Rampart street) and from Duane

---

* As the remaining nuns expected the French Revolution in miniature in New Orleans, they allowed these papers to be sent to Havana for safety.

street to the Esplanade. The houses near the river were of brick, roofed with tiles; a levée crowned with willow and orange trees protected the town from periodical overflows. The *plaza*, a green lawn with diagonal walks, was crowded late and early with the air-loving citizens. Above this rose the cathedral of Almonaster (a Spaniard who spent $2,000,000 on his adopted city), an exquisite structure with white turrets and shining cross, in and out of which women veiled in Moorish style, and attended by slaves, might be seen gliding, often laden with votive offerings. The silvery bells of the convent echoed the mellow tones of the cathedral chimes as they rang out the *Angelus* morning, noon, and night. The cabildo, the calaboza, the hospitals, and the forts, all teeming with religious and historic associations; their own loved convent, then visible from the river; the houses daubed with violet or saffron, pink or white, a mosaic of colors, were surrounded by open galleries and *jalousies*, decked with flowering shrubs and shaded by moss-draped trees — perhaps the nuns, as they lay rocking in the river, tried to enjoy these sights. Before them was the busy levée — old *negresses* with Indian baskets full of rice-cakes, singing in "gumbo French" the nutritious qualities of their *belle calla*; colored wenches bringing Marseilles jars to be filled by the water-carriers; picturesque gypsies selling nut-cakes in the arcades of the courthouse, about the corners of old quadrangular buildings, or among the shadows of a many-pillared colonial villa. On these warm days merchants put their goods on the *ban-quettes*, and waresmen praised their wares in many a dialect. Towards sunset negroes danced the *bamboula* and the *calinda* in vacant patches, and jabbered and sang in the barbaric jargon of Sene-gambia.

No doubt the poor nuns wearied of these sights and sounds, and were heartily glad when a favorable wind arose. Gradually they lost sight of the twin turrets of the cathedral and its glittering cross, swept down the river and out of the dreary passes by which it glides into the sea. Many a time has the writer been actually depressed in going through these chan-nels, in which, whatever way one looks, one sees, perhaps, the bleakest prospect on earth. How must the poor nuns have felt! Their voyage across the gulf was tedious. They reached Havana on June 23d. As they were entirely unexpected, no prepara-tions had been made for them. The Bishop sent six to the Convent of Santa Clara (Poor Clares), six to Santa Catalina (Dominican nuns), and four to Santa Teresa (Carmelites).

On the twenty-fifth of July Mother Ramos was consoled by a kind letter from Madrid signed by the king, in reply to hers of October, 1802. His Catholic Majesty expressed himself as much pleased with the good the nuns had effected in the past, and graciously invited them to continue their useful labors in Ha-vana. He granted each Sister a monthly pension of twenty-seven dollars, payable till his death, and strongly recommended the Ursulines to the fatherly care of the Bishop.

The people of Havana welcomed the refugees with tender, respectful kindness, and began at once to build them a magnificent monastery. To this they went in carriages, escorted by the Governor and all the nobility of the city (1804). Many distinguished ladies joined them, and the training of the novices and the education of the future teachers of the Order were confided to the only Irishwoman in the band that fled from New Orleans, " Sister Felicitas Carder." Twelve Spaniards, three Frenchwomen, and herself composed this band. The splendor of the new house was a genuine surprise to the Sisters, especially the finely-carved stalls and the sparkling chandeliers in the chapel. It is particularly and gratefully noted that each Religious had her own cell, which contained a " leathern bed, two chairs, and a clothes-press in the shape of a table."

Fearing that it might be inferred that they were fugitives from their monastery because they left it late at night, the nuns took care to record that their passports were regularly signed, that they were escorted to the ship by the highest religious, civil, and military officials, and, finally, that the hour of departure was not chosen by them, but appointed by the captain. They reiterated that the only motive of their departure was " to save themselves from the impious revolutionary government of France." The French claimed authority over the property of Religious, and confiscated such property in France. It was said that Laussat meant to sell the New Orleans monastery or turn it from its sacred purpose. All manner of wild rumors were afloat. Spain, by her commissioners, O'Farrell and Salcedo, ceded the colony to France, November 30, 1803. Twenty days later the United States took possession of Louisiana, having purchased it from France for fifteen million dollars.

It comes not within the scope of this paper to recount the story of the Havana Ursulines. We shall merely add that what they had feared in Louisiana came upon them, after a short period of prosperity, in Cuba. The Government closed their novitiate, and compelled them to leave the cloister and put off their sacred garb. After suffering in many ways for years, they were allowed to reassemble in community in 1824. But the beloved Mother Ramos, the joy and consolation of her daughters in all their afflictions, did not live to see this happy time. She died October 23, 1823. Their chief friend during their long and grievous persecution was Very Rev. Don Bernardo O'Gahan, Canon of the Havana Cathedral. Queen Isabella II., whose confessor was made first Archbishop of Havana, has been a generous benefactress to these nuns. On one occasion Her Majesty sent them a gift of twelve thousand dollars.

Early American times may be said to belong to the Spanish period, not only because there was no social or religious change for many years, but also because there was in the breast of every one either a hope or a fear that Spain would retake Louisiana. When the stars and stripes replaced the tri-color, and *Nouvelle-Orleans* and *Nueva-Orleans* had given place forever to *New Orleans*, the nuns were more uneasy than ever., And not causelessly, for nothing could be more dark and threatening than the aspect of public affairs. The Creoles did not take kindly to the new order of things. And so little was the genius of the American Government understood in her latest acquisition, that people supposed to be well informed kept the nuns in continual agitation; to-day, they were to be expelled; to-morrow, their property, which was considerable, was to be confiscated; next day, the utmost concession granted them was leave to stay in their convent till the present inmates should die out.

Internally, the nuns were doing well. Two subjects had been recently added to their staff, and their boarders numbered 170. Under these circumstances the Superior, Mother Farjon, addressed a letter to Bishop Carroll, which he forwarded to Mr. Madison, then Secretary of State, later President, who sent the following courteous reply, July 28, 1804:

" I have had the honor to lay before the President your letter of the fourteenth of December, who views with pleasure the public benefit resulting from the benevolent endeavors of the respectable persons in whose behalf it is written. Be assured that no opportunity will be neglected of manifesting the real interest he takes in promoting the means of affording to the youth of this new portion of the American dominion a pious and useful education, and of evincing the grateful sentiments due to those of all religious persuasions who so laudably devote themselves to its diffusion. It was under the influence of such feelings that Governor Claiborne had already assured the ladies of this monastery of the entire protection which will be afforded them after the recent change of government.

"I have the honor to be, with great respect, etc.,

JAMES MADISON."

Mother Farjon wrote direct to the President, who consoled her with the following reply:

"*The President of the United States to Sœur Thérèse de St. Xavier Farjon, Supérieure, and the Nuns, etc.:*

"I have received, Holy Sisters, the letters you have written to me, wherein you express anxiety for the property vested in your institution by the former Government of Louisiana. The principles of the Constitution of the United States are a sure guarantee to you that it will be preserved to you sacred and inviolate, that your institution will be permitted to govern itself according to its own voluntary rules, without interference from the civil authority. Whatever diversity of shade may appear in the religious opinions of our fellow-citizens, the charitable objects of your institution cannot be indifferent to any; and its furtherance of the wholesome purposes of society by training up its young members in the way they should go, cannot fail to insure it the patronage of the Government it is under. Be assured it will meet with all the protection my office can give it.

"I salute you, Holy Sisters, with friendship and respect,

THOMAS JEFFERSON."

The first American governor, Claiborne, treated the Ursulines with great deference. On taking office he assured them, on the part of the President, of the protection of the United States Government. Early in his administration a comedy was put on the stage in which the religious state was ridiculed; the Lady Abbess invoked the interference of His Excellency,

who at once communicated with the mayor, " to whom
belongs the duty of checking the abuses of the stage."
A courteous reply, in which the Governor expresses
great regret that the feelings of these pious ladies
should have been wounded, concludes:

"The sacred objects of your Order, the amiable characters
that compose it, and the usefulness of their temporal cares, cannot fail to command the esteem and confidence of the good and
virtuous. I pray you, Holy Sisters, to receive the assurances of
my great respect and sincere friendship. I salute you, etc.,

.   WILLIAM CLAIBORNE."

No one could be more kind and respectful to the
Sisters than the Protestants, Madison and Claiborne,
and Jefferson, who is usually classed as an infidel.
When Jefferson died, leaving his family destitute,
Louisiana, mindful of his courtesy, voted his heirs ten
thousand dollars.

But despite the kindness of these officials, many
within the convent and outside were extremely unset-
tled. Having changed rulers three times in twenty
days, they could not believe they were at last under a
stable government. The sale or cession was very unpopular. There were sympathizers with Spain, and
Jacobins, and Burrites, and " dangerous Americans,"*

*Among the Americans who posed as friends of Spain was
Wilkinson. "I shall always be ready," said he, "to defend the
interests of Spain with my tongue, my pen, and my sword."
"Thank you, dearest friend," said Governor Miro. "I am anxious to become a Spaniard, the first opportunity." "You! a
Spaniard, Sir," exclaimed Miro; "Oh, no! That cannot be. Continue to dissemble and work underground. Retain your American pen, etc. You can serve us better in that guise." "Thus

who wanted back Spanish rule. In external appearance and accomplishments Claiborne contrasted poorly with O'Farrell, the "lordly Casacalvo," whose "exquisite politeness" * rather embarrassed the republican Governor. The people, accustomed to see only fine linguists in high places, complained that neither Claiborne nor his colleague, Wilkinson, could speak a word of French or Spanish.

Religion was in a deplorable state. Father Hasset died in 1804. Father Antonio Sedella, who, for attempting to introduce the Inquisition in 1789, had been summarily dismissed by Governor Miro, had found his way back. He was again dismissed by Vicar-General Walsh in 1805, but appealed to the parishioners and was reinstated by them. The affair was brought to the civil courts, and there were Valesians in New Orleans as well as in Ireland. The fourth of July was celebrated by a grand High Mass and *Te Deum* in the Cathedral. Death removed Father Walsh, but not the ecclesiastical troubles that had harassed him, which ended in a schism. The aged Father Olivier, appointed Vicar-General by Bishop Carroll, December 27, 1806, was the only priest in the city who had faculties.

Since the expulsion of the Jesuits, the Capuchins spoke Spanish pride and honor," says Gayarré. " Is there on record a more striking specimen of withering contempt?"

* When reproached for returning the salutation of a negro with as much gracious respect as he would that of a prince. Casacalvo mildly asked : " And do you suppose that I would suffer myself to be outdone in politeness by a negro?"

had been directors of the Ursulines, but from the opening of the century they appear no more in that capacity. Their directors since have been Fathers Olivier, 1806, Moni and Sibour, 1822, Richard, 1834, Janney and Roussillon till 1842, when M. l'Abbé Perché succeeded till 1870, when he was raised to the episcopate. The Jesuits then, after the lapse of over a century, resumed their direction.

In 1812 Bishop Carroll sent Rev. William Dubourg, a native of San Domingo, to regulate affairs; but so many obstacles were raised by those who should have aided him, that he placed the city under an interdict. The Cathedral was closed, and in the Ursuline chapel only was Mass celebrated. The chaplain being over eighty, the nuns feared they might soon be deprived of Mass and the sacraments, and they petitioned the Holy Father to allow them to go to France, where peace now reigned. His Holiness himself deigned to reply in the following letter addressed to Mother Marie Olivier:

"MADAME:— Your letter of May 2d, reached us only towards the end of September. We are very sensible of your good wishes for our preservation and the success of our enterprises, always directed to the glory of God and the advantage of the Church. As to the inquietudes that agitate you regarding your spiritual direction, they cannot last, for M. Dubourg has received from Us Bulls, and has been consecrated at Rome, by our order, Bishop of the diocese of New Orleans, to which he will soon return. You may, then, be tranquil as to your future, and give up the project of going to France; you can do much more for religion where you are. Therefore we exhort you to redouble your zeal for young persons of your sex and for the eternal salvation of your neighbor. We have your community continually present to our mind, especially in our prayers, to obtain for you all the graces you need, and we give you, with effusion of heart, our Apostolic benediction.

"Given at Castel Gandolfo, near Rome, the sixteenth of October, 1815, of our Pontificate the XVI. year.

PIUS-VII., PP."

Abbé Dubourg officiated at the thanksgiving for the success of the American arms in the battle of New Orleans. From their galleries and dormer windows the nuns could see the smoke rising from the plains of Chalmette and hear the sharp report of rifles and the thunder of cannon, January 8, 1815. All night they watched before the Blessed Sacrament, beseeching the Lord of Hosts to give victory to the Americans. Over the entrance of the monastery was exposed an image of Our Lady of Prompt Succor, still religiously preserved by the New Orleans Ursulines. That morning Abbé Dubourg said Mass in the convent chapel for the same intention. There were present only women and children; the men were on the battle-field. Humanly speaking, the English were certain to win. Never had the nuns been in such danger. The horrible watchword of the enemy was *Booty and Beauty*. Had the day gone against Jackson, he would, had he survived, have blown up the city. "For," said he, using energetic expletives which we forbear from quoting, "New Orleans shall never fall into the hands of the British."

A magnificent pageant celebrated this great victory. General Jackson entered the city in triumph

January 23, 1815. In the midst of the historic *plaza*, now Jackson square, a triumphal arch was erected, supported by symbolic figures. Under this he was crowned by a fair girl who represented Louisiana. He moved slowly through an avenue of lovely girls representing the States and Territories, with silver stars on their foreheads, flags in their right hands, and, hanging from their left arms, baskets of flowers, which they emptied beneath the feet of the preserver of New Orleans. M. Dubourg received him at the church door.

It is doubtful if any who witnessed the procession of July 13, 1734, were present January 23, 1815, though some of the Creoles and negroes live to a great age. But many were there — the whole city turned out to do honor to its savior — that remembered the picked veterans of Spain who paraded the same square and drew up before the church, under another warrior of the same race — a race always enamored of religion and poetry and military glory. But the gallant O'Reilly was judge and savior, whereas Jackson was savior alone. There was not, as he poetically said, a cypress leaf in the laurel circlet that crowned him.

The conqueror * visited the nuns to receive their felicitations and thank them for their prayers and vows in his behalf. Nor did he ever omit to call

---

* There were nuns in the convent when Jackson visited it who could describe for him the later French governors and all the Spanish governors.

on the nuns on his subsequent visits to New Orleans. Jackson was the last great soldier that passed into the cloisters of the old monastery, and the only President of the United States that ever stood within its precincts.

After the battle of New Orleans the convent school rooms were turned into infirmaries, and the nuns resumed their *rôle* of hospital nurses. Their schools flourished more than ever. The people were now thoroughly reconciled to American rule, and all hopes or fears of again becoming an appanage of any European power had perished forever. In 1817 Bishop Dubourg brought the nuns nine postulants from Europe. In 1821 he wrote to Quebec for a few experienced members. His letter shows the state of the convent: "In point of numbers the house gives me no cause for alarm, but when I consider the age of the ancient pillars of that edifice, and that, at the moment, not remote, of their fall, there will remain only feeble reeds to replace them, I cannot be tranquil as to the consequences." This metaphorical language was meant to convey that, as the nuns were all very old or very young, there were none in the prime of life to succeed the elders. "Send us, then," he continues, dropping metaphor, "three or four professed nuns of mature age, good judgment, and formed to the practice of virtue, to fill the void between the aged and the young." It was far easier to travel from Quebec to Europe than from that city to New Orleans. But volunteers were found for the perilous journey, and three nuns, whose ages ranged from thirty to forty, came to aid their New Orleans sisters, "a precious acquisition" which all received as "a boon from heaven." Three Ursulines, driven from Boston in 1834, took refuge with the New Orleans nuns, to whom they rendered important services. One of these ladies, Irish by birth, still (1887) lives.

The nuns built in 1821 a spacious monastery three miles from the city, capable of accommodating four or five hundred pupils. To this they removed,* without ceremony of any kind, in the vacation of 1824. Three nuns and a novice took up their abode in it July 26th. Two weeks later several other Sisters and the boarders followed, the Superior and some others remaining in the city till the closing of the day-school in September. The early dwellers in the new home had many privations; having no cooking apparatus, their meals were sent from the old house. Once their caterer did not come till evening, nor was his arrival a source of much comfort. He presented only empty dishes, his cart having upset on the way. Even at this late date, depredations by Indians in the suburbs of the city were not unknown, and the nuns were so much afraid that they could not sleep. Finally, one of the bravest, Sister Marie Olivier, offered to keep watch while the others slept. But neither Indians

* One of the nuns had not been outside her cloister since her entrance, in 1760. This aged lady was overcome with tears and emotion when obliged to pass beyond the *grille* on the way to her new home in 1824.

nor other robbers made their appearance in her hours of patrol. She was kept busy chasing rats, which ran in every direction making dreadful noises. For two months the nuns had Mass on Sundays only, Monseigneur Dubourg himself officiating as their chaplain and director. The community then (1824) numbered twenty, two of whom are still living (1886).

Bishops Dubourg, Rosati, De Neckère, and Blanc are mentioned with grateful affection in the Ursuline records. They never left the city without paying farewell visits to the Sisters and begging their prayers. And on their return they would at once call on them. Their visits were frequent and most paternal. Ceremonious receptions were given them only on their feasts. Within the convent they were as fathers in the midst of their families. The pupils would continue their games before them, or gather around them to hear their amiable words. Bishop De Neckère used regularly to give the Religious lessons in astronomy, philosophy, chemistry, and natural history. He took the greatest delight in instructing those scholars who corresponded by their intelligence and application to his paternal devotion.

The French, Spanish, and early American governors paid the Ursulines ceremonious visits at stated times, and any cause of complaint they referred to these gentlemen was immediately removed. When Louisiana became a State in 1812, and Claiborne, who had governed by appointment since 1804, was elected governor, he and all officials under him, especially his Secretary of State, MacCarthy, showed them every possible courtesy. Apart from the troubles of the Church, which were a keen source of grief to these good Religious, a long era of peace and prosperity began for them with Claiborne's administration. Johnson was the last governor who paid them an official visit and a New Year's call, in 1828. Jackson visited them the same year. Though men of French descent and men of the lineage of O'Reilly and O'Farrell have since occupied the high position of chief magistrate of this State, the courtesies shown the nuns by the earlier governors have been discon‑ tinued since 1828.

Madame Duchesne, of the Sacred Heart Order, who came to New Orleans in 1818, and shared the generous hospitality of the Ursulines, says they edu‑ cated nearly all the girls in Louisiana. She found in the convent almost three hundred boarders receiving a Christian education, besides many *negresses* and *mulattresses* who assembled for catechism every even‑ ing. "The blacks," she writes, "gather around Abbé Martial (the convent chaplain) with the fervor of the early Christians gathering about St. Peter, and when the signal gun obliges them to withdraw, they com‑ plain of not being allowed to remain all night at their pious exercises." This is not the description com‑ monly given of the black and yellow people, the quadroons and octoroons, by those who have never read their secret history in the letters and diaries of the Religious who labored among them, and who would have us believe that all the Africans spent their evenings in the wild and terrible orgies of Congo square.

Madame Duchesne, who had been a Visitation nun before the Revolution, was charmed with her sojourn among the daughters of St. Ursula, as nuns still living who were boarders in 1818 can testify. Without the walls she found little to console her. There were but two priests in a city of 15,000 souls. Including the chaplains of convent, barracks, and hospitals, there never had been less than seven priests of various nationalities on duty in New Orleans during the Spanish domination, all being paid by the king of Spain. O'Reilly considered eighteen priests necessary for the spiritual wants of the Louisiana * of his day. The Sacred Heart nun speaks disparagingly of the state of morals where she had expected to find only " primitive families, simple, innocent, and pure." The Louisiana girls did not edify her, yet her companion, Madame Audé, wrote a little later: " The children are obedient and have excellent manners." First impressions of new countries are often misleading, because exaggerated. Vice is bold and readily leaps to the surface ; virtue is modest and too often timid. There was more good in New Orleans than could be seen at a glance, and had Madame Duchesne labored a few years in the city her views would have been considerably modified. The beautiful devotion to the Sacred Heart had been in-

* The population of Louisiana in O'Reilly's day was over thirteen thousand.

troduced by the Ursulines, and Madame Duchesne mentions a picture of that divine object in the sanctuary and a book of " Devotions to the Sacred Heart of Jesus" published in New Orleans. The Ursulines lavished on this good woman and her five companions the most delicate attentions, and provided them with comforts and even luxuries. On leaving for St. Louis, in July, 1818, the Sacred Heart Sisters received from their generous hostesses a gift of 1,500 francs. Almost all the Religious who have since settled in New Orleans have received hospitality and kindness from the Ursuline nuns. They were formerly wealthy and gave freely of their abundance. Poverty was almost unknown in New Orleans before the Civil War, from which the Ursulines suffered more severely than any kindred institution. Nor have they yet regained their former prosperity. While the teachers have never lost their high literary reputation, it is sad to think that their pupils are now counted by tens where they were once hundreds.

The archives of this oldest monastery in the United States contain instances of heroism in its early teachers which find their counterparts only in the Lives of the Saints.

There was Sister Farjon. Born at Avignon of pious parents, she was attracted in girlhood to the pleasures of the world. Being sent at fifteen to the Ursulines, her heart, under their judicious training, turned entirely to God, and she showed the germs of the excellent qualities that blossomed and bore fruit in after life. Her mind was most penetrating, and she worked successfully to overcome the difficulties one experiences at that age whose early education has been neglected. At sixteen she entered the novitiate. Humility and obedience were her favorite virtues and the hidden life of Christ in God her peculiar attraction. Her gayety, her obliging and gentle manners won her the love of all. Her great talent was for teaching the young, whom she made excellent scholars and trained to the practice of solid virtue. She had a strong desire for the foreign mission, and in response to an invitation from the Superioress of New Orleans, made known to her by an old Jesuit who had spent twelve years evangelizing the Indians of lower Louisiana, Sister Xavier, with two young Religious, set out for New Orleans in 1786. Here she divided her attention between the slaves and the scholars. But it was in the office of Superior, which she held twelve years, that her virtues shone with greatest lustre. To her fell the difficult task of building up the Order after the departure of the Spanish Sisters. Like most of the early members, she worked on to the last. Seeing her end approaching, she comforted her sorrowing children, bade them be of good cheer and not leave New Orleans, for God would send them help, which came to pass as she had predicted. She died in the odor of sanctity, March 10, 1810.

There was Felicité Alzas, who left the world before she knew its vanity and entered the Ursuline Convent, where "she trod the paths of perfection with the steps of a giant." In 1786 she came with two other nuns to the aid of New Orleans from France. The French archives say they were coldly received by the Spanish Ursulines, who placed them in the lowest grade, and even counseled them to return. But this was probably because they could not receive French women without leave of the King of Spain. This was obtained by an old Jesuit friend who, not wishing the New Orleans house to lose such promising subjects, wrote to the Catholic king in their behalf. His Majesty immediately ordered Bishop Cirilo to have them admitted as full members, which was done in November, 1786. If Mother Ramos felt any coldness towards Sister Alzas, it soon vanished, for her natural acuteness showed her what a treasure the house possessed in her. After filling all the other offices, Mother Alzas became Superior in 1827, at the age of seventy-five. Happy by nature as by name, she was all goodness to her daughters, and it was admirable to see her, despite her great age, taking part in all their little amusements. She had a special love for the sick, and might be seen every evening, lantern in hand, visiting them to assure herself they wanted nothing. This holy nun preserved her faculties to the last, and could read the finest print by candlelight without glasses. It is said that she asked and obtained of St. Joachim the grace of never falling into dotage.

The nuns were never weary of extolling the charity and humility of Mother Felicité. Her maternal goodness drew subjects to the house. She loved to replace any Sister that might be absent from a duty, to help at sweeping the dormitory and ironing the clothes. Children and ignorant people had a particular attraction for her. She sacrificed to them her time and her rest. The venerable Mother had great conformity to the will of God. And when several young Religious were describing their ardent desires of perfection, after hearing them patiently, she said: "And I, my children, desire no more love of God, no more of any virtue, than He pleases to give me." To a nun who expressed surprise at her joyousness under afflictions she said: "For a long time, my daughter, my soul has been established in peace, and nothing can trouble it." Her fifty years' residence in New Orleans had been singularly checkered — she saw the dreadful conflagrations (1788 and 1794) that left thousands homeless; the hurricane that desolated the city in August, 1795; the revolt of the negroes, who, excited by the success of the San Domingo revolution, conspired to butcher all the whites in the colony,* but worst of all, the schism that all but ruined religion in Louisiana. The death of Charles III. was a loss to the nuns, and it was in their chapel, as the parish church had recently been burned, that grand funeral rites were held in his honor, and a solemn *Requiem* celebrated for the repose of his soul, May 7, 1789. Like other favored souls, Mother Alzas was tried in

* After this, the importation of slaves into Louisiana was prohibited, the Cabildo having petitioned the King of Spain to that effect.

many ways, but she joyfully drank the chalice of afflic-
tion. In 1796 yellow fever for the first time ravaged the
city,* and though the nuns escaped, they had much
to suffer from the consequences of the plague. This
good mother despised the pains of this life, having her
heart set on the glories of eternity. Such was her
reputation for sanctity that she was honored at home
and abroad, and consulted by many on delicate matters
of conscience. She loved to instruct and console the
slaves, to whom she was a kind mother. Her last illness lasted but a few hours. She resigned herself entirely into the hands of God. To the Sisters, whom
she had loved and served so faithfully, she said : " Do
as you please with me." She died October 13, 1835,
in the eighty-sixth year of her age, having spent
seventy years in religion.

There was the musical Mother de la Clotte, whose
songs resound through her sweet story. Born at
Montpellier of a highly distinguished family, she was
imprisoned during the Revolution, and made herself
the slave of her fellow-captives. When set free the
fair girl sought to bury her beauty and mental gifts in
a cloister, and for this end came to New Orleans in
1789, *via* Baltimore, where Bishop Carroll detained
her till December 21st, "on account of the heat." She
was specially devoted to the duty of teaching, and

---

* The Intendant, Morales, remarks that the yellow fever selected Flemish, English, and Americans for its victims, and spared
Spaniards and blacks. There has never been a case of yellow fever
among the Ursulines.

though a lover of silence and recollection, she could not bear to be absent from her beloved schools, even when Superior. It was believed that this saintly woman never lost her baptismal innocence. She died after a few days' illness, December 20, 1827.

There was Mother Gensoul, a saintly girl in the world, a saintly nun in the cloister. In 1792 she had to fly; the most stormy years of this dark period she spent with her relatives. With another Ursuline, Sophie Ricard, who had been reared a Protestant, but converted by seeing the profession of a nun, she opened a school at Montpellier, and both followed their vocation as well as they could during the Reign of Terror. In 1810 she desired to join the New Orleans Ursulines, now reduced to seven, but her Bishop would not allow her. She referred her case to the Pope, who, himself, deigned to calm her perplexity. December 31, 1810, she reached New Orleans, having been detained over the sickly season in Baltimore by Dr. Carroll. As the nuns heard her carriage lumbering up the narrow street towards their convent, they felt that her coming was a realization of the comforting prophecy of Mother Farjon.

The good Mother now resumed the religious habit she had been compelled to put off eighteen years before. Her graciousness and affability charmed everyone, particularly the young. She had a tender devotion to the Sacred Heart of Jesus, which was increased by a miraculous dream, in which she seemed to see this Heart burning with love for men, adored by angels who were as nothing in His presence; a little above was the Eternal Father under the appearance of an old man. Struck with astonishment, she resolved to paint what she had seen, and the result of her labors was placed within the sanctuary.

Mother Gensoul had a lively devotion to Our Lady of Prompt Succor. Before the battle of New Orleans she made a vow to have a solemn Mass of thanksgiving every year if God would give victory to General Jackson. The statue of Our Lady of Prompt Succor was placed on the altar while Abbé Dubourg offered the Holy Sacrifice to the God of armies, begging Him to deliver the city from the threatened danger. Women and children joined in his supplications; the fathers and sons were all on the battle-field.

To this day a solemn Mass is sung every year in the Ursuline chapel on the eighth of January, which is a legal holiday, and a hymn composed by Mother Gensoul is sung after Mass, "because," say the chronicles, "a great army commanded by generals proud of their ability was cut in pieces, while on the American side six only were killed and seven wounded." Years, sorrows, and labors at length told upon the iron constitution of Mother Gensoul. To Bishop Dubourg, who entered the infirmary just before her death, she spoke her last words: "I thirst." "Yes, Mother," said he, "but it is for God!" "O God, my God," she murmured, "I thirst for Thee. How lovely are Thy tabernacles! My soul longeth and fainteth after the courts of my God." This apostolic woman, teacher of youth, friend and mother of Indians, negroes, and slaves, passed from earth, March 19, 1822, aged over seventy years.

There were Mothers Coskery, Ray, O'Keeffe, and others; but we must here close the edifying record, merely remarking that Mother O'Keeffe still lives (1887), and, though an octogenarian and in failing health, is a most saintly, charming, and accomplished woman, with whom it is a treat to converse. . . .

Once, when bound for the bright southern seas, we glided past the lower horn of the river's crescent in the blaze and brilliancy of noontide. The sweet, soft breeze, laden with the odor of lilies, and the aroma of the white-starred orange tree and the pink oleander, scarcely ruffled the glassy waters that reflected the changeful sky. The landscape reposing in the luminous atmosphere was exquisitely peaceful. Rising out of the river, embowered in fresh, green shrubbery, is a huge white pile whose windows innumerable look out on blooming meadows, giant oaks, fields of maize and sugar cane, mirrored in the yellow river. What bewitching combinations of light and shade, of blue sky, old-gold waters, pale-green leafage, and blossoms of·every hue. A sylvan paradise, the beauty of which we have no words to depict, surrounds the Ursuline Convent. We have gazed upon the scene when the moonbeams quivered on the foliage, and made fantastic figures as they played among the ancient trees, silvering the whole, by their magic touches, into dreamy, indescribable loveliness.

How many associations has the Mississippi for the inmates of that convent since it bore their ancestresses in religion to this fertile spot. Where are the gentle Sisters, the ardent priests, the mailed warriors, who came hither with chivalrous promptitude to win souls to the good God? From their belvideres the Religious of to-day can look into the depths of the river on which their predecessors shed such a glamour of poetry and romance. Where are they now? Do the ancient nuns never see phantom boats, guided by the spirits of the great ones of old, moving over its fair bosom in the dusky twilight or the white moonlight?

Alas! all — even the "faithless phantoms," and the pale ghosts, and the fair wraiths, have departed. But the deeds of daring, of brave men, and the gentle virtues of saintly women, and the sweet lights of holiness, have cast a halo around the old place and glorified it forever.

The place remains while those who gave it undying interest have passed away. Yet the walls still echo sweet children's voices, and the song of the cloistered virgins is heard by angels, if not by men, and the old white monastery looks out forever from its leafy bowers on the eddying, whispering river.

THE CHURCH OF THE ATTAKAPAS—
1750-1889

I

ABOUT 6 A. M., August 16, 1887, Père Jan, Pastor of St. Martinsville, was found dead in his poor, dusty room. He had retired at nine the previous night to pray rather than to rest, though a man far up in the eighties might well have been weary after so full a day. He had celebrated two Masses and preached at each, heard many confessions, given Holy Communion to the greater number of his congregation, presided at Vespers, and held the Blessed Sacrament aloft over his people, for the last time, in solemn benediction. He lay against the bed partially kneeling—had not even undressed. The peaceful, smiling expression of his venerable countenance showed that the beautiful soul had departed without a struggle. The doctor declared he must have died some seven hours previous. So the Blessed Virgin had taken him on her greatest feast.

His death was telegraphed to New Orleans, and people asked each other: "Who is this Père Jan?" Save a few of the clergy, nobody seemed to know or care. He had lived between the porch and the altar; had never been in the city save in passing on his arrival in this country, thirty-seven years previous.

To his simple flock he was all the world, but otherwise his life was as solitary as if he had lived in the Thebaid.

Yet the old priest who lay dead in St. Martinsville had seen stirring times. He had lived through the latter years of the first French Republic; remembered the fleeting glory of the great Napoleon's empire; shared the anxiety of the Hundred Days; and rejoiced like a loyal Breton, as he was, at the restoration of the Bourbons and monarchy.

Ordained May 26, 1826, by Archbishop de Quélen, at Notre Dame, with sixty others, among whom was Archbishop Purcell, of Cincinnati, he said his first Mass on Trinity Sunday at the Convent des Carmes, memorable as the scene of the massacre of so many priests in 1792. The Abbé Surrat, his intimate friend, who attended him, lived to witness scenes scarcely less horrible than those of 1792, and became the victim of another massacre, second in atrocity only to that of the *Carmes*, when he was assassinated by the Communists in the fair city by the Seine forty-five years later.

On the return of Charles X. from Rheims, Père Jan acted as chief of the *mâitres de cérémonies* at the grand *Te Deum* at Notre Dame. Often did the simple priest in far-away St. Martinsville smile to think that he, on so great an occasion, had given the order *laisser passer* to so many distinguished personages, among others his friend, Mgr. de Frayssinous, Minister of Public Instruction. A few years later he

7 97

saw the flight of the same Charles, that typical Bourbon, who could neither learn nor forget.

He had been the friend or fellow-student of nearly all the churchmen of the Paris of his day, and among them all loved Lacordaire best.

It was the apostolic life of this holy priest that first drew the attention of the writer to the remote region blessed and sanctified by his labors. We shall return to this latest and greatest Apostle of the Attakapas.

II

SOUTH CAROLINA is divided into districts, Louisiana into parishes; the divisions of the other States are counties. Five Louisiana parishes cover the ancient Attakapas country: St. Martin, St. Mary, Iberia, Lafayette, and Vermillion, lying between the Mississippi and the Mexican Gulf. Ecclesiastically, the Attakapas region once formed but a single parish, extending from Grand Coteau to Berwick Bay, and from the Atchafalaya to the Gulf of Mexico, an area of some thousands of square miles. A commandant ruled this fair country, politically known as the " Poste des Attakapas."

Into these green savannas white men found their way very early. The first permanent settlers were a few families driven from Canada by the English. Their descendants are scattered over the wilds of Louisiana to-day. Some settled at the "Poste des Attakapas," as the Broussards, Martins, Le Blancs,

Voorhies, Arcenaux, still numerously represented in St. Martinsville and its vicinity. Some New Orleans men, more adventurous than their brethren, "prospected" in these prairies, and a few settled down, "the world forgetting and by the world forgot," with Indian brides, whose dark eyes and swarthy complexions may be traced in their descendants to-day. The traditions of the country assert that the first of these migrations occurred between 1750 and 1760, during the administration of the Marquis de Vaudreuil and Governor Kerlerec.

The immense plains, stretching to the Gulf, afforded such facilities for raising cattle that the immigrants chose a pastoral rather than an agricultural life. Bayous of pure, limpid water furnished delicious fish, and game was abundant. Much of their time was therefore spent in hunting and fishing. But the extraordinary richness of the soil, which yields several crops a year, did not long remain undiscovered. Indigo, cotton, rice, and tobacco soon varied the green monotony of these fertile pampas. Sugar cane was introduced by the Jesuits in 1751, and seed cane distributed throughout the various plantations. This made a great addition to home comfort. But in 1795 sugar became a gold mine to Louisiana, when the syrup the cane yields was made to granulate on Boré's plantation near New Orleans.* This was a boon to the dwellers

---

* Etienne de Boré, a wealthy, influential planter, signalized himself by his humanity and charity to the Jesuits when they were suppressed in Louisiana, 1763. It was he who gave a home to the

in the Attakapas. Nowhere are there finer sugar plantations than on the banks of the Tèche.

The first pale-faces who arrived here found Attakapas Indians scattered throughout the territory.
They had given up the man-eating propensities from
which they took their name, and tradition assures us
that there were among them many Christians.

By an arrangement, the wisdom of which has been
often questioned, the Capuchins of the Province of
Champagne attended to the spiritual wants of New
Orleans, while the Jesuits preached the Gospel to the
outlying Indian tribes. So, when the adventurous
Canadians pushed westward to the Tèche country,
they found the Indians partially Christianized and
civilized. One Jesuit preached to them in their native wilds,— Father Viel,* who, besides his ministra-

venerable Father Baudouin, S. J., a Canadian, whose health was
irretrievably broken by his labors and sufferings among the Indians.
He would not allow the holy missionary to be driven, at the age of
seventy-two, from the country in which the greater part of his life
had been spent. Mr. de Boré was grandfather to Charles Gayarré, the historian of Louisiana.

* Etienne Bernard Alexandre Viel was born in New Orleans
in 1736, and died in France in his eighty-sixth year. After the
suppression of the Society of Jesus he lived for many years in
Attakapas, where he was much beloved. The greater part of his
life was spent in teaching. Many considered him the greatest
living Latinist. Judge Gayarré told the writer that he was a fanatic in his love for Latin, and thought nothing fit to be published
except what was in Latin. He translated Telemachus into beautiful Latin verse, and the work was splendidly brought out by some
distinguished men who had been his pupils. Gayarré, in his youth,
saw that work and others from the same learned pen.

tions to them, taught a school for the children of the dwellers in this romantic region.

III

EVEN in the days of Bienville, who left America forever in 1747, the Attakapas and the pale-faces had met. The romantic story of Belle-Isle is repeated to-day under the spreading oaks that fringe the sparkling bayous, and by the hunters and fishers of the Salt Marsh Parishes. In 1719 he sailed from France with many troops and emigrants. Losing their reckoning in a storm, they made land at St. Bernard's Bay, Texas. The captain sent ashore for fresh water. Belle-Isle and four other officers remained on land when the boat went back with her casks replenished. While awaiting their return for a second cargo the loiterers found so much to interest them that time passed quickly, and on reaching the shore they saw to their dismay that the vessel had departed.

The unfortunate men found they had exchanged the perils of the ocean for those of the wilderness. They hoped, but in vain, that the captain might send a boat back for them. The keen gnawings of hunger they stayed with berries, worms, and insects. Belle-Isle's hunting dog was doomed, but he could not slay it, and the poor animal escaped when another essayed to do the deed.

One by one his companions died of hunger. He buried them and "watered their grave with his tears." After the burial of the last, his truant dog returned with a wood-rat, which gave master and dog a dainty meal. Once, while his master slept, a panther stealthily approached him, which the dog attacked and vanquished, but was so badly lacerated that his master compassionately put an end to his sufferings.

Again alone in the wilds, Belle-Isle reverently knelt to thank God for his safety, and implore His further protection. By traces of human footprints he was guided to a pirogue tossing in a stream. Crossing to the other side, he saw Indians feasting. They were man-eaters (Attukapaw). The cadaverous Frenchman they regarded as a spectre. He made signs that he was hungry, whereupon they offered him human flesh and fish. No need to say he chose the latter.

The Indians spared his life, intending to fatten him for a barbecue. They took him to their village and appropriated his miserable belongings. He was made slave to a widowed squaw, who treated him well, and whose papooses he aired in a cradle fastened to his bare shoulders. The prospect of being sacrificed to their deities, and having his flesh served up at their revels, retarded his improvement. He soon acquired their language and had the happiness to learn that the warriors in council assembled had decided it would be base and treacherous to kill a stranger who had come to their wigwams for hospitality.

His mistress allowed him considerable liberty. He accompanied the braves on their hostile excursions. Human flesh and venison were the delicacies prepared for these expeditions. Once, when he unwittingly ate a piece of dried human flesh, the savage commissary said: "You improve. You will soon be a true Attakapas, and 'eat man' as well as any of us." This, with the powerful aid of the imagination, brought about an inversion of the muscles of the epigastric region; a violent upheaval and the loss of a dinner followed.

After some years, deputies from a distant tribe came to smoke the calumet with the cannibals. Seeing Belle-Isle, they remarked that there were palefaces in a neighboring nation also. He questioned them. Fortunately he had preserved his commission as an officer. On the reverse of it he wrote with a crow-quill and ink manufactured from soot:

"I am M. de Belle-Isle who was adandoned at St. Bernard's Bay. My companions died of grief and hunger. I am a captive among the Attakapas." This "talking paper" he begged an Indian to convey to the French Chief in New Orleans, who would liberally reward him. Another Indian tried to take it, but he escaped by swimming across the river, holding the letter aloft that it might not get wet. After a journey of 150 miles, he reached the French post and delivered it. On hearing it read, the people wept aloud after the manner of the Indians. Being asked what troubled them, they said they were grieving for their brother, a prisoner among the Attakapas. The Indians offered to rescue him. Ten went, all well mounted. On reaching the Attakapas village, they discharged their muskets. The savages took the report for thunder. A letter to Belle-Isle ordered him to surrender himself to his red visitors, and his hosts, terrified by the roar of musketry, did not dare to oppose his abduction. The woman whom he had served wept piteously, and it was with difficulty he tore himself from her. Bienville richly rewarded his deliverers and sent a valuable present to the Attakapas. A deputation, which, to the great delight of our hero, included his adopted mother, came to New Orleans to thank the Governor and form an alliance with the French. The Chief, pointing to the former captive, said to Bienville: "This white man, my father, is your flesh and blood, but by adoption he is one of us. His brothers died of hunger, but had they been met by my nation they would to-day be alive and free."

From that period the Attakapas always treated strangers humanely, and gradually abandoned their barbarous custom of eating human flesh.

The above incidents became the occasion of sending missionaries to the friendly Attakapas. As late as 1776, Galvez, when preparing to do battle with the English, recruited among them and other tribes 160 Indian warriors. It is noted that in this campaign they refrained from doing the slightest injury to the fugitives whom they captured, and even brought the babes they found with their mothers ambushed in the woods in their arms to Galvez. But the partial suppression of the Society of Jesus in 1763, and its total suppression in 1773, deprived these intelligent barbarians of their spiritual fathers. They dwindled away, and many wholly lost the faith once delivered to them by saints.

In 1804, when Father Isabey, a holy Dominican, made his way to the " Poste des Attakapas," he suffered much hard treatment from the Indians he met on his way, remnants of the Attakapas, now entirely extinct. Among other cruelties to which they subjected him was the pulling off of the nails of his fingers and toes. Francis Chauvet, who lived in a wooden hut facing the Tèche, and died there, a centenarian, not many years ago, distinctly remembered and graphically described the maimed condition of this worthy priest when rescued from these cruel savages.

IV ∴

BUT long before the granulation of cane juice, indeed before the captivity of the hapless Belle-Isle, events occurred at the other end of North America destined to give new settlers to the blooming llanos of the Attakapas. Nova Scotia (Acadie) had been peopled by Normans and Burgundians, who reclaimed thousands of acres from the muddy waters of the Bay of Fundy, and lived by their daily toil in peace and plenty. They had schools, churches, priests, even musical chimes, which, thanks to our American poet, will ring out forever in song and story. By the Treaty of Utrecht, 1713, Louis XIV. ceded Acadie to Queen Anne. The inhabitants were to retain their lands on swearing allegiance to the British monarch. But they refused to take any oath that could bind them to bear arms against France, and, though known later as French Neutrals, their new masters refused to believe in their neutrality.

They were cajoled, deceived, lulled into a false security by vague promises, and, as they held the best lands, their enemies finally decided on a wholesale spoliation. The terrible vengeance wreaked on these sturdy farmers will ever remain a shameful blot on the blurred escutcheon of England. They were accused of aiding their brethren in Canada and inciting the Indians to rebellion. And it was known that in the attack against Beauséjour some Acadians had battled under the lilies against the British flag.

On September 5, 1755, the Acadians, in response to an official mandate, assembled in their chapels to hear important details as to their future relations with the British Lion, then represented by the unspeakable George II. With sad amazement they perceived the handwriting that was against them. Their smiling farms were to be devastated, their houses leveled. Ships were in readiness to take them they knew not whither. The roads from the chapels to the shore were alive with men, women, and children, weeping, praying, or mournfully chanting their favorite hymn to the Sacred Heart of our Savior. Now began their melancholy exile, "exile without an end and without an example in story."

They were scattered throughout the British Colonies from New Hampshire to Georgia, among people whose language they knew not and whose creed they abhorred. Everywhere they were regarded as " an intolerable burden," and they retained under all circumstances " an unconquerable dislike to the English." * Husbands and wives, parents and children, were separated. Many escaped to some French settlement. Those who remained were for the most part gradually absorbed by the population — one of many circumstances which show how the genuine Anglo-Saxon stock, if there be any such in America, has been " watered."

The army chaplains of the French detachments that came to America during the Revolution to help the patriots in their struggle against England, were often surrounded by people of Irish and Acadian lineage who had never before seen a priest.

After wandering for a decade as helots and paupers, some 600 Acadians made their way to New Orleans. Their sorrowful faces, as they drew up on the Levée and the old Place d'Armes, evoked the deepest sympathy of their compatriots in the little town over which the spotless banner still waved. The Ursulines, the only nuns from the St. Lawrence to the Gulf, re-

---

*During the Civil War several Louisiana regiments were composed largely of " Cayjuns" (Acadians), who, regarding the war as a fight against the Yankees, descendants of their ancient enemies, the English, fought furiously. Their " Cayjun " battle-cries, prolonged shrieks like the war-whoop of the Indians, struck terror into the hearts of their opponents. The Unionists are charged with wreaking awful vengeance on St. Martinsville and every other haunt of the wild and vengeful Acadian.

ceived many of the women and children. The doors of every house were thrown open to the rest.

Nothing could be more different from the snug farms and smiling meadows of "Acadie, the home of the happy," than the New Orleans of that day. It was bounded rear and sides by a cypress swamp; in front was the river, ever threatening to submerge its one-story houses and palmetto huts. The population was about 3,000, of whom perhaps a third were blacks; and it is certainly no slander to say that neither race was overburdened with energy. In the centre of the town, facing the river, was the modest brick church erected in 1725, which was swept away in the terrible conflagration of 1788.

The religious state of New Orleans at this epoch was deplorable. In 1763, the Superior Council issued a decree of banishment against the Society of Jesus. From this blow the Church of Colonial Louisiana never wholly recovered. The baseness and tyranny of this insignificant body, composed almost entirely of wicked or ignorant men, are indescribable. The property of the Jesuits was confiscated and sold for $180,000. Their chapels were leveled to the ground, and the faithful in many places left without priest or altar. Among the sacrilegious wretches that aided in this infamous work, Lafrénière, of the Superior Council, stands conspicuous. And his fate, and that of his confederates, a few years later, was a terrible instance of Divine retribution.*

* Lafrénière and four others were shot in New Orleans in 1769, for high treason. Felix del Rey, O'Reilly's lawyer, spoke

The Acadians found a struggle for supremacy going on between Fathers Hilaire de Génovaux* and Dagobert. † In 1766 the Superior Council expelled the former and made the latter, who bore a most unsavory reputation, head of religion in Louisiana. The former was for some time pastor of the Attakapas, but nothing is known of his career at that "Poste" save that he kept no records, or, if he did, they were afterwards lost, as Father Barrière charitably suggests.

The mere sight of the Bourbon *fleur-de-lis* thrilled the hearts of the Acadians and kindled gleams of triumph in their sad eyes. But their joy was allayed when they learned that Louisiana was, theoretically, a Spanish province. Louis XV., like his great-grand-

of him with withering contempt as an unfaithful officer and the chief instigator of conspiracy against his king, whose money he was receiving as Attorney-General while driving his fellow-citizens to rebellion against him.

*Génovaux quarreled with the Jesuit Vicar-General, and joined the Spanish friars against Père Dagobert. He professed to be neutral. Dagobert besought Governor Unzaga to prevent Génovaux from abusing him, "as he was in the habit of doing every day."

† The writer can hardly believe Dagobert was as bad as a late historian has painted him. If he were, his conduct could scarcely have escaped the eagle eye of Count O'Reilly, who lived within a few yards of him, and who would have had him removed for far less than his accusers say against him. The chief authority against him was Cyrilo, who came to supplant him, and who at that time did not understand French, and was, moreover, ignorant of the customs of Louisiana. On the arrival of the Spanish Capuchins, Dagobert had been over fifty years in New Orleans and was at least seventy-four years old.

father, Louis XIV., grew tired of paying the expenses of a colony that brought him no return. In 1762 he ceded his broad lands below the lakes to other powers, and the parts in which we are now interested fell to Spain. But the Catholic king was in no hurry to accept the gift his royal brother had thrust upon him. And, as no representative of the majesty of Spain appeared for years, people began to imagine — the wish being father to the thought — that the transfer announced by Louis XV. to Governor Abbadie, in April, 1764, had not taken place even on paper, and that the Treaty of Cession was but a sham instrument.

Other bands of Acadians appeared on the scene. Many had tried the French West India Islands, but under torrid skies they could not live. In February, 1766, 216 Acadians were added to the population of Louisiana. The Acadian Coast, on both sides of the Mississippi, above New Orleans, was colonized by Acadians. Rations and instruments of husbandry were supplied them at the expense of the government, and many made their way to the flowery meads of the Attakapas.

It was certainly for God and their country that some 7,000 Acadians suffered the horrors of an exile unexampled in history. But the constant and bitter persecution to which they were subjected in "the house of bondage" broke their spirits in many instances; nor could they withstand that worse ordeal, intimacy with free-thinking Frenchmen. Bishop Carroll notices the deterioration of the Acadians in Balti-

more. Something similar might be observed even in
the remote Attakapas, and early in the next century
Father Dufour informs us that only six people attended his first Mass in St. Martinsville. The vicious
Frenchmen who labored with a zeal worthy of a better
cause to disseminate irreligion, corrupted the Acadians
wherever they were exposed to this evil influence.
At an earlier epoch they became the accomplices or
tools of the vile men who arrogated to themselves
supreme power in Church and State before the arrival
of O'Reilly. They were among the armed insurgents
who paraded the streets of New Orleans, and sustained
the Supreme Council when that body ordered the expulsion of Governor Ulloa, in 1768. In the report to
his government of this insurrection, Ulloa charges the
Acadians, with the Germans, with being guilty of ingratitude, "they having received nothing but benefits
from the Spaniards."

Indeed, the inhabitants of the Attakapas received
only kindness from the Spaniards. When they complained to O'Reilly, he listened gently to their grievances, and rectified them, as far as possible, on the
spot. De Clouet,* who was commandant of the

---

*Opelousas was governed from Attakapas; but in 1787, as the
population had largely increased, Opelousas was made a distinct
command under Nicholas Forstall, while the Attakapas remained
in charge of Chevalier de Clouet. Forstall (possibly Forristal), was
an Irishman, and carried with him everywhere a huge genea-
logical tree, which showed his descent from the Kings of Ireland.
He was an upright, pious man. Many of his descendants bearing the name Forstall may yet be found in Louisiana. Judge

" Poste " in his time, is to-day represented by numerous descendants in the vicinity of St. Martinsville, and much information referring to these early days may be gathered from this ancient family. As to the Indians, O'Reilly officially declared that it was "contrary to the mild and beneficent laws of Spain to hold them in slavery." His closest attention was given to everything regarding the divine worship. He even requested the commandant to keep the church at Natchitoches clear of dogs during divine worship. The *alcaldes* and *alguazil* or mayor, with the *escribano*, were commanded to visit all prisoners every week, and the governor several times a year. The humane and Christian regulations established in Louisiana by this great man reflect high honor on Spanish colonial legislation.

V

WE HAVE seen that the Attakapas country was peopled chiefly by Canadians and Acadians, originally of the same stock. The religious wars and other disturbances of New Orleans, the civil and ecclesiastical headquarters, found but little echo in this peaceful region. The "Poste" was seldom without a priest. There is a regular succession of pastors up to 1889. Except in administering the sacraments of baptism and matrimony, and burying the dead, the pastor had little to do for the white male portion of his congre-

Gayarré told the writer that he had seen the above Forstall Genealogy.

gation. Governor Unzaga says: "The men never confessed after their first communion — would think it hypocrisy to do so."* But they were all anxious to have the ministrations of the Church when fatal illness seized them.

The Acadians have kept distinct from the Louisiana Creoles, and have been strangely unprogressive. † " My mother cooked in this manner, so shall I." "My father got along without that invention, so can I." "What was good-enough for our parents will do for us." These and similar responses are given in Acadian *patois* to those who speak to them of modern improvements. They are called " Cayjuns," a corruption of "Acadians," and the Creoles rather look down on them for their peculiar habits and strange dialect. They dwell mostly in unpainted structures called *maisons d'Acadiens*, small but solidly built cottages of cypress:

"Near to the bank of the river, overshadowed by oaks from whose branches
Garlands of Spanish moss and of mystic mistletoe flaunted,
Such as the Druids cut down with golden hatchets at yuletide,
Stood secluded and still the house of the herdsman."

The Acadians usually marry young and have large families. Among them the cradle is never empty.

* Much the same is said by Cyrilo in his report to the Bishop of Santiago de Cuba. But both reports refer, perhaps, only to New Orleans, and are probably exaggerated.

† Several Acadians have attained eminence as lawyers and soldiers

They are a peaceful, industrious race, strongly attached to their homes and families. Among their faults and those of the Creoles are a habit of marrying relations, and sometimes a passion for gambling, and very sad the consequences often are. Though both races fled from English tyranny in Canada and Nova Scotia, they have never been anxious to receive settlers of other races. A more liberal spirit is now beginning to prevail among the foremost inhabitants. Conservative as the Gallic races are, the railroad, immigration, and the introduction of the English language will have swept away their exclusiveness before the close of the nineteenth century.

The headquarters of the Attakapas is St. Martinsville, a village of some two thousand souls. But places of equal or greater importance now stud that romantic region. St. Martin is no longer, as before the war, a little Paris. Its beauty even then could not have been of the architectural order, for there are no remains of any buildings save the plainest. But boundless prairies dotted with sheep and cattle, vast plantations of sugar cane, the majestic trees that shade the bayou, endless hedges of wild roses, "the flowers that bloom in the spring" in tens of thousands, but, above all, the winding Tèche, make the parish of St. Martin, "a thing of beauty and a joy forever."

The religious history of this region may be gathered from the church registers and from tradition. The inhabitants have preserved many of the peculiarities of speech and manner that characterized their ancestors, and have never lost the Faith.

The oldest register is copied from that of Pointe Coupée, a district visited by all the political and religious celebrities of early days, from O'Reilly to Peñalvert. Though much worn, one can count on it eighty-two baptisms and twelve marriages from 1756 to 1773. The " Poste des Attakapas " had at first no resident priest, and the sacraments were administered there by Father Didur of Pointe Coupée, and Friar Valentine, of Natchitoches. Register No. 1, in the archives of St. Martin, is a small folio bound in parchment, in a very dilapidated condition. Here is a copy of a note on page 1, which gives interesting details of the origin of the Church of the Attakapas :

"In Nomine J. Amen.

" This book has been made to serve as a register for Baptisms, Marriages, and Burials, in the Parish of the Poste des Attakapas, beginning from 1765, Father John Francis officiating. . . . This colony belonged to France, but by the Treaty of Peace it was ceded to Spain. The Pastors that succeeded Father John Francis are Rev. Hilaire de Génovaux, French, and Rev. Joseph d'Arazena, Spaniard. No register of Father Hilary's administration can be found. We do not think he neglected to note what happened, but that his register was lost. Father d'Arazena took possession of this Parish, January 20, 1782. He wrote two small books in which baptisms, marriages, and burials, of whites and of blacks are noted. These were left to Father Gefrotin, a Dominican, who succeeded him in 1783. Another register was found which helped to replace things in order. . . . These originals are of great use in enabling us to give correct records. . . . We beg pastors to use this and no other."

Father Marceda became pastor in 1787, Father de

Deva in 1788. As a rule, priests did not remain long at this Poste. In 1791, Father de Deva was succeeded by Father George Murphy, an Irish secular priest. He labored in these parts with great zeal from 1789 to 1794, and was noted for his gifts as a preacher. He exercised the sacred ministry in various languages, among them English, French, and Spanish. During his incumbency, we find the first mention of St. Martin as patron of the Poste des Attakapas. It was made in 1793 by his assistant, Father Pedro de Camora.* In the book of burials, Father Murphy speaks of the Church of St. Martin,† February 6, 1794.

After more than four years' fruitful labor, Rev. George Murphy left the humble parsonage of St. Martin.

The transfer of Louisiana to Spain was, on the whole, favorable to religion. The Catholic kings showed great zeal for the progress of the Gospel. In

---

* Perhaps this priest is identical with Rev. Peter de Zamora, who came to Louisiana with Sebastian O'Farrell, Marquis of Casacalvo, and received faculties from Very Rev. Thomas Hassett, April 11, 1804.

† This would indicate that Longfellow was a little premature in calling the capital of the Attakapas St. Martin. It began to be generally so called only in the beginning of the present century. Over the high altar of the church is an old painting of St. Martin dividing his cloak with a beggar.

Le Sieur Louis Charles de Blanc, captain in the armies of the king of Spain, was civil and military commandant of the Poste des Attakapas in 1800. The writer thinks that he is the first commandant of whom it is recorded that he resided at St. Martinsville. His descendants are numerous about the old Poste.

1772 Father Cyrilo and four other Capuchins came to New Orleans to replace their lax French brethren, who, however, refused to be replaced. Headed by the famous Père Dagobert, they had so won the people, and prejudiced them against the Spanish Clergy, that Governor Unzaga feared to remove them. Governor Miro, however, supported Cyrilo, and some semblance of order was drawn out of chaos. Cyrilo wrote very disparagingly of religion in Louisiana. "It is more difficult," said he, "to weed the garden of New Orleans than it was to plant it in the beginning."

Up to this time no bishop had visited Louisiana, and no priest had been empowered to administer confirmation. The king of Spain desired that his Louisiana subjects might receive that great sacrament, and, on his recommendation (1779), the Holy See appointed an auxiliary to the bishopric of Santiago de Cuba, who was to exercise his functions in Louisiana. The austere Cyrilo, consecrated in 1781, was chosen for this office — a choice that did not give universal satisfaction. Being really a holy and zealous man, the bishop infused new life into the country parishes, which he visited assiduously, and he was a terror to the evil-doers who have made the ecclesiastical history of the time and place so painful to the Catholic student. In 1786 he issued a pastoral, in which he eloquently urged his flock to attend Mass on Sundays and holy days, and censured the wicked custom of the negroes who, at the vesper hour every Sunday, assembled in a green, still called Congo square, to dance the bamboula and throw the wanga, and worship the serpent, with hideous rites imported from Africa by the Yolofs, Foulahs, Bambarras, Mandingoes, and other races of the dark continent.

While changes went on at headquarters, the Church of the Attakapas, save for the appointment or confirming of a pastor, seems to have been left severely alone. There is no record, so far as we can ascertain, that the zealous Bishop Cyrilo ever evangelized "the black, white, and brown" dwellers on these "sultry savannas." He visited many other country churches, as is evident from the registers, which he caused to be kept in Spanish, not in French as heretofore. The many Irish clergy scattered throughout the territory over which this prelate held spiritual sway,— Fathers Burke, Walsh, White, Hassett, O'Reilly, Crosby, Barry, Savage, McKenna, etc.,— who had been accustomed to make these entries in Latin, are commanded to keep their books henceforth in Spanish. But no order of this nature is recorded in the Attakapas register till March 26, 1796.

The reward which so often comes to the zealous and saintly in this life overtook Bishop Cyrilo in the midst of his labors for souls. He was suspended by the king,* and commanded to return to his province, Catalonia. A long letter, dated November 23, 1793, from Charles IV., signed *Yo el Rey*, gave him this unwelcome news, and in 1794 he left Louisiana forever.

---

* The king of Spain as "Protector of the Council of Trent" assumed great authority in Church matters.

He was delayed at Havana for want of means to take him to Spain in compliance with the royal ukase, and was still in that city in 1799, the incumbent of Havana refusing to pay his salary till the king interfered. Well might this holy man, persecuted by his brethren, his king, and the abandoned souls for whom he toiled, exclaim: "I have loved justice and hated iniquity, therefore I die in a strange land."

On October 19, 1796, the "Poste des Attakapas" saw a bishop for the first time. On the twenty-sixth of March, the pastor, styled by Bishop Peñalvert "Don Miguel Bernardo de Barrière," made the first Spanish entry in his register, probably because he had on that day received official notice of the coming of his bishop. This visitation is the only one made during the Spanish domination.

In the Bull which makes New Orleans the see of a diocese bounded north and east by the diocese of Baltimore, and south and west by Linares and Durango, Pius VI. gives as his reason for forming Louisiana and Florida into a separate diocese "the miserable state of religion and ecclesiastical discipline" in these parts. Don Luis Peñalvert y Cardenas,* having been the right hand of the bishop at Havana, was well aware of the deplorable condition of the diocese confided to his pastoral care. His coming was hailed with delight by the Governor, Baron Carondelet, who

---

* According to Spanish custom, he bore his mother's name as well as his father's. His parents were Don Diego Peñalvert and Doña Maria Luisa de Cardenas.

had reported adversely on Church matters in his province, and seen with grief the unsuccessful efforts of Cyrilo to correct abuses. The bishop's instructions to his clergy show that he was filled with the spirit of God and an ardent zeal for souls. From the St. Martinsville register, " Parroquia de San Martin des *Atacapaz*," we gather that he made a careful examination of all the records that could be found, noted their defects, and put them in the best order possible. The great distinction always kept up in Louisiana between people of unmixed European origin and the other races, is apparent from these records, as the "whites, the blacks, and the browns" are entered separately in the lists of baptisms, marriages, and burials. As in New Orleans and other parts of Louisiana, there were in the Attakapas, negroes, Indians, Mestizos (children of the white and the Indian), griffe (of the African and the Indian), mulatto, mulatre, mulattress (of the white and black). These mixed races the bishop calls *browns, morenos.* Later, however, cognizance was taken but of two classes: the whites, Europeans and their descendants, and the colored.*

* To evade O'Reilly's merciful law, which forbade the enslaving of Indians, these poor people were often classed with the mulattoes as colored.

The Spaniards were most kind to the Indians. In May, 1784, Indian congresses were held with great pomp at Pensacola and Mobile, at which Count Arthur O'Neil and Governor Miro presided. Of the treaty framed on that occasion, here is an article: " In conformity with the humane and generous sentiments of the Spanish nation, we (the Indians) renounce forever the custom of raising scalps, and making slaves of our white captives," etc.

Bishop Peñalvert's entry in the *Atacapaz* register is signed simply: "El Obisbo de la Luisiana."

The bishop did not forget the *Atacapaz*. Three years later he speaks of that district as one into which evil men had penetrated — adventurers who "have no religion, acknowledge no God, and have deteriorated the morals of the people."

Louisiana was soon to lose this zealous prelate. In 1801 he was made Archbishop of Guatemala. The diocese was now governed by Canon Thomas Hassett, head of the Cathedral chapter, with whom was associated Very Rev. Patrick Walsh. These worthy and learned Irish priests, who had labored long in the diocese and were most useful in a cosmopolitan city as speaking several European languages, were not destined to live many years under the American flag.* Father Hassett, whose health was broken by the sever-

---

* Fray Antonio Sedilla, known traditionally as Père Antoine, came to New Orleans, in Governor Miro's time, to introduce the Inquisition; but Miro shipped him back to Spain at once. He returned and ingratiated himself with the people, who supported him in his rebellions against Administrator Walsh and Bishop Dubourg. The stories of his immorality are probably exaggerated. He lived forty years in New Orleans, baptized and married almost everybody. His closing years were edifying. He went barefoot, wore a coarse brown habit, and a rope as his girdle. It is said he received from the people thirty to forty thousand dollars a year, and gave all to the poor. He lived in a hovel behind the Cathedral. Several persons still living knew him well. Gayarré described him as a prodigy of ignorance, not able even to speak or write his own language correctly, and, as a director, very easy. He died in 1829. The Legislature adjourned to attend his funeral.

ity of his apostolic labors in a climate which had never agreed with him, died suddenly in April, 1804. The closing years of Father Walsh were embittered by the frequent rebellions of Fray Antonio Sedilla. After an illness of five days, the administrator died, August 22, 1806. Posthumous honors of every description were lavished on a priest who had during life won the respect of friend and foe. Father Walsh's official title was "Vicar-General and Governor *ad interim* of the diocese." His remains lie beneath the sanctuary of the old Ursuline chapel. The cathedral being under an interdict, in consequence of the usurpation of Sedilla, this was the only place in the city in which Mass could be offered or the sacraments administered. Besides, Father Walsh was a benefactor of the Ursuline community.

VI

THE French in Louisiana have been singularly barren of vocations to the priesthood. The first century and a half produced one, the learned Father Viel. The bishops of Louisiana have always been natives of other countries. In the diocese of New Orleans to-day there are among the secular clergy only two priests of Creole parentage. Several youths of that race have, however, joined the Jesuits and other religious bodies. In 1794 Father Viel became seventh pastor of Atta-kapas, or rather exercised his priestly functions there when required, for, we regret to say, he is marked in the register, "Not approved." A writer of distinguished ability, he consoled himself in the troubles of life by devoting his leisure hours to the muses. Though "not approved," he is known traditionally as an excellent priest. The distinguished men whom he had educated comforted his old age by their filial attentions, and published a magnificent edition of his works.

Father de Barrière, an *émigré*, eighth pastor of this "Poste," arrived* March 8, 1795, and remained till 1804. His name occurs from time to time till 1830, and is also found in the registers of Opelousas and Lafayette, where he was pastor successively. He returned to France and died in his native city, Bordeaux.

As time wore on the early settlers were joined by friends and relatives, and it was decided to build a village. A surveyor named Johnson drew the plan, but the progress was slow. The houses were very plain, and did not extend further than what is now Main street. The oldest inhabitants of a few years ago remembered the last years and death of the centenarian, François Chauvet, who lived near the bayou. When he arrived at the "Poste," Main street was part of a vast prairie. He worshiped in the first chapel, a small frame building, memorable, says tradition, for the visit of Evangeline. The poor presbytery was, in 1795, the oldest house in the village. That the church was built in 1770, may be inferred from the fact that

---

* Father de Barrière lived about a mile from the village, but walked in every day to say Mass. The church was small and poor. On Sundays he remained about the church all day.

it was at that period Mr. d'Hauterive gave the land the church and its dependencies now occupy, and on which a large part of the town is built. From this donation arises the obligation of many property holders to pay rent to the church. It must be remembered that during the Spanish domination the inhabitants paid no taxes. The clergymen were liberally paid by the king of Spain, who even furnished necessaries for the church. Spanish galleons brought their hundreds of thousands of solid money from Mexico to Louisiana every year to pay the expenses of Church and State.

From 1802 to 1840, 2,198 baptisms of blacks are registered. Up to 1887 there are recorded in the archives of St. Martin 19,692 baptisms, 3,527 marriages, and 7,227 burials.

Father Gabriel Isabey exercised the ministry at St. Martinsville from 1804 till his death, of heart disease, July 21, 1823. During his administration the ecclesiastical extension of the parish was divided. This priest was greatly beloved. He had a pleasant face, was tall, well proportioned,* and possessed of elegant manners. His gentleness and amiability gained all hearts, and when he died there was general mourning. He owned a plantation, of which his nephew, Mark, took care. Little children were greatly attached to him. A venerable lady told us, that when she was four or five years old, she went to his door, and call-

---

* The writer has a miniature of Father Isabey which bears out this description.

ing his old servant, Sylvain, by his pet name, said: "Vain-vain, where is Isabey?" The good priest came out and gave her cakes and candy. The memories of childhood are never forgotten, and to her latest breath she recalled this incident with pleasure. Vain-vain could not survive his master. He ran through the village, exclaiming in his picturesque jargon: *Maite mouri, Négue mouri.* His intense grief deprived him of the little sense he once had. He bought a loaf and got a bottle of water, and laid them on Père Isabey's grave: "Cé pour *vouyage* là," said he. He wandered in the wood, which at that time surrounded the church, striking his head against the trees and crying out: *Maite mouri, Négue mouri.* A few days later the body of the poor Congo was found floating on the Tèche.

Even the animals loved this good man. After his funeral his favorite cat disappeared, and every one was asking: "Where is Père Isabey's cat?" But the poor animal was soon forgotten. Years after, when the church was about to be enlarged, the whole village assembled to see the remains of Father Isabey exhumed. The skeleton of the cat was found at the foot of his coffin.

Father Borella, an Italian, came to St. Martin at the age of fifty, August 20, 1819. He was pastor of the parish from the death of Father Isabey till his own, January 21, 1836. He left $16,000 to enlarge the church. His grave in the cemetery being neglected, his remains were removed to the church, where they now repose.

In 1826 and 1827 multitudes of Congo negroes
used to assemble every Sunday on the green before
the church and dance under the trees. This gave no
small annoyance to the pastor, the dances being part
of the hideous rites with which these benighted people
worshiped their idols. But gradually they became
Christians, and the horrible ceremonies entirely disappeared.

Under the administration of Father Borella the
parish was again divided. Of Father Brasseur, who
succeeded him, 1830 to 1840, no traditions seem to
have been preserved. The same may be said of
Father de St. Aubin, 1840 to 1841. In 1842 the fourteenth pastor, Father Martin, arrived. He was seventy
years old, and soon became paralyzed, except as to
his tongue. A priest, aged thirty, Father Bérel, assisted. This poor young man became very ill, and a
charitable woman took care of him. One day she left
him in charge of a colored servant, and coming in the
evening to see how he fared, she found him alone and
dying. She raised his head on her arm, and he cried
out: "A little water, for the love of God." But before she had time to assuage his thirst, he was dead.
Father Lucas was curate from 1843 to 1845.

Father Dufour, fifteenth pastor, had a very
pleasing countenance, and, despite a frankness that
sometimes gave offense to those he reproved, was
generally beloved. He had a great gift of eloquence.
The first Sunday he officiated only six persons were
present at Mass. Yet he preached a most powerful

sermon. His auditors spread his fame as an eloquent speaker, and the second Sunday eighty came to Mass. The church was soon too small for the congregation. But this brilliant man could not long content himself in such a Sleepy Hollow. He left on April 29, 1848, deeply regretted. The ancients still speak of him with admiration and affection. Of his successor, J. Jacques Fontbonne, no details have reached us.

About this period the shrill whistle of the steamboat was heard for the first time on the Tèche. *Le Correo*, Captain Curry, began to ply regularly between New Orleans and St. Martinsville. The inhabitants built a beautiful steamer which they called *Attakapas*. The captain belonged to a family well-known in these regions, Delahoussaye. Every arrival of this handsome "greyhound" of the river was announced by a volley of musketry.

VII

THE seventeenth pastor, Ange Marie Felix Jan, was born at Pontivy, April 11, 1802. The official record of his birth is dated: "Le vingt et un Germinal de l'an dixième de la République Française, une et indivisible." He was baptized stealthily in a hospital. Becoming an orphan at a tender age, he was placed by his godfather and guardian, Ange Marie Chassin, at the Jesuit College of Ste. Anne d'Auray, where he remained seven years. A letter from the president, which the old priest carefully preserved, bears high testimony to his literary ability and good conduct, and describes his life as most Christian and edifying. He desired to become a Jesuit, but his guardian opposed him, and he entered the Sulpitian College at Paris, 1823. In 1826 he finished his philosophy and theology, and was ordained May, 1826. The ceremonies began at 6 A. M. and were not over till 2 P. M. Père Jan always spoke with enthusiasm of Archbishop de Quélen. "Ah," he would say, "Monseigneur was not handsome, but what dignity, what nobility in his demeanor, especially when he officiated! And with what fervor and piety he celebrated Mass!"

The young priest made a series of resolutions which are those of a saintly soul, and to which he adhered to the end of his long life. Love of the Blessed Virgin was almost a passion with him. From childhood he recited the rosary every day.

His first charge was to teach the catechism classes for four hours a day. He was so devoted to this duty that, even as an old man, he loved to recall this period, and spoke of it as the happiest of his life. He was exceedingly modest, and it was but rarely he raised a little the veil which covered his life in France. The superb ceremonies that celebrated the coronation of Charles X. were never effaced from his memory. The grand tableau made by the princes, cardinals, ambassadors, and all the great orders of the State, gratified his natural love of the beautiful; "but," he would say when describing the scene, "the most imposing figure there was Monseigneur de Quélen."

Père Jan, like the other members of his family, was a royalist. In this he never changed, and towards the close of his life showed the deepest feeling at the death of the Count de Chambord. He related that when that prince was only five years old, he and other seminarians met him with the Duchess de Guyon in the gardens of the Tuilleries. The Duchess asked the young people if they would like to see the prince. "Oh, yes, Madame la Duchesse, we should be most happy," was the reply. But princes of five are, happily, like other children of the same age, and the royal child, intimidated by the crowd of young men, hid his face in his hands. But in a moment he recovered the self-possession taught him from the cradle; and when the lady said: "Salute these gentlemen, Monseigneur," the charming child advanced most graciously and murmured in his sweet voice, "good morning, gentlemen." The seminarians gave a hearty cheer for the Count de Chambord.

A second time Père Jan sought to enter the Society of Jesus, but his confessor said: "No; go back to Brittany." He obeyed, simply, and we next hear of him as curate of the Cathedral of Vannes. Here, as everywhere else, he won golden opinions, and we have the written testimony of the senior canon as to the great sanctity of his life and his zeal for souls. Equally fruitful in virtue was his sojourn at Nantes, as the bishop and clergy of that city bore witness.*

* Père Jan preserved the letters received from the ecclesiastical authorities under whom he had worked, probably because he

Among his penitents at Nantes was a Carmelite nun, Madame Fidelis, who escaped the massacre of 1792, and sought refuge first with her family, who were rich, and then in Spain. When the evil days were over, she returned, hoping to gain admittance to some cloister. In Spain she had endured all sorts of privations, and lost her health, she said, by the heat of the Spanish sun. She rented a little room near the cathedral, and never left it but at daybreak to hear Mass. The rest of the day it was carefully barricaded. She was nearly ninety and very delicate. Père Jan often visited her. One day he found her very sad. " I have suffered agonies," said she, "because my servant, being angry with me, opened the doors and windows and let in the sun's rays." And she wept bitterly. The young priest consoled her and promised to come every morning to see that the sun was not allowed to molest her. In gratitude she gave him a beautiful gold cross of ancient workmanship, which a few years before his death he presented to the writer of this article. He established a foundation Mass to be said every feast of Our Lady of Mount Carmel for poor Madame Fidelis after her happy death, and always offered Mass for her soul on the sixteenth of July.

Seven Visitation nuns who had been driven from their monastery came to Nantes; Père Jan gave them a house, and found them means to live in community.

did not wish to be identified with such of his clerical countrymen as had come to Louisiana without being sent or invited and without the proper credentials.

Their Superior, whom he highly esteemed, gave him a curious silver cross that had belonged to one of the first Visitation mothers. This relic he bestowed a few years ago on the Convent of Mercy, St. Martinsville. Among these Visitandines was " une Janseniste," whom he could not convert, and who, to his great grief, died as she had lived.

Père Jan was placed over the *Young Workmen* at Rouen in 1838, and made *aumonier* of the Hotel Dieu a little later. Desiring to participate in the good works of the Trappists, he was aggregated to them in 1842. In 1848 he was sent as missionary apostolic to Hayti; and his adventures in that isle, where he at first gained the good will of the terrible Soulouque, would fill a volume. Having received from this worthy himself a peremptory order to quit, he put himself under the protection of the French consul. But he was obliged to leave, and on returning to France, in May, 1849, after visiting Nantes and Paris, he spent some time in the Château de la Motte with his devoted friend, Madame la Marquise de St. Léonard, partly, it is said, to escape the mitre, and partly to mature his plans for devoting himself to the foreign mission, for which he had always had a great desire. In January, 1851, he presented himself to Archbishop Blanc, who had invited him, and was just then in need of a pastor for St. Martinsville. He merely passed through New Orleans and never returned, devoting himself to the welfare of his people with an energy that never relaxed. He never left his post even for a day, never left his house save for the church, the schools, or the sick. He was a priest for over sixty years, during which his daily Mass was omitted only three times. Tobacco he never touched, save a little in the form of snuff, and he was a total abstainer. When not among the sick or in the schools, he almost lived in the confessional.* Money he never mentioned. If some were given him, it merely touched his hand for a blessing, and then went to the poor, especially those who had seen better days — a numerous class in Louisiana since the Civil War. The annuity that came to him from his patrimony in France went the same way. That he might be better able to help the needy, his dress and food and sleeping-room were those of a pauper. Though he lived on corn meal and milk, his constitution was wonderfully strong. He walked bare-headed at every funeral, taking no notice of rain, mire, or sunshine. He attended sick calls many miles away, and after riding over the prairies almost all night, would be at the altar next morning. If he were delayed, he would say Mass at any hour, going directly to the church on his return and ringing the bells to give notice to his flock. His curious little buggy might often be seen flying over the prairies, for he always kept a fleet horse. But he was often obliged

---

* This was especially the case at Easter-tide. Père Jan was in the confessional at daybreak. About seven o'clock he left it to say Mass. After his thanksgiving he returned. After each confession — in case of persons who lived at a distance — he would give the absolved penitent holy communion. He seldom broke his fast until after 3 P. M.

to go on foot where his horse could not carry him.
Two days before he died he spent the night searching
for a poor colored man that had asked for his ministrations. The weather had been very wet. The prairie
verdure was hidden in many places by muddy water.
His steed, which the boys used to call the "lightning
flash," could not "pull through" the mud, but the old
man did. Leaving his turnout in a quagmire, he half
waded, half dragged himself through the obstructions
—and the writer is inclined to think that anybody
who has not been in St. Martinsville in a rainy season
knows not what mud is—he reached home coated
with dirt and wet to the skin, and, after such a night,
was on the altar in less than fifteen minutes.

In March, 1881, Père Jan founded St. Martin's
Convent of Mercy, whose astonishing success he often
declared to be the chief consolation of his old age.
This was in a great measure due to his incessant exertions in its behalf, and the Sisters of Mercy mourned
him as their kind father and best benefactor. They
were glad to be able to ease him a little on their arrival by taking charge of the First Communion and
Confirmation classes which, including "white, black,
and brown," numbered thousands, and with which he
had never had help before.

When the bells, even those of the neighboring
Protestant churches, announced the sad news of the
death of this patriarch, the whole village mourned,
business was suspended until after the funeral, stores
and offices closed. While his remains lay in the church,

hundreds touched them with beads and medals to preserve as relics. People spoke of miracles wrought by
contact with his precious earthly tegument. And a
hardened sinner who had publicly defied God and man,
no sooner gazed on his sacred remains than he wept,
and said: "I will make my peace with God as soon as
a priest comes for the funeral."

A solemn *Requiem* was offered for him on August
17th, and his remains were laid beneath the sanctuary
from which he had blessed and instructed his people
for nearly forty years. The voice of the people proclaimed him a saint, and he had certainly led the life of
one — a life of prayer, penance, and labor. He was a
man of splendid education and brilliant intellectual
gifts, yet, for the love of God, he chose to wear out
his life among poor Cayjuns and negroes. He had no
congenial society; few, if any, of his parishioners were
his equals intellectually. In manner he was a perfect
gentleman, and was as courteous and gentle with the
humblest of his flock as with the highest in the land.
He had a remarkably strong countenance and a wealth
of hair white as cotton bursting from the pod. He
seldom wore a hat — the one he had was half as old as
himself; his cassock was brown and threadbare; but
though his plump figure were draped with an Indian
blanket, it could not hide his distinguished air; the
culture derived from the polished society in which the
first half of his life had been spent remained to the
last. And, however awed people were by his undoubted
sanctity and his perfect devotion to "mankind of

every description," especially the lowliest, the universal verdict was, "Père Jan is a gentleman — a real gentleman." And this from aristocrats of his flock, who, while admitting that the king can make noblemen, declare that "it takes three hundred years to make a gentleman."

Save for God and his work, the loneliness of Père Jan's later years would have been terrible. His early friends, Lacordaire, Purcell, Varin, and so many others, had all passed away. One of his pupils, the aged Bishop de Goesbriand, still survives. But they never met in America. How often must the old priest, amid the vast solitudes over which he roved alone under the midnight moon, in search of souls, fearless of the evil men* or beasts that infested them -- how often must nature have sighed "for the touch of a vanished hand," and, still more, for "the sound of a voice that is still?" Or, rather, were not sufferings and privations joyous things to him who had borne the yoke of the Lord from his youth? Did he not realize a thousandfold

*Père Jan was utterly fearless in every way. On his first coming to St. Martinsville, his great devotedness to the colored, bond and free, was not relished by some of his aristocratic parishioners. He told the writer that on several occasions men stood up in the church and drove their slaves from the Communion rail. They had evidently intimidated some of his predecessors. But Père Jan soon showed these people, whose gentlemanly propensities had been maturing for centuries, that the poorest slave was as much to him as the highest magnate, for it was only for the immortal soul he cared in either. They thought that negroes should not be allowed to kneel at the same railing as they, but Père Jan was no respector of persons.

the truth of the beautiful promise: "Son, give me thy youth and I will guard thy old age?" Was he not able to say with the spouse in the Canticles: "All things, my beloved, the old and the new, I have kept for thee." No regret clouded the green and beautiful old age of this holy man. He had given the whole substance of his house for love, and despised it all as nothing.

VIII

HITHERTO we have given sober history, but we cannot wholly forget that poetry and romance have cast their bewildering spells over the Attakapas. It is alive with weird and fantastic legends of the man-eating Indians, the early missions, and that beauteous flower of Acadie, Evangeline. For long stretches the solitude of the Tèche, whose meandering course lies through "the green Opelousas" and the fertile fields of St. Martin, is as unbroken as when her bark navigated its sluggish waters. It is spanned by arches of live oak and cypress, whose dark, thick foliage, draped with Spanish moss, gives the whole a melancholy yet most poetic aspect. The noise of engine and paddles seems strangely discordant on the silent river. The echoes of the "Canadian boat songs" of the men "who rowed through the midnight, silent at times," come down to us through the misty avenues of time. The trills and roulades of the mocking bird make the morning joyous. There is little undergrowth between the heavy trunks; but one frequently catches delicious vistas of the bright green and golden yellow of the cultivated fields beyond. Down to the water's edge grassy slopes in many places roll in graceful curves, and from out the cool shadows of numberless groves comes the sweetest forest music.

Towards St. Martinsville a sweep around a point of live oaks, "bearded like a pard," brought the boat to "Evangeline's Bend." The immortal trees that sheltered the cannibals and waved their branches to welcome the sad exiles of Acadie, lean lovingly over the bayou and embrace each other in the skies. One seems to be in a gorgeous cathedral, whose roof is interminable. The whispering winds, the dim religious light, the preternatural calm of these scenes, fresh from the hand of God, make this summer-land of intense sunshine and cool shadow and quivering moonlight glorious "beyond the muse's painting."

Around the oldest town on the Tèche poetry and romance will linger as long as our gentle troubadour's *Evangeline* survives, whether we regard that maiden as a beautiful creation of fiction, or, according to the traditions of these parts, a genuine heroine who lived, loved, and suffered, and, like the sweet-smelling balms of the east, gave out her best fragrance only when her heart was broken. Upon the details of the heartless eviction of her people romance has lovingly seized and the poet has turned the magic light of his genius, till the gilded halo of song and story veils, as with a beauteous haze, the harsh outlines of sombre historic truth. Evangeline, with Father Felician, began her search for Gabriel, the silent hero of the tale. They accompanied a band of exiles down the Mississippi, passed the Golden Coast, and entered Bayou Plaquemine. Her heart told her that

" Through these shadowy aisles had Gabriel wandered before her."

Tradition asserts that their meeting with Basil, the blacksmith, took place at St. Martinsville. In the first church * erected here she heard Father Felician's Mass ere she set out again on her sorrowful quest. In front of it was the *plaza* or square, still unfenced, and, save for a bronze statue of Père Jan,† unadorned, as when her dark eyes looked their last upon it. Around the church was the parish cemetery. Several graves and ruined tombs may still be seen to the right, though since the opening of a new cemetery — now an old one — no interments have been made near the church.

Our first glimpse of St. Martinsville was idyllic. The evening was of perfect clearness; the sun was setting slowly, and the young moon rising as we passed the old-fashioned drawbridge, and moved upon the shining waters beneath the shadow of hoary trees, garlanded with wreaths of gray moss. The repose of the scene was preternatural. Save the lowing of the Attakapas kine on the distant prairie, and the tinkling of the sheep-bells, no sound broke the solemn stillness. The white spire of the old church on its red base stood

* The old people say this church was burned.

† This statue was erected by the exertions of Père Jan's successor, Rev. A. B. Langlois, who, besides being an excellent priest, is an accomplished botanist.

out finely against the darkening sky, the CROSS, which has stood aloft in this place for a century and a half, keeping loving watch over all. It was high water, and everything on the banks was mirrored in the clear depths. We sang softly the Acadian hymn to the Sacred Heart of our Savior. And the writer pledged herself to return to these fairy scenes by dipping her hand in the Tèche and tasting of its waters. For whoever drinks of these waters must revisit its umbrageous shores ; yea, as a sterner proverb hath it, must return thither to die.

The cloisters of a Carthusian monastery are not more silent than St. Martinsville. A thriving outpost when most of the great cities of our country were not, it seems now, in the serene evening of life, dozing over the bright memories of the past. The broad dusty thoroughfares felt scarcely a footfall. The stores were open, but no one was in them. Around a strongly built brick church the town lies. The architecture is of a past era. Cottages shingle-roofed and bricked between the uprights, close Creole doors and shutters, an occasional tile roof — it was like stepping into the Attakapas capital some eighty years ago. On Sunday this other village of Grand Pré shook off its slumberous spirit, and the charming mist of poesy seemed to evaporate. Hundreds of carriages arrive from all points of the prairie, pirogues anchor in the bayou, cavalcades of horsemen on Creole tackies come trooping in from the various roads in clouds of yellow dust, processions of bright-eyed children wind out of the convent gardens, and by ten o'clock the spacious church is full of "white, black, and brown," summoned by the sweet-sounding quintet of bells, of which the old place is proud. Mass does not begin directly. Père Jan is hearing confessions. About eleven High Mass begins. The choir is good, but the strongest voice in the village belongs to the saintly octogenarian.

No non-Catholic place of worship stands within the limits of St. Martinsville. It is, to a great extent, French in race and feeling, though not without Fitzgeralds, O'Rorkes, and other names of Celtic origin, which, however, have long since been thoroughly Gallicized. New settlers have come with the railroad, and every one now speaks English. The women have discarded the Spanish mantilla, universal when the writer first knew St. Martinsville, and taken to modern millinery.

But nothing can rob the old place of the glamour of poesy that envelops it. Within the convent square is Evangeline's tree, a giant oak, from whose shade "the maiden descended down to the river's brink, where the boatmen were already waiting." Sometimes in the cool of even', when the moon is growing old, *on dit*, a slight figure with sad eyes and streaming hair is seen gliding among the shadows of this oak and among the ruined tombs of the ancient cemetery by the tall, red church. And the children hurry past these haunted spots with terror in their wide, dark eyes; even at noon, they say: " Perhaps Evangeline is under the convent oak, for she, too, was a Sister of Mercy." And, verily, when the moonbeams assume fantastic shapes, flitting among its shadows, imagination may easily create for us once more that fair girl, all in flowing white, her soft, black eyes gleaming through her nut-brown hair; and with true poetic feeling cordially would we welcome such a ghost.

"Faded was she and old," says the poet, "when in disappointment her long journey ended." But never is Evangeline faded or old to us. To us she is always beautiful, and young, and "fair to behold, that maiden of seventeen summers." We see her in the summer of All Saints, "the sunshine of St. Eulalie," where "the simple Acadian farmers dwelt in the love of God and man." We see her on the flowery surf of the Attakapas prairie, now dotted with substantial plantation homes, and huge sugar-houses. We see her when the dying

"Looked up into her face, and thought, indeed, to behold there
  Gleams of celestial light encircle her forehead with splendor."

We see her as a fair wraith ascending from her northern grave and revisiting the land of the cypress and myrtle.

And to this one fair spirit, so thoroughly Catholic, and so touchingly described in the exquisite imagery of the poet, more than to any belted knight or squire, the Church of the Attakapas owes the dreamy mist of poesy that floats about her groves and waters, and the halo that gleams from the oldest temple of God on the Attakapas prairies.

FORTY YEARS IN THE AMERICAN WILDERNESS

I

THE song that pictures Fionula, King Lir's lonely daughter, sighing for the beaming of the day-star, craving, with tearful eagerness, to hear the sweet bells of heaven, whose music was to announce to her the glad tidings that her spirit was freed from its thraldom, is assuredly one of Moore's finest. By some magic spell, this princess was imprisoned in the form of a swan, and doomed to wander over the bright waters of Eire's fair lakes and streams, until the star of Christianity should arise over the Isle of Destiny, and the bells for the first Mass ring out in joyous peals through the morning sunshine:

> " When will the day-star, mildly springing,
> Warm our isle with peace and love?
> When will heaven, its sweet bell ringing,
> Call my spirit to the fields above?"

Why do we open with this exquisitely poetic legend the unholy subject we are about to treat? What have the touching wailings of this royal virgin to do with our story? Certainly no glamour of poetry, no witchery of romance, have cast their spells of enchantment over the beginning, or the progress, of the hideous burlesque of religion which lured to a doom worse than death so many beings made in the image and likeness of God.

Though of them may be said, as of their chosen prototypes in the desert: "They always err in their hearts, and have not known my ways," yet there was an element of natural goodness and probity among the so-called "Latter-Day Saints." Many soon learned, not, indeed, to prefer the gates of their Zion to all the tabernacles of Jacob, but to abhor them as the gates of hell, gates to which the poet alluded when he said: "Who enters here leaves hope behind."

Many years ago, when he who styled himself king, prophet, and priest of Mormondom, was in the zenith of his power, two *religieuses*, going west on some business of their order, stopped at Salt Lake City. They spoke with several of the wretched women of the place, and listened kindly to their tales of sorrow. One of these abject beings, who was strangely affected by their presence, spoke to the following effect: "I have been long looking for this. If these holy women settle among us, our atmosphere will become purer. And since they have come hither, even for a short time, our religion will never again be to us what it was before their coming." And she burst into a passion and tempest of tears, which, she said, were of joy rather than sorrow.

Had this unhappy creature been sighing, like the princess in the song, for the arrival of something better and purer than her surroundings? And was the advent of these dark-robed daughters of the Faith a sign unto her? Unfortunately, we were not able to follow up her history. But, by some occult association of ideas, the circumstance recalled to our mind the beauteous white bird in whose graceful form was hidden the virgin daughter of the royal Lir, singing, with the swan's sweetest notes, to the stormy river:

> " Silent, O Moyle! be the roar of thy water,
>   Break not, ye breezes! your chain of repose,
> While, murmuring mournfully, Lir's lonely daughter
>   Tells to the night-star her tale of woes."

II

IF THOU seekest a beautiful vale, *circumspice*, here it is; behold it! Perhaps "there is not in this wide world a valley so sweet." We have all heard: "See Naples and die." And a prelate, whose poetic soul revels in the beautiful, wrote of another charming spot: "After Killarney, heaven." We say: See Salt Lake City, and live and admire. Keep the lovely picture in your mind's eye until your dying day. But for this go not down into it. Look at it from the lawns and orchards of Camp Douglas or Prospect Hill, or from any bench or plateau on the hillside. It lies at the base of the Wasatch, sloping towards the west and south. It is girdled with mountains, some bleak and forbidding in aspect, others of emerald brightness, and superb in their beauty and symmetry. In the early summer sunlight the skies are blue, the air balmy. Clustering trees of every shade of green half hide the wide-gabled houses. The bushes are laden with blossoms, and fragrance. The limbs of the fruit trees are pink and yellow with flowers. The amber air is filled as with some delicate aroma by the upspringing blossoms. Quaint abodes, like toy-houses, peep from between the trees. There are seas of waving corn, and green patches of alfalfa, and lazy, lowing kine, and wide stretches of pastoral country dotted with sheep, in the broad valley that slopes to-wards the distant Salt Lake — the dead sea of this new Palestine. The peaks and battlements of the far-away hills, white with eternal show, the turtle-like back of the spacious tabernacle, the rows of Lombardy poplars, which form huge, whispering walls between the abodes of the "saints," and the jungles of sunflower and golden rod that brighten the green sward, give such changeful effects of radiant coloring as are rarely seen outside of the tropics. The panorama of lake, mountain, valley, residences, gardens, public buildings, is kaleidoscopic, ever-changing, and full of charming contrasts. Long lines of fruit trees, trim white houses, tideless, dreamy, slumbering waters that flash every hue of the rain-bow, — the Oquirrh Mountains, now like feudal castles, again with splintered peaks, gilded by the burning sun, — sometimes all this is seen as it were swimming in the air. The amber haze mellows every outline. The hills are wedded by wondrous bridges. The sluggish Jordan leaps to the inland sea, whose calm bosom shimmers in the sunshine. It is that beautiful optical illusion — the mirage. The blue heron, the sacred pelican, the white sea-gull, the graceful swan, the restless prairie-chicken, --- on a closer view you may see some of them poised in the air, or breasting the waters, or resting on the swamp, or balancing their lithe forms on some sparkling pyramid of salt, apparently enjoying the picturesqueness of the scene, and, like ourselves, fascinated by its beauty.

Laid down between the feet of the mountains, amid groves of cottonwood, maple, and oak, and rows of sentry-like poplars, with the great Salt Lake gleaming like sunshine on the distant horizon, is the "Temple City," the "Mecca of the West," the New Jerusalem, which has charmed every eye that ever rested on its varied beauties — at a distance.

III

FATHER DE SMET one day met Brigham Young and his scouts wandering about the haunts of his Indians, and believing them to be immigrants in search of homes, he directed them to a cañon many miles in length, stating that at its end they would find a valley which the hand of man could transform into a land flowing with milk and honey. This territory, which the Mormons entered July 24, 1847, was bleak and forbidding in aspect; the serrated peaks of the Wasatch Mountains bold and rugged; the briny inland sea, sullen and listless, or bright and stirring, according to wind and weather; the dreary waste adorned with tufts of sandgrass and bristling with gray-green sage; the stillness, unbroken save by the screaming of wild birds, the whistling of the cañon

winds, or the barking of the prowling coyotes;—
"this was their welcome home."

So sure was Captain James Bridger of the perennial barrenness of the soil that he offered a thousand
dollars for every bushel of corn wrung from its fastnesses. But Mr. Young was better informed. No
doubt Father de Smet, who at that time was ignorant
of the peculiar views with which he imbued his satellites, knew what the Indians knew, that where the
sage-bush abounded corn would grow, and enlightened
him as to that fact. When he reached the valley, he
told his followers that the Lord had commanded a halt.
But he knew well this was the last spot at which they
could stop; the bleak, inhospitable, alkali desert was
beyond it.

Many disciples came hither in the dusty wagons,
drawn by slow, patient oxen, that passed in trains
over the desert and through the rocky defiles, and,
later, some of the wealthier by the pony express or
the lumbering stage-coach. Some escaped from the
holy city, despite the argus-eyed Brigham and his
myriads of spies. One hundred and fifty of these
gave Father de Smet a dreadful account of the in-
ternal and external condition of Zion. But the
prophet had defenders. On March 20, 1850, Colonel
Kane, one of the many whom his oily tongue had
deluded, lecturing at Philadelphia before the Pennsyl-
vania Historical Society, "On the Mormons," declared
that he had found Brigham Young "sharing sorrow
with the sorrowful and poverty with the poor," and

extolled him as a man of rare natural endowments, which he undeniably was. In June appeared a Mormon paper, *The Deseret News*,* and on September 20th, of the same year, an auspicious year for the prophet, President Millard Filmore appointed him Governor of Utah, partly through the recommendations of Colonel Kane. This at once gave him a position and an influence of which he made the most.

Utah was part of the territory acquired from Mexico in 1848, and originally contained 225,000 square miles. The name is of Indian derivation, and is said to signify "home on the mountain." Salt Lake City† was incorporated June 11, 1851, its population being nearly 5,000. Missionaries were sent in every direction to increase the flock. "Stakes in Zion," as Mormon settlements are called, were established in several places. They were then much more arbitrary in their conditions than now. The peculiar feature of the sect, which had been more than suspected, but always emphatically denied, had not yet been made public. The revelation establishing the "patriarchal order of marriage" is said to have been made to Joseph Smith, July 12, 1843. Smith's widow and four sons denounced it as a forgery, and headed a schism. In 1845, a formal denial was given

---

* This paper is the official organ of Mormonism. Deseret is understood by the Mormons to mean "home of the honey bee." Governor Young wanted Utah admitted into the Union as the "State of Deseret."

† In 1880 its population was over 20,000; at present it is nearly 45,000, of whom over one-third are Gentiles.

by the " Church " in these strong words: " Inasmuch as the Church of Christ has been reproached with the crimes of polygamy, . . . we declare that we believe that one man should have but one wife." Yet in 1852, "the revelation of the celestial law of marriage" was made public.

The next year the Spanish wall, nine miles long, was built of mud and adobes around the little city. Every property was surrounded by a high wall of mud and cobble-stones. Brigham's quarters, in particular, were walled in like Moorish fortifications. Some of these have crumbled away, and others have given place to less unsightly fences. They were intended to keep out Canaanitish Indians and ungodly Babylonians; but they were needed to keep in the discontented victims of the abhorrent system now forced upon the better element. For, be it recorded to the honor of human nature, polygamy met with strenuous opposition from men and women — opposition unavailing before the powerful will and iron hand of the man who riveted it upon his law and gospel. Neither did it ever become universal — it was practised only by a small fraction of the population. Many defections were due to the engrafting of it on the Mormon creed, and those who remained, agreeing to differ with Governor Young, were obliged to keep their opinions to themselves or get beyond the radius of his circle. But, apart from what was euphoniously styled "celestial marriage," the Mormons would scarcely be allowed to rest in peace in any country. They were everywhere accused of incendiarism, fraudulent dealings, and other crimes, and were often in open conflict with the State authorities. Politically, their vote would always be a unit, and, cast on either side, would secure the victory. Any one party's vote, *plus* the Mormon vote, could put in that party's candidate. As a factor in local politics, the Mormon vote could always be relied on to control elections. Even to-day (October, 1889) the Governor of Arizona, in his official report, attacks the Mormons, and says: "They are a curse to the country." He charges them with sending colonies to other territories in order to hold the balance of power, and declares that they vote just as the interests of their church dictate. Hence the feeling against them in Illinois, which culminated in open warfare. The charter of their city, Nauvoo, a place of some 15,000 inhabitants, was repealed in 1845. Joseph Smith and his brother Hiram were killed fighting a mob, and the whole Mormon population expelled from the State.

They crossed the Mississippi to Iowa. Later they crossed that State to the Missouri. Camps of Israel, as their resting-places were called, were laid on the site of the city now known as Council Bluffs. Near Omaha were the famous Winter Quarters, to which the prophet came more than once in the early days of the Utah invasion. Florence now occupies the site of the deserted quarters. From this starting point, band after band of Mormons moved in wagon-trains towards the promised land. Year after year these Ishmaelites, their hand against every man and every man's hand against them, wintered in this obscure corner of Nebraska, and in early spring set out on their perilous journey over the American desert. These expeditions sometimes had a versifier. Here is a stanza of a song composed by a Mormon woman, Eliza Snow:

" The time of winter now is o'er,
   There's verdure on the plain,
We leave our sheltering roofs once more
   And to our tents again."

IV

WHILE the bulk of the new sect migrated to Utah, many remained in their earlier haunts, especially about Council Bluffs, then called Kanesville, from Colonel Kane, who organized the Mormon battalion for Governor Young. These were mostly followers of Joseph Smith, son of the originator of the sect, who claimed to be the rightful head of the church, and deemed Brigham an usurper. A dividing line was drawn very early between the Josephites and the Utah Mormons, but many of these latter only tolerated, from motives of policy, the religion and politics of the spurious prophet.

It was reserved for the nineteenth century to produce a sect * which revived some of the worst horrors

* The Book of Mormon, called by one of the " apostles" the Golden Bible, is said to have been taken from a sort of romance by Rev. Mr. Spaulding, which contains a supposititious history of the wanderings of the Lost Tribes, and their final appearance in America. Save where it quotes from the Sacred Scriptures, it is a tissue of absurdities and contradictions.

of the lowest type of paganism. The leaders of this loathsome caricature of a theocracy, while professing to be divinely inspired, led lives diametrically opposed to those of the men and women usually selected by heaven as the medium of celestial communications to their fellow-mortals. They did not belong to the Negro, Indian, or Mongolian, or any of the races commonly ranked below the Caucasian.

The controlling authority of the Mormon church has always been exercised by Americans of Anglo-Saxon lineage. It is even said that several of the first "Twelve Apostles" came from families that had participated in the struggle for national independence. It is not, therefore, quite correct to speak of Mormonism as an alien organization. It was always wholly non-Catholic. Even in seeking recruits, the Mormons rather avoided Catholic countries. Spaniards, Italians, French, Irish, Mexicans, are sought in vain among the Latter-Day Saints. Its disciples were drawn mainly from the lowest grades of non-Catholic nations. But into this seething vortex men and women of ordinary education, and a few of more than average ability, from the Old World and the New, have been drawn. Time and again have deluded creatures turned their backs on home, friends, and country, to seek salvation in this awful fanaticism. The Catholic faith seems to have been the only *ægis* capable of protecting souls from this stupendous parody on things decent, fitting, and spiritual.

Religiously a fraud, chronologically it was an anachronism, and one wonders how the fanciful tales of

its origin and progress ever obtained credence. In
1820 Joseph Smith, an illiterate lad of fifteen, sees a
glorious vision. In 1823, the angel Moroni,* in a
white robe, and with a countenance like lightning,
makes known to him the existence of metal plates
covered with an ancient record. After his marriage to
Emma Hale, in 1827, an angel delivered to him the
plates of the book of Mormon, which had been buried
1,400 years. On these were written the law, in several
ancient languages. By the application of the seer
stone or peep stone, and a sort of spectacles called the
Urim and Thummin, Smith read them off in English,
sitting meanwhile behind a blanket, that the sacred
records might be screened from profane eyes. All
this is reported to have happened in Ontario County,
New York. Several who swore to its truth, afterwards
declared the falsity of their testimony. On the walls
of the Assembly House these romantic details are
illustrated by a series of colored daubs. The wingless
angel shows his treasure to Joseph, under a tree which
bears a provoking resemblance to the Charter Oak of
the school histories; Aaron anoints him with the
order of Melchisedeck; Peter, James, and John elevate
him to higher privileges; John the Baptist confers
other favors. A Scotchman who has been in Salt

---

* Moroni is described as son of the prophet Mormon, from
whom the sect takes its name, but the Mormons say their correct
name is " Latter-Day Saints." The Scotch gentleman who acts
as beadle in the tabernacle informed the writer that Mormon
angels have no wings.

Lake City some thirty or forty years, and bewails the days of its greatness when Brigham was sole ruler, explains these mystifying pictures, and his hearers are as wise when he concludes as they were before he started. How such absurd ravings could attract, or, having attracted, satisfy, disciples is simply inexplicable.

Yet, for many whose feet rested not on the Rock of Peter, the fables of the ubiquitous Mormon propagandists possessed an alluring charm. The Happy Valley, the City of the Blest, the true and only Zion "where indeed the wicked cease from troubling and the weary are at rest," but, above all, the great prophet who was to the excited imaginations of the earlier pilgrims a sort of sanctified grand lama or great mogul, did not the overworked, ill-paid toiler of "effete" Europe long to enter his home of perennial sunshine,* whose skies were always blue, and whose fields wore eternal verdure? Was he not eager to breathe the same air with the holy patriarch, that man of heavenly (?) visions, and to worship in the place where his feet had trod?

Happily, many were disillusioned. Some who went out in families and had wealth and position at their back, returned home disgusted and humiliated. That many were too poor to retrace their steps, it would be foolish and inconsequent to deny. For them there

---

* In point of fact, Salt Lake City (4,354 feet above sea level) is intensely cold in winter and intensely hot in summer. It is only now beginning to be drained. For many months of the year it is perhaps the dustiest spot on earth.

was no release. Poverty and superstition helped to force them into a vise, and while some were ever in rebellion against their pitiless fate, others seemed to grow accustomed to it. Neglected wives and mothers may have accepted their bitter lot with unsanctified resignation. Some were deluded into the belief that the forlorn lives to which they were condemned were crosses from heaven to win them crowns of glory ever-lasting. Homes were dreary, though full of children; wives were widowed, but not by death. With pathetic deceit some declare they are happy under such circumstances, but the tear-dimmed eye and the anguished countenance give the lie to such declarations. There is a terrible pathos in the lives of women, otherwise respectable and intelligent, who find themselves in the interior of households directed by the shining lights of Mormonism.

Mrs. C——, who lives near Temple Block, a staunch Mormon, but not a polygamist, affirms in the strongest terms that there is no happiness in any polygamous family of her acquaintance. The wife of a bishop, who came to her for consolation, said: " For sake of peace and good-will, I have tried to like the wretch who usurped my place, but found it impossible. There are no feelings in my home but feelings of hate and envy." "Those who profess to be happy in their plural relations," added Mrs. C——, "are cunning women who know how to get cloaks and dresses by wholesale from their husbands, while the more honest cannot get them by retail."

When the women believe in the absurd teachings of Mormonism,— how the air is filled with spirits waiting to be born, how such beings can select the time and place of their birth into earthly probation, how they are eager to be born in Zion, how the millennial dispensation is at hand, after which no more spirits can be reclaimed,— that the patriarchal order into which they were given in marriage is to be eternal in heaven, with the rewards and emoluments thereof,— they are upheld under the tortures of their lives by hope. But that good and bright women could ever have been satisfied with such speculations, or with the men that taught them, is simply inconceivable.

Lofty enthusiasm was, indeed, simulated by fanatics or hypocrites; but being only simulated, its fruits were as Dead Sea apples. Where materialism of the lowest type prevailed, no ideal world of beauty could exist. "There is something dry in the reality of things," said Madame de Staël, a little peevishly, "and we try in vain to get rid of it in our daily affairs." What would she have said had she been able to look behind the Eagle Gate? There realism went beyond dryness. Disenchantment, discontent, misanthropy, and sometimes the implacable hatred of the infernal furies, were the monstrous fruits of this "Variation of Protestantism." Though they understood not the meaning of the term, the celestially-espoused women of Utah were to a great extent the most pessimistic creatures on the face of the earth. Considering the plausibility of the crafty autocrat of Zion, the rough and ready eloquence of Mormon missioners, and the ignorance and isolation of many Catholics, it is a grand thing that, while wealth, position, and in some cases intellectual ability, have been lured into the acceptance of a system diametrically opposed to every fine instinct of womanhood, yet no Catholic maid or matron was ever beguiled into believing in this "patriarchal order." Many have chafed under their hard lot, for it is the women chiefly who must bear the shame, scorn, and anguish consequent on plural marriage. Some have left husbands who broke God's law by multiplying wives, and reared their children by the sweat of their brow. One poor English woman, whose eyes were dim, not from age, but from weeping, said that when her husband brought home a girl whom he called a plural wife, she told him to choose between them. He selected her rival. She at once left his premises, taking her six little children, whom she supported henceforth by working for Gentile families. He took another consort, and still another. Years passed slowly for the struggling woman thus sadly widowed. The "plural wives" died. Then did the worthless wretch return to his first choice. She had prospered, she could support him now as well as his children. But the outraged creature drove him from her presence, nor could she speak of him without loathing. "No religion could be from God," said she, "which causes the inexpressible torture I have seen in the weary years of my life in the wilderness."

The Mormon men * seemed dull, vulgar, and clownish; no doubt there are many exceptions. "When I look at them," said a prominent Gentile, "I think their horrible system should be uprooted by fire and sword." Not so the writer. It should never be glorified by persecution. Left to itself, it will tumble to pieces. When Mormons break the laws by bigamy or other crimes, they suffer, not as martyrs, but as evil-doers. Yet it is their policy to pose as victims.

The Mormon women look shapeless and slovenly; their faces soulless, their eyes fishy, dead. Seen in thousands issuing out of the tabernacle on a fine Sunday afternoon, with their slatternly figures and slouching gait, they do, indeed, appear "the off-scouring of all." Nothing blithe or gay about them as they waddle along; no glow upon the cheek, no sparkle in the eye, no trim, graceful robes, no womanly dignity. Those whom we saw were downright ugly, and had a wizened appearance. In some the expression was repulsive and defiant, in others, repulsive and sad. Many of the children are afflicted with physical deformity, and not a few are said to be idiotic. The deaf and dumb have increased of late years. The

---

*N. P. Willis's description of "British Workmen" fits the lower type of Mormon men: "Utter want of hope in the countenances of the working classes — the look of dogged suspicion and animal endurance of their condition of life. They act like horses and cows. . . . Their gait is that of tired donkeys. . . . Their mouths and eyes are wholly sensual. . . . Their dress without a thought of more than warmth and covering. . . . Their voices are a half-note above a grunt."

groups have a decidedly foreign appearance. Light hair and the Scandinavian cast of features predominate.

The peculiar institution was made subservient to the temporal weal of the apostles and elders. By organizing and directing trade to his own advantage, Brigham Young accumulated enormous wealth. In the poorer classes, too, avarice often had something to do with the multiplication of helpmates. These wretched creatures supported the children, or, in a country where labor was high, supplied servants without wages to their masters. They minded the chickens and cows, sold or bartered butter, eggs, honey, and farm produce in general. As much exterior decency as was compatible with the condition of affairs was generally observed, for the Destroying Angel was abroad, and woe to the hapless wight that fell under his vengeful wing. But under a semi-respectable appearance, there existed the vices of the cities of the plain.

Neither sensuality, nor so-called spirituality, ever turned the heads of the rulers* aside for one moment from what seems to have been their main purpose — the achieving of opulence. The financial was inextricably interwoven with the law and the prophets, as

* There is no man of remarkable ability among the Mormons. The only one who approaches such a plane is a man who, " to further his own ends, has been ever ready to use duplicity, perjury, and dishonesty with his fellow Mormons and with the United States; a man of supreme selfishness, and a crafty worldling."

expounded by the lights of Mormondom. Being rapt in ecstasy, July 8, 1838, Joseph Smith spoke thus:

"O, Lord, show unto me, how much thou requirest of the properties of thy people for a tithing."

Here is the answer:

"Verily, thus saith the Lord, I require all their surplus property to be put into the hands of the Bishop of Zion, for the building of my house and for the laying of the foundation of Zion, and for the priesthood, and for the debts of the presidency of my church.

"And this shall be the beginning of the tithing of my people.

"And after that, those who have thus been tithed shall pay one-tenth of all their interest annually, and this shall be a standing law unto them forever, for my holy priesthood, saith the Lord.

"Verily I say unto you, it shall come to pass that all those who gather unto the land of Zion shall be tithed of their surplus properties, and shall observe this law, or they shall not be found worthy to abide among you."

At first there was little or no money in Utah. Everything was done by barter. When a man took his families to a place of amusement he paid his fee in "collateral," consisting, perhaps, of a barrel or two of potatoes, or a wheelbarrow full of turnips, or some dozens of adobes. But at no time were the new lights able to say with one of the genuine apostles, "Silver and gold I have none." From the promulgation of their tithe system they grew prodigiously rich. The rank and file worked; the profits swelled the exchequers of the heads of this nefarious system.

For the first twenty years after their arrival the Mormons were, it may be said, the sole occupants of Utah. Being a thousand miles from the frontier, they deemed themselves secure from further molestation. In 1854 the President appointed Governor Steptoe in Mr. Young's place. But Young refused to stir from the gubernatorial seat, and set the Chief-Executive and the world at large at defiance. "I am, and will be, governor," said he, "and no power can hinder it until the Lord says, 'Brigham, you need not be governor any longer.'" The new appointee considered it unsafe to enter the city, and Brigham remained governor *de facto*. The saints were now in open rebellion against the United States, and the Mormon War followed. In 1857 the army of Utah, consisting of 2,500 troops, was sent to reduce them to submission. Brigham cut off the supply trains. The territorial militia went out to reconnoitre. The "enemy" was snowbound one hundred miles east of the capital. The saints determined to evacuate the country, and leave it as they found it, a wilderness. But, through arbitration, a peaceful solution of the difficulty was found. The new Governor, Alfred Cumming, appointed by President Buchanan, was allowed to take his seat, and the belligerent Mormons were pardoned.

The army remained in Utah until 1861. In 1862 Colonel O'Connor and his command settled at Camp

Douglas, within easy range of the city. The Mormon leaders have always keenly resented the military occupation of their country as an element of antagonism, and a menace to peaceful, law-abiding citizens. But the soldiers have been a blessing to the place.

VI

BY FAR the most remarkable product of Mormonism was Brigham Young, of Vermont, who began life as a glazier. He was supreme in Church and State. A Catholic lady, his neighbor for many years, said to the writer: "No Russian autocrat ever held his subjects, body and soul, in so firm a grasp as Brigham Young." They were literally his, to have and to hold. His temper was generally under perfect control; his conversation easily drifted from monologue to grotesque rhapsody; his unctuous words were seasoned with scriptural allusions, and emitted in a clear, finely modulated voice, with which one could not readily connect any disposition to cruelty. His gentle condescension and quiet self-possession sometimes threw strangers off their guard, and made them wonder whether this bland, courteous gentleman was in reality the terrible Brigham. He would describe his sufferings with a pathetic air, and pose as a victim with so much grace that tears sometimes bedewed the eyes of an impressionable listener. He rather liked the *rôle* of a persecuted saint, a taste still common among his disciples. He could be ebullient, sarcastic, and naively exultant by turns, and was not in the least repelled by irresponsiveness.

Wearing a sort of spurious tiara as king, priest, and prophet, Brigham Young played the triple part with consummate ability. He did hard things in a kindly fashion, kept the rabble on his side, and was worshiped by his motley *clientèle*. He knew everyone in his territory, and, by a judicious distribution of his favors, gained the good-will of the multitude. Of his wonderful personal magnetism, there can be no doubt. And did we not know that there are persons whose affectations in the course of years have become natural, and whose illusions have finally become to them realities, we should say that he was at once a profound hypocrite and a crafty fanatic.

Apparently large-hearted and generous, the prophet was really most grasping and avaricious. He understood perfectly the art of throwing a herring to catch a whale. The tithes must be paid into the Tithing House in money or kind, but if he ground his people as in a mill, he always "spoke them fair." He was ready to administer the estates of wealthy widows, but to have surer control he appointed himself spiritual spouse to such ladies. "Deal you in words," was an advice he followed to the letter. If women complained of their hard lot in the pleasant valley by Jordan's stream, he spoke, with hands and eyes uplifted, of the perfect blessedness reserved for the Latter-Day Saints in the heavenly Jerusalem during all eternity. A Catholic who knew him well spoke of

him in terms more strong than elegant. Another said
to the writer: " Mr. Young was always a civil-spoken
gentleman. He never put his hands behind his back
when I asked him for a subscription." He gave this
lady twenty-five dollars for the Land League in Ireland, and he sent a like sum for a hospital to be erected
on his old hunting grounds in Omaha. But those
who knew him best declare that he was close-fisted,
and not at all inclined to part with his money. It
was necessary to his scheme to give land to every
man* capable of working it. The wealth of the place
was to be chiefly agricultural, and every farmer increased the wealth of the church. As all hands had
to pay their passage in labor, the immigrants were,
for the time being, little better than slaves. Like
Queen Elizabeth, Brigham was willing to take with
both hands, but would scarcely give with his little
finger.

But the great man walked about among the laborers, shook hands with them occasionally, called them
by their names, inquired how their families did, seemed
to believe their stories and to trust in them. They
were as ciphers, every one of whom pushed him up a
place higher; obscure, ignoble builders of his prosperity. They swelled his retinue, and he made them
feel he was interested in their welfare. When crickets
or grasshoppers destroyed their crops, there was

---

* Until 1871 the Mormons had only squatters' titles to their
property. At that date only three or four city lots were owned
by non-Mormons.

always plenty in his larder, and he more than once invited them to partake of it. "Ah," said a poor woman to us, "I was never hungry when provisions were scarce. The president with his own hand gave me plenty of breadstuff." This woman did what many another did who was better than her surroundings. She declined to be superseded by the women her husband called wives, left his roof-tree, took service in the family of the prophet, and lives to testify how well he provided his household with the flesh-pots of Egypt. "No one was ever hungry in his house," said another, who had suffered the pangs of hunger in early times of scarcity. Both these women execrated the vile institutions which left so many homes, practically, without husbands or fathers. As the prophet usually gave separate establishments to the women on whom he bestowed his hand, things did not look as gloomy in his premises as in the homes of the poor, but in all cases the scenes between the rival women may be more easily imagined than described.

"No one but a Mormon woman," said a poor, faded creature, "can know the torture, the horror, of this diabolical custom.

"You think it wrong, then? You are not deluded into believing it right?"

"Oh, no. I never could believe such abominations."

"Well, now, the head of your religion practised these abominations. How can you follow his teachings in other points?"

"Oh, that is entirely different. *He* was right whatever he did."

No one can doubt the sincerity of these people when they laud this man to the skies. He thoroughly imbued them with a belief that he was the centre of a theocracy on the model of the Bible, and the source of every spiritual and temporal blessing they enjoyed. When they worked for him they had enough to eat, a great point with these stout bread-winners. When he made tours, or, what the old English would call "progresses," through the country, young men, unasked, went out before his carriage to remove stones or other obstructions from the rocky roads lest his sacred person should be jolted. On his arrival at Mormon hamlets, little girls in white, with sashes of celestial blue, used to march and gambol before him. Every material misery found a counterpoise in him. He sought to eliminate all the supernatural of which he was not the medium. He listened gently to the woes of the plural consorts who came to him for a remedy which he could not give. Similar woes disturbed his own castles. But after a few soft words from him, they would submit to their hard lot with patient endurance from which no perfume of genuine piety exhaled.

It is significant that while so much is made of Joe Smith, one hears but little of Brigham Young in the city he founded. No picture or memento of him hangs in the Tabernacle or Assembly House. It is the present policy of the Mormons to keep polygamy

as much out of sight as possible. And Mr. Young,
like Henry VIII., is especially famous for his matrimonial transactions. He left his families millions of
dollars. A grandchild of his told a Catholic lady that
when he was dying, illumined perhaps with "the light
that enlighteneth every man that cometh into the
world," he said: "I never had a wife but one, and
that was my first."

VII

THE beehive is the adopted emblem of Mormonism, and much parade has always been made of Mormon industry. But, leaving out the homes of the
wealthy bishops and other high officials, Mormon
homesteads are often as slovenly looking as their mistresses who lounge on the doorsteps or hang over the
gates and fences, in cotton gowns and sunbonnets.
They greatly disappointed us. As a rule, the homes
were not neat, tidy, or well kept. Considering their
years in the desert and their opportunities, we failed
to perceive the Mormons had done anything extraordinary. Gardens and farms showed great lack of
cleanliness; weeds and tangled grass were rank and
abundant, bushes untrimmed, withered branches hanging from fruit trees, broken limbs from shade trees.
The usual complement of tin cans, old hats, shoes, and
rubbish in general that one sees in remote western
towns was not absent here. Few of the poorer dwellings, whether of adobe, log, or frame, or all combined,
will bear a close inspection. Of flowers we saw scarcely

any. The little brooklets or runnels were dry, the dust stifling. Water was very scarce. Those who used the hose to water their lawns could use it only for a stated period. We were surprised at the general untidiness, especially on the outskirts; a people who did little else might have their places bright and clean. "The sights," however, are always in good order. The Mormons are on dress parade before strangers, and seem feverishly anxious to make a good impression. Their worst features are held in abeyance. To see them at a discount one should visit, unannounced, the suburban quarters and back settlements. We have heard of the unspeakable Turk; in rustic haunts, where the people are not civilized by Gentile contact, may be seen the unspeakable Mormon. Denmark, Wales, England, Switzerland, Sweden, Scotland, Germany, and the States, have contributed to establish these outlying camps of Israel, formed of dugouts, log-cabins, and huts, with a sprinkling of houses of more decent type. The barbaric hordes that followed in the wake of the prophet have not lost all their barbarism.

Some of Brigham Young's children married Gentiles —a Jew is a Gentile in Mormondom. This he affected to consider an indelible disgrace. And as he had in earlier days consigned his rival, Rigdom, to the devil, "to be buffeted for a thousand years," so he solemnly delivered his own children to Satan forever, and cursed them with all his might. This was severe from a potentate who laid claim to constant angelic or divine guidance, and whose talent and shrewdness were seldom at fault.

The Mormonism of thirty or forty years ago is now but a tradition. "Ah," said an official of the Tabernacle to the writer, "you should have seen this town in the early days, before the railroads brought in the trash of the continent," *i. e.*, the Gentiles. The people were driven like sheep to the market-place by a few fox-like demagogues who assumed a priestly* power terrifying to the abject. They had been coaxed into the wilderness by the mellifluous words of the president and his silver-tongued auxiliaries, and were secure in their iron grasp. They came to the Tadmor of the desert, or rather to the rich corn-fields and blooming orchards which the Jordan laves. They found a shabby little town, shaded by saplings — an ugly, dismal place, whose streets were enlivened by pigs and goats, and adorned at irregular intervals by heaps of offal and decaying vegetables. The dwellings were silent as the Sahara, save for the bawling of children. The low cottages, five or six in the same yard, had additions on the sides and rear for the different families. Here and there, on the dusty street, one might see a deserted wife airing her progeny. The cottage occupied by Brigham Young in his humble early days is now the property of the convent

---

*The officers of the Melchisedek priesthood are high priests and elders. The officers of the Aaronic, or lesser priesthood, are priests, teachers, and deacons. These preside. The office of the Seventy is to travel for recruits.

of which it forms a part. It contains four large apartments (each can be shut off from the rest) and three
entrances. The doors and windows are screened with
wire gauze to keep out insects, which are very annoying in Utah during the hot weather. In one room is
a trap-door, through which Brigham more than once
escaped when the United States authorities were wishing to see him. Many of the early houses, with their
succursales, and a few of the original log-cabins remain.
Even to-day there are large expanses of swamp and
sage brush between the Temple City and Ogden. Although still profoundly disappointing to one who has
often heard of it as "combining the cleanliness and
activity of Young America with the picturesqueness
and dignity of the Orient," it has greatly improved
since its earlier decades. But this progress is
due chiefly to the presence of the progressive Gentile.

The exodus of the pilgrims from Nebraska, and
their establishment on the beautiful plain at the foot
of the Wasatch range, would, it was supposed, place
them beyond the reach of Gentile interference forever.
There were no soldiers, no railroads, no telegraph.
Heretofore their peculiar ways had brought them into
conflict with their neighbors. The new Jerusalem
would have no neighbors. Unfriendly Gentiles would
disturb them no more. Ere the saints would have
spent "Forty Years in the Wilderness" they would
have established an empire more compact than that of
Charlemagne and grander than the dream of Napoleon.

But the railroads, the mines, and the soldiers brought a "change over the spirit" of such dreams.

The Mormon leaders, notably Young, opposed the development of the mineral resources of the country. The locality of valuable mineral ledges was kept secret by his order, though he thorougly understood their value, lest the Gentiles should profit by them. The Mormons trade only with each other, give work to each other, and boycott the Gentiles in every possible way. Zion's Co-operative Mercantile Institution, irreverently called "the Co-op," which has several branches, handles business to the amount of six million dollars a year. Through this institution the church considered herself entitled to crush out all competition.

When enterprising people like the four Walker brothers sought to do a little business on their own account, and encouraged outside capital to come to their aid in developing the silver* ledges of the Wasatch, they immediately fell under the ban of Brigham's displeasure. Their tithe-offerings did not suit him. He wanted thirty thousand dollars more than the amount they presented. Tithe collecting is an art in which these apostles have always been distinguished experts. To-day, Presiding Bishop Prescott, a Virginian, admits that the revenue from this source amounts to seven hundred thousand dollars a

---

* From any of the heights around Salt Lake City one may see spiral wreaths and columns of black smoke arising from the silver-ore smelters.

year. He declines to make any statement as to its use. "The people," said he, "are asked to believe in the honesty and business sense of their bishops, without an annual array of figures which might or might not lie."

VIII

ONLY the lethargy or stupidity of the masses could make fraud and pillage on this gigantic scale possible. The calumnies uttered against the Jesuits by their enemies would be true if applied to the "Aaronic" priesthood. "The end," the enriching of the rulers, justifies any "means" whatever. One-tenth of everything goes into the treasury of the church. Mormondom is divided into stakes. At the head of every stake is a stake bishop. Every stake is divided into wards, presided over by ward bishops. Ward bishops get orders from stake bishops, and these make returns to the presiding bishop and his cabinet of two. Blind, unquestioning obedience is rigidly enforced. Apostle John W. Taylor, the czar of all the Mormons, has just warned his flock of the pernicious tendencies of the day, and the danger that lurks in criticism of those over them. "The men at the head of the church," says he, "have the spirit of revelation — they are prophets and seers, and we cannot retain the spirit of God and be constantly finding fault with them."

The prophet was once abroad, but the iconoclast is abroad to-day. Revolts and rumors of revolts are common in the holy city. There were, indeed,

upheavals and commotions in the days of the redoubtable Brigham. The Godbeites and others spoke, and
with no uncertain tone. They declared that President
Young was not lord of their temporalities, and that
the elders should confine their guidance to things
spiritual. When the Walker brothers were asked for
an enormous sum as their "tithing," the demand met
with a stern refusal. But the dictator, who would
brook no opposition, excommunicated the rebels, and
worked with all his might to ruin their business.

The church is weaker now than in early days, and
it is kept up chiefly through its missionary* channels.
The Catholic Church, without showing the slightest
aggressiveness; the railroads, which daily pour in
throngs of witnesses; and the freedom which the
pointed guns of Camp Douglas insure, have perceptibly
weakened what seemed to be a vital force in this
hideous fanaticism, and have begun its overthrow.
Some Mormon women have married Catholics and become exemplary members of the true Church. In
fact, all the Mormons who wed liberals of any denomination embrace the religion of their spouses, which
shows that Mormonism carries no conviction to the
minds and hearts of its votaries. Many of the

---

* "A Perpetual Emigration Fund" is collected to bring out
new recruits. At first, Europeans were brought to Winter
Quarters, *en route* for Utah, by way of New Orleans, whence
they ascended the river to Omaha. But, since the opening of the
railroads, they go from the Atlantic seabord by trains. Probably
about half of the Mormons are foreigners, though this may be an
underestimate.

daughters of Zion tell their Gentile friends that, though Mormons, they do not believe in the teachings of Mormonism.

Would that all who fall away, or rise up, from that superstition embraced the Catholic faith. Here is what Rev. Mr. Lamb, a Baptist minister, who has lived many years in Utah, says:

"At the annual conference held in Provo, April 4, 1886, one of the leading speakers confessed, with a sad heart, that one-third of all the boys and young men in Utah, between fifteen and thirty years of age, are infidels. This statement was fully confirmed by subsequent speakers. And my own observation is, that this infidelity among the young people is even more widespread than the above admission would indicate, and is being shared by a rapidly increasing number of the older members."

So severe is the tithing tax on the rich that, among those who accumulate wealth, some quietly drop aside out of the church without joining any other. These, and the large class that side with every party, are called "Jack Mormons." Genuine apostates are quite numerous, and their testimony as to the rulers is by no means complimentary. These men must have money. Their subjects, whose allegiance is due to ignorance and superstition, live simply. They must not buy from Gentiles or give them work. The Gentile must be starved out. A prominent "saint" was wont to affirm that God was a business God, and that if the saints had kept their business to themselves they would not be punished by the presence of the Gentiles; their money would remain among themselves. A man with many wives and children needs a good allowance.

Brigham Young improved to the utmost his opportunities of acquiring wealth. The last — said to be the nineteenth — reversion of his hand he bestowed on one Amelia Folsom. He built her a showy mansion with a Mansard roof, a tower and cupola, set in the midst of a beautiful lawn. It is now the executive mansion of the Mormon hierarchy, though still called the Amelia Palace. To each of the abject women whom this American Turk selected for dishonor he gave a local habitation, if not a name. The first wife was Mrs. Young; the others were simply called Miss, with the given, we cannot say Christian, name, the ˙ chief being "Miss Amelia," according to a custom common in Utah. The children of a first marriage consider themselves on a higher social plane than the offspring of subsequent so-called marriages contracted amid the orgies of the Endowment House.

Immense pains have always been taken to imbue the young with the doctrines of Mormonism. They were forbidden to hold intercourse with Gentiles, and so far this isolation has, to a great extent, kept them in darkness. But as the Gentile population increases, the young saints, much to the discomfiture of the patriarchs and high priests, become ashamed of Mormonism. At the county election held in Salt

Lake City, August, 1889, several Gentiles were elected because many disaffected Mormons voted the liberal ticket. An intelligent Catholic gentleman who has long resided in Utah writes:

" If the Government were to break up the school trustee system, for of course when there are Mormon trustees * there will be Mormon teachers and Mormon pupils, and appoint its own superintendent and teachers, and adopt its own text-books, which, in this case, might contain a full account of the true nature of Mormonism, the enlightenment of the children would be secured."

So far the number of Mormons who embrace the Catholic faith is small. The Mormon ranks are recruited from non-Catholic countries. The prejudices of early years are strengthened by the Church's inflexible teachings of self-crucifixion as compared with the loose morality of Mormonism. The condition of the children is deplorable. They are often taught by their jealous aunts — plural wives are so-called — to hate one another, and encouraged to tantalize their deserted mothers. Besides, many fathers are ordered off on missionary work. Some are absent three or four years, others get " revelations," establish new families, and never return. In either case the children are left to their own sweet wills, and, says a Gentile resident, " it is not surprising that in the outskirts of

* Several Gentile trustees have been elected, but the Mormons are scheming in every possible way to get full supervision of the schools.

the town the nights are often rendered hideous by the whoops of the young Mormon hoodlums," called also " yaps."

Like Brigham Young, the Mormons love to pose as victims. With them prosecution is persecution. They insist it is their religion that is persecuted when they are punished for breaking the law, and, "my father is in the pen," is a common boast among the children of polygamists. There is profound policy in viewing the question as they choose to view it. As long as it bears a religious aspect, so long will law-breakers arrested for crime proclaim themselves martyrs. Queen Elizabeth, with extraordinary cunning, tried to deprive martyrdom of its heroism by enacting that the Catholic religion was treason, and punishing its adherents as traitors.

IX

BRIGHAM'S own special demesne near the Temple Block, and stretching far to the east, was strongly fortified. A gateway in the Spanish wall called the Eagle Gate, with huge bulging buttresses on either side has over the keystone of the arch that spans it a golden beehive, on which is perched an immense eagle with outstretched wings. The wall is broken here and there by round towers. Near it are the historic Beehive and Lion Houses, so-called respectively from the ornaments on each portico. Other houses have their faces turned to the rear of this dead wall. They were once tenanted by the miserable women who accepted, or were compelled to accept, life with the patriarch and other high mightinesses. Trap-doors and underground passages are said to exist. In digging cellars and sewers skeletons have been found. All this gives a color of probability to many a weird and ghastly tale. The crumbling walls seem to re-echo the sharp shrieks and dismal moans of the poor sultanas who wept and struggled for freedom. One of these, the fifteenth consort of Brigham, actually did escape, and applied to the United States Court for a divorce in 1874. But in earlier days there was neither ingress nor egress, save through the suave but terrible sultan.

An inmate of the Beehive House says that Mrs. Young, when faded and broken, almost annihilated herself to keep some hold on the capricious affections of her husband. He breakfasted with her every morning, and she, like Rebecca of old, prepared the meats he loved. She showered attentions on the women who had supplanted her. She was politic, and could smile when her heart was breaking. Poor woman, the end was not worthy of the means; she could not keep the heart of her fickle husband, for he had none.

The saints were not allowed to contribute to Gentile charities, but their own church assessments were very large. The building up of Zion has always been an expensive work. The church was the great merchant. Emissaries in foreign lands, Blood Atoners, Destroying Angels, could not live on air. The expenses of the Temple have already run into millions.

The Destroying Angels do not now exist as a public factor in Mormonism, but the principle that established them in bygone days, and prompted them to
perform their abominable cruelties, still exists. It is
well-known that the prophet would brook no resistance. When some rebel was missing it was understood
that he had been put out of the way for the good of
the church. Many a dark, mysterious tale was whis-
pered of such or such a man who was seen going into
the Tabernacle or behind the Eagle Gate, and whose
place in the city knew him no more. The Mountain
Meadow massacre is an indelible stain on Mormonism.
Over a hundred emigrants from Arkansas, *en route* for
the Pacific slope, stopped at the holy city to buy provisions. Brigham did not want these strangers to mix
with his saints, lest such intercourse might foment the
discontent of many to whom Utah had been a land of
promise rather than of performance. All were driven
out and massacred by the Mormons and Lamanites, or
Mormon Indians, September 9, 1857. Many years
later, John D. Lee was taken out of Zion's fold and
executed for his share in that shocking transaction.
Something similar happened, but on a smaller scale,
when the "Morrisites" seceded on the polygamy question. They settled in Weber Cañon, entrenched themselves behind stockades and corrals, and were living in
peace, when one day the Destroying Angels burst furiously upon them and left many weltering in their gore.

A middle-aged man, son of Mormon parents, but a
Gentile by choice, who remembers vividly the Moun-

tain Meadow massacre, is a warm admirer of Governor Young, whom he knew intimately. He told the writer that Young was not responsible for all the murders which anti-Mormons lay to his charge; that he had sent a messenger on his fleetest horse to stop the Mountain Meadow massacre. "But," said he, "he wronged himself and his cause by allowing the vilest evildoers to escape unwhipt of justice." Unhappily, however, he cannot be cleared of complicity in these dastardly deeds.

In a material sense, he had executive ability and several other qualities of a great ruler. He made much show of what he called religion, and was always ready to affirm that whatever commands he laid on his dupes were the results of direct revelation.* He inculcated apparent honesty and truthfulness, and insisted on industry. But even of material progress he allowed but a modicum. The mines must not be worked, nor skillful metallurgists introduced, for fear of bringing in the Gentiles. Neither did he care for railroads. But if he could not hinder these projects, he helped, or pretended to help, them. In the laying of the transcontinental railway between his old quarters, Omaha, and San Francisco, he was a heavy

---

*An old resident of Utah writes: "Some Mormon leaders are hypocrites of the most arrant type; no better proof can be given than their claim of being in direct communication with God, of having seen Him, etc. In making this statement each knows that he is a liar. Some bishops lay no claim to having seen the Almighty or received revelations from Him. But they profess to believe the statements of those higher in power."

contractor. The Mormons built the road between Salt Lake City and Ogden. The modest prosperity that rewarded Mormon efforts in the days of Young's power and prestige was due in a great measure to his watchful eye, his inspiring language, and the partial absence of alcoholic stimulant. The real progress which has made Salt Lake City a notable commercial mart, is due chiefly to the incoming of the Gentiles and Gentile enterprise.

Joe Smith and Brigham Young were men of infamous lives, but, over and above personal merits or demerits, the latter had one quality the former had not, the faculty of being interesting. He attracted attention. People liked to hear of him. He was the personification of absolutism. No one was allowed to air an opinion contrary to his. But though they were as wax in his hands, he never trusted fully to the *vis inertiæ* of the masses. He was the grand archee of the Danites, a secret society sworn to do his will, right or wrong. A few years more of the rule of this despot would have reduced his followers to primeval barbarism. Most of the obloquy of a horrible state of affairs fell on the women. They were emphatically the injured party. History tells us how ferocious women can be. But even had they a competent leader and a capacity for organization, what could the spiritless women of the beehive do against the sensual, avaricious wretches supposed to be their husbands?

Singularly enough, Brigham Young always got on better with Catholics than with any of the sects that settled in his capital. He expressed real love for them, and even condescended to affirm that they would be next *below* the Latter-Day Saints in heaven. To this day the Mormons say: "Oh, we like the Catholics and their bishop! He always treats us like gentlemen." When certain ministers urged the bishop to sign a petition to the Government to have them rooted out he very properly declined to interfere. They had always been kind to him, and in following a religion which he deprecated they were only exercising their private judgment, like other non-Catholics. But they had no real love for the true religion, nor would it ever have entered the boundaries of Utah if the apostles and elders could have kept it out. The first priests who penetrated President Young's capital were persecuted by his followers, and nothing of this kind was done but by his inspiration and connivance. Threatening letters were sent them; a coffin was hung on Father Kelly's door, and he was privately informed that he would be put in a state to occupy it if he did not withdraw from Zion. Ostensibly the sanctimonious prophet was ignorant of all this, and no one would have dared to implicate him. The sturdy priest laid the letters and the coffin before his half-dazed eyes. With the composure and dignity of a leader in Israel he prudently "accepted the situation." Seeing that Catholics could not be kept out, he declared himself their protector. Mass was celebrated in a poor log-cabin, some miners and emigrants forming the congregation. To the Sisters, who were there in 1870, he said: "I am certain I did all a man could do to convert your priest to my religion, and without any success. But I am not so certain that he could not have converted me to the Catholic faith had he remained long enough and tried hard enough." Something like friendship sprang up in him for this bright, sunny priest, of whom he often spoke with affectionate admiration.

Brigham begged the Sisters to remain in his city to teach the children. "I am very anxious," said he, "for good, moral schools for our young people." When a convent was opened some years later, Mormon children* flocked to it. Intercourse with them brought out curious details of their domestic life. Two children, of the same father and different mothers, being about the same age, were called "papa's twins." The largest families number sixty-five, and families of thirty or forty are not uncommon. A theatre manager, while in Salt Lake City, wanted a certain space for his posters. He asked the owner for leave to use it. "Certainly," was the reply, "but I want some tickets for my family." Inquiry elicited the fact that the family numbered forty-one, and the manager thought it cheaper to hire his advertising space.

The bishops soon put a stop to sending Mormon children to the Convent school. Placing an importance

* Even the Destroying Angel put his children at the Convent school, but he would never enter its precincts. When he wanted to see them he would stand on the opposite side of the wide street, and send a messenger across to have them sent to him. When invited to the convent he would say: "I cannot go into that holy house, I am too wicked," or "Don't ask me, I am a bad man."

on early impressions, which people of greater intelligence in other respects might copy with advantage, they agreed that children subjected to the teachings and example of the Sisters could never grow up good Mormons;* and they opened Mormon schools, to which the children were compelled to go. As a rule, the leaders were never unkind to the Sisters, but they did not wish them to invade their territory. Their head-dress seemed to mystify the women. "Madam," said one, very kindly, "have you a headache that you wrap your head up so? I can give you something to cure it." Another stopped two Sisters in the street, and said: "What disgraceful creatures you are! You should be ashamed to come among the saints. How dare you lead lives against nature and the prophet?" They did not realize that a life may be above nature or supernatural without being against it. A few told sorrowful tales, but seemed sincere in their belief that some awful deity, whom they could not define, exacted of them the dreadful sacrifice their peculiar institution involves. We did not see a solitary cheerful face among the Mormon women; many faces bore the hard look that unsanctified suffering gives.

Fort Douglas is a great protection. Once a lovely girl of fifteen was dragged from her mother's side and hurried beyond the Eagle Gate, to be sealed to a "Twelve Apostle man." The girl watched her oppor-

---

*Mormon children are taught to ignore all creeds and governments save the Mormon creed and the theocracy of the Mormon church.

tunity, and, with the connivance of a friend, fled to the barracks for protection.

Thrilling tales are heard on all sides, but the old days of terror have passed away never to return. One Englishwoman declared that she had been a saint since her eighth year; another was born a saint. In addressing them one must say, "arc you a saint?" not "are you a Mormon?" A gentleman having shown us great courtesy, we ventured to ask, " are you a saint, sir?" "No, madam," said he, "I am a sinner from the Island of Saints." In Utah sinners are preferable to saints. Bishop Scanlan* has gained the good will of the Mormons more than the representative of any other denomination. When at Silver Reef, in southern Utah, he was held in such high esteem by the leaders at St. George, that they invited him to perform service in their Tabernacle. St. George is an exclusively Mormon settlement, almost on the boundary line between Utah and Arizona. High Mass was sung, the Mormon choir assisting, and, according to the report in the official paper of the Mormons, the *Deseret News*, Mr. Scanlan preached a very interesting discourse on the principles of the Catholic faith. The Tabernacle was crowded. "Mr. Scanlan appears to be a man of considerable information, and, considering his faith, appeared liberal in his views. . . . He said: 'I believe you are wrong, and you think I

* Utah was once under the spiritual jurisdiction of the ordinary of San Fransisco, and Archbishop Alemany visited Salt Lake City three times.

am wrong; but this should not prevent us from treating each other with due consideration and respect!' It is to be hoped that he may retain this feeling in practice as well as in sentiment." Brigham Young was extremely polite to the Catholic clergy and Sisters. When he met them in the street he would stop his carriage, uncover his head,* and make a deep salaam. Sometimes he would make a sign to them to approach. And the big, showy man, in gray suit, with a red scarf about his neck and the shiniest of boots, would graciously inquire how they were doing, and emit his best wishes for their health and prosperity. One day two Holy Cross Sisters called on him at the Lion House, and, after some desultory conversation, asked whether he would be pleased to give them some help towards building their hospital. He had no ready money just then; all was invested, much to his regret, as it deprived him of the pleasure of aiding them. The rest of his answer deserves to be put on record *verbatim.* " But," added this high priest, considerately, "whenever you feel that you need any spiritual advice or direction, apply to me, and I will instruct you!" And so he dismissed them with his blessing. So great was his zeal for their salvation that he was baptized for them, as he had been vicariously baptized for George Washington and others.

The present attitude of the United States Government and the aggressive and progressive policy of the liberals are calculated to suppress polygamy; but resi-

* Yet Brigham never doffed the hat to any one, even a prince.

dents in Utah say that it is still prevalent, while it is . extremely difficult to convict an offender. A friend who has been long in the territory says: "The Mormons are a lying, hypocritical, contradictory people; without honor or honesty, conscience or principle." But for their time and opportunities they are few. The whole of Utah does not contain as many people as New Orleans,* and of these less than sixty per cent are Mormons. As for healthfulness, Salt Lake City is not more healthy than other western towns. It has been singularly unhealthy for children, as its populous cemetery shows. Diphtheria has been peculiarly fatal in the holy city, and malarial diseases are by no means unknown. People boast of the number of old men and women as a proof of the salubrity of the climate; but, if we take into account the fact that most of the adults are foreigners who did not leave their homes until the perils of childhood were passed, a death-rate of over 10 in 1,000 would be very large.

XI

BRIGHAM YOUNG died August 29, 1877, at the Amelia Palace, and was buried September 2d. The

* One who investigated this subject writes: "Polygamy does not, where practised, show a greater number of children born in that state than does monogamy. For example, two men with ten wives each will not show as large families collectively as where the same number of women are married each to one husband." The official church report for 1888 places the number of the "faithful" in Utah at 125,000 souls. The whole population is about 215,000. In 1880 the males were 5,055 in excess of the females.

people grieved for him. The ladies, about a score, who considered themselves widowed by his demise, roamed the streets disconsolate, each carrying a large towel to receive her tears as she lifted up her voice and wept. The shrieks rent the air. "The prophet is dead," was heard in every variety of tone. He had been thirty-three years their great Head Centre, and it had never struck the common people that he might, could, would, or should die. He was buried in a large green square near the Eagle Pass. Many tons of granite have been placed over the body. Perhaps it was feared that the grave might be rifled. It is further guarded by a tall iron railing. Four of his consorts are buried in the same field. Should the others decline to marry again, the same posthumous honor will be accorded their remains. Some of his descendants have become Catholics.

Nothing can be more bleak and desolate than the Mormon graveyard on the bare hillside. Thickly are the graves planted in the sandy bench, where the wind often howls and whistles dismally. Some have headstones, others pillars, others curious little headboards coming to a point on the top. The husband is sometimes buried at one end of the family lot, his consorts in the order of their respective deaths beside him. One man had four babes lying at his feet, all born in 1870. On several women's tombstones are carved two hands clasped in the Odd Fellows' grip, with the legend, "She was true." In the cemetery no soft green turf can be seen, no trees worthy of the name; it is a piece of the original desert, planted with the dead, and contains no sign of faith, hope, or peace, no touching appeal for the eternal rest and perpetual light which poor humanity craves. In descending the lonely mountain side, it was a relief to see the grave of a penitent sinner.* Some kind hand had placed upon it a rustic cross, on which were scratched the consoling words, " May he rest in peace. Amen."

Neither where the Mormons worship when living, nor where they lie when dead, is any emblem of Christianity to be seen. In the huge ugly Tabernacle, where eight or nine thousand people have sometimes assembled, there is no token of Christian faith; no cross, no dove, no reminder of death, judgment, or heaven; no gentle Jesus gazing down on them from the gray walls. Only lions couchant and a beehive adorn the unsightly edifice. The preaching in Mormon assemblies is said to be in keeping with the decorations. If Gentiles are present, they are preached

---

* In Utah criminals condemned to death are not commonly hanged. They are shot on their coffins. The above-mentioned, being sentenced to death, asked for the Sisters. He told them he wished for a priest. The Mormons had offered to bring one, but he feared one of themselves would personate a priest to extort from him secrets about others, and about the situation of certain mines. The Sisters were naturally shocked; but the criminal said: " They are capable of worse than that; I have been with them so long that I know the depths of their depravity." They brought him a genuine priest, and he made his peace with God. He lived a few moments after being shot, and was assisted and consoled by the priest to the last. R. I. P. He did not wish to be interred in the Mormon Golgotha,

at; if only Mormons, the crops, the weather, and other mundane subjects are introduced.

Descending from the unexpressibly dreary hiding-places of the dead, "the valley lay smiling before me." Mazes of orchards, farms, garden patches, with far-away sunny peaks, diversified the grand panorama. But it is all of earth, earthly. Among the turrets of the temple there is no suggestion of heaven. From the elliptical dome of the graceless, unwieldy Tabernacle no symbol of redemption, no towering CROSS arises. The beautiful valley has perhaps seen more sin, and sorrow, and unsanctified suffering than any other vale on earth. Amid its picturesque scenery only the Catholic college, hospital, and cathedral give a ray of hope for the purity and sanctity of the future. Only the Catholic Church can speak to the intelligent Mormon with authority. It is the sole institution he respects, though his passions be in conflict with her pure teachings. He sees little difference between the simultaneous polygamy grafted on his religion by Brigham Young and the successive polygamy legalized wherever divorce holds sway.

The Catholic Church purified the pagan world of the Cæsars, and made her austere virtue a commonplace thing among a people just converted from the worship of Bacchus and Venus. It is more difficult to reclaim those who have fallen from their high estate as Christians into the vices of heathenism. But we can pray, and hope, and say a word in season. Something has already been done towards attracting these misguided people to her communion. More will follow. May this only true civilizer, this divine institution for the saving of souls, make a lasting home among the smiling gardens of Utah. And may every erring child of the falseness and fanaticism of the Mormon patriarch, renouncing sin and cleaving unto righteousness, find rest and salvation in the chaste embraces of our mighty Mother, the Holy, Catholic, and Apostolic Church, One and Indivisible.

[Judge Anderson, after a calm, impartial, and exhaustive investigation, has decided that membership in the Mormon church is incompatible with allegiance to this nation; that the teachings, practices, and aims of that church are antagonistic to the government, and utterly subversive of good morals; and that an alien who is a member of that church is not a fit person to be made a citizen of the United States. He therefore denies the application of several men who have taken the Mormon oaths, to become citizens. (See Salt Lake City *Tribune*, December 1, 1889, and previous numbers.)

In view of the overwhelming mass of evidence from Mormon authorities * by which the learned judge arrived at this decision, Bancroft's " Utah," vol. 31 " Pacific States Series," must be considered, in many parts, mere romance, more like the work of a Mormon pamphleteer than of an impartial historian, as a scathing review of that work in the same paper shows.]

* Journal of Discourses, *Deseret News*, etc.

I

T IS about thirty-four years, so far as we can ascertain, since the first mass was said in Salt Lake City. The celebrant was Rev. E. Kelly. The place was an old adobe building on the site of the present church. The Mormon capital was then under the spiritual jurisdiction of Right Rev. Eugene O'Connell, Bishop of Grass Valley, California. In December, 1866, Father Foley became second resident-pastor. Utah passed from Bishop O'Connell to Bishop Macheboeuf, and from him to Archbishop Alemany, who, in January, 1871, appointed Rev. P. Walsh pastor. Father Walsh built the present church, which was dedicated November 26, 1871, under the patronage of St. Mary Magdalen. It is situated on the west side of East Second street, about 200 feet north of the northwest corner, and is 34 by 60 feet, exclusive of the sanctuary. The basement is built of stone, the rest of brick. The style is said to be Gothic, but it did not strike the writer as distinctively such. It has a clean, neat appearance, but is rather small for the congregation. Sometimes it is called in the holy city "The Little Church around the Corner."

In August, 1873, Father Scanlan succeeded Father Walsh, and thirteen years later became Vicar Apostolic of Utah. All Hallows College, St. Mary's Academy, St. Joseph's School for small boys, convents and schools at Ogden, Park City, Silver Reef, and three hospitals are but a few of the good works set on foot by this zealous prelate. Catholics in Utah have increased a hundred per cent during the last ten years. In no other part of America have they had such a struggle for existence. They came at the risk of their lives. Not open warfare, as in parts of New England, was to be dreaded as much as secret assassination, taught and justified under the name of "blood atonement" by the Latter-Day Saints, who, as avenging angels, sometimes destroyed members of their own body, through love, to procure them a more certain admission to the Mormon heaven, and were always ready, when so directed, to destroy the intruding Gentile, through hatred. The priests were threatened and circumvented in every possible way. But Father Kelly averted serious consequences by a bold stroke of policy; he put himself under the protection of the arch-conspirator, Young, himself, and caused it to be generally understood that, if he were made away with by the belligerent Indians,— always convenient scapegoats for Mormon atrocities,— he had friends in high places who, like the twenty thousand Cornish men of the ballad, " should know the reason why."

Poorer and meaner, then, in a worldly sense, than the beginnings of the Church in the Cenacle, in the upper chamber, or on the morning of Pentecost, were the beginnings of the Church in Utah — a handful of miners, smelters, stokers, besmeared and begrimed, led by apostolic men, whose garments were poorer than the coarse raiment of their disciples, who felt the pinching of hunger, and whose privations gave additional zest to their cheerfulness. But " Jesus stood in the midst of them," and Mary was their shield. And so, having nothing, they possessed all things.

II

BEFORE the opening of the railroad, few, * besides the saints, found their way to Salt Lake City. Occasionally, some trappers and traders, a Mexican caravan, or a band of Indians fresh from the war-path, stood without the walls begging admission; but as a rule the inmates were little disturbed by pilgrims from the outer world. The soldiers and the railways made it comparatively safe to enter the capital; the Gentiles began to come, and not a few of them came to stay in Zion.

In 1870 Right Rev. James O'Gorman, Vicar Apostolic of Nebraska, sent two *religieuses* of his vicariate

* Gold-seekers and other emigrants, going by land to California, sometimes visited Utah, not always a safe proceeding, as the Mountain Meadow massacre showed. But this terrible blot on his memory King Brigham desired should be forgotten. The cairn, — who would expect to find a Celtic cairn in Utah? — the stone on which was engraved, " Here one hundred men, women, and children, from Arkansas, were massacred in cold blood, early in September, 1857," and the red-cedar cross, with the words, " Vengeance is mine, I will repay, saith the Lord," were all destroyed by order of Brigham. When the massacre of these emigrants took place, Young was Governor of Utah, Commander-in-Chief of the Militia, and Indian Agent.

to the western portion of the continent on some business connected with the good of religion, and it was
arranged that their itinerary should include Salt Lake
City. At that period, and indeed until his death in
1877, Brigham Young was *de facto* king of Utah, and
had been privately anointed king in an early period of
his despotism. Immigrants had come in myriads. Before 1853 fifteen thousand had found their way to the
region of the blest. The saints were in a chronic state
of oriental prostration before the terrible Mokanna,
some of whose sons and daughters assumed superiority
over their fellow-citizens, as being of the " blood-royal "
of King Brigham.

The *religieuses* reached the holy city in June, and
never could they forget the beautiful appearance it presented as they moved towards it. In form it seemed
semicircular. Beyond it, lying, as one might say, at
its feet, was the vast sheet of water known as the Great
Salt Lake. On almost every side, sheltered by the
Oquirrh and the Wasatch ranges, its rich lawns and fra-
grant meadows contrasted charmingly with the bleak
hills and alkali deserts in its vicinity. Travelers arriv-
ing in early summer, when the place looks its best,
were wont to call it the " Pink City," from the thousands of peach trees scattered in every direction, whose
limbs and branches were covered with the beautiful
pink blossoms of that luscious fruit.

Their descent into Zion rather drove away the illusion as to its extraordinary beauty. ´ The streets were
over one hundred and thirty feet wide, and seemed

wider because many of the dwellings were set far back from the sidewalks. Being unpaved, they were seas of mud, or saharas of stifling dust, according as rain or sunshine prevailed. On either side were artificial brooklets, in which water from the mountain streams sparkled in the sun, and from which the gardens were watered by means of a hose, for rain seldom falls in the sacred city. The houses were mostly low, one or two stories, and each had peach and apple trees in front, and in the rear, currant and gooseberry bushes, with some kitchen vegetables. Around them were hideous walls of mud and adobes, and the gates at the entrance were prison-like. Indeed, a great part of the town was surrounded by a wall, never finished, of which little remains save some weed-grown mounds. It has crumbled away, as will, also, the fanaticism it was erected to protect. At one place there were several rows of low huts, connected by boards. A lady asked a boy: "Whose house is that?" pointing to one of them. "My father's," was the reply. "And the next?" "My father's." "And the next?" "My father's." "Why, your father seems to own them all?" "No, only five; my mother lives in the first, and my four aunts in the others." Plural consorts in Utah were called aunts, and were regarded as intruders by the real wife and her progeny.

The visitors were soon in the heart of the shabby little town. It was a bright day in leafy June, and the cloudless sky, the balmy air, the mountains towering above the city on every side, "seemed to proclaim," wrote one of them, "Great is the Lord, and holy is His name." About Salt Lake City there is a peculiar optical illusion as to distances, owing to the extreme clearness of the air. "How far off do you think that mountain is?" asked a friend of one of the *religieuses.* "I should say, about half a mile," was the reply. It was twenty-five miles distant.

III

NEVER was town or city "boomed" or puffed into fictitious renown like the Mormon capital. At this epoch it was really only a mean, straggling little collection of huts, houses, and dugouts, and so it would be still were it not for the incoming of the hated Gentile. Its site, on the "alluvial cone" of City Creek, was in what its projectors styled the Jordan Valley. No lack of ground room here ; it was divided into ten-acre squares, each square into eight lots, which were afterwards divided and subdivided. To walk around one of these blocks is to walk half a mile. Except the area, and the heads of some of the saints, almost everything about the concern was small—small houses, small gardens, small schools, if any. Even the migrations and Mormon wars were small affairs. In fact, there were not saints enough in the territory they loved to call "the State of Deseret" to make a decent strike or riot in a third-rate city. Mormonism was then what it is now, a mere local nuisance. As long as it remained pent up among the mountains, and hidden from the rest of the world, it might, perhaps, live. But it could never keep its head aloft before the cloud

of witnesses which the railroad poured in, or coexist
with daily Gentile intercourse, unless reinforced from
foreign shores. Yet the poor creatures, who formed
the rank and file, were daily told it was their destiny to
bring the nations of the earth under their heel; that
they were the chosen people who would rule Babylon
from the high places, and that they would long since
have taken possession of the earth. had not iniquity
abounded and the charity of many waxed cold.

Passing a street full of stores, built of sun-dried
brick, Temple Block, once the centre of the city, was
reached. It is on a square of ten acres, surrounded by
a high wall, which has several gates. Within the enclosure are the Temple and the huge, ugly, turtle-
shaped Tabernacle. The dreariness of the scene is
enlivened by green growing things on every side, especially young trees planted in straight rows across the
big blocks. The pretty houses nestling among orchards
and gardens belong chiefly to the Apostles, and the
lesser lights of Mormonism. The best are owned by
the "Prophet, Seer, and Revelator," Brigham. The
Lion House, on the northern side, where most of his
consorts live, has a large lion sculptured on the portico,
"resting, but watchful," a delicate compliment to the
owner, who styles himself "the Lion of the Lord."
The house is rather picturesque, with pointed gables
and narrow dormer windows projecting from the steep
roof. It was half embowered in trees, and climbing
plants, for the Prophet, who had the best of everything, had the finest gardens between the Missouri and

his dwelling. A row of offices connects this with his official mansion, the famous Beehive House, a large white building, balconied to the roof, with an observatory on the top. Its chief ornament is a huge gilt beehive, the beehive being the symbol of industry in the Home of the Faithful. Near these buildings were the storehouses for the tithing levied on all; to this day one may see people bringing offerings to the tithing-house. Behind his houses were corrals and stables for his flocks and herds. Temple Block and the Prophet's Block were walled in like forts; the sameness of the fortifications was broken by bulging bastions. Before the tithing stores the wall still stands as it did when Brigham Young was king; by other parts it has crumbled away, or been replaced by less unsightly fences.

The temple was going up slowly. Before the railroad era, the pale granite used in its construction was brought in as required by bullock teams. It was ominous that Mr. Ward, who designed it, and who sculptured the lions couchant over the Lion House, seceded from the religion of the saints, and became, as Brigham said, a vile apostate. More than a quarter of a century has passed since that untoward event startled the denizens of the holy city, and the massive temple is still unfinished. Defections have always been common among those who could get away. Hence the oft repeated counsel to the saints in other lands "to flee to Zion," and seek rest "in the chambers of the Lord in the mountains," to replace the backsliders.

In the Endowment House, near Temple Block, are administered the secret ordinances of Mormonism. Other official buildings may be seen from the balconies of the Mormon pontiff, but none very imposing. The log-cabins of early days have almost entirely disappeared. Adobe cottages are scattered over the sloping ground, some in picturesque situations on the borders of streams, in the midst of smiling meadows, or crowning grassy knolls. Wings were often added to the original huts, and these dismal *succursales* were appropriated to "plural" consorts. Specimens of primitive abodes, with roofs slanting inward and board windows, still remain. The Three-Wife House, a long, low, one-story building, was pointed out as a sample of the best structures of the Royal epoch. It is only from an elevation these places could be traced, as they were pent up behind hideous ramparts of mud and cobble-stones. Some dwellings stood back among clumps of trees, giving no sign of the life that was within them, save the inarticulate noises of bawling babies. Much of the squalor, degradation, and misery of this oasis in the desert was gracefully draped by the umbrageous trees and luxuriant climbing plants of the summer season.

IV

CAMP DOUGLAS is said to cover the first spot in Utah claimed in the name of the United States. It was a capital offense to entertain a soldier; "no soldier shall sleep one night in Salt Lake City," the Mormons constantly protested. One evening, so some old residents say, Colonel O'Connor, U. S. A., with two or three comrades, came into the city unarmed. The great Brigham at once heard of the intrusion. "Are they armed?" he asked; being told they were not, he said, magnanimously: "Let them come; their intentions are peaceable, or they would not have come hither without arms." Soon after, the stars and stripes were planted at the camp, to float over a place which heretofore defied every king, emperor, and president on earth, and acknowledged only the terrible Brigham. But the saints had no welcome for the star-spangled banner.* More than once has it been insulted in Utah; perhaps the only place on earth where it has been trailed in the dust, and set at half-mast on the Fourth of July.

The *religieuses* were guests of two Irish ladies whom they had known in Omaha, at the Townsend House, the best hotel in the place. A little before there were no hotels. Gentiles were not encouraged to come in; the few who came boarded in Mormon families, who regarded them as heathens, and never allowed them to know anything of their domestic concerns. But the railroads brought so many Gentiles that lodging-houses became a necessity. One of the hostesses, Mrs. McClosky, described herself as grand-niece of John

* The Mormons were taught that they owed no allegiance to the government at Washington. Though never as numerous as the population of a tenth-rate city in the United States, they swore to revenge on this nation the blood of Joe Smith, and bring all the countries of the earth into subjection to the saints. They were constantly threatening to unsheath the sword of the Almighty, not only in word but in deed.

Philpot Curran. Her husband kept the largest livery stables in the city. The other, Mrs. Williams, was a convert to the faith. The proprietors of the inns were Mormons; the work was done and the guests were waited on by their so-called wives, the only domestic servants among them. The worst physical inconveniences of this heavenly Jerusalem were fleas and sandflies, which all but assassinated newcomers. They are felt even now, despite the wire screens that barricade doors and windows.

In those days, which already seem so distant, it was deemed only right and proper that Gentile visitors should pay their respects at Camp Douglas, as an earnest of their sympathy with the United States, heretofore considered in Utah as a weak, heathenish, foreign power, destined to bite the dust, and one day beg for bread and quarter at the gates of the saints. The President had foolishly tried, with scarcely a shadow of success, to usurp the mitre of the Mormon Mikado. At no time has loyalty to the Washington government been a feature of the patriotism of the Utah hierarchy. The ladies brought their guests in a carriage up the winding road of some five miles. One of the Sisters wrote to a friend: "I assure you it gave us indescribable pleasure to see the United States flag waving aloft once more. It was like meeting an old friend. We had not seen it since we left Nebraska." When the carriage stopped at the top of the circuitous path that led to the fort, the party was cordially welcomed, and received with great courtesy, by Colonel Morrow, then in command, with whom the *religieuses* were already acquainted, The extreme beauty of the scene from the pink city in the valley to the vague blue of the distant mountain range was not unappreciated by the group. After some commonplace talk about the capital and its approaches, the colonel spoke of the horrid fanaticism that desecrated a spot to which nature had been so bountiful. He was an Episcopalian, but he "loved the Pope better than any other ecclesiastic, and hoped His Holiness would come to the United States if Victor Emmanuel should presume to treat him badly."

If it was necessary to call at Fort Douglas, it was still more essential that all birds of passage should alight at the Beehive. The colonel offered to escort the *religieuses* to the official residence of the potentate at whose nod so many thousands trembled. Their hostesses deemed it risky for them to go unattended. But after studying the matter in all its bearings, it seemed that such attendance, on the part of a military man,* might not be pleasing to the powerful magnate whom all were eager to propitiate. The most affectionate feelings that ever prevailed between the controlling powers of the Mormon church and the United States officials might be described by the words "armed neutrality." "You are perfectly safe, said the colonel "in going without the escort I should feel honored to give

---

*The United States officials did all they could to propitiate the Mormons, and overlooked much provocation given them by people who were always wanting to pose as martyrs or victims.

you. You will be graciously received on your own account. But be not surprised if the Prophet* does not remove his hat in your presence. Many royal princes and other high dignitaries from Europe and elsewhere, have called on him, but he has never uncovered his head to any of them." Brigham often declared, with characteristic modesty, that he was second to no man living, and would doff the hat to none.

The party descended from the fort and drove past Temple Block and the thoroughfare now known as Brigham street, thinking of the meeting to take place the following day, from which the *religieuses* recoiled. The Lion House and the Beehive House were in their route, giving no sign of their seventy or eighty inmates. Half hidden in their pale green shrubbery, they looked calm and lovely sleeping in the noonday sunshine. But their beauty was that of a convict ship on the southern seas, and the gleaming whiteness of their walls was as the whiteness of sepulchres, which hides all manner of corruption.

V

NEXT day, at the hour appointed for the audience, the two *religieuses* presented themselves at the Beehive, the official residence of Governor Young. They were received at the porch by some apostles, and ushered into a spacious reception room, at one end of which was a platform about one foot high and twelve

---

*King Brigham was frequently called "The Prophet," though, as a rule, his forecasting was very unfortunate, and his prophecies never verified.

feet deep. On this were thirteen seats, arranged in a semicircle; the centre seat was a sort of throne for Brigham; the six on either side were for his chief bishops. Dozens of cane and walnut chairs were placed in close rows down the sides of the room. The floor was of oak and walnut in alternate strips. The walls were decorated with pictures, poor specimens of art, of the great personages of a sect in which all proclaim themselves saints. The visitors were escorted to chairs about midway down from the platform, which was occupied by Brigham and the elders. When the ladies appeared he and the others arose. To their great astonishment, the Czar of all the Mormons uncovered his head. He then made a deep salaam and moved towards them.

Brigham was then in his seventy-first year, but looked more like a well-preserved man of fifty. He was among the few who improve in appearance as they grow older. As "a sharer in the adversity of his people, their companion and friend," there was nothing to distinguish him; he was simple in taste and habits, and dressed in homespun. But later he became fashionable. At all times there was something remarkable in his foot-gear. Sometimes his feet were encased in moccasins, sometimes in embroidered slippers; on this occasion, they were hidden in shining French boots of the latest fashion. He had had a season of dudishness; he could use the curling-tongs, and was even seen with his hair in papers; artificial curls should have killed him as a prophet; but, no. It was said, he was quite vain

of his small, well-formed extremities, which attracted
more attention than his head, save when his favorite
consort curled his hair.   The gray frieze and red scarf
of former days were discarded; he appeared in a suit of
fine broadcloth of the newest cut, looking like an English yeoman in Sunday clothes.   He seemed to have
lost the bluster and swagger of other days, and acquired
some of the ease and graciousness we associate with a
gentleman.   With his intimate associates, however, he
was as coarse and arrogant as ever.   The self-restraint
he practised before Gentiles was creditable, and hid his
worst points.   He looked nearly six feet high, rather
stout, and had a kindly though fox-like expression, and
a habit of glancing furtively at his guests, which many
felt embarrassing.

On seeing him approach, the *religieuses* stood up to
await him.   Making another bow, he shook hands with
them very warmly, begged them to be seated, and said
effusively: " Ladies, you are the first of your high calling that ever came among us.   Need I say you are
most heartily welcome?   I hope you have come to
stay and teach our children."

Now, we regret to say that Brigham's thoughts and
words did not agree when he spoke thus.   Being himself uncultured, he considered education rather in the
way for his followers, and preached only the gospel of
work.   Until forced by the presence of Gentiles, he
would scarcely allow schools at all.   To desire education was to be " Gentilish."   To sew, weave, work in
the garden, cook, be smart in the dairy, he considered

education enough. Books would puff up, and make the readers despise their fathers and husbands. So far as he could achieve it, education was neglected or despised. To wish for it was to seek the flesh-pots of Egypt, and prove that the leaven of the gospel had not yet fully worked in the heart. It was commonly said of Orson Pratt, the best scholar in the sect, that he would apostatize : " His learning will lift him up till he topples over." It was said that Brigham himself never read a book through; he studied men and things. When the subject of a grammar school was discussed, in very ungrammatical language, the elders agreed that, if grammar is truth, " the sperit will lead us jest into it a kinder nateral like, and if it aint, I aint a gwine to bother my brains and pay my money about it."

With obsequious politeness, Brigham inquired what mission of mercy had brought them to his city, and expressed a willingness to share in their good works. He graciously asked about the several institutions in which they were interested, their rules and duties, and expatiated on his own benevolent projects. They mentioned a plan on foot for the erection of a Catholic Church in his city, at which he professed to be pleased and surprised. He besought them to go among his people, who would receive them well and be proud to aid them. They mentioned that a priest would make a collection in the ensuing week for the new church, and " his people " would then have an opportunity of showing their generosity. A church was greatly needed for Catholic settlers and the many Catholics that sojourned at Salt Lake City, *en route* for the Pacific slope — all of which he knew better than themselves.

There were then about sixty Gentile families in the city, most of whom had come in after the entrance of the soldiers.

Brigham had a pleasing countenance, but not a strong one. He assumed great dignity, so much so that "we thought it out of place," wrote the elder *religieuse*. He had poor conversational powers, lectured rather than conversed, and required his visitors to be good listeners. He did the talking, in the form of harangue, rhapsody, or simple narrative. On this occasion he took his guests quite into his confidence, spoke of his woes, not domestic, but political, of the Mormon problem, — there was no problem in his eyes. Like President Davis in the days of the Confederacy, he wanted only to be let alone. As though he were a sovereign prince in the time when the divine right of kings was admitted, he always spoke of the dwellers in Utah as "my people." He told of their adventures from the time they poured through the Emigration Cañon until the recent attempt of the Washington government to disturb them. He was maligned, persecuted, threatened. It was wicked to report that people could not come and go without let or hindrance, or that justice would not be done to Gentiles in Utah, where the judges and juries were all saints. He described his grievances in pathetic language, and appeared deeply affected at the picture his fancy had painted of the sorrows that encompassed him. His health was not as good as he wished his *clientèle* to think. "I suffer much from rheumatism," he said, plaintively; "at times I am obliged to use this cane to support me; but I suppose we must suffer something," sighed this "seer, prophet, and revelator." He was extremely plausible. His easy, gentle manner and low-toned monologue made the listeners drowsy, but did not put them to sleep. His talk was convincing. "I listen, and my companion listens," wrote Justin McCarthy, describing his interview with the prophet, "and Brigham Young talks on; and I do declare and acknowledge that we are fast drifting into a hazy mental condition, by virtue of which we begin to regard the Mormon president as a victim of cruel persecution, a suffering martyr, and an injured angel!"

But no sensation of this nature came over the *religieuses*. They were disgusted rather than edified, for they had learned something of the inner lives of the Mormon oligarchy. Many years after, one of them wrote: "Stern duty compelled us to hold intercourse with this man. But we felt ill at ease the whole time we were in his presence. A creeping sensation comes over me whenever I think of our visit to the Beehive House, when Brigham Young ruled it.

A little before this period, a Mormon, named Godbee, had openly separated from the president, and headed a schism, his followers being known as Godbeites. They were quite numerous, and owned several good stores filled with cotton, linen, woolen stuffs of all colors, and many other useful commodities. They absorbed a good deal of trade, and to attract customers in this eminently religious town, they placed over their shops, in rude fresco, some scenes from the Old Testament, and words from the Proverbs. The most striking scene was a representation of Gideon's Fleece. Condign punishment awaited every Mormon that traded in these places, especially after the signs were put up. Circumstances arising from this rebellion formed the chief trouble of the Prophet at this time, as he diffusely explained.

One of the guests said she hoped the Godbeites might find their way to the true religion, and she was happy to learn that a church to the true and living God would soon be erected.

"You take great interest in religion, then?" said he; "from this I conclude you are not an American?"

A singular conclusion for an American bishop of bishops, who protested he had no interest in anything *but* religion.

"Not by birth," was the reply.

"May I ask, madam, your native country?"

"Ireland, Mr. President; I was born in Dublin."

The great man pondered awhile.

"You have read the history of your country, and know what your people suffered for their faith for centuries. I do not find such a spirit of unity, stability, and endurance anywhere as I find in the Catholic Church."

The *religieuses* remarked that they had met many Latter-Day Saints who said they had been taught to revere the Catholic Church next to their own. The president gave his shoulders a French shrug, and said, smiling: "Yes, yes; we have faith in the Redeemer." Were it not for their intuitions, and a slight knowledge of his previous career, they might have thought that this sanctimonious creature was not far from the kingdom of God. He inquired what they thought of his religion. They replied, they knew little of it, adding: "But we do know, President, that Christ established on earth the One, Holy, Catholic, and Apostolic Church, to which we belong, and which you admire."

Brigham, who "was a law unto himself," asked if they thought they could do anything without the aid of the Spirit? "Certainly not," was the reply; "does not the Holy Scripture declare that no man can say the Lord Jesus, but by the Holy Ghost?"

Then he spoke of a pioneer priest of Salt Lake Valley, to whom he seemed greatly attached. Father Kelly would have been removed by a Destroying Angel, or reported scalped by some belligerent Indian—the missing were often accounted for in that way—but the great ruler knew well that if one priest were slain a dozen others would rush in to replace him. "He and I," said he, "had many pleasant chats. I don't know why he discontinued his visits. Had he come often, I cannot say what effect they might have had on me. But I never could induce him to become a Latter-Day Saint." He said much more about this priest, and then went on: "There are many things in the Catholic Church I greatly admire." He paused, and the guests took this as a sign that he wished to close the conference. But, with great dignity and composure, he waved his hand and signaled them to remain. One of them ventured to say:

"Mr. President, have you ever thought that the knowledge of these things is perhaps a grace from God, of which He means you to profit?"

Instead of answering, "Mr. President" detailed the sufferings of his people: "We were in Omaha, twenty-five years ago, starving. I wrote for help to some of my fellow-bishops of your church, thinking they might relieve us."

"Did they send you anything, Mr. President?"

"Yes," he returned, in a hollow whisper; "they sent me twelve dollars and a half."

Then he expatiated on the wonders his people had done in the wilderness; how they brought seeds and agricultural implements over the mountain range,— all other pioneers did the same,— planted trees which grew, promoted agriculture by artificial irrigation. "This place was a wild mountain-slope; my people have made it what it is." The self-complacency and conceit of the Prophet surprised them; for, considering the time and labor expended on it, they could see nothing remarkable in the progress of the Pink City of Zion.

He returned to the sufferings of the Irish, and said "they were like his own people"; they being the

purest race on earth ; his people, the most licentious!
He had sent apostles * to them about the famine time,
and after. He regretted they did not join the saints.
They were good farmers. He had English, Welsh,
Scotch, Americans ; they were the only English-speaking people unrepresented among the Mormons. No
doubt he knew well that if they wanted to barter their
faith for this world's goods, they need not come as far
as Utah. They did come, however, but not as disciples, to his paradise. They are among the teachers,
professors, merchants, miners, smelters, of Utah. And
none are more highly respected in the Mormon country to-day than the bishop, clergy, sisters, and other useful citizens of the nationality † he professed to admire.

The elders, in semicircle on the platform, wonder-
ing, perhaps, what kept their chief so long, arose

* When Moore wrote his fine song, "The Irish Peasant to His
Mistress," the "Mistress" being the Catholic Church, he would
have been infinitely amused could he have looked into the future
and seen a man of Brigham's character attempting to convert his
country-people. The "Peasant" would scarcely have answered
the strange apostle, but would address his "Mistress" in the impassioned words :
   "Cold in the earth, at thy feet, I would rather be,
   Than wed what I love not, or turn one thought from thee.

† On Sunday, February 9, 1890, one hundred gentlemen, of
Irish birth, assembled at the Walker House, Salt Lake City, for
the purpose of forming an Irish Legion, and inviting their countrymen by birth or extraction throughout Utah to join them.
Their president was the veteran, General O'Connor, who has been
fighting for liberty in Zion for twenty-seven years. The victory
of the Liberals, February 10, 1890, was the Mane, Thekel, Phares,
of the Mormons, who are doomed as a political power.

one by one, and advanced slowly until they were in close proximity to the party. Heretofore "the seer, prophet, and revelator" had spoken in a low, confidential tone, and in a subdued manner, but now he lifted up his voice and described his sufferings, "though loth to allude to them." He explained with fanatical energy the evil deeds of the Gentiles, and the simple, holy lives of his followers. Several times he lost the thread of the discourse, and the strangers could make no sense of his words, when to their relief he paused, after prophesying that the time of warfare would soon come. Calling one of his bishops, he dispatched him on an errand. He returned, with a yellow envelope, which he gave to his master, who handed it to the elder *religieuse*, saying: "Accept this; it may be of service to you, or you can distribute it among the poor at my old hunting grounds near Omaha. I wish you would establish yourselves here to teach our young people. I want them piously raised."

The beneficiary thanked his excellency, and said: "We hope to hear soon of the erection of a church and of a resident-pastor in your city. Then, Mr. President, Sisters will gladly come to teach your children." He sermonized on the importance of a good moral training, the bishops * listening with rapt attention. Finally, he asked, as a special favor, that the *religieuses* would step into his private office and sign their names in the Visitors' Book, saying: " I will value your signa-

---

* The hierarchy always spoke with enthusiasm of Brigham, and treated him with reverence, especially in presence of Gentiles.

tures more than all the others on my records." They
complied with his graciously-given request, and withdrew more eagerly than they had come, the high priest
invoking blessings on them to the last, with great
effusion and fervor. He remained under the portico,
bowed again and again as they entered the carriage,
and stood gazing after them as long as it was in sight.
Certainly, nothing could be more reverential or gracious than his reception of them, and they took care to
send him a message thanking him for the same. On
reaching the hotel, they found that the yellow envelope
contained twenty dollars.

Living in the Lion and Beehive houses were some
nineteen women, whom the Prophet euphoniously
called wives. None of these appeared at the above interview. They were busily engaged as cooks, seamstresses, housekeepers, housemaids, and one grim-vis-
aged woman kept school for the "Young" children.
With the exception of one German and two English
women, all the consorts of the Prophet were Americans,
several being from New England. Save the reigning
favorite,* who ruled Brigham for the time, these women
worked hard; their wants and those of their children
were supplied with a very frugal hand. In early days
they were arrayed in cotton gowns and sun-bonnets.

* The person who ruled the dictator for the longest period,
was Amelia Folsom, a native of Massachusetts, whom he "married," according to the Mormon rites, in 1868. He may be said to
have discarded the rest for this lady. He died at the elegant
mansion he erected for her, called the Amelia Palace, August,
1877. "Miss Amelia" is living still at Salt Lake City.

These were deemed too stylish, and if there could be anything uglier, in an æsthetic sense, he achieved it in the "dress reform" called the "Deseret Costume," which he planned and inaugurated — a short gown of linsey, a long, shapeless sacque of antelope skin, and a high, untrimmed hat, with a narrow brim. Even *his* despotic authority could not establish this hideous *mode*, and, after a season or two, it was seen no more. He was ferocious in his denunciations of feminine vanity. It was the text of many of his rantings in the tabernacle; but, being grasping and stingy, he preached nothing more frequently than retrenchment and economy.

Every subterfuge was resorted to to keep the Gentiles in ignorance of the doings of his families. It was well-known that some of his children were bad, and others exceedingly disorderly, haughty, and arrogant. However, as has frequently been the case in Mormon families, more than half of his children, who were mostly girls, preceded him to the tomb. Nor were his cold, steely eyes ever seen to moisten when death took away any of the miserable mothers, or robbed the crowded nurseries of their babes.

Gentiles brought in the fashions, and the women of the Beehive discarded the sun-bonnets. Once, Brigham took an extraordinary freak of generosity. He actually went to a milliner, and ordered bonnets for his consorts. They were made and duly delivered, and, having examined them minutely, he expressed himself much pleased. When the milliner, a poor woman, presented her account, $275, he returned her a receipted bill for the amount, which, he said, she owed the church for tithing! Great was her dismay, but there was no appeal from the dishonesty of the autocrat. He had always a great facility for taking advantage of his opportunities; the creditor cowered beneath his steady, unflinching gaze, and the shrewd, turbulent, illiterate Vermonter gained a victory, of which an honest man would be ashamed.

Among the public buildings was a wretched theatre, lit with oil-lamps, on the boards of which the Prophet's daughters and others acted. He had some histrionic and musical ability, uncultivated, of course, and was a clever mimic. Some of these qualities passed to his descendants; one became an actress in San Francisco.

"All the women we saw," wrote one of the visitors, "looked broken-hearted. It seemed as if depression and sorrow stalked abroad everywhere. We were glad when the time came to leave the Pink City. Every day we saw women in the street, perhaps shopping. Each had with her from three to six or seven children; she carried the smallest, the others held on to her or to each other. There was no mistaking them for anything but Mormons. This sort of exhibition took place daily. Soon after, we heard that such displays were forbidden. The children had mostly light hair and fair complexions. Some of the women looked like Swedes and Danes; others were English, Welsh, Scotch, German. All dressed pretty much as emigrants from Northern Europe dress when resting at Castle Garden,

New York — long skirts, shawls, bibs, handkerchiefs on the heads. We heard there were Mormon schools, but did not see any."

All who have visited Salt Lake City have noticed the extreme plainness of the women. "I protest," wrote one, "that only in some of the *Crétin* villages of the Swiss mountains have I seen creatures in female form so dull, miserable, moping, hopeless, as the vast majority of these Mormon women." To use a harder and more emphatic term, their ugliness is not merely negative, but positive. The writer has asked many what they thought of the Salt Lake women. "Oh, the sallow, wizened creatures! I never saw such women," is about one of the most complimentary answers received. This is the sad consequence of the iniquitous system that bears so heavily on the hapless women of the Beehive, destitute of happiness in the present and hope for the future. The sullenness or apathy seen in the face was very annoying to the saints, who boast of the happiness of the Mormon women, living like turtle-doves in their snug nests in Zion. The sad experiences of a hideous life have carved deep lines about the eyes and mouth, made the faces hard and grim, and robbed them of the softness, tenderness, and grace which appertain to women.

Brigham's house — it could not be called home — was the best regulated in Utah, "a pattern to the saints." The women waited on themselves. Their time was spent in washing, cooking, mending, dairy-work. Each consort was supplied, in rotation and by weight, with necessaries. Later, it was found more economical to have a general table. He dined with his families daily at the Lion House. Some seventy or eighty sat down to dinner, each mother being surrounded by her own children. Every evening, at seven, they assembled in the drawing-room of the same establishment to receive the benediction of the patriarch. If the women complained of their grievances, Brigham's remedy was "more work." He had often to scold and threaten. He advised them to "round up their shoulders to endure the afflictions of the world," and declared he "would rather go to heaven alone than have scratching or fighting about him." He protested he "would do something to get rid of whining women,"—all this from the platform of the tabernacle, before the assembled thousands, and where he knew they could not retort.

Brigham reproached these wretched creatures* for being unhappy, "wading through floods of tears"; the bitter jealousies and constant acrimony displayed in their galling lives annoyed him. Outsiders he received rather kindly at times; those of his own household he politely and affectionately termed "everlasting fools to complain of anything." And if he happened to be "too

---

*If it was thus in Brigham's household, what was it in others? It may be asked: Why did not those wretched creatures endeavor to escape? Before the railroads came in, and for long after, it would be impossible to get away. The town was full of the spies of Brigham. Besides, to run away was to abandon their children and deprive themselves of a living, such as it was. And, as a rule, they had no means, and no friends to whom to go, and in any case they dreaded Mormon vengeance.

full of the spirit," the mildest name he had for some who had once been his idols, was "termagants." For their illness he had no sympathy. "They get sick to shirk work," he would say.

Fanaticism does not always teach patience. The "peculiar institution" engendered the worst passions in the human heart. Brigham professed to be able "to give the word of the Lord" on every subject, but he could never keep peace in his own mansions. Another luminary, Jedediah Grant, affirmed that, "if they could break asunder the cable of the church, there is scarcely a mother in Israel but would do it this day." But the tyranny of old has passed away forever. Gentile ascendancy is now an assured fact. And it will be woman's own fault if she should not in future receive the position Christianity accords her, and which is her right.

A friend, resident in Utah, says that the Mormons are not up to the average in intellect; that their importations from non-Catholic countries are of a class whose intellect is little above that of the brute. According to Mormon teachings, they must obey the priesthood in all things. Their thinking is done for them, somewhat after the manner of Russian serfs. Physically, the Mormons are a muscular people; the animal prevails in every way. The proportion of deaf and dumb is greater than in the rest of the United States. And of lunatics born in the Territory, the proportion was $10\frac{1}{4}$ per cent in 1886 to $12\frac{1}{2}$ in 1887, in the State lunatic asylum.

There are several superior Catholic educational establishments in Utah. All Hallows College, directed by Marist Fathers; St. Mary's Academy, by the Sisters of the Holy Cross; a large Academy in Ogden; another in Park City; hospitals in Salt Lake, Ogden, Silver Reef, and several schools, all founded by Bishop Scanlan.

On the Sunday prior to their leaving the holy city, the *religieuses* heard Mass, which was offered about seven in the morning by Rev. Father Foley, in a log-cabin about 30 by 17. He had to say a later Mass at Ogden. There were fifteen long benches, or forms, stretching the length of the room. About sixty men, many of them miners, and six women were present, most of them being of Irish birth. Everything about the humble church was as poor as the stable of Bethlehem. But the Adorable Victim was offered up to the Eternal Father, and the purest of Virgins was invoked. And the priest on the altar, and the *religieuses* who received from his hands the Bread of Life, were they not the "chaste generation" who feed on the "wheat of the elect and the wine that maketh virgins?" After Mass the priest besought the great God to enlighten and bless the city, and make it, indeed, a holy city, and give to the dwellers therein light to know His will, and grace to do it. And when all knelt to offer the Rosary for this intention, the prayers of great, strong men, like the voice of many waters, were heard ascending to heaven. And who will say that these and many such prayers have not been gloriously answered, when the answer is more than faith would ask, and can be seen and felt? The beautiful Convent, where every accomplishment is taught under the auspices of Mary; the handsome College, where the youth of the Territory, when they ask for intellectual bread, will not receive a stone; the spacious, well-appointed hospital where consecrated virgins assuage the anguish of every sufferer, whether Greek or barbarian, bond or free; the children of two religious congregations teaching the young in Zion itself; the bishop and clergy reverenced by a people who, in earlier days, would have stoned them, as well as by their own loving flock,—surely a glorious response to prayer. Verily, the finger of God is here. This is the change of the right hand of the Most High.

ABOUT THE UTAH SAINTS

I

THE Mormons have always regarded the island of Great Britian as their best recruiting-ground. On Christmas Day, 1837, their leaders held a conference at Preston, at which they announced that their disciples in England alone numbered a thousand. Forty-one left England for Utah, June 6, 1840, being "the first saints that gathered from a foreign land." From those early times to the present, Mormonism has been gaining a steadily increasing number of its adherents in Great Britain. Every State in the Union is also represented among them. And it is somewhat singular that little has been done to place before the English-speaking world the real nature of a sect which has attracted so many of the just and the unjust, despite its awful fanaticism. To develop the tenets and policy of the Latter-Day Saints in a single article would not be possible. But, without describing their baptism for the dead, their celestial marriage (a euphemism for polygamy), polytheism, the deification of Adam, whom Brigham Young blasphemously styled "the god of the universe," we will give some information, gathered on the spot, of the workings of this peculiar offshoot of Protestantism, merely premising that its distinctive features were polygamy, *plus* politics, farming, and commerce. To build up the kingdom, to possess the earth and the fulness thereof, to gratify passion, to make money — behold the ends which were held to justify the most atrocious ways and means since Joseph Smith "made a gathering of the saints" in Ohio and promulgated the "Book of Mormon" early in the thirties.

Away among the western mountains of North America, in a picturesque valley, whose inhabitants of a generation or two ago were wont to describe themselves as living "a thousand miles from everywhere," on the southern slope of a spur of the Wasatch range is the capital of Mormondom, called from the dead sea towards which it looks, Salt Lake City. By the "saints," indeed, it is styled Zion, or the New Jerusalem. And the sluggish stream that laves its banks is euphoniously called the "Jordan River." But to the Gentile world Zion is known by its more commonplace name. In early days it was described to outer barbarians as *Great* Salt Lake City. To the name of every new place in the west it is customary to add, with reference to the future rather than the present, the imposing word *City*. But in visiting such places one need not strain the eyes looking for the spires and domes of a vast metropolis. Cities could not always show one decent house or twenty log-cabins. To reach the *terminus* of a street in a "city" we have had to pass in review the drapery of the population hung out of windows or on clothes-lines zigzag on the street. But similar drapery may be seen about the palaces of Genova la Superba. When these humble hamlets do really become cities they usually drop the appellation.

Denver, when merging from a mining camp into a town, was Denver City. Now that it has become a great railroad centre, with an immense population, the prophetic term has been dropped, and it is simply Denver. Who now speaks of Omaha City or Sacramento City? But we have still Salt Lake City and, for an obvious reason, Kansas City and Mississippi City. And under one aspect few places have more right to the title than the Mormon capital. From the first, Zion has had bishops enough, such as they were, to equip half the great cities of Christendom. They were more numerous than any other officials of Church and State. And a city, according to a European usage not introduced into the United States, was held to be the seat of a bishop.

In their Scriptural style the early Mormons used to describe their piebald village as dowered with the beauty of Carmel and the glory of Libanus. Here dwelt Brigham Young, the prophet of the Most High, and hither came multitudes from the ends of the earth "to worship in the place where his feet had trod." Here the glory of the Lord had descended on His chosen one, and the saints exclaimed with enthusiasm: "Our feet have stood in thy courts, O Jerusalem!" Even the physical beauty of the shabby little town was extolled, and, in the glory of her vineyards and cornfields, she was likened to "a bride going forth to meet her beloved." Much of the beauty and freshness ascribed to Zion and its environs was doubtless due to the contrast with the territory through which they were reached. Pleasant was the refreshing greenery of the holy city to the wayfarer who had just passed through prairies interminable, where the sun goes down. as he sinks at sea—a dreary, treeless, rainless expanse, where every species of growth is spinous, a desolate alkali desert, a blighted arid land, on which one might fancy "the Lord had rained fire and brimstone out of heaven." Even the spray of the unpoetic garden-hose, which one sees everywhere in Salt Lake City, is grateful after the white dust of the wilderness, which irritates the eyes, throat, and nostrils. And the patches of alfalfa, so common throughout Zion, are as squares of earth jeweled with emeralds, after the blinding glare of the white sun on the white ground, or the white moon on the saline plain, where the effervescence of salt resembles frozen sand. Lovely is the pink-limbed peach tree after the dusty sage-brush which assumes the neutral tint of the wilderness, where there is no color save in the sky. And cheering are the broad, dusty streets of Zion to pilgrims who have traversed the ocean-like steppes, *Llano Estacado*, where the Indian sets up stakes in the drifting sand to guide him aright through this deserted bed of some prehistoric sea.

It was homelike, too, to see the crowds pouring out of the tabernacle in thousands of a Sunday evening, when one had been familiar with the Indians draped in bright-colored blankets, which they wear as gracefully as a Roman might wear his toga. But their matted hair and greasy faces are rather repulsive to the dainty Caucasian. The sleek, fat cows behind Brother Brigham's corrals were a pleasanter, if less romantic, sight than the fleet antelope skipping over the gray savannahs. Even the low, squat houses of pre-Gentile days, every chimney of which represented a separate family, looked fair and cozy after the white tents and camp-fires of the wilderness. And how restful to the eye were the green grass and the golden corn when one had come through bald, bare cañons, or over the Rockies, so desolate in their grandeur—some hoary, weird, grotesque, framing their great heads in the sky; others covered with aspen, beech, and pine; their tints contrasting with the brown and gray of the heavy granite boulder and the pale brightness of the milky quartz!

When Brigham led his followers into the Happy Valley, they were, indeed, separated from the whole world, and completely at the mercy of this despot. Gigantic peaks stood as sentinels over the sacred city. Tremendous as were the difficulties of getting out, they were purposely exaggerated. The knowledge that every avenue of escape was closed exerted a powerful influence in forcing them to abide by their fate. By law or otherwise, there was, practically, no redress: "Who entered here left hope behind." Surrounded by barriers almost impassible, of desert and mountain, Utah, and especially the holy city, formed the last and securest stronghold of the Mormon exodus. *L'Etat c'est moi!* The temporal governor and spiritual ruler, Young, an irresponsible despot, was prophet, high priest, and anointed king, whose counsellors might advise, but must not presume to direct him. To strengthen the hands of the Church—*i. e.*, himself—missionaries who would compass sea and land for a proselyte, were sent to the heathen—*i.e.*, every one not a "Saint." Mormon membership is recruited from all religions save the Catholic. Rank and file, who worked under the *ægis* of the Beehive, the Mormon escutcheon, emblem of the industry Young pretended to deify, were mostly ignorant dupes. The best thing this "Prophet, Seer, and Revelator" did was to preach the gospel of work. So far as he could achieve it, the men and women of the Beehive earned their bread in the sweat of their brow, "No drones in this hive," was his text for many a discourse. "It is a fixed law," said he, "that every man, with few exceptions, is intended to live on his own earnings. No man has a right to eat his daily bread without producing as much in the scale of life as he consumes, and that, too, by some kind of honest physical labor." His disciples mostly became farmers, or laborers, or wrought at mechanical trades, or entered into mercantile business. The richer they became, the more they enriched him. When he purchased property, he graciously allowed them to pay for it, but held it in his own name. As trustee-in-trust, all moneys of the Church passed through his hands. He continued to add house to house, field to field, mine to mine, and to increase his investments and bank deposits till he became a millionaire many times over.

From the first, the Latter-Day Saints, whether east of the Missouri or in the "Valley of Ephraim," were antagonistic to every form of government save their own miserable caricature of a theocracy. The credulous Mormon was taught that his church would overthrow the government at Washington, assume control of the Republic, and finally possess the earth. This monstrous ambition created a civil war in Missouri, and excited the people of Illinois to drive the Saints by force of arms from their borders. Hence, the retreat to Utah, "a thousand miles from everywhere." Here, secure from all interference from the outside world, the arch-Mormon gathered in disciples who brought him the mammon of iniquity, and, in still larger numbers, those who carried neither purse nor scrip. The chiefs "counselled"—a "counsel" being the strongest kind of command—"the Saints" to be ready to carry fire and sword to the very gates of the capital. However wild in theory and impossible in practise their designs were, the leaders were ready to sacrifice the rabble for their achievement. Though mostly Americans by birth, the controlling powers never regarded themselves as such, but as citizens of Zion. Full of bombast and hypocrisy, they were chronic rebels to the flag that protected them. When the great Civil War broke out, no Mormon handled a musket on either side. President Young, Czar of all the Mormons, spoke the sentiments of his associates and dupes when he said: "The North prays for the destruction of the South, and the South prays for the destruction of the North, and I say 'Amen' to both prayers."

Often did he point a moral with that Titanic struggle. And not a few of his satellites hoped that the

Mormon Church, whose comparative insignificance they knew not, would one day march to victory over the mutilated remains of both armies. To be at variance with the government seemed essential to their status as Mormons.

Brigham Young,* undoubtedly, possessed many of the qualities of a great ruler. His suave, plausible manners endeared him to the people, who certainly cherished his memory more than that of any other leader. He would walk about among the laborers on the roadside, descend from his carriage to inquire about a sick brother, shake hands affectionately with some small farmer, and effusively, with eyes and hands lifted heavenward, invoke the blessings of Abraham, Isaac, and Jacob on the admiring bystanders. We have never heard a Mormon speak against Brother Brigham. More than one hapless woman who spoke with loathing of the horrors of polygamy, placed him above the divine law : " He can do what he pleases ; whatever he does is right." Others bear the wretchedness of their forlorn lives as the heaven-appointed cross destined to win an eternal crown. Their faith in Mormon fanaticism seems unshaken, and they accept their bitter lot

* Brigham Young has been called a psychological freak. His parents were ordinary, his children scarcely average, and not one of his ten brothers or sisters showed any talent whatever. He was a man of splendid appearance; the carriage of his massive head was majestic; he was considerably above middle height, and in his costume wore combinations which would suggest the ridiculous on any one else. But we have never heard of any one daring to laugh at this formidable despot.

with sad resignation. But since the incoming of the Gentiles many shake off the degrading yoke.

From the first, polygamy, though indignantly repudiated by the leaders, was a characteristic of this latest phase of Protestantism. The founders and higher officials — Smith, Young, Kimble, Grant, Taylor, Wells, all Americans of English lineage — were, without exception, polygamists. In early days this was carefully concealed from the outer world; later, it became their boast. All were consummate hypocrites, ready, when the so-called good of the church required, to assert unblushingly what they knew to be false. Truth, honor, honesty, were unknown qualities among them.

The polygamous feature of this fanaticism attracted much attention from the fact of its bearing so heavily on women. Mormons married two or three sisters at once, and occasionally a mother and her daughter, and even granddaughter. Brigham Young married the sisters Clara and Lucy Decker. His daughters, Fanny and Luna, married George Thatcher; Mary and Caroline, Mark Croxal; Alice and Emily, Hiram Clawson. On these points there was no law save the will of the Prophet. And what God had joined in lawful wedlock — or not joined, as in case of unlawful marriages — he was willing to put asunder for a consideration of ten dollars, the ordinary divorce fee. Money made in this way he declared he gave to his consorts for pin-money, but it was well known that it never got nearer to those poor sultanas than his own pockets. He did, however, allow them the windfalls of his blooming orchards, by which they made a pittance in a region remarkable for its fine peaches and apples. Save in the secret archives of the Endowment House, where the occult ordinances of Mormonism took place, no record of marriages was kept. Passing over the "wives" of earlier years, the nineteen women who lived under the roof of the Prophet and ate his bread in the sixties and seventies, derived no social distinction, even in the holy city, from being espoused to the Protestant Sultan. Except the favorite, usually the lady on whom his High Mightiness had bestowed the latest reversion of his hand, all were merely servants without wages — cooks, housemaids, care-takers, laundresses, teachers for the ever-increasing progeny, who did the work and kept everything clean and orderly about the premises. Their wants were frugally supplied; necessaries, but no luxuries, were seen in their tidy quarters at the Lion House or the Beehive. In the Beehive most of the consorts and their children lived. Seventeen of these degraded women were Americans, who were continually boasting of their Anglo-Saxon descent; one was a German, and one an English woman who proposed for the Prophet, offering, like Jacob, conditions reversed, to serve seven years for him. She did work for him for that space, and received the coveted prize. Their son was greatly petted by Brigham, who used to call him "My English boy." The favorite of the moment ruled the capricious tyrant with a rod of iron. No "plural wife " ever held this precarious post so long as Amelia Folsom, a Massachusetts woman, on whom he bestowed the seventeenth nuptial ring he distributed. Among the sights of Zion, in the midst of a spacious lawn, is the elegant mansion he built her, called the Amelia Palace. It perpetuates the memory of their unholy connection in the city that witnessed their sin, but, unhappily, not their repentance.

II

WHEN we conjure up a vision of Catholic women as we remember them in the long ago — maidens with the innocence of children, matrons with the modesty of maids — we have sometimes wondered if they ever thanked God that they had never seen, nor, indeed, could they imagine, the awful miseries of their sister women in the Mormon valley — *hac lacrymarum valle* — which nature has made so fair. Looking at the hard, disagreeable, ugly faces of the Mormon women who met us at every turn in the City of the Blest, we recalled the sweet, patient, holy countenances grouped about us in childhood — the matron about whose lineaments lingered the graces of virginity, and the maid through whose bright eyes looked an angelic soul. Whence the difference, yea, the contrast, between woman and woman, maiden and maiden? Ah, it is due to faith — virtue. The Catholic belongs to a Church that teaches all holiness. In the Mormon women virtue is in abeyance, if not annihilated ; vice in the guise

of religion usurps its place, and some of its hideous-
ness shows even in "the human face divine."

A Catholic friend who has lived many years in
Utah writes: "I took the census of 4,000 souls, four-
fifths of whom were Mormons. I found two married
women of English birth whose parents were Catholics.
They had left England in early girlhood. Both were
illiterate, had received no instruction as Catholics, and
were Mormons, not from any belief in the doctrines of
Joe Smith or Brigham Young, but on account of the
earthly paradise promised them. Another woman had
been baptized a Catholic, she did not know where. I
asked if the Mormons were good to her. She said
'yes.' I asked in what this goodness consisted. 'They
let me live there,' she replied, pointing to a mud hovel
on the roadside."

God be praised! Catholic women never accepted
the "celestial exaltation" which women are declared
to receive by becoming the "plural wives" of Mormon
elders. The Mormon elders and most of their wives
continually boast of their Anglo-Saxon lineage. The
Irish, who may be considered the representative English-speaking Catholics, have been conspicuous only by
their absence. Years ago, Henry Ward Beecher, who
had little sympathy with the Irish race, and less with
the Catholic religion, in lecturing on his "Circuit of
the Continent," gave utterance to the following remarkable words when describing his sojourn in Salt
Lake City: "Be it said to the credit of the Irish race,
that I have not found a single Irishman or woman in

the whole Mormon system. Whether this is due to the teachings of the great Roman religion, or to some inherent virtue in the people, I cannot say, but such is the fact."

To a considerable extent the Mormon women were "gathered in" from the lower strata of womanhood in non-Catholic countries, and were the offscouring of all. But women of education (so-called), of wealth and social standing, have been inveigled into this monstrous and pernicious superstition. One of these, who, unasked, gave the writer much information about these peculiar creatures, said: "If it were known that I told you all this, it would get me into great difficulty with our people." They were captivated by the rude eloquence of bishops, elders, and the "quorum of the seventies," who preached, in words of striking sound and little meaning, the glory and fulness of the everlasting gospel, the gifts and graces of the spirit, sedulously concealing the doctrines of polygamy and blood atonement, and every other repulsive feature of this crude fanaticism.

No wonder that unspeakable wretchedness of body and mind have absorbed from female faces among "the Saints" all beauty and comeliness, and wrought in them the hard look that unsanctified suffering produces. The degraded creatures from whom womanly dignity, sweet refinement, and sustaining self-respect had vanished, and in whose souls the discordant elements of malice, hatred, and strife had made their abode, were the slaves, rather than the toys, of capricious tyrants whose boorishness was the least of their foibles.

In Salt Lake City, and throughout Utah, the writer was struck with the preternatural ugliness of the women. Issuing from the Tabernacle, squatting on their door-steps, or lounging about the gates of their dwellings, one could note the hard, wizened features, the defiant, repulsive expression. Having mentioned this all-pervading absence of personal comeliness to friends who rather doubted that it existed to such a remarkable extent, and remembering that tastes differ, we sought other evidence as to the personal appearance of these people. To the query: "How do you find Mormon women as to looks?" an Irish gentleman who has lived many years in Utah, replied: "Decidedly ugly, and this ugliness is more marked throughout the Territory than in the capital. The cast of features is more than plain." Domestic unhappiness and social degradation have furrowed the features and drawn hard lines about the eyes and mouth, making the faces grim and repulsive. We inquired of Gentile visitors and found that they were impressed as we were. Indeed, visitors to the Valley of the Saints have been all but unanimous on this subject. Ann Eliza Webb, a Mormon by birth, and a so-called wife of Brigham, admits the ugliness of the women, but says: "They are pretty enough as children. When the curse of polygamy is forced upon them, they grow hard, or die in their struggles to become inured to this unnatural life."

The Mormons have attracted attention and created excitement out of all proportion to their numerical insignificance. In Utah they are far below 200,000.

Many apostatize, but their places are filled by disciples allured by Mormon propagandists in all parts of the globe. The fanatical energy of the governing elders has not slackened. They have publicly renounced polygamy, but "plural wives" now appear as nurses or servants, and the law reaches few of the wily transgressors.

In 1850 President Filmore appointed Brigham Young governor; in 1854 another governor was sent out, but Brigham would not be replaced. "I am, and shall be, Governor of Utah," said he, "and no power shall remove me till the Almighty says, 'Brigham, I don't want you in this post any longer.'" He kept his word. To the time of his death, 1877, he broke every power sent to break him, and was, *de facto*, supreme ruler to the last. For thirty-three years he may be said to have nominated every officer in Utah. He was president of the "Saints," and all legislative, executive, and judicial offices were in his gift. In no instance did the people vote, save as "counselled." Many acts of the legislature were passed simply to convey valuable property to Young, at once the grantee and the governor, whose approval was necessary to the validity of the grant. Nor did this state of things die with the terrible high priest. As late as 1882 the Legislative Assembly consisted of thirty-six members, all Mormons. They met to do the bidding of their chiefs, the United States paying their mileage and *per diem* salaries. It was the aim of the leaders to form a separate independent State, an empire within an empire, destined to crush all other governments and to inherit the earth. They ruled Utah, held the balance of power in Idaho, and wielded a potent influence in Arizona, Colorado, Wyoming, and Nevada. They declared themselves, like the Israelites in Egypt, aliens in the land that bore them. The alienism that began with Joe Smith over sixty years ago, has descended from sire to son into this last decade of the nineteenth century. Hence, Gentiles have contended that Mormons should be denied the privilege of voting so long as their fealty is not given to the Washington government, that "the political fangs of Mormonism should be extracted" by the withdrawal of franchise. In public the "Saints" affect the deepest reverence for the laws. But their works agree not with their words. Instead of bringing offenders to justice, they screen them from the officers of the law, and when refractory citizens are tried and punished, they pose as martyrs rather than transgressors.

Federal officers who entered the territory when Brigham Young was king, were traduced and persecuted unless they were as wax in his hands. When, in 1870, he conferred the franchise on women, he was hailed by advanced female suffragists as a liberal, high-minded ruler. But this made elections a greater farce than ever. Every woman voted as her husband dictated, and no man voted except as "counselled." To increase the voters so as to entitle Utah to be admitted into the Union as a State, Mormon leaders resorted to the most unscruplous measures. It was judicious to provide against a contingency that might arise should

Mormon and Gentile votes result in a tie, were men the only voters. Such a calamity could now be easily averted. The poor Gentile went to the polls with one or, at most, two votes. The Mormon drove up triumphantly with wagons full of wives and children, every one, even the babe in arms, having a vote to deposit. Suffrage became the veriest sham. One of Brigham's consorts says that when ordered to vote she begged to be excused, as she knew nothing of the candidates; but her lord sternly bade her go to the polls, naming his coachman as her political instructor. She never learned the name of the person for whom she voted, but suspected it was that "calamity of his time," George Q. Cannon, an Englishman, high in office, who more than once had been a convicted criminal. Swedes and Norwegians who could not speak a word of English voted according to the "counsel" of the elders, without the formality of naturalization. Dead "Saints" voted by the proxy of the living. More than we commonly understand by "the quick and the dead" were represented on petitions sent to Congress. Men were known to "christen" their beasts of burden, give them names and surnames, and make them sign or vote — by proxy.

The Prophet was a declared enemy to education, but when the establishment of schools became compulsory, he was equal to the occasion. The school system became, practically, a scheme to erect Mormon meeting-houses at public expense. In these were taught all the abominations of the sect. And as Catholics are taxed for schools they cannot conscientiously use, so the Gentiles in Utah were forced to support the Mormon system, while maintaining separate schools for their own children. Our modern Mahomet often declared that he would never give a dollar to educate another man's child, that education is a foe to labor, and puts children in danger of becoming "loafers and horse-thieves"; perils to which he exposed his own progeny, when he sent some of them to Gentile colleges. But, he was above all law. His descendants used to boast of their royal lineage, and take liberties on account of it. There was an absurd story, devoutly believed in the New Jerusalem, of a traveling scion of the House of Young, who refused to give the *pas*, in Hyde Park, to a son of Queen Victoria; and the genuine princes who visited Utah were regarded as offshoots of the effete royalties of Europe, and infinitely inferior to the vigorous sons of Brigham, which, from a physical stand-point, they probably were.

As will be readily conjectured, nothing was done to keep the children of the Rocky Mountain "Saints" clean of heart. How could purity be thought of amid such base environments? But to attach them to the Mormon church and polity, every effort was used, and in the most effective manner. Many immeasurably higher in the scale of morality might take lessons from the value "the Saints" set on early impressions and associations. It was well said: "Give me the child for the first seven years and do as you will with him afterwards." The future of Mormon children is overshadowed by early associations to a greater extent than any one unacquainted with their peculiar ways could imagine. They are indoctrinated with Mormon tenets, taught to exalt their own and despise every other "persuasion." Intercourse with Gentiles was forbidden as contamination.

Some one said that if a man were permitted to make the ballads of a nation, he need not care who made its laws. The ballads of Utah engraved in the tender hearts of children the pernicious principles of a disgraceful sect. Doggerel, dignified by the name of poetry, striking couplets, sharp epigrams, were committed to memory, or sung from the church hymn books, by the camp-fires, on plains glittering with salt crystals, within the bare walls of the huge, ugly tabernacle, on the school-bench by day, and under the roof-tree at night. The Deity was thanked for having mercifully brought the choristers into the bosom of the Church of the Latter-Day Saints, and taught them a faith, whereby they were to be savingly converted. Some were sung to bold defiant airs, with staccato movement; some to music, appealing and sonorous; some to easy negro melodies. Brigham's favorite air was "Gentle Annie." The singers were "the chosen few," whose mission was to build up the waste places of Zion, and make the desert blossom like the rose. They sang the glories of the promised land, the city of refuge, where "the Saints" were beyond the reach of their enemies, with none to molest them.

Catholics who were formerly Mormons, have often expatiated on the extreme difficulty of shaking off their early impressions. Nor could they readily forget the coarse rhymes in which their earlier creed was enshrined. Snatches of these were often unconsciously warbled, even by some who had learned the glorious " Porta manes et stella maris" of the Universal Church.

Some effusions sung in the tabernacle could not be quoted here. Absurd, utterly worthless, beneath criticism, as most of them are, they always crystallize Mormon tenets. If the more intelligent Mormon could despise the angry denunciations of cunning elders, and rid himself of early associations, the greatest obstacles to his conversion would be removed. But under a system of utter subjection to a despot, freedom was annihilated. The people, irreverently styled in non-Catholic phraseology "the masses," were as "dumb, driven cattle," and rarely had any one the spirit to "be a hero in the strife." "To resist was fatal, and it was impossible to fly." A recalcitrant member who, after the first or second admonition, refused to submit to the great Moslem, soon "disappeared," and his place knew him no more.

III

IN AUGUST, 1866, Father Kelly, of Grass Valley, was made pastor of Salt Lake City by Right Rev. Eugene O'Connell, to whom the Holy See confided Utah Territory in 1865. Father Kelly bought the ground on which the little cathedral now stands. In

1868 a Catholic bishop visited Zion for the first time, and said Mass at the residence of Judge Marshall, whose guest he remained for a fortnight. Among the names of the first Catholics are O'Reilly, Barron, Byrne, Kennelly, Vaughan, Dahler, and Simpkins.

Father Foley succeeded Father Kelly, and early in 1871 opened a subscription list for the erection of a church. Though few, and mostly poor, Catholics were so generous that the church was finished in a few months, and dedicated to St. Mary Magdalen, November 26, 1871. In 1873 Rev. Lawrence Scanlan devoted his energies to the spread of the true faith in Salt Lake Valley; in 1887 he became Vicar Apostolic, and later bishop of the holy city. Under the able administration of this zealous prelate religion has made rapid strides. The church in which the sacred mysteries have been celebrated for a score of years is now too small for the constantly-increasing congregation, and zealous Catholics hope that the spires of a splendid cathedral will soon overlook this New Jerusalem.

More quickly than any other means would the spread of Catholic doctrine destroy this new Islamism, and hence Young would never have allowed the Church to gain a foothold had he been able to keep it out. The establishing of soldiers, many of whom were Irish Catholics, at Fort Douglas, on a plateau above the city, and the immense number of miners, smelters, stokers, of the same religion and nationality, that flocked to Zion after the opening of the railroads, in 1869, made it impossible for him to keep it out.

Young and other Mormon lights showed much esteem for Catholics. A high official said to the writer: "We all like the Catholics. They do not annoy or persecute us; they treat us like gentlemen." If Catholics spoke of the peculiar institution, they felt that it is only Catholics who could do so with authority. For they saw little difference between their own system and the progressive polygamy practised wherever divorce holds sway. Some of Young's descendants have renounced polygamy, and a few have become Catholics. A grandson of his was elected city marshal of Zion on the Liberal ticket. During the campaign he spoke of his people as misled and benighted, and never alluded to his royal pedigree. Several intelligent Mormons say that it is useless to uphold their doctrines against the sea of enlightenment with which emigration is flooding Utah, which has grown quite commonplace, and is no longer the Western Wonderland. Graded streets, castle-like edifices, gas, electric lights, and other modern improvements brought in by the Gentiles—who quickly emptied the exchequer, and were even so fashionable as to go in debt—have quite changed the aspect of the rural village, with dusty streets, adobe or frame cottages, embowering shrubbery, and little runnels like those of Berne—the holy city of Brigham's day. In a Christian aspect, things are brighter to-day than they have yet been in the stronghold of the "Saints." It has been proclaimed, and in no uncertain tones, that the Mormons must conform to the law or cease to exist as a body. This would, at one fell swoop, destroy the most debasing feature — polygamy. Loyal subjects will not stand on the same plane with fanatics who assume to have a mission to uproot every government. The Royal Brigham made them slaves; the Catholic Church shows them the blessed " freedom wherewith Christ has made us free." The Gentiles now outnumber the Mormons, and recent victories show that Utah is at last a fit abode for the brave and the free. The decision of Judge Anderson, in refusing to admit to citizenship men bound by the horrible oaths of the Endowment House, embodied an impartial epitome of Mormon subterfuge and treachery. But this fanaticism dies hard; it has not only nine, but nine hundred lives.

The incoming of non-Mormons has not done all that optimists expected; nevertheless, its effects are felt. Even fashion has contributed to wound this moral cancer in the breast of the nation. It costs money to dress fashionably, and "plural wives" are not always content to be servants without wages. Even in the Valley of the Blest, women will assert themselves, and "Saints" copy style from their Gentile sisters. The cotton gowns and sun-bonnets of early days, and the hideous " Deseret Costume " of linsey and antelope-hide, designed by the Prophet for the women of the Beehive, could no more be revived to-day than could the laws and usages of the Saxon Heptarchy.

A great work has been begun in Utah by Catholic agencies. Ecclesiastics, with their helpers, in exemplifying the purity and sanctity of Catholic teachings before men steeped in every abomination, have caused many a sinner to say, as did St. Augustine, when he considered the virtues of the genuine Saints: "Cannot I do what these have done?" When Mormons enter the Church, their allegiance is transferred from the Sultan of Zion to the President of the United States, and they cannot be good Catholics without being good citizens.

Suffrage, the acknowledged palladium of the free-man's liberty, is free, and Gentiles have been voted into office in Utah. The law, sustained by a healthy public opinion, is doing away with the more loathsome features of this abhorred system. But among the de-termining causes which will destroy this moral leprosy, grafted by sensual, avaricious men on a false religion, the most powerful is the spread of Catholic principles. Where woman was most degraded, woman must reign a queen—the Woman clothed with the sun, the moon under her feet, and the stars of heaven for her diadem. Mary, the purest of Virgins, will sanctify the fertile vales and blooming gardens of Utah. The great Mother of Mercy will look lovingly on these poor children of fanaticism, and her glance creates purity.

In 1870 Brigham Young invited the Sisters of Mercy to his city, and when these Sisters visited him he showed them every courtesy. He used to say that he had never met his superior, and there was no one on earth to whom he would raise his hat. He refused this courtesy to royalties visiting his capital. "The master should hang his hat on the peg the Almighty made for it—his head, of course," said Bishop Kimball, one of his sycophantic admirers. But he did doff his hat to the Sisters, gave them, unasked, twenty dollars for their charities, and showed them to their carriage with extreme politeness. He invited other Sisters to come to him whenever they needed spiritual advice and direction! In 1875, when Sisters came to stay, Mormon children went to them in great crowds, but were soon "counselled" to leave, the Mormon oligarchy being convinced that children educated in a convent could never become good Mormons.

Brigham died August 29, 1877, being as old as the century. One of his daughters said his last words were, "Joseph! Joseph!" His disciples understood that he called on Joe Smith, who had led him into Mormonism, either in reverence or in reproach. Some Catholics, to whom he had showed kindness, hoped against hope that he was calling on St. Joseph!

Like Joe Smith, he was a persistent violator of the ten commandments. If his hand did no murder, murders were done at his instigation by a secret society sworn to do his will, the Danites, Avenging Angels, or Destroying Angels. A profound hypocrite, an able politician, as leader of the Saints for thirty-three years, he showed much executive ability. Many of his children were girls and preceded him to the tomb. In early times he would not allow his disciples medical aid, but undertook to cure the sick by the laying on of hands. When ill himself, however, he always had as many physicians as could be got. He left nineteen widows and some fifty children. His millions were divided among his families. No restitution was made to those whom he had robbed or cheated, and, as far as we could ascertain on the spot, he died as he had lived. His grave, in a large green near his old dwelling, behind the Eagle Gate, is one of the sights of Zion. Several of his consorts are buried near him, an honor which will be accorded to any among the rest who may die without contracting another marriage.*

Brigham Young told the Sisters of Mercy who visited the holy city in the zenith of his power and fame, that he had heartily wished and earnestly tried to induce an Irish colony to join the Saints in Utah; and he boasted that whatever he set his heart on he accomplished. An Irish colony came, but not in the guise for which he had hoped. The bishop and most of the clergy and religious are of that nationality—the zealous clergy, who have erected schools, churches, and hospitals, and the dark-robed daughters of the faith, who gather in the little ones of Christ, are as the lightning-rods of Utah to turn the divine vengeance from

---

*Both as a prophet, and as a Thaumaturgus, the enterprising Brigham was very unfortunate. But the credulity of the Salt Lakers was inexhaustible. When he said, "Do you believe that I know what is coming? That I can work this miracle?" The answer was an enthusiastic "Yes." Once, Joe Smith said he would walk dry-shod over a river; but he paused on the brink, and asked his followers, "Do you believe I can do what I say?" They replied in the affirmative. "Well, then," said he, "that is the same as if I had done it!" an answer which did not shake the implicit faith of the advanced or the neophytes in the founder of Mormonism.

her people. These are chief among the causes which will determine the gradual, if not rapid, overthrow of this latest development of the Reformation. Disciples will be attracted to the true faith by seeing in the children of the Church illustrations of the sanctity which Mary fosters in those who love her. God, himself, by His omnipotent grace, will work, sweetly and peaceably, this "change of the right hand of the Most High." The deluded victims of a vicious system will become "the clean of heart," destined to see God, and pronounced "blessed" by the mouth of the Word Incarnate. "O, how beautiful is the chaste generation in glory; the memory thereof is immortal."

A GLANCE AT THE LATTER-DAY SAINTS (?)*

I

MANY years ago I saw, in Dublin, in an obscure alley not far from Sackville (now O'Connell) street, a queer looking edifice on the
door of which was painted: CHURCH OF THE LATTER-
DAY SAINTS. Though entirely ignorant of everything
concerning these recently sanctified people, it struck me
as a great piece of boldness that their sect should have
"a smoke of its own" in the fair metropolis of my

*The distinguished writer of this paper ought to have put
forward more plainly the fact that she has been in Utah and has
seen what she describes. Some circumstances mentioned in her
private letter might have usefully been embodied in the article.
" It seems I am the only Catholic that has ever touched the subject, and I am, perhaps, inordinately proud that there are no Irish
among these *misérables*. These shocking people interest me
greatly. Please join me in praying for their conversion. The
Bishop, Dr. Laurence Scanlan, is a Tipperary man; the priests,
nuns, teachers, miners, smelters, etc., are mostly Irish. Polygamy
— if it can be proved, which is difficult — is now punished by imprisonment. So, as a friend writes to me, 'the car of progress
will now rattle over the rocks of Utah.'" Another part of this
letter speaks of some Catholics in Mexico. " Nearly all are Irish,
strange to say: for Irish immigration has not turned south as
much as we would like." So the Irish Nun has even traveled far-
ther than the Irish Emigrant.

"Quæ regio in terris nostri non plena laboris?"

country. I knew there had been no Irish heresiarch, and that consequently the "Saints" must have been established and propagated by foreigners. The name was a good one. It was cleverly chosen — a taking name, in fact. Persons shaky in other forms of Protestantism ought to be able to find a secure haven among "Saints," a refuge from the unrest and instability which periodically crop out in the crews and passengers of every barque not moored to the Rock of Peter. And what more could seekers after higher things desire than to be admitted among the "Saints," former and latter?

The period when the sign of a new religion offended my Catholic instinct was, though I knew it not, the golden age of the Latter-Day Saints. They were scarcely settled in the fastnesses of the Rocky Mountains, a thousand miles from civilization, or, as they themselves said, "a thousand miles from everywhere." Their high priest, Brigham Young, was Governor of the Territory of Utah, whose authority, supreme and absolute in spiritual and temporal things, it was hardly less than death to question. No railroads, no telegraph, no soldiers, disturbed the solitude of the holy city. Under the guidance of Young, the Mormons were making the desert blossom like the rose. They, an insignificant handful of ignorant creatures, were taught to regard the United States of America as a poor, mean power, which they could "whip" any day they felt inclined to make the exertion. It was their intention utterly to rout that heathen confederation, and they were often told in Sunday harangues that the heads of the same would soon be seen begging their bread at the gates of Zion.

II

BRIGHAM YOUNG, who for over thirty years wore the triple crown of king, priest, and prophet in the new Zión, the headquarters, the Rome of the Mormons, was born in New England in 1801. A glazier by trade, he was a Methodist and a Baptist by turns till 1832, when he embraced Mormonism. His personal magnetism and keen practical sense were of immense use to Joseph Smith, founder of Mormonism, who made him one of the newly-organized quorum of the Twelve Apostles in 1834. Brigham now began "to preach in tongues to the Saints," and though neither saints nor sinners understood him, the manner in which he transacted all business committed to him proved his superiority, and his promotion to the higher grades was rapid. In 1840 he preached the new gospel in England. He would compass sea and land to make a proselyte, and success rewarded his exertions. He often afterwards spoke of the "gullibility" of the English. Although not very clear as to what he believed himself, he was able to give them satisfying reasons for the faith they understood to be in him, and many left all that was dear to them to follow his lead.

Though entirely uneducated — he spent but thirteen days of his life in school — intercourse with the world had polished his manners, which could be very pleasing when he wished. His personality was not to be despised. A rather handsome, though sinister-looking face, and a tall commanding figure, attracted his audience before he opened his mouth to utter the unknown sounds which were understood to be the gift of tongues. When he spoke "American," his "inspiration" showed to better advantage, and he seldom failed to "bring many to the truth," as he pretended to understand it.

Fraud, dishonesty, and worse crimes distinguished the Saints everywhere, and they were driven out of Ohio, Illinois, and Missouri, places they had "opened to the preaching of the gospel." Joseph Smith was shot, and the next in rank, Sidney Rigdon, assumed his office. Brigham soon removed Sidney's candlestick, denounced his revelations as from the devil, cut off himself and his followers, cursed him, and finally "delivered him over to Satan to be buffeted for a thousand years." Even his opponents admired his stern intrepidity. He was elected President by an overwhelming majority. The minority he at once cut off, root and branch. Everything flourished, directed by his strong will, and the improving status of the saints soon showed that there was an able and firm hand at the helm.

Brigham determined to found an empire in the Rocky Mountains, then Mexican Territory, and though nothing could be more difficult than to bring his disciples to this, he accomplished it. Many who crossed the Mississippi in the hope of one day "worshiping under their own vine and fig tree, where none should make them afraid," won only nameless graves in the great American desert. But he administered the affairs of the survivors with skill and energy, and bent them all to his designs by his dogged pertinacity and resistless influence. He made himself feared, loved, and venerated by the people whom he cajoled, fed, scolded, and praised; but, above all, they learned to dread his iron hand. When the crops failed and famine stared them in the face, he told them they were cursed for their unfaithfulness; but he found them food.

Brigham was invariably courteous to strangers, and quite willing to gratify the curiosity of which he was the object, so long as it was respectful. When gentlemen of the press visited his city, he showered attentions upon them. They were at once taken hold of by his sycophants, and shown the bright side of the loathsome system of which he was the head. Though himself illiterate, he showed the highest appreciation of the literary personages who visited his capital, and was obsequiously polite to them. Hence, the glowing accounts that often appeared of a rather insignificant region. Writers were surrounded by Mormon officials and never allowed to see for themselves. They "wrote up" the holy city rather from a Mormon standpoint than from their own unbiased researches. The Mormons were prohibited under the gravest penalties from taking the Gentiles into their confidence on any subject whatever.

III

IN THE Lion House and the Beehive House, two handsome residences connected by a range of business offices, lived and worked the redoubtable Governor Young. The former was devoted chiefly to his nineteen consorts and their numerous children ; the latter might be called his official residence. The women derived no social prominence from being the so-called wives of the great man. They all dined at his table in the Lion House, each mother being surrounded by her own progeny, while Brigham and his latest favorite occupied a separate table at the head of the dining room. Neither were they allowed to live in idleness ; each had her appointed tasks, and all were servants without wages. Save one German and one or two Englishwomen, the legal wife and the " plural wives " were all natives of America, several being of New England. These unfortunate women were scarcely ever mentioned in Utah. Their wants were supplied with great frugality. Though Brigham soon became one of the wealthiest men in the world, having a " faculty" for turning the most unlikely things into gold, he was close-fisted and even stingy to the last. There was rarely a servant on his premises. His consorts and daughters did the menial work of his extensive household, while his sons-in-law and sons were expected to busy themselves in farming, herding, branding cattle, and mechanical work. The versatile "seer, prophet, and revelator " held the makings of his wives' gowns, and measured them out very sparingly. In early days sun-bonnets and cotton dresses were their uniform, and the Czar of all the Mormons signalized himself by devising a still uglier garb — a high hat with a narrow brim, a shapeless sacque of antelope skin, and a short, tight skirt of linsey. This, the famous "Deseret Costume," he made all the women "Saints" wear, but even his power was not able to perpetuate so hideous a *toilette*, and after a few seasons it gradually dropped out, and only his senior spiritual bride, Eliza Snow, who gloried in having been the first polygamous wife of Joe Smith, appeared in the Deseret Costume.

Considering that Brigham was always a *de facto* king in Salt Lake City, and had even been anointed king, it is a little singular that his consorts had no social standing, but remained cooks, housekeepers, seamstresses, to the end, with little variety save from the drudgery of the kitchen to that of the laundry. Vice spread through all the ramifications of this fanaticism, but the worst of its degradations were imposed on women; to them only a bare support was given in lieu of the virtue and liberty they had been compelled to barter. It was considered wonderful that the royal Brigham took off his hat to some Sisters of Mercy who visited his city in 1870 on business of their community. He never uncovered his head to the women of the Beehive. Mormon prints and pictures show that he even wore his hat at meals, when all his consorts and families were present. Indeed, he was accustomed to declare that his superior did not exist on earth, and therefore there was no one in whose honor he could be expected to lift his hat. Sometimes he could not well remove it, for during a season in which he was unusually given to vanity, his hair of a morning was done up in curling

papers and hairpins. The lady on whom he had bestowed the latest reversion of his hand prepared him to
appear before his callers at his daily levée in all the
bravery of well-oiled ringlets. Towards the close of his
life he dressed in the latest fashion.

IV

THE sons of Brigham Young, like the sons of royalty
in general, were celebrated for what is vulgarly called
rowdyism — whiskey, fast horses, furious driving; besides which all were polygamists. His daughters, said
to be the boldest maidens in the holy city, were early
"married into polygamy," with his fullest approbation.
Though his consorts lived in retirement and with great
economy as to furniture, food, and apparel, his descendants were accused of taking on airs on account of their
blood royal. Indeed Brigham was not at all satisfied
with the doings of his children, though his family was
the best regulated in Utah, "a pattern to the Saints."
He had a sort of phonetic way of quoting Scripture,
and would render a well-known text, "according to his
experience": "Train up a child, and away they go."
Though he was a declared enemy to education, one of
his consorts was schoolmistress to the children of the
rest, and, as they grew older, he gave them other advantages, even sending some of them to college. But his
liberality in this respect never extended beyond his
own children.

The greatest virtue a Mormon can possess is to pay
his "tithing" promptly. The Church was the universal

merchant, and through "Zion's co-operative stores" and their branches, the first Presidency organized all commerce to their own advantage. While the heads of the church reveled in luxury, the people had but a bare subsistence. Despite Brigham's perpetual preaching of industry, there were some drones in the hive, and not a few were supported by their wives. But profits of all kinds fell into his hands. One of his wives, so-called, who escaped from him in 1874, in the legal proceedings she instituted against him, declared that he was worth eight million dollars, and had a monthly income of forty thousand dollars besides. Events since have proved that she correctly estimated his goods and chattels, yet he denied that his income exceeded six thousand dollars a month — an immense sum at that time in Utah, especially for a man who had no rent and little taxes to pay.

To-day, thanks to Gentile enterprise, the Mormon capital is a beautiful city, especially when viewed from a distance, and in spring and summer. Trees, gardens, cornfields, patches of vivid green, starred with golden rod and sunflowers, bright sky, sparkling waters, contrast finely with the sombre gray and brown of the surrounding mountains. The temple built of white granite has cost millions. The Assembly House, used in cold weather for Sunday meetings, is a fair, graceful building. The tabernacle is grotesquely ugly; even the saints themselves irreverently compare it to a huge gopher or land turtle. It seats eight to ten thousand people, and, as the walls are almost all doors, it could in case of accident be emptied in three minutes. There is no sign of religion in it. Its gray walls are bare and unsightly. Lions couchant and a beehive are the only adornments of this temple of fanaticism.

Mormonism is a materialistic religion ; one of the hymns begs some not well-defined deity to

> "Celestialize and purify
> This earth for perfect Mormons."

Their aspirations begin and end in earth. The most desolate spot in the whole world is, I think, the Mormon cemetery. No sign of faith, hope, or love ; no solemn trees, no green turf, no soaring cross, no emblematic dove. In family "lots" wives lie at the foot of the husband in the order of their decease. The mortality in early days was immense, especially among children. It was said that the deceased children of Brigham would fill a fair-sized graveyard.

V

THE handsomest dwelling house in Utah is the mansion known as the Amelia Palace, built by Brigham for his favorite, Amelia Folsom, a native of Massachusetts. It is erected on a beautiful lawn, surrounded by trees and gardens, and would be a splendid residence in any city. Here Brigham died August 29, 1877, to the grief and wonderment of many of his disciples, who thought their prophet would never see death. His widows roamed the streets disconsolate, weeping into immense towels, and shrieking in every variety of tone: "The Prophet is dead!" Every one of them, save the contumacious Ann Eliza, who, instigated by some Gentile barbarians, had instituted proceedings against him, was a widow "well left." Each had a house and lot. Amelia is quite wealthy.

As to religion, I fear the wretched high priest died as he had lived. A descendant of his told a Catholic lady at the time that he frequently muttered on the last day of his sinful life: " I never had a wife but one, and that was my first." He had ample opportunities of knowing the truth which would have freed him from his unruly passions; but avarice and sensuality and ambition were strong in his craven soul to the last, so far as can be ascertained. As early as 1866 a priest ventured to reside in the holy city — a Father Kelly, sent thither by the Archbishop of San Francisco, in whose diocese the New Jerusalem then was. Everything was done to drive him from this difficult mission. The saints whittled about his poor hut day and night.* Nothing of this kind was ever done but by the instigation of the Prophet; if he did not commit murder with

---

*An obnoxious stranger was frequently "whittled out of town." Mormon men and boys would surround his house in perfect silence. Each had a knife and a stick of wood. When the unfortunate Gentile appeared, they all began to slice off pieces of wood, bringing their knives as near to his face as possible. They followed him everywhere, but never actually touched him. To see sharp knives flashing continually about his head and face was more than the bravest man could stand. Few could bear it for a day. When these persons left, they were said to have been " whittled out of town."

his own hands, it is certain that he inspired, suggested, or even commanded many a one. The priest boldly appealed to him for protection. He was astonished (!) that any had behaved so inhospitably to the interesting stranger, whom he immediately covered with the *ægis* of his protection, and the priest was henceforth unmolested. Brigham expressed the greatest friendship for him, asked him many questions, professed himself "almost persuaded" to become a Catholic, but virtually concluded every conference in the words of another who preferred the honors of this world to the glory of the next: "I will hear thee again concerning this matter."

Brigham expressed a strong desire for Irish disciples. He considered the class of Irish likely to be induced to emigrate excellent farmers, and was most anxious to have them settle in his territory in large numbers. His missionaries were not at all successful in the Emerald Isle. Indeed the Irish have always been conspicuous among the Mormons only by their absence. Brigham told an Irish lady that he always did what he set his heart on, and that he would live to see plenty of Irish in Zion. So he did, but not in the way he expected. It was not Irish bishops, priests, religious, and laity that he courted, but this was the only Irish immigration he ever saw. When Father Kelly said Mass in a hovel in the den of vice that Salt Lake City then was, his congregation consisted of a few Irish soldiers from the neighboring camp, and some miners and smelters. Fervently they besought the good God, through the intercession of the purest of Virgins, the Maid without a stain, to plant His holy Church in this fair land, and create a chaste generation in this modern Gomorrha. Soon after, the railroads opened up this unexplored region to the Gentiles, and Mormonism, which cannot bear the light of day, was no longer cloistered. The spread of Catholic principles more than any other means would cure the loathsome ulcer on the breast of a great nation. From the first the Catholic Church has been respected by the Mormon, who sees little difference between his own "celestial ordinance" of simultaneous polygamy and the progressive polygamy sanctioned by divorce. Nor is it easy to persuade him that he has not as much right to interpret the Bible in favor of his peculiar institution as the non-Catholic has to interpret it in favor of monogamy.

The sagacious Brigham, a man of unusual administrative ability and great natural gifts, saw this, and he often seemed on the verge of conversion. He admitted that he tried hard and in vain to convert the first priest he met in Utah. But he often averred that this priest could have converted him had he remained long enough and tried hard enough. It is certain that he showed more respect to Catholic clergy and religious than to any other persons, even princes. And when, to the wonder of America, Sisters settled in Zion, the patriarch declared himself their protector, would stop his carriage if he met them in the street, and graciously inquire how they were doing. He even invited them, should they be in need of spiritual advice or direction, to come to him, assuring them they would always find him ready and willing to instruct and direct them!

But, indeed, the astute Brigham had quite enough to do to give advice and direction in his own household. Bitter quarrels, intense animosity, indescribable scenes of violence, results of a vicious system that brought the worst passions to the surface, were not unusual in his wide domestic circle. Sometimes he was obliged to threaten to drive all his consorts away, and "go to heaven alone." More often he consoled them with empty promises. The older ones, known as "Mothers in Israel," he promised to rejuvenate in the resurrection; with the younger ones he used diplomacy, and to all in general he declared that they must bear their miseries cheerfully, for "he would not have whining women about him."

Verily, the most wretched women on earth were in this happy valley by Jordan's stream. To see them pour out of the huge, ugly tabernacle of a bright Sunday afternoon was to look upon a sea of faces from which all love and graciousness seemed banished, and on which sin and sorrow and unsanctified suffering had left indelible traces. They were of every age and of almost every country. True, they were to a great extent of the lowest and most degraded classes. But there were among them, too, women of education and so-called refinement, who had been lured into this seething vortex by the deceitful tongues of Mormon missionaries. Why did not these leave? Because they could not. There was neither ingress nor egress save through the terrible Mokanna; if they did leave, they would lose their way of living, such as it was; and, worst of all to a woman's heart, they would never again see their unfortunate children. Poor creatures, they regarded their fate as the inevitable to which they must, per force, reconcile themselves. And, in the midst of the tortures of their hideous condition, they would say, with a sort of blasphemous resignation: We are made to suffer; we must go on suffering; we must bear our awful cross; we must live our religion. God wills it.

Every English-speaking country was represented among the Mormons, as I have said, except Ireland. This was a great grief to Brigham Young. He was willing to give the Irish "a refuge from famine and danger." He looked for them in Ireland; he sought them earnestly among the Irish settlers in England, Scotland, Wales, America; he sent his most eloquent apostles into the highways and byways of the world to compel them, so to say, to come to his banquet, but not one of them came. Surely this is a grand thing for the island of genuine saints. That they should be faithful in their own country, where they are so shielded, is not surprising in the light of their past record; but we must thank God specially for their fidelity in other lands, where wealth and social position, and in several cases intellectual ability, succumbed.

They are now in Utah in large numbers, and they have contributed their share to the victories won over the Mormons within the past year by the other settlers

—victories which have broken the power of the Saints and are the beginning of the end of their hideous caricature of a theocracy. May they ever preserve intact the faith once delivered to the saints. May they remain in the future what they have been in the past, the chaste generation whose memory is immortal. Under the protection of the Mother of Mercy may they continue to bring up their children in the fear and love of God and the practise of holiness. And, appreciating the freedom of which they were of old deprived in their own fair land, may they ever preserve to themselves and to others that higher and more blessed freedom wherewith Christ hath made us free.

THE NINE-DAYS' QUEEN

HE most superficial student of history can hardly fail to observe that the *heroic* vanishes from royalty, especially female royalty, with the Catholic faith. The great qualities of the Saxon, Norman, and Plantagenet queens of England, for instance, have never been reproduced in their Protestant successors. I speak not of the sainted queens—Protestants have disclaimed sanctity from the beginning. "How dare you mention such persons in my presence?" asked the godly Edward VI., in a rage, when an Anglican prelate, from old habit, swore "by the saints," before his youthful majesty. Heroic sanctity has never been achieved, or even deemed possible, outside of the one fold whereof Christ is the Shepherd. I speak merely of high courage, extraordinary filial, conjugal, or maternal devotedness, intense patriotism, great penance wherever great faults were to be expiated, and lavish charities to the orphan, the student, the plague-stricken, and the stranger.

There is one lady, however, who, at first sight, seems to be an exception to all this. She wore a crown for nine days, and the people called her the "Epiphany Queen," and "The Nine-Days' Wonder." Although Jane Grey, or more properly, Jane Dudley, has never awakened in the public mind at large either interest or enthusiasm, yet there is no character in history more completely taken on faith by the few who have written her praises. Her very faults are canonized. Mrs. Sandford * told our grandmothers that Jane would not have been so amiable had she been less submissive (*i. e.*, in the matter of usurping her sovereign's throne). "Her graces," said she, "like gems whose brilliancy is increased by an opaque setting, gathered strength in her adversity." Miss Strickland † has exhausted the language of eulogy in describing one whom she affirms to be "the most noble character of the royal Tudor lineage, endowed with every attribute that is lovely in domestic life, while her piety, learning, courage, and virtue, qualified her to give lustre to a crown." "Early wise," "sweet and saintly," "peerless," "heavenly-minded," "angelic," "lovely," "innocent," "candid," "divine," are but a few of the flattering epithets which this celebrated biographer showers upon her youthful heroine. Catholic writers, too, have been fascinated by the qualities with which some have invested her, no less than by her tragic fate. The *Dublin Review* ‡ testifies that she "left a loved and honored memory to the world—the memory of a victim, almost a martyr." A popular essayist and novelist of our day affirms that Jane Grey was incomparably more noble than the two beheaded queens of France, Mary Stuart and Marie

---

* Life of Lady Jane Grey, in English Female Worthies, vol. 1. London: 1833.

† Lives of the Tudor Princesses. By Agnes Strickland. London: 1866. Also, Lives of the Queens of England, by the same.

‡ October number, 1875.

Antoinette. "She suffered to the full as deeply as either"—a great mistake—"and yet," he asks, with evident surprise, "what place has she in men's feelings and interests compared with theirs?"*

The poets have come to the aid of the essayists, biographers, and historians. The laureate of England makes poetic license verge on the impossible in his eloquent description of the saint of his drama:

> "Seventeen—and knew eight languages—in music
> Peerless—her needle perfect, and her learning
> Beyond the churchmen; yet so meek, so modest
> So wife-like, humble to the trivial boy,
> Mismatched with her for policy!"†

And there are few more beautiful passages in English poetry than that which Sir Aubrey de Vere puts into the mouth of Jane, in the parting interview which he imagines between the Duchess of Suffolk and her child, the length of which precludes its insertion here.

Strange it is that the contemporaries of this unfortunate lady were unable to perceive, or unwilling to acknowledge, the existence of these marvelous qualities which have dazzled her modern panegyrists. Her early patroness, Catharine Parr; her sometime fellow-student, Edward VI.; her royal cousins, the Princesses Mary and Elizabeth; her sisters, Lady Catharine and Lady Mary Grey, all good scholars and ready writers, failed so utterly to be struck with the wonderful, if

---

*Justin McCarthy, in Modern Leaders. New York: 1872. Sheldon & Co.

†Queen Mary. A Drama. By Alfred Tennyson. London: 1875.

not miraculous, gifts and graces with which the nine-teenth century has invested their hapless relative, that no allusion is made to her erudition or her sanctity in their letters, memoirs, or journals. I cannot find any evidence that she was loved or revered by a single contemporary, even of her own or her husband's family. If I am wrong, some one will have the goodness to enlighten me, but I really find little to support Jane's fame as a scholar, save the rather interested testimony of Roger Ascham,* while her title to sanctity has been manufactured by no less a personage than the veracious martyrologist, Fox.† Indeed, if Jane's contemporaries were of the same opinion as her admirers of to-day, she would certainly have figured as a Protestant saint —a distinction to which she was fully as well entitled as her handsome, deceitful relative, King Charles, "the Martyr," sole incumbent of the Protestant calendar.

Even the boy-king, Edward VI., whose wife Jane was brought up to be, was perfectly insensible to her charms, and indignantly spurned the idea of marrying her,‡ saying he would have a foreign princess, "well

* Ascham's Schoolmaster.

† Fox's Book of Martyrs.

‡ Edward Sixth's Journal. This prince was the son of a private gentlewoman, the detestable Jane Seymour, which connection gave the youthful majesty of England near relations named Smith, one of his mother's sisters having chosen a husband of that homely name. Another of the queen's sisters was married to one Cromwell, grandson to a blacksmith at Putney. The haughty young Tudor had already more kin of low degree than he cared to acknowledge.

stuffed and jeweled." He was actually engaged to the Princess Elizabeth of France for some months previous to his premature death.

Mary Tudor was one of the most thorough and elegant scholars that ever graced a throne. In point of years she might have been Jane's mother. Much intercourse took place between the cousins, and Mary, both as princess and as queen, showed great and constant kindness to the cadet branches of her family. Yet so far as I can discover, there is no evidence that this learned princess ever perceived in her cousin the uncommon intellectual endowments and saint-like virtues, the mere recital of which charms posterity. That Mary was not insensible to extraordinary ability is proved by the fact that, even amid the stormy scenes of her early maiden reign, she found time to examine and correct the Latin exercises of another cousin, related to her in exactly the same degree as Jane, the boy-prodigy, Darnley, who is allowed to have entirely surpassed the far-famed progress of his cousins, Edward VI., Queen Elizabeth, and Lady Jane Grey.*

By their deeds, rather than by the speeches and sentiments attributed to them by partisan writers, ought the men and women of history to rise or sink in our estimation; and the more virtue they can be proved to possess, the more pleasing the task of the biographer. But truth ought to be the first ingredient of history;

* Life of Lady Margaret Douglas, who, through her son, Darnley, husband of Mary Stuart, is ancestress of almost every royal personage in Europe.

nor can a good cause be really advanced by falsehood. An excellent authority affirms that for the last three centuries history has been little else than a conspiracy against truth. The lies of history during that period have been chiefly in the interest of Protestantism, and with what results? Protestantism was never less respectable than it is to-day; its brightest minds, its purest hearts, have sought and continue to seek rest in the maternal bosom of the Unchangeable Church. We will endeavor to give in these pages all that remains of an acknowledged Protestant heroine when fact is separated from rhetoric, the sober, historical truth,—so far as it can be discerned at this distant period,— of a youthful lady of demi-royal descent, who would probably have left no "footprints in the sands of time," during Queen Mary's* reign, had she not usurped a throne, and, as a consequence of her temerity, mounted a scaffold.

The grandmother of Lady Jane Grey is celebrated in contemporary chronicles as the fairest princess in Europe. Born towards the close of the fifteenth century, Mary Tudor, youngest surviving child of Henry VII. and Elizabeth of York, was, at the age of ten, affianced to the Archduke Charles of Austria, afterwards the renowned Charles V. At sixteen she married the mature widower, Louis XII., King of France, who, dying in less than three months, left her a not very

---

* Had Jane lived to the next reign, she would certainly have been persecuted by Queen Elizabeth, as her sisters Catharine and Mary were.

disconsolate widow. Charles Brandon, a favorite of her brother, Henry VIII., was dispatched to France for the purpose of escorting the princess to England; but was previously obliged to take a solemn oath before the king and the all-powerful Wolsey, that "he would not abuse his trust by any particular manifestation of partiality towards the young queen consigned to his guardianship."

Oaths, vows, or promises were never deemed very sacred by that handsome miscreant. Undeterred by the fact that two or three living ladies * claimed him as a husband, he broke his oath at the earliest opportunity; the marriage ceremony was performed over himself and the royal widow of six weeks, in Paris, February 12, 1515. As Brandon had been domesticated in her father's family from infancy, and is said to have been the first object of her girlish devotion, the princess could not have been ignorant of his matrimonial entanglements. And even if she were, her virtuous sister-in-law took care to send a special messenger to Paris to warn her that the captivating Suffolk was not free to contract matrimony anew. Indeed, a recent writer † has severely censured the Spanish queen for endeavoring to prevent this iniquitous connection. But this person, so far from being able to write history, is incapa-

---

* He deserted his first wife, a daughter of Sir Anthony Browne, and married her cousin, Lady Mortimer. The Church compelled him to return to his lawful wife. His third venture was the heiress of Lord Lisle, by whom he had his title, Viscount Lisle.

† W. H. Dixon, in History of Two Queens.

ble of giving a truthful description of a famous city *
which he traveled thousands of miles to see and examine.

The mother of Lady Jane Grey, Frances, eldest
daughter of Charles Brandon and Mary Tudor, was of
illegitimate birth; hence it was often argued that the
crown could not descend through this lady. Her sister
Lady Eleanor † Brandon, however, was universally allowed to be of legitimate birth; the claimants on her
father's hand died before she was born, although it was
not till 1529 that Cardinal Wolsey had the marriage of
the princess with Suffolk confirmed.

Henry Grey, Marquis of Dorset, was the father of
Jane. Grey repudiated his wife, Catharine Fitzalan,
daughter of the Earl of Arundel, to form a more lofty
alliance with a niece of Henry VIII., a crime which the

---

* Americans who have read this gentleman's description of
Salt Lake City will credit him with a rather lively imagination.
Mr. McCarthy remained almost as long in that capital as Mr.
Dixon, but could see nothing of the beauties out of which the latter
made the larger part of a volume. "Oh, Hepworth Dixon," he
exclaims, after a careful survey of the morally and physically
filthy capital of Mormondom, "how could you write so about its
theatre? Or was the beautiful temple of the drama which *you*
saw here deliberately taken down, and did they raise in its place
the big, gaunt, ugly, dirty, dismal structure which *I* saw, and in
which I and my companions made part of a dreary dozen or two
of audience, and blinked in the dim, depressing light of mediæval
oil-lamps?"— *Mr. McCarthy, in Galaxy.*

† See Life of Lady Margaret Clifford, daughter of Eleanor
Brandon, who claimed precedence of the sisters of Jane Grey, as
being of legitimate descent.

deserted wife's kindred avenged when Grey's daughter usurped the throne. Grey was not royally descended, as his pensioner Ulmer,* a German Reformer, erroneously states. As soon as monastic spoils began to be scattered among the greedy courtiers of Henry VIII., Dorset became, as Ulmer writes, "the thunderbolt and terror of the Papists, their fierce and terrible adversary." †

This Grey was about as wicked as his slender ability would permit ; a bad son, a bad husband, a bad father, a bad brother, a bad subject. The churchmen of those times were reluctant politicians ; the king was obliged to seek their services owing to the ignorance, incapacity, and drunkenness of the nobles ; and Suffolk and Dorset, grandfather and father of Jane, are particularized among such nobles as being "almost illiterate." ‡ They are not, therefore, invested even with the interest that often attaches to clever rogues. There is no evidence that Frances Brandon surpassed her worthless mate in intellectual endowments, education, or moral rectitude ; or rather there is abundant evidence that she did not. Judging by the letters which remain, the Queen Duchess herself had more intellect than her immediate descendants. Some of the best of these are addressed to her redoubtable brother, Henry VIII.: "My most dearest and right entirely beloved lord and brother," and subscribed, "Your loving *sister*, Mary, Queen of France."

* Zurich Letters.
† Ibid.
‡ Burke's Men and Women of the English Reformation, vol. i.

This princess is that "Mary bright of hue," whom Sir Thomas More represents the dying Elizabeth of York praying God to make "virtuous, wise, and fortunate." This prayer was not granted, though we may well hope that the follies of her early years were expiated by the sorrows and sufferings amid which she closed her short and troubled life. Queen Elizabeth of York has been highly eulogized for her graces and virtues. Her biographers style her "Elizabeth the Good." But if this royal lady be judged by her children who reached maturity — Margaret, Queen of Scotland, a woman of scandalous life, Henry VIII., and Mary, the Queen-Duchess, her character as a mother would scarcely stand very high.

It is not from parents such as we have described that saints or scholars usually spring. Lady Jane Grey did not certainly *inherit* the virtues and abilities with which her eulogists invest her. We shall see that she was little more fortunate in her friends, companions, and tutors, who were, for the most part, mere sycophants of the party in power, apostates, church-robbers, and friars of infamous life, who gloried in their shame, and whose greatest boast was that they had made vows to the Most High and violated them.

It is not perhaps the most gracious task in the world to take down from its pedestal a popular idol; and such a few of our contemporaries have sought to make Lady Jane Grey. Her memory as a Protestant saint and martyr is endeared to the Protestant mind — though she was rather a Calvinist than a Protestant —

and her tragic fate has shrouded her with a lurid glare which some have mistaken for the aureola of sanctity.

The history of Lady Jane Grey has several points of resemblance with that of her cousin, Arabella Stuart, who married a descendant of Jane's sister, Lady Catharine Grey. Both — one through Mary Tudor, one through Margaret Tudor — were great-granddaughters of Henry VII., and their demi-royal descent caused their ruin. The elder Disraeli* might have said of Jane what he says of Arabella: "She is said to have been beautiful, and not to have been beautiful; her very portrait, ambiguous as her life, is neither the one nor the other."

No chronicler has deemed it worth while to give the date of Jane's birth,† so far as we have been able to discover. Her pictures would lead to the belief that she was born several years earlier than the period usually assigned. Her age at the time of her usurpation of the throne, July, 1553, is variously given as sixteen, seventeen, and eighteen. In a letter from Ulmer to Bullinger, dated April, 1550, Jane is stated to be about fourteen years of age. If so, she must have been born in 1536; and there is every reason to believe that this is correct, as Ulmer was domesticated with her family at Bradgate, and might easily have heard, from Jane or her parents, her exact age. She

---

* Curiosities of Literature, vol. iii.

† Lingard mentions Jane as sixteen and as seventeen, in the last year of her life.— Hist. England, vol. vii. Fuller says she was eighteen.— Holy State, p. 311. Miss Strickland says she was born in October, 1537, and, later on, that she was exactly fourteen in May, 1551!

could scarcely have been born earlier, as her parents were married in March, 1533, and Jane's birth was preceded by those of a brother and sister who died in infancy. It may well be that Jane was born about the time of the disgrace of the unfortunate Anne Boleyn,* and the exaltation of her vile rival; and that as her parents were peculiarly given to deserting the setting and worshiping the rising sun, they called their infant *Jane*, to compliment the triumphant beauty whose star was then in the ascendant.

Bradgate, in Leicestershire, is universally allowed to have been the place of Jane's birth. Fuller thus describes it: "This fair, large, and beautiful palace was erected in the early part of the reign of Henry VIII., by Thomas Grey, second Marquis of Dorset. It is built principally of red brick, of a square form, with a turret at each corner." Bradgate must indeed have been one of the fairest homes in England. Its ruins may be traced to-day, in a rural spot of exquisite beauty, five miles from the town of Leicester. A tower still stands which local tradition points out as the birthplace of the Nine-Days' Queen.

*Anne Boleyn was beheaded a little after noon, May 19, 1536; the royal widower of a few hours married Jane Seymour on the morning of the 20th. The reformers vied with each other in doing honor to the successor of their murdered patroness. In the dedication of Coverdale's Bible, the names *Henry* and *Anne* were introduced, but as Anne was beheaded between the printing and the publication, J for *Jane* was printed over the letters which composed the name Anne, and the wife-killer associated with the new object of his caprice, on the fly-leaves of the Bible.

The early days of Jane are involved in the completest obscurity. Who baptized her? Who held her at the font? What were the first religious impressions she received? Did she ever make her first communion? Was she ever confirmed? At what period was she transferred from the nurse to the governess? Had she ever a governess? At what time did Aylmer become her tutor? These particulars elude all our research. We know, however, that she was not long alone in her nursery. Lady Catharine Grey was two years younger than her more celebrated sister; while the youngest child of Henry Grey and Frances Brandon, Lady Mary Grey, was not born till 1545, when her sister was about nine years old.

The first glimpse history gives of the "divine Jane" is in 1546, when we find her installed into some office about the person of Henry VIII.'s last Queen, Catharine Parr. She had, therefore, all the advantages likely to accrue from being frequently in the presence of her royal grand-uncle, when that degraded monarch was at his very worst, which certainly was after his marriage with his Protestant queen. The fact that Catharine Parr accepted the sixth reversion of the bloody hand of Henry VIII. a short time after the death of her second husband, his lawful wife, Anne of Cleves, being yet alive, is sufficiently eloquent of her character. One of Luther's descriptions * of the first Anglican Pope was

* "Luther called Henry VIII. 'the grossest of all pigs,' which he probably was, and 'of all asses,' which he certainly was not."— *My Clerical Friends*—MARSHALL.

never more true than at this period. He was sunk so low, that his sister-in-law, who subsequently stood in the same relation to Catharine, says truly, "that no lady that stood on her honor would venture on him." When he proposed for Christina, Duchess of Milan, that princess informed him, with infinite scorn, that if she had two heads she would place one at the disposal of his majesty.

Jane was much in the company of Catharine Parr. This lady had become a disciple of the "new learning" during her second widowhood, and was intimate with most of the reformers, who were accustomed to meet at her house. There is little doubt that her conversion to the "godliness" of the age was due to her love for Sir Thomas Seymour, one of the leaders of the anti-Catholic party, and subsequently her fourth husband. Perhaps, too, Jane's Protestantism was partially confirmed by her love of the handsome Edward Seymour, whom she frequently met at court * and to whom, with the consent of her parents, she was contracted at an early age. Neither Henry VIII. nor his son ever thought of her as the future queen-consort. Henry's latter years were spent in carrying fire and sword into Scotland, to seize the person of its infant queen, Mary Stuart, for the bride of his heir-apparent. This scheme was given up only when Mary was contracted to the dauphin; after which Edward was betrothed to that prince's sister, Elizabeth of France.

---

* He was usually in attendance on Prince Edward, his cousin-german.

We know not the date of Jane's residence at court, nor the length of time it continued; but we have some idea of the kind of persons whom she met there; her house at Bradgate was the rendezvous of the most infamous men that ever disgraced Christianity. No doubt she oscillated between the court and Bradgate. Her father constituted himself a sort of protector-general to a set of vile wretches, who, having appalled their own people by their crimes, came to hapless England to reform the Church:

> " With every crime they stocked the nation,
> To fit it for a reformation." *

Of these divines and their English compeers, the acute Bishop Doyle † says: " If these men have reconstructed the Church on the foundations of the prophets and apostles, the Manichean system must be true, and the evil principle has prevailed over the good." " They were," says Dr. Littledale, a Protestant clergyman of our day, " utterly unredeemed villains." ‡

The first Christians sold their lands, and gave the money to the Apostles for the poor; the "reformed" English — especially Jane's relatives — stole the goods of the poor to enrich themselves, and created that terrible evil unknown in the Ages of Faith, and with which no power but the Church has ever been able successfully to grapple — *pauperism* — a word hideous in the

* Ward's Cantos.
† Life of Dr. Doyle, Fitzpatrick.
‡ Lecture on " The Characters of the First English Reformers."

mouth of a Christian. Jane's grandfather, Brandon *
was infamous even among the courtiers of Henry VIII.,
as the suppressor of thirty monasteries. Her mother,
with the rapacity truly worthy of a niece of Henry
VIII., contrived to become mistress of almost all the
Carthusian property in and about London. The first
Christians had but one heart and one soul; no two of
the reformers, English or foreign, agreed on a single
doctrine.

Historians have spoken of Henry's queens as Catholic or as Protestant. The truth is, his queens and his
courtiers were of the religion, or phase of religion, which
the new pope dictated. Not one of them, after the
saintly Catharine of Aragon, ever dared to oppose his
will. If they had done so, they might have prepared
for martyrdom; and the spirit of martyrdom in his wives
died with his Spanish queen. It is, however, certain
that, with the exception of Catharine Parr, who died
delirious, all the women whom the royal pope married
sought to be reconciled to the Catholic Church when
death approached. Henry, indeed, kept the title † he
had won in his young and glorious days, but, as in the
case of Queen Victoria, ‡ his successor as " Head of the
Church," it might be asked: Of *what* faith was he
" Defender "? Jane knew well that he tied Catholics

---

* He died while Catharine Parr was queen, leaving two sons
of his last wife.

† Defender of the Faith.

‡ The question was recently put, in Parliament: " Of *what*
faith is Queen Victoria defender? "

and Protestants to the same stake. Poor Charlotte Brontë, in her strictures on Julia Kavanagh's *Women of Christianity*, says that "Protestantism is a quieter creed than Romanism—it does not set up its good women for saints, canonize their names, and proclaim their good works." I am afraid the quietness of Protestantism in this respect is akin to the quietness of death; and its creed, being as uncertain to-day as in the days of the first Anglican pope, Miss Brontë, though eldest daughter of one parson, and first wife of another, did not undertake to explain.

Lady Jane Grey could not have been long at court without learning that her patroness, Queen Catharine Parr, was ambitious to add the higher crown of authorship to her matrimonial diadem. The work by which this lady sought admission among royal authors contains several passages worthy of the picturesque right hand of Cranmer:

"Thanks be given to the Lord that He hath now sent us such a godly and learned king, in these latter days, to reign over us, that, with the force of God's word, hath taken away the veils and mists of error, and brought us to the knowledge of the truth by the light of God's word. . . . Our Moses, and most godly wise governor and king, hath delivered us out of the captivity and spiritual bondage of Pharaoh. I mean by this Moses King Henry VIII., my most sovereign favorable lord and husband, one (if Moses had figured any more than Christ), through the excellent grace of

God, meet to be another expressed verity of Moses's conquest over Pharaoh (and I mean by this Pharaoh the bishop of Rome), who hath been, and is, a greater persecutor of all true Christians than ever was Pharaoh of the children of Israel."

The woman who could apply such gross flattery to Henry VIII., "the impersonation of evil," as that monarch is aptly styled by Mackintosh,* was a fitting nursing-mother for the "miserable apostasy"† known as the Reformation.

The youthful Jane knew perfectly well the vicious and cruel character of the crowned wretch whom her patroness thus flattered. She knew that he had murdered his late queen, "a very little girl,"‡ and still more recently butchered his aged relative, Margaret Plantagenet, who, with the lion-like spirit of her dauntless race, refused to lay her aged head on the traitor's block, and bade his minions "take it as they could."§

* English Hist., vol. ii.
† Baring-Gould.
‡ *Parvissima puella* — HILLES.
§ Prescott rather innocently observes, in his Charles V., vol. iii., with reference to the Marian persecutions: "The English being *remarkable for the mildness of their public executions* (!), beheld, with astonishment and horror, venerable persons condemned to endure torments to which their laws did not subject even the most atrocious criminals." The fact is, there was not one *illegal* execution in Mary's reign. Parliament made the laws, and the Queen allowed them to take effect. That is *her* share in the persecutions that disgraced her reign. But, verily, no style of killing could be a novelty after the days of the royal Bluebeard. The Countess of Salisbury was hacked to pieces, Anne Askew

Jane was old enough to remember these, and a hundred other instances of his demoniac cruelty. How it must have blunted her sense of justice to hear such a monster flattered. As to her moral training, she was certainly worse off at the court of such a woman than she would have been with her unprincipled parents.

The interest which Catharine Parr took in the young Jane Grey must be considered in connection

and many others were racked and burned; several were boiled to death at Smithfield. See *Gray Friars' Chronicle*, printed for the Camden Society, 1852. Father Middlemore's flesh was torn off with red-hot pincers, the cruel executioners searching for his heart, which the martyr told them was "in Heaven, where his treasure was." "The executioner," says Pole, "suspended the embraces of that fell tyrant, Death, and thus prolonged the sufferings of his victims." The common punishment for treason — and every one knows how easily treason was committed under Henry VIII.—was so horrible that nothing more dreadful could be devised. Some forty years later than the period of which we write, Queen Elizabeth was so exasperated by the Babington conspiracy (1586) for the rescue of the Queen of Scots, that she ordered her Council to invent "some new device" to punish its perpetrators. But Burleigh informed Her Majesty "that the punishment prescribed by the letter of the law was to the full as terrible as anything new that could be devised, if the *executioner took care to protract the extremity of their pains* in the sight of the multitude."—*Letters of Burleigh to Hatton*—LINGARD. Does Prescott write in ignorance or in malice ? As to venerable persons, the English mob never saw any more venerable than More, Fisher, and the Carthusian monks, whose prior, Father Haughton, was hanged till half dead, disemboweled while yet alive, his heart cast into the fire, his trunk divided into four pieces, and, when half roasted, sent to the four most important cities of the kingdom ! O, Prescott, shame !

with the darling project of that Queen, who desired to perpetuate her influence over the future monarch of England by providing him with a wife in the person of his cousin. If Jane possessed a tithe of the qualities and fascinations with which posterity has endowed her, she ought to have won the heart of the princely boy. But, poor girl, scarcely one of those who knew her, loved her; and yet her more unfortunate contemporaries, Mary Tudor and Mary Stuart, had qualities to evoke in those about them the most passionate attachment.

When Catharine Parr was in serious danger of being added to the list of Henry's conjugal victims, 1546, we find Jane in attendance on her person. Jane must have learned on this perilous occasion how deeply the Queen was attached to the Reformed doctrines, when that frightened mother of the Reformation saved her head by disclaiming all theological knowledge but that of which the royal wife-killer was the exponent. When Catharine visited her sanguinary master on the evening of the day which had almost proved fatal to her, Lady Jane Grey * is mentioned as carrying the lights before her mistress, a ceremony during which etiquette required that the candle-bearer should walk backwards, facing the Queen.

Catharine and her ladies had been borrowing books of an unfortunate lady who had recently left her husband to preach some new gospel. When Anne Askew was condemned to death, the Queen and her party

* Speed's Chronicle.

were terror-stricken lest the poor fanatic might mention them as her disciples. But, with a nobility of soul which deserved a better fate, Anne guarded their secret even on the rack. Henry was terribly incensed against this young woman, who did not protest exactly in his way, for "having brought prohibited books into his palace and imbued his queen" and his nieces whom he unceremoniously calls "Suffolk's daughters," with her doctrine. This passage would seem to show that Jane's mother and aunt, Lady Frances and Lady Eleanor Brandon, the Marchioness of Dorset, and the Countess of Cumberland, were at court at this time, and that both were disciples of the hapless lady who became the scapegoat for the royal party.

Anne Askew was burned alive. There is no evidence that her royal friend interceded for her, or indeed for any other "martyr." In the midst of her sombre honeymoon, a period at which she must have had some influence, three Sacramentarians were roasted alive at Smithfield. Some of the worst of Henry's bad acts were perpetrated during the queenship of Catharine Parr. With all the changes and distractions of a court life, and frequent traveling hither and thither, Jane's opportunities of acquiring learning were not by any means propitious. The awful death of her redoubtable great-uncle, Henry VIII., in January, 1547, wrought a great change in her position and prospects. Whether Jane was at court or with her parents at this period, we have no means of ascertaining. Catharine Parr was not present when Henry's appalling death-scene was enacted; and it is possible that Jane attended her in her retirement; in which case that youthful lady must have been edified to see that the royal widow engaged herself to contract her fourth marriage, and probably contracted it while the colossal remains of the first Anglican pope was still above ground.

The will of Henry VIII.,* the provisions of which were known only to his council and queen, placed Jane † immediately after his daughters, Mary and Elizabeth, in the royal succession, entirely passing over the posterity of his weak and vicious eldest sister, Margaret Tudor. Hence, there was a distant prospect that Jane might be a queen-regnant, if not a queen-consort.

The death of Henry VIII. was "very evil." He continued his tyrannies to the last.‡ Harpsfield and Saunders mention that the dying monarch evinced an ardent desire to be reconciled with the Church, which he had so barbarously persecuted. But Henry had slaughtered, or driven far from him, every ecclesiastic who would have dared to tell him the truth. The

* "Considerable doubt was entertained of the authenticity of the will attributed to Henry VIII. Under Mary it was pronounced spurious by the privy council; by Elizabeth it was never suffered to be mentioned."—LINGARD.

† "The heirs *masles* of the Lady Frances," and failing these, of the Lady Eleanor, "but," says honest old Spelman, "the name of Brandon was clean put out in the second generation."

‡ "Surrey of the deathless lay," was his last victim, and the tyrant's death alone prevented the execution of the father of the poet, the aged Duke of Norfolk, and of Catharine Parr herself.

murderer of More, and Fisher, and Forest, and Abell—
the wretch who had made the blood of God's saints
flow like water—deserved to hear the truth no more.
His gigantic corpse remained above ground from January 28th till late in February. On its way to Windsor
it was laid for the night among the broken walls of
Sion, the prison of the young queen whom he had
murdered exactly five years before, and then were verified the awful words of Friar Peyto, who had compared
him to Achab, and told him to his face from Greenwich
pulpit, "that the dogs would in like manner lick his
blood." Blood oozed from the body and saturated the
pavement of the dismantled church, and when the
plumbers came to solder the royal coffin they found a
dog beneath it, which lapped up the blood of the re-
lentless tyrant.*

Save the mother that bore him and the wife who
glorified his early days of kingship, no woman ever
loved Henry VIII., except his daughter Mary. The
boy-king severely censured her for the filial grief with
which she bitterly bewailed his woeful end. The crown
consoling him for the loss of such a father, he commanded his subjects to dry their tears—a command
which they could not obey for a very obvious reason.
In his capacity of Head of the Church, the Pope of
nine summers informed the public that "a prince who
led so holy a life, and governed his people with such
justice as Henry VIII.," was sure of going straight to
heaven; and was, in fact, now enjoying eternal happi-

* Burnet, The Sloan Collection, etc.

ness.* The troublesome and tedious ceremonies of canonization were entirely dispensed with.

Henry left two widows, his Lutheran queen, Anne of Cleves, who was living in retirement at Richmond, and ultimately became a fervent Catholic; and his Protestant queen, who at once provided herself with a mate, no other than Thomas Seymour, the vilest profligate of a most licentious court. Strype informs us that she rather courted him, than he her; † and in one of her letters she tells him that she would have married him after the death of her second spouse had not the king stepped between them. It will be remembered that it was during her second widowhood, of two or three months at most, that she adopted the views of the Reformers, and it can scarcely be doubted that Seymour's handsome face and dashing figure were the agreeable medium through which this change was wrought in the religious sentiments of the gay widow, who was anything but a " widow indeed."

Lady Jane Grey seems to have been with her parents during the courtship and clandestine marriage of her late mistress, for we find that as soon as the marriage was made public, namely, about three months after the burial of the late king, Sir Thomas Seymour ‡ offered to purchase the wardship of Jane from her parents, he and his wife being determined to marry her,

* MSS. Harl.

† Ecclesiastical Memorials.

‡ Deposition of Jane's father, the Marquis of Dorset, Tytler's Reigns of Edward and Mary.

if possible, to the young king, and thus perpetuate their influence over their sovereign. The parents of Jane readily acceded to this proposal. The guardianship of their daughter was transferred, "for a consideration," from them to Seymour, and Jane was again domesticated with Catharine Parr.

Seymour had a double object* in wedding the frolicsome widow of his late master. 1. The acquisition of the wealth which this prudent lady had accumulated while queen, and of the dowers which she enjoyed as widow of two wealthy lords and a king. 2. To gain more easy access to Catharine's stepson, the new king, and win him over to his purposes. The chief of these purposes was to thwart his brother, the Protector, who had just helped himself to the royal title of Duke of Somerset, and who was eager to marry his daughter, Jane Seymour, to the young king. The bold move of the bridegroom, in obtaining possession of the person of Lady Jane Grey, and purchasing the right to marry her to whom he would, checkmated Edward Seymour most provokingly, and fanned the flame of enmity already kindled between the ambitious brothers.

One circumstance rendered Catharine Parr's residence most unsuitable for the virtuous bringing up of a young woman. The princess Elizabeth was domesticated with her stepmother from the time of her father's death. Here, indeed, the child was the mother of the woman. How could Jane Grey escape contamination

---

* Pictorial History of England, a voluminous compilation by Craik and Macfarlane, vol. ii., book v.

in such companionship? Elizabeth Tudor, in her fifteenth year, was what she had not ceased to be in her seventieth, a bold, bad woman. So far as can be ascertained, Seymour was the first, and certainly not the least infamous, of Elizabeth's lovers. The fact that he was brother to one of her father's wives and husband of another—that he was brother to the woman for whose sake her mother had been sent to the block—did not in the least deter Elizabeth. The fact that Elizabeth was an orphan, a daughter of his late king, and sent to his wife for protection, did not deter Seymour. Mary endeavored to draw her sister from the ill-regulated household of Catharine Parr, by offering her a home with herself, on the ostensible plea that the queen-dowager had outraged their father's memory by her hasty, indecorous marriage; but the daughter of Catharine of Aragon knew exactly how matters stood, and endeavored to save the reputation of Anne Boleyn's daughter by withdrawing her from temptation. But Elizabeth preferred the license of her present home.

These disgraceful amours utterly ruined the character of Elizabeth, and rendered miserable the life of Seymour's wife, who was finally compelled to send the princess from her house a few months before her death, which occurred in September, 1548. Elizabeth is the only unmarried princess of England whose conduct was investigated by the royal council, and who was compelled to write a "Confession" of her misdeeds while yet a mere girl. It would seem that intercourse between the vicious pair was not quite broken up by separation. "It is probable," says Miss Strickland, "that the alarming change in Catharine"—after the birth of her only child—"was caused by the whispers in her lying-in chamber relating to her husband's passion for her stepdaughter, and his intention of aspiring to the hand of the princess in case of her own decease."* Nobody seems to have dreamt of removing the youthful Jane Grey from the contamination of such surroundings. Her parents thought more of the money the sale of her wardship brought them than of the morality of their child, then at the tender age of twelve. Surely Seymour's house was a model house; it was filled with English and foreign reformers, who held divine service therein two or three times a day. "Seymour,"† says Latimer, "gets him out of the way when the daily prayer begins, like a mole digging in the earth." Verily he was not so much of a hypocrite as those who attended the daily prayer and led such vicious lives.

Poor Catharine was happier even in the lifetime of Henry VIII. She was not then tormented by jealousy, and she could resort to her literary labors, such as they were. "She spent her own leisure hours in compiling into the form of prayer the inspirations of a diseased brain."‡ Never had an ill-used wife greater need of prayer. Lady Jane Grey remained in her household to the end. Having given birth to a daugh-

* Life of Catharine Parr.

† Latimer's Sermons, first edition.

‡ Audin's Life of Henry VIII.

ter, the queen died delirious eight days later. Lady Jane officiated as chief mourner at her funeral. Sir Thomas brought her to Hanworth when all was over, and such was the favorable impression she made on the heartless widower, that he deliberated which he would select for his next wife, the Princess Elizabeth or Lady Jane Grey.

It would be strange indeed if the precocious Jane acquired either virtue or learning in so vicious a school as the licentious household of Catharine Parr. Neither could daily intercourse with Seymour, Elizabeth, and the immoral apostates on whom Seymour's wife lavished her friendship, have been at all beneficial to so young a lady. If Jane were "truthful and conscientious,"* she could have had but little real respect for her much-married patroness,† whose duplicity she knew to be perfect. She was aware, too, that it was not the virtuous indignation of the Christian matron, but the jealousy of the neglected wife, that the scandalous behavior of her wicked husband and her shameless stepchild awoke in the breast of this unfortunate lady.

Seymour desired at first to send Jane home to her parents, but he speedily changed his mind and wrote a second letter to her father, in which he evinces the greatest anxiety to keep her. Elizabeth was perfectly

---

* Strickland.

† While Catharine Parr was queen she used to attend Mass with the king in the morning and hold Protestant worship privately, her own chaplains officiating at both. Jane often shared as well as witnessed her deceit, as she was in attendance on her person.

willing to marry this bold, bad man, if the consent of the council could be obtained. To act without this would invalidate her title to the crown. That Jane did not strongly reprobate the heartless conduct of this worthy pair to her late patroness, may be inferred from the fact that she continued on excellent terms with both.

The answer of Jane's father to Seymour is a remarkable production. " It bears,"* says Miss Strickland, " no token of the imbecility of mind, under which his partisans have been driven to shield the reproach of his vices." But it not unfrequently happens that persons who are imbecile as to honor, uprightness, truth, and virtue, are wonderfully quick-sighted and clear-headed when there is question of making money.

After many thanks and flatteries, Dorset goes on:

"Considering the state of my daughter and her tender years, wherein she shall hardly rule herself without a guide, lest she should, for want of a bridle, take too much head, and conceive such an opinion of herself that all such good behavior as she heretofore hath learned by the queen's and your most wholesome instructions should either altogether be quenched in her, or, at least, much diminished, I shall in most hearty wise require your lordship to commit her to the guidance of her mother, by whom, for the fear and duty she oweth her, she shall be more easily framed and ruled towards virtue, which I wish above all things to be plentiful in her." †

* Tudor Princesses.
† State Papers, in Tytler. Hayne's Burleigh Papers.

Here follow allusions to the necessity of putting Jane under the "eye and oversight of her mother" and "the addressing of her mind to humility, soberness, and obedience," which would seem to show that she was not exempt from the faults and foibles of other girls. If she had borne anything of the repute of a saint her father would not have written in this strain. His object was not, however, to get his daughter home and place her under his wife's tutelage, but to drive a better pecuniary bargain. His wife, actuated by the same base motives, joined in her husband's request, and Jane was returned to her parents. But it was no part of their policy to keep her. Their letters to Seymour bear the date of September 19th, and we find them in London, four days later, negotiating for the sale of their child. They received £500, the first instalment of her whole purchase-money, £2,000, an enormous sum for the time. By the following letter, still extant, Jane acknowledges the Lord-Admiral Seymour, as her guardian :

"To the Right Honorable and my singular good lord, the Lord-Admiral, give these.

" My duty to your lordship, in most humble wise remembered, with no less thanks for the gentle letters which I received from you. Thinking myself so much bound to your lordship for your great goodness towards me from time to time, that I cannot by any means be able to recompense the least part thereof, I purposed to write a few rude lines unto your lordship, rather as a token to show how much worthier I think your lordship's goodness than to give worthy thanks for the same; and these, my letters, shall be to testify unto you that, like as you have become towards me a loving and kind father, so I shall be always most ready to obey your godly monitions and good instructions, as becometh one upon whom you have heaped so many benefits. And thus, fearing I should trouble your lordship too much, I most humbly take my leave of your good lordship.

" Your humble servant during my life,

" JANE GRAYE."

Indorsed : " My Lady Jane, the first of October, 1548."

It would have puzzled Jane Grey to explain in what consisted the goodness of Lord Seymour which she lauds so highly; and the " Adonis of the Court " bestowing " godly monitions and good instructions " on his young ward, places that gentleman in rather a new light. The letter was evidently written at the dictation of her parents, who were not oblivious of the fact that Seymour, by the terms of their late contract, still owed them £1,500 for the wardship of their daughter.

Lord Seymour came at once to Bradgate for Lady Jane. He would take no receipt for her purchase-money, saying merrily, " The Lady Jane herself is in pledge for it." "And," says Miss Strickland, "for the vile consideration of a few hundred pounds, the parents of Lady Jane Grey saw their sweet child carried away from them by one of the greatest profligates of a profligate court, after having declared, under their autographs, which exist to this day, that he had no one in his establishment by whom her education was likely to be properly finished." *

Jane continued with Seymour, residing now at one, now at another, of his magnificent seats. In the winter he brought her to his town residence, Seymour

* Tudor Princesses.

Place, where she came under the influence of the notorious Bucer, from whom she imbibed the Calvinistic views she seems to have retained through life. The fact that Jane was allowed to have any intercourse with this wretched man, would indicate that Seymour was not very choice as to the persons whom he allowed to approach her. But that such a man was her religious monitor is preposterous. Four times had he stood up at the altar of Hymen; and as he had an extensive domestic establishment to maintain, he tried to live on princes and princely families. He may be considered a patron saint of Mormonism, as his name is signed, with the names of Luther and Melanchthon, to the "Church Dispensation," * whereby the licentious Philip of Hesse was permitted to confer the name and style of *wife* on two women at the same time. It was the public boast of this clerical miscreant that he had taken oaths and vows to the Most High, and violated them.

It was reported about this time that the Lord-Admiral meant to marry his ward. "When Thomas Parry† was conferring with Lord Seymour regarding his marriage with the Princess Elizabeth, he proposed going to see her." Parry "had no commission to say her grace would welcome him." "It is no matter now," said the widower, "for there has been a talk of late ; forsooth, they say now I shall marry the Lady Jane." There was no hope of marrying her to the

* See the whole document in Bossuet's Variations.

† Hayne's State Papers.

young king; but the Protector was as little satisfied that she should marry his brother. He applied to the Marquis and Marchioness of Dorset, demanding that their promise of espousing Jane to his eldest son should be ratified; but this worthy pair had not as yet received the whole of her purchase-money.

Speaking of his ward to Parr, Marquis of Northampton, Seymour said: "There will be much ado soon for my Lady Jane, Dorset's daughter; for the Lord Protector and his duchess mean to do all they can to obtain her for their heir, young Hertford. However, they will not succeed, for her father has given her up wholly to me, upon certain covenants between us."

Death frustrated all the ambitious projects which had been so long ripening in the plotting brain of Thomas Seymour. Arrested on "thirty charges," he claimed to be confronted with his accusers. But this act of justice was denied him, and the bill for his attainder passed both Houses, almost without opposition. The warrant for the illegal execution of this unfortunate man was signed by his brother, Edward Seymour, the Lord Protector; by his sister's son, King Edward VI., and by his friend and spiritual adviser, Cranmer. Latimer, who was a party to all the intrigues of Seymour, described his execution as an act of justice, averring that he had led a sensual, dissolute, irreligious life, and that God had clean forsaken him. " He was a covetous man, an horrible, covetous man; he was an ambitious man; I wish there were no more in England; he was a seditious man; I would he had left no more

behind.him. He died irksomely, dangerously, horri-
bly."* One scarcely knows which to reprobate most,
the unnatural brother, the cruel nephew, or the false
friend, to whom a wicked, and perhaps not unrepentant
sinner, appealed for consolation and assistance in his
last awful need, and who should, as a friend, and, still
more, as a minister of religion, have dropped the veil
of charitable silence over the mangled remains of the
murdered reprobate who had sought his ministrations.

Sir Thomas Seymour survived the consort whose
death seemed to open so wide a field to his ambition about six months. He was beheaded on Tower
Hill, March 20, 1549. Among the charges brought
against him were his precipitate marriage with Catharine Parr, his presumptuous courtship of the Lady
Elizabeth, and his design to marry the king to Lady
Jane Grey. Jane's father, Dorset, and Catharine Parr's
brother, were the chief witnesses examined against
against him on the last-named point. Jane was with
him at Seymour Place up to the moment of his arrest.

Jane was once more returned to her parents, who
were by no means disposed to give her a hearty welcome, being extremely dissatisfied at the failure of
their ambitious schemes. She was now in her fourteenth year. The king continued quite insensible to
whatever charms of mind and body she possessed, and
there is no evidence that her former *fiancé*, the son of
the Protector, renewed his suit. Her father had

* Latimer's Sermon on the Bad Life of Sir Thomas Seymour,
a most uncharitable, unchristian production.

already offended that powerful magnate by refusing to have her contract with Hertford ratified, and had recently to undergo several severe examinations before the king's council, as to his motives in selling the wardship of his eldest daughter to the king's uncle.

Whatever learning or accomplishments Jane acquired were probably stored up at this period. I do not see how she could have devoted any regular time to study while at court with Queen Catharine, or while traveling with that lady and her fourth husband from one magnificent estate to another, from Chelsea to Hanworth, from Sudeley Castle to Seymour Place, in the slow and ceremonious mode in which great people moved about in those days.

One John Aylmer had been appointed by her father as domestic tutor to his children. This Aylmer is described by Becon* as "a young man, singularly well learned both in the Latin and Greek tongues." Aylmer was an immoral man and a hypocrite; † his friend Roger Ascham bore a similar reputation. No conscientious father or guardian would have allowed such men in their families; still less intrust young girls to their care. Poor Jane was singularly unfortunate in her friends, and in those under whose tutelage she fell.

---

*Becon was an English Reformer. It is impossible to say how often he changed his creed. The Jesuit Waterworth styles him the "Prince of Scurrility."— *Origin and Development of Anglicanism.* I quote the Reformers wherever they refer to Jane or her connections, but cannot vouch for the accuracy of their statements.

† Hatton's Letter-Bag; Archbishops of Canterbury.

Aylmer was subsequently made a bishop by Elizabeth. He was the friend and companion of Fox, and the corrector of the work of that famous and infamous martyrologist; "upon which account," says a panegyrist of Jane, "we may read with greater confidence (?) Fox's minute and interesting account of her."

Ascham is our sole authority for the following anecdote, which, if true, is less creditable to Jane's filial affection than to her classical tastes. One day, having called at Bradgate, he found that all the family had gone out to amuse themselves in the park, except Lady Jane, who was reading Plato in the original. When Ascham asked her why she forbore to join in the merry pastimes of her family, she replied that all their sport was but a shadow of the pleasure she found in studying Plato. And, growing more confidential, she replied in answer to a second question: "Good Maister Roger. I will tell you a truth, which perchance you will marvel at. One of the greatest benefits that God ever gave me is, that he sent me so sharp and severe parents and so gentle a schoolmaster. For when I am in presence either of father or mother, whether I speak, keep silence, sit, stand, or go; eat, drink, be merry, or sad; be sewing, playing, dancing, or doing anything else, I must do it, as it were, in such weight, measure, and number, even so perfectly as God made the world, or else I am so sharply taunted, so cruelly threatened—yea, presently, sometimes with *pinches*, *nips*, and *bobs*, and other ways, which I will not name for the honor I bear them—so without measure misordered, that I think myself in hell, till the time comes when I must go to Maister Elmer, who teacheth me so gently, and with such fair allurements to learning, that I think all the time nothing while I am with him. And when I am called from him, I fall on weeping, because whatsoever else I do but learning, is full of great trouble, fear, and whole misliking, unto me. And thus my book hath been so much my pleasure, and bringeth daily to me more pleasure and more, that, in respect of it, all other pleasures, in very deed, be but trifles and troubles unto me." *

Jane and "Maister Roger" must have been alone when this conference took place; she would not have dared to speak so disrespectfully of her parents had she been attended as her rank required. One can hardly believe that a girl of fourteen would be allowed to confer alone with a man of Ascham's character or position. The young lady could use very strong language, too, although there is no evidence that swearing was among the accomplishments of her girlhood, as was the case with her sometime companion, the Lady Elizabeth.

* *The Schoolmaster*. Ascham is said to have written this book at the request of Sir Richard Sackville, as an argument against cruelty towards scholars. His friend Aylmer was Bishop of London at the time. Whether Jane spoke so freely to Ascham of her parents, or whether Ascham spoke in this way *for her*, and for a purpose, must remain undecided. It is just possible Ascham found Jane in *punishment*, and that her solitude on this occasion was not through love of Plato, but to expiate some of those faults for which her parents were accustomed to give her *pinches*, *nips*, and *bobs*, as she elegantly expresses herself.

It is well known that the Reformation was forced on England by foreign soldiers and foreign theologians. The latter class found a liberal patron in Jane's father. His house was their home. No matter how despicable these exiles were, morally and spiritually, the Marquis of Dorset allowed them to mingle freely with his wife and daughters. The material aid he bestowed on them, they repaid by the most fulsome flattery of himself and his family. In the letters of these men we trace some particulars of Jane. She added music to her more abstruse studies, and is blamed by them for devoting too much time to it. Her passion for dress gave them much anxiety. Fond as Aylmer is said to have been of his pupil, and cordially as she is supposed to have reciprocated his affection, he was afraid to correct her on either point, which argues badly for the sweetness of her temper. He writes to Bullinger desiring *him* to admonish his pupil as to "what embellishment and adornment are becoming in a young woman professing godliness. Moreover," he adds, "I wish you would prescribe to her the length of time she may properly devote to music, for in this respect the people of England err beyond measure, while all their exertions are made for the sake of ostentation." This *Zurich Letter* was not intended for the eyes of the Dorset family, and cannot be considered at all complimentary to Jane.

The wonderful letters ascribed to this demi-royal lady I pass over; because if they be genuine, of which there is considerable doubt, it would be impossible to separate the productions of the pupil from the corrections of the master. Sir Harris Nicholas, who has investigated the matter most thoroughly, assures us that there is no ground whatever for most of the marvelous stories which have been narrated of Lady Jane. He doubts, and with reason, her extensive knowledge of Greek. A young lady who devoted so much time to dress, and to the study of music "for ostentation," could not spare much leisure for the classics.

The deaths of Jane's two uncles on the same day, of the plague, raised her parents to the rank of Duke and Duchess of Suffolk. A severe illness of the new duchess called Lady Jane to her sick-chamber at Richmond; but though apparently sick unto death, she recovered. One longs to know whether Jane roamed through the spacious apartments of this newly-acquired monastic property. If so she must have met a sight appalling to any one who possessed the slightest nobility of soul. When her father became owner of this suppressed monastery he found in one of the side chapels the embalmed and unburied body of poor James IV. of Scotland, killed at Flodden Field. Instead of giving decent burial to the remains of this brave and unfortunate monarch, who was moreover his wife's uncle by marriage, the newly-made duke permitted the body to be thrown into an old lumber-room, among timber, lead, and other rubbish; in which state Stowe saw it, as he informs us in his *Survey of London*. Jane was old enough to feel rightly about the indignity put upon the fallen warrior. If she expressed her feelings it would probably have availed nothing, for her parents were thoroughly base and un-principled.

From Jane's childhood, she had much intercourse with her royal cousin, the Princess Mary. Mary was exceedingly kind to the younger branches of the royal family. In her accounts are several entries of presents to "my cousin Jane," who paid many visits to her formidable kinswoman during the latter years of her life. Sometimes when the whole family of the Greys, consisting of father, mother, and three daughters, visited the princess, Lady Jane remained with her after the departure of the rest. At the Christmas of 1551, festivities were kept up in Jane's family for nearly a month, during which the Greys hired players for the entertainment of their guests. Jane made all these "progresses" on horseback; and they must have left her scant leisure for Plato. In the spring of 1552 she suffered from severe illness.

On her recovery she began anew her correspondence with the Swiss Reformers, and sent a present of gloves and a ring to the lady who was styled by courtesy Madame Bullinger. In the summer of 1552 Jane visited her royal kinsman, Edward VI., but, though he received her kindly, he was as blind to her charms as ever. Later on she paid a visit to her cousin, the Princess Mary, who presented her with a rich dress. "What shall I do with it?" asked Jane of the lady who brought it. "Marry," replied the messenger, "wear it to be sure." "Nay," returned the little hypocrite, "that would be a shame to follow the Lady Mary who leaveth

God's word, and leave my Lady Elizabeth who fol-
loweth God's word." *   Jane knew perfectly well what
the Lady Elizabeth was; and the Princess Mary was,
perhaps, the only woman of principle and uprightness
with whom she was acquainted.   But Mary was suffering grievous persecution for her faith at this period, and
Jane, mean little creature that she was, found it perfectly safe to strike one who was already under a cloud.

Another incident gives one a still worse impression
of the character of Jane.   While she was on a visit to
the Princess Mary, Lady Wharton, a Catholic, in passing by the chapel door, paused to make a genuflection
before the Blessed Sacrament.   Lady Jane, who knew
very well why her Catholic companion bowed, asked
"if the princess were in the chapel," and on receiving a
negative reply, said, "Why, then, do you courtesy?"
"I courtesy to Him that made me," was the natural
reply of Lady Wharton.   "Nay," retorted Lady Jane,
"but did not the baker make Him?"

One of Jane's panegyrists — she has had no biographers — calls this a "lively sally."   The wit of this
"sally" is within the compass of the intellect of an ordinary child of six; the blasphemy is revolting, and
argues an irreligious mind.   The impoliteness of insulting Mary's religion in her own house is a poor proof of
Jane's "extreme amiability." †   If Jane, in her numerous visits to her connections, could deport herself in no
better style than this, it is no longer surprising that, in

* Aylmer.

† Burke's Men and Women of the Reformation, vol. ii.

her hour of need, she found herself friendless. She must have had a peculiar talent for making enemies.

These anecdotes are recorded to Jane's credit; but to appreciate rightly the audacity of that young woman, insulting in a most uncalled-for manner a royal kinswoman, double her age, and her hostess, we must not view the hapless Mary Tudor by the lurid glare of the Smithfield fires. At this period Mary was known only for her virtues. Amid the most extraordinary and heart-rending trials and temptations that ever beset a royal maiden, she had led a life of unswerving integrity, every day of which was marked by acts of kindness and beneficence. It is said that Mary, having heard these "precious anecdotes," never after loved her cousin Jane as before. Very likely; how could she love or respect a young woman who repaid her princely hospitality with gratuitous insults to the faith for which she had suffered, and was still suffering, bitter persecutions, and for which she would have deemed it an honor to shed her blood?*

*The above story is related by Fox, Strype, and Speed. Aylmer, when he became one of Elizabeth's bishops, relates the former in his *Harbor for Faithful True Subjects.* He tells another precious story in the same. Speaking of the visit of Mary of Lorraine, Queen-Regent of Scotland, in November, 1551, during which Jane appeared at court, with her mother, in great splendor of attire, he insinuates that the beauty and rich apparel of the blooming dowager, and her train of Scotch and French ladies, wrought a complete revolution in the already too magnificent appointments of the English belles; and he adds that the Princess Elizabeth was the only lady about the court who was not carried away by this evil example. " So that all the ladies went

The miserable reign of Edward VI. was now drawing to a close. Edward Seymour had followed his
brother to the block, the first and last victim of an iniquitous law which he himself had made. Jane's father
joined the dominant party, now headed by the crafty,
unscrupulous Dudley, who, like his predecessor, helped
himself to a dukedom, and is historically known as
Northumberland. Jane's family removed to the neighborhood of the court. They lived partly at Sheen and
partly at Gray's Inn, the former being contiguous to
Sion House, the favorite country residence of the new
duke. As the Seymour's were in disgrace since the
violent death of the Protector, it is not probable that
young Hertford renewed his proposals for the hand of
Jane; neither would her parents have bestowed her on
the impoverished heir of a fallen house. She was now
in her eighteenth year. It became expedient to dis-
pose of her in marriage, and her parents' choice fell on
Guilford Dudley, a youth of nineteen or twenty,* the
only unmarried son of Northumberland.

with their hair frounced, curled, and double curled, except the
Lady Elizabeth, who altered nothing, but kept her old shame-faced-
ness." The truth is, the Queen-Regent, having just lost her son,
was attired from head to foot in the deepest mourning, as were
also her ladies, their very faces muffled in black, according to the
lugubrious etiquette of the French court at that period. And
Elizabeth, not relishing the contingency that the ladies of the
Grey family might take precedence of her on a state occasion, did
not come near her brother's court during the stay of his distinguished guest.

　* Guilford's elder brother, Robert, is said to have been born at
the same day and hour as Queen Elizabeth, which Camden attri-

Jane positively refused to become the bride of this ill-mannered boy, and consented only when her father and mother beat her into a reluctant compliance. From the few particulars we have of her life we cannot close our eyes to the fact that she possessed no firmness of character, and could be beaten or scolded into anything. She was not even free to marry young Dudley, being legally contracted to another; and if she had possessed a tithe of the virtue attributed to her she would have suffered death rather than break her faith to the man to whom she had plighted it, and who actually *was* her husband according to the law of God, insomuch that Queen Mary subsequently treated her marriage with Guilford as a nullity.

On Whitsunday, 1553, Jane Grey became Jane Dudley. At the same time her sister Catharine was married to Lord Herbert, and her sister Mary solemnly betrothed to her kinsman, Lord Grey, of Wilton. Both

---

butes to a mysterious conjunction of their planets. If this be correct, and if it be certain that Guilford was the youngest son of his parents, he could not have been twenty, as Miss Strickland states, when he was married to Jane, May, 1553. He is the founder in Christian countries of the heathen practice of calling people by surnames in preference to Christian names. This custom is confined to English-speaking countries. It was only because Northumberland could not mate Guilford with Lady Margaret Clifford that he selected for him a daughter of the aspiring house of Grey; the title to the royal succession being considered better than that of Jane Grey's mother and family, as her (Margaret's) mother, Lady Eleanor Brandon, was not born till after the death of the ladies whom Charles Brandon styled his spouses, previous to his lofty, but unlawful, alliance with Mary Tudor, sister of Henry VIII.

lords deserted their ladies. These luckless marriages were celebrated with extraordinary pomp, much to the annoyance of the populace, who evidently thought such gorgeous nuptial festivities in very bad taste, it being known that their young King, who was related to almost all the contracting parties, was then in a dying condition. Ill as he was, he did not forget to order the master of his wardrobe to deliver a wedding present to the young bride, who did not object to it as on a former occasion, though it consisted of apparel far richer than that which Princess Mary had given her out of her poverty. The dying monarch's gift was an ominous one. Cloth of gold and silver, jewels, rich tissues, all from the forfeited effects of Jane's murdered father-in-law, and her imprisoned mother-in-law, the late Duke and the Duchess of Somerset. Among the manors and domains granted her was one equally ill-omened, Stanfield Hall, from the church tower of which swayed the blackened corpse of Kett, the Hospital Monk,* hung in chains, after being dipped in pitch to preserve it, and clothed in the monastic habit. The frightful memento of the ruin of a religious house, oscillating forever in the wind, must have been a weird spectacle for a youthful bride. We soon find Jane with her mother at Sheen, also a suppressed monastery.

The amiable Agnes Strickland, who has written so eloquently of the loveliness of Jane's character in

---

* The body of the brave monk, William Kett, dangled from the highest tower of his monastic church till the day of Queen Elizabeth's death, March 25, 1603.

domestic life, has not failed to inform us that she was at continual variance with the members of her own family. The case was not altered when marriage removed her to a new family. The same authority informs us, not noticing the inconsistency of her statements, that Jane "had a deep dislike to her husband's father and mother; she dreaded and distrusted the one, and abhorred the other;" feelings which a person eminent for "holiness," or "extreme amiability," certainly would not have entertained. Indeed, we have this under Jane's own hand, in a letter to Queen Mary:

"The Duchess of Northumberland promised me, at my nuptials with her son, that she would be contented if I remained at home with my mother. Soon after, my husband being present, she declared 'that it was publicly said there was no hope of the king's life' (and this was the first time I heard of the matter); and further observed to her husband, 'that I ought not to leave her house,' adding, 'that when it pleased God to call King Edward to His mercy, I ought to hold myself in readiness, as I might be required to go to the Tower, since His Majesty had made me his heir.' These words, told me offhand and without preparation, agitated my soul, and for a time seemed to stupefy me. Yet they afterwards seemed to me exaggerated, and to mean little but boasting, and by no means of consequence sufficient to keep me from going to my mother." Jane evidently resisted the entreaties of her mother-in-law, for she proceeds: "The duchess was enraged against me, and said that 'it was my duty, at all events, to remain near my husband, from whom I should *not* go. Not venturing to disobey her, I remained at her house four or five days;" a great concession, considering that these domestic altercations took place during the honeymoon. She carried out her own will as to leaving her mother-in-law, for we find her in Chelsea a little later, and dangerously ill.

Meanwhile the king, whose death was hourly expected, expired on the sixth of July, the anniversary of the judicial murder of the greatest layman of the age, Sir Thomas More. The royal boy, at the dictation of the plotters by whom he was surrounded, left the crown to Lady Jane Dudley, entirely passing over her mother, Frances Brandon, through whom Jane derived her royal descent from Henry VII. and Elizabeth, heiress of the brilliant house of York. Why Lady Frances was set aside in favor of her daughter, no historian has adequately explained. The death of the king was concealed for four days, and on the tenth of July, Jane, having come by water to the Tower, was there publicly received as queen. At Sion House she had already received the homage of her parents, of the father and mother of her husband, and of several members of the council. Ridley, the usurping Bishop of London, harangued the populace at St. Paul's Cross on the illegitimacy of the sisters of the deceased king, and the blessings likely to result to the country from the prospective reign of Jane Dudley. But his bold and eloquent words evoked no enthusiastic response in the multitude. Their hearts were with the persecuted heiress of the crown, not with the triumphant Grey and Dudley factions.

Meanwhile, Mary Tudor, whose life had been heretofore so retiring, so gentle, so benevolent, now that she had a right to maintain, showed the lion-like spirit of her sturdy race. Her proceedings in this most critical conjuncture evince extraordinary courage and prudence. She fled towards Cambridgeshire with her retinue, and was sheltered by the hospitable Huddlestones during the first night of her perilous queenship. Her enemies were on her track. Early next morning, but not before she had assisted at Mass, Mary journeyed towards her house at Kenninghall, some say in the disguise of a market woman. On turning her steed to cast a last look on the hospitable roof that had sheltered her, the venerable pile burst into flames in her sight. Her enemies thought the fugitive heiress was within the walls. "Let it blaze away," said Mary, "I will build Huddlestone a better house." The present stately mansion, Sawston Hall, built at her expense, remains to prove how magnificently Queen Mary kept her promise, and how grateful she was to the friends of her adversity.

The measures taken by the new sovereign from this time until she displayed her royal standard from the towers of Framlingham Castle, are matters of general history. "Had Elizabeth been the heroine of this enterprise instead of Mary," says Miss Strickland, "it would have been lauded to the skies as one of the grandest efforts of female courage and ability the world had ever known. And so it was," the same lady generously adds, "whether it be praised or not."

All authorities, or nearly all, assert that Jane received the news of her elevation with anything but exultation. In the letter which she wrote to excuse her conduct to Queen Mary, she asserts the same, though she admits that she at once (having recovered from her very natural surprise) accepted the position, saying: "If to succeed be indeed my duty and my right, God will aid me to govern the realm to His glory." Jane threw all the blame on her mother-in-law, which was rather ungenerous, as that lady's husband had just had his head cut off. Sharon Turner will not acquit her of all blame. "Jane Grey had descended," says he, "from her social probity to take a royalty which was another's inheritance, and, although importunity had extorted her acquiescence, yet her first reluctance gave testimony, even to herself, that she had not erred in ignorance of what was right; and no one but herself could know how much the temptation of the offered splendor had operated beyond the solicitation, to seduce her to accept what she ought to have continued to refuse."*

When it is remembered that Jane was educated to become a queen-consort, that she knew that by the will of Henry VIII., only Mary and Elizabeth, last surviving members of a short-lived family,† stood between her and the crown, it is very difficult to believe in the

---

* History of Edward and Mary.

† No Tudor, except Elizabeth, lived to be old.

ignorance of the laws which she pleads when she endeavors to shirk responsibility of her doings as " Nine-Days'
Queen," on the shoulders of her aiders and abettors.
I cannot see that Jane, judged by her actions, ever
rises above the commonplace, though she sometimes
falls below it. I say nothing here of her personal ingratitude towards Queen Mary. An honorable woman
would lay her head on the block, rather than be guilty
of that execrable vice.

The public occurrences of the *nine days*, are recorded
in general history; the private life of Queen Jane was
disturbed by the extravagance of her husband, who insisted on being crowned king. Jane soothed him by
promising to make him king by act of Parliament,
which it appears she had no notion of doing. She told
two of her council next day, that she was willing to
make him a duke, but not a king. Guilford, however,
swore he would be no duke, but King of England. He
was actually called *King Guilford* by his own faction,
and in several foreign dispatches. It appears by her
letter, already referred to, that King Guilford " struck
her, and swore at her on several occasions "; also that
she was "*maltreated*" by his mother. This unfortunate young woman seems to have been utterly incapable of winning the respect or affection of those about
her. Not one of her cabinet remained loyal to her,
while her much maligned rival was followed by many
thousands who served her cause at their own expense.
To add to her difficulties, the King Guilford business
was making her ridiculous. Part of her brief queen-

ship was spent upon a sick-bed, poisoned, as she charitably suggests, by her unbeloved mother-in-law. In
common justice it must be remembered, that the Dudleys and others, about whom Jane speaks and writes
with such unchristian bitterness, * have never had any
opportunity of repeating *their* version of the story.

The following is the cautious and accurate Lingard's
estimate of the Epiphany Queen:

" Jane has been described to us as a young woman of
gentle manners, and superior talents, addicted to the
study of the Scriptures and the classics, but fonder of
dress than suited the austere notions of the Reformed
preachers. . . . Modern writers have attributed to
her much, of which she seems to be ignorant herself.
The beautiful language which they put into her mouth,
her forcible reasoning in favor of the claim of Mary, her
philosophic contempt for the splendors of royalty, her
refusal to accept a crown which was not her right, and
her reluctant submission to the commands of her

---

* In the succeeding reign, the enemies of Jane's brother-in-law,
Robert Dudley, the most favored among the favorites of Elizabeth the Unclean, used to say that " he was son of a duke, brother
of a *king* (Guilford), grandson of an esquire who was put to death
as an extortioner, great grandson of a carpenter; the carpenter was
the only honest man in the family, and the only one who died in
his bed." Despite her many promises of marriage to Leicester,
it was said, and it proved true, that Elizabeth would never marry
so mean a peer as Robin Dudley, noble only in two descents, and
both of them stained with the block. This Dudley lived to have
several wives, two of them simultaneously, whom he facetiously
styled his Old and New Testaments. Guilford Dudley's family
was much beneath the family of Jane Grey.

parents, must be considered as the fictions of historians, who, in their zeal to exalt the character of their heroine, seem to have forgotten that she was only sixteen years of age." *

We could wish to make this article exhaustive, but the space at our disposal forbids, and we must pass over the better known incidents of the "nine days." What need to give in full the lengthy proclamation in which "Jane, by the grace of God, Queen," sets forth her titles and her claims? Was she not rather like her ancestress, Eleanor of Aquitaine, "Queen by the wrath of God"? Mary put down the rebellion almost without a blow. Her illustrious grandmother, Isabella the Catholic, could not have adopted a more prompt, vigorous, and merciful policy. For her future disquiet, she forgave almost everyone concerned in the late plot to effect her ruin. Even Jane's father, who had borne arms against her, Jane's mother, who had held up the train of her usurping daughter, Jane's Lord Chancellor, Goodrich,† who had sent her an insolent message during his brief tenure of office under Jane, all were pardoned. True, "Guilford Dudley and his wife" were tried, and pleaded guilty in the historic Guildhall, but it was understood that Jane would never have to pay the penalty of her treasons.

Charles V. advised his cousin to allow the law to take its course, but Mary replied, "that she could not find it in her heart to put her unfortunate cousin to

---

* Lingard's History of England, vol. vi.
† Lives of English Chancellors, Campbell, vol. ii.

death." The queen, whose clemency was so ill-requited, added, that Jane had been but a puppet in the hands of Northumberland, and, knowing well that she had been compelled to marry a man with whom she never could be happy, took the earliest opportunity of asserting that she could not legally be Dudley's* wife, as she had been validly contracted to another. In fact, it was not possible that Mary could do more in favor of her rival than she did. Jane's prison was a palace; she was allowed to recreate in the queen's gardens; and even on Tower Hill her friends might have free access to her. The Harleian chronicler records that he dined in her company, in the rooms of the lieutenant on which occasion she remarked, with good reason: "The queen's majesty is a merciful princess." Her remarks on her father-in-law were not so edifying. His head had fallen from the scaffold a week previously, "but," says Miss Strickland, "she had not yet forgiven him."

* Guilford Dudley, with his brothers, John, Ambrose, Robert, and Henry, was confined in the Beauchamp Tower, a military structure of the twelfth century. They were allowed to take exercise on the leads, and, except in the case of Guilford, their wives had access to them. Robert's wife was the celebrated Amy Robsart, whom Scott has immortalized in Kenilworth. In the prison-room occurs twice the name JANE, written, perhaps, by one of the Dudleys who suffered so much in her cause. It is said to be the only memorial of Lady Jane preserved in the Tower. As, however, Jane was not beloved by her husband or his family, it is just possible that the name JANE was inscribed by Guilford, in memory of his mother, whose name was Jane, and who passionately loved her tall, handsome, youngest son. The monument of this lady is still to be seen in Chelsea Church.

Jane's father, with his brothers, Lords Thomas and John Grey, were soon again in arms against the sovereign who had so recently pardoned them. Suffolk attempted to purchase his own pardon by betraying his friends and even his own brother. But he had put it out of the queen's power to pardon him now, and his daughter, who had been a sort of hostage for his loyalty, shared his ruin. Mary's councillors declared that revolt and insurrection would never cease while her rival lived, and Mary was persuaded to sign the death-warrant of "Guilford Dudley and his wife."

Feckenham procured a respite of three days. Guilford desired to see his wife, a wife who was to cost that aspiring youth his head, the queen consented, but Jane declined. I would like her better if she had gratified his last expressed wish, for it may be that he wanted to ask pardon for "the blows and curses" with which he had afflicted her during the eight or nine weeks of their married life, previous to their imprisonment. But even misfortune awakened neither affection nor sympathy in this ill-matched pair, at least not in Jane.

Feckenham, "the amiable abbot," * whose charity to the poor "allured the minds of his adversaries to benevolence," † came to the Tower to console the last days of this unhappy woman. She accepted his ministrations, thanked him for his kindness and humanity, and even embraced the venerable divine ‡ on the scaffold, but I deem it impossible to say in what phase of

---

* Froude.   † Camden.   Feckenham died in prison for his faith, in the reign of Elizabeth.   ‡ Bishop Godwin.

Protestantism she died. She had been made a widow about an hour before her death. Crucifix in hand, Feckenham stood by her side to the last. Jane wore a black cloth and velvet costume of great elegance. She addressed a few words to the spectators, saying that she most justly deserved the punishment she was about to receive, for allowing herself, although unwilling, to be the instrument of the ambition of others. She confessed that "when she knew the word of God she neglected it, and loved herself and the world," and thanked Him that He had given her a respite to repent. Having asked the prayers of the people, she suffered her two maids to remove her outer robe, while she herself tied a "fair handkerchief" before her eyes and besought the executioner to dispatch her quickly. She had just repeated the psalm, *Have mercy on me, O God, according to Thy great Mercy.* She now felt for the block, saying, "*Where is it? What shall I do?*" and, being guided to the spot, knelt down, and cried out: "*Lord! into Thy hands I commend my spirit.*" She laid her head on the block, but the five minutes allowed for "royal mercy"—a period of horrible suspense—elapsed before the powerful headsman did the deed of blood. At one blow her head was severed from her body, about noon, February 12, 1554. Guilford, whom she had married nine months previously, was beheaded on Tower Hill; Jane, on account of her royal descent, suffered on the green* within the Tower. Both were

* The precise spot, nearly opposite the door of St. Peter's Chapel, is indicated by a large oval of dark flints. Here, too,

buried in the church close by, between the mangled forms of Anne Boleyn and Catharine Howard.

Thus perished, in her eighteenth year, the unfortunate Lady Jane Grey, "through her own want of firmness in the first instance,"* and in the second place, as Stowe justly says, "for fear of further troubles and stir for her title." No human being can read her sad story without sympathy and regret. It is hard to think, even after three centuries, of the fair head of a girl of eighteen rolling from the scaffold. Queen Mary regretted the political necessity more than the parents and sisters of the victim; though that princess was not one to feel *repentant* for doing what she deemed to be her duty. The weird stories of the bleeding form of Jane haunting the royal pillow of her successful rival have their source in some lively imagination. Mary was sorry for her luckless cousin, but I doubt if she ever felt the least remorse of conscience for allowing the sentence of Judge Morgan, on "Guilford Dudley and his wife," to take effect. Nevertheless, I am heartily sorry that Mary did not, at all risks, continue to exercise in their regard the royal prerogative of mercy. Still Jane's early death has been the best friend to her fame.

In personal appearance Jane was not grand or noble. Her features were very small, her forehead so high as almost to amount to a deformity, but the expression

Anne Boleyn and Catharine Howard had been murdered. The instrument used at Jane's execution is shown. See Bayley's History of the Tower of London.

* Flanagan's History of the Church of England, vol. ii.

sweet and pleasing. In height she was little more than a dwarf, and was therefore accustomed to wear gilt *chopines** (cork soles), which elevated her about four inches. Her dress was of the richest, and her portraits show her rather vulgarly overladen with finery. That in the Earl of Stamford's collection is by far the most pleasing. Tytler admits that " Plato left his pupil leisure for the *toilette*." All her portraits represent her older than she was ; but much unhappiness checkered her young life, and pangs of the heart, no less than years, leave their impress on the countenance.

Poor Jane Grey, the Epiphany Queen, the Nine-Days' Wonder, how little have they studied your sad story, who paint you as a paragon of human learning and divine perfection ! No one regrets your tragic fate more than I, but truth is dearer to me than the sweetness of an historic memory.

But Jane's mother, was ever woman so tried ? Her daughter, her son-in-law, her husband, his brother — all fell beneath the axe within a few days. Could anything console her under such bereavements ? Must not the life current have frozen in her veins, and her heart turned to stone, at these horrors ? What wonder, if, like Rachel, she refuses to be comforted ; like Niobe, weeps herself into a statue ?

Alas, alas, Jane's father was scarcely cold when her mother, emulating the cruel Henry VIII., who plucked " his Mayflower," Jane Seymour, before the blood of Anne Boleyn was dry on the scaffold, married her

* Disraeli's Curiosities of Literature.

groom, Adrian Stokes, a youth of twenty. "Some call the Reformation a tragedy," says Erasmus, "but I call it a comedy, because every new scene ends in a marriage." Was this marriage, certainly one of the most revolting in history, a tragedy or a comedy? The beheaded Duke of Suffolk had been Frances Brandon's husband from her sixteenth year. He was beheaded February 24th, 1554; his brother, Lord Thomas Grey, March 8. On the twentieth of November, 1554, the mother of Jane Grey gave another heir to the crown, whose father was a groom, and who bore the plebeian name of Stokes! Her sisters, Lady Catharine and Lady Mary, were completely neglected by their mother, who was absorbed in her young spouse; but Queen Mary had pity on these desolate girls, took them into her service as maids of honor, and lavished on them the affection denied them by their worthless mother, as they bore honorable testimony when they were being persecuted to death by their cousin, Queen Elizabeth.*

* Lady Catharine Grey married her sister Jane's betrothed husband, Lord Hertford; Lady Mary, a dwarf and deformed, married the largest man in London, Sergeant-Porter Keyes. For these "offenses" both ladies were imprisoned, and died state prisoners. They were, besides, entirely destitute, their mother having bestowed all the property in her gift upon Adrian, the groom. Like so many families enriched by Church plunder, the wealth of the Greys did not reach a second generation. Henry Grey, Jane's father, was so notorious for his plunder of churches and monasteries as to draw upon himself the animadversions of a man fully as infamous as himself, Thomas Cranmer,* who besought him to cease his robberies and sacrileges. Even the "gentle Jane," on her marriage, was dowered with church plunder.

* Strype's Cranmer.

I

THE first great battle between the Jacobites and the Williamites occurred July 1, O. S., 1690. The writer stood on the historic spot 200 years after that strangest of battles, between sire and son, had driven the one forever from Ireland, and almost secured to the other the crown he had coveted since the day of his marriage with his uncle's heiress. The astute and ambitious prince married his cousin for her expectations, not for affection. Many years elapsed before any love appeared on either side. His eye was always fixed on the throne which would be hers if her fair Italian stepmother bore no son. And should it come to her, it would be his, for, as he elegantly said, later: " He would not be his wife's subject, nor would he be tied to her apron-strings." From the hour of his marriage, he did all he could to create or foment discontent in England; and shortly after the birth of his wife's brother, he came over as the " Deliverer."

The Boyne, which laves the southern frontier of Louth, the smallest county in Ireland, and forms part of the northern boundary of Meath, one of the largest, rises out of a holy well in Kildare, and is named after St. Boyne, Within four miles of its mouth is the ancient town of Drogheda, situated in two counties and two dioceses. From its heights, or from the splendid viaduct that spans the river, may be seen the famous field on which William III. was victor and James II. vanquished. From the town to "King William's Glen," north of the river, or to "King James's Hill," south, is about a mile. You can go by the south side, cross the bridge at "the field," and return by the Rampart on Meath side; there is no mistaking the fatal field. It is marked by a massive obelisk, 150 feet high, on a huge irregular granite boulder, some 20 feet square. The date is in the Old Style. Other nations were ten days later. Rather than "quarrel with the stars," they followed the Gregorian, or New Style. Obelisks are not common in Ireland. An ugly one marks the spot on which George IV., the next king who visited Ireland after William III., landed at Dunleary, now Kingstown. On the rocky base of the Egyptian landmark that overshadows the Boyne is the following pretty inscription:

"Sacred to the memory of King William III., who, on July 1, 1690, passed the river near this place to attack James II. at the head of a Popish army advantageously posted on the south side of it, and did, on that day, by a single battle, secure to us and to our posterity, our liberty, laws, and religion. In consequence of this action, James left the kingdom and fled to France.

"This memorial of our deliverance was erected in the ninth year of the reign of George II., the first stone being laid by Lionel Sackville, Lord Lieutenant of the kingdom of Ireland, 1736."

The people of Drogheda, a most Catholic place, have always before their eyes this remarkable pillar, which says that this battle secured to their country her liberty, laws, and religion. Even to the Williamites in Ireland, nothing was *secured* till the honorable capitulation of Limerick. Nor were the liberties and religion of the people restored to them, even partially, till over a century later. And the laws were made so unjust, cruel, and repressive of everything the people gloried in, that it has been said, and not entirely untruly, that the ordinary idea of patriotism with the Irish peasant was: "To be agin the law."

II

THE ground towards the battlefield is varied by low green hills. Suddenly your horse makes a quick turn, and, behold, you are in the beauteous valley of the Boyne. Within a few yards of the obelisk, the river is spanned by a handsome iron and stone bridge, with latticed iron sides, painted white. Heavy piers of limestone support it. Visitors sometimes record their sentiments on the dead white of the parapets. Every available spot was covered with pencil scribbling. Some sentences were patriotic, others affectionate. Strange, there was not a line complimentary to the "glorious, pious, and immortal memory" of the peevish manikin whose name is inseparably connected with the sweeping river.

From the bridge are seen some fine country residences. Old Bridge House, in the midst of smiling meadows that slope to the water's edge, is a charming and stately home. A rising ground, thickly wooded, leads to Donore Hill in the waving plains of fertile Meath.* From this height James viewed the contest he shared only vicariously. The spot on which the timorous, irresolute prince stood, in an ancient church-yard sanctified by a ruined church, is marked by a group of ash trees. Further off is Duleek, whither a part of his army retreated after the fight. On the ancient bridge, built 1587, some of his cannon were placed.

III

JAMES landed at Kinsale, March 12, 1689. The house in which he rested, now an apothecary's shop, has little to distinguish it from its fellows, save some ancient stucco work. In Cork, he slept at the Dominican Priory, whose site is now occupied by a handsome Convent of Mercy, St. Marie's of the Isle. The Mayor of Cork, 1688, was Patrick Roche; the Sheriffs, Messrs. French and Morough. The Mayor, 1689, was Dominick Sarsfield; the Sheriffs, Messrs. Mead and Nagle. James heard Mass at the Franciscan Church, North Side, of which no vestige now remains. He was supported through the streets by two Franciscan Friars, and followed by several members of the same Order, in their brown habits. His host was the Earl of Clancarty; he created Tyrconnel, who met him

---

* It is said that one acre in Meath is worth two acres else-where, because of the great fertility of the soil.

in Cork, a duke, and thus Frances Jennings became a duchess long before her sister, Sarah of Marlborough. James was the first sovereign who visited Ireland since the Plantagenet epoch. Everywhere he was received with open arms; his early reputation for bravery made his supporters hope they had a king equal to the emergency that had arisen. On Palm Sunday, March 24th, he made his triumphal entry into Dublin. As he rode through the streets multitudes cheered him on every side; tapestry hung from the windows of the rich,—the poor draped theirs with blankets. The season being ten days later than the date, O. S., vegetation was advanced, and green boughs and spring flowers added to the decorations. A solemn *Te Deum* was sung in Christ Church, in thanksgiving for the king's arrival.* His Majesty issued a proclamation convoking a Parliament for May 7th.

It has been acutely said that James II. was a Catholic in religion and a Protestant in politics. His chief enemies were the descendants of those English and Scotch fanatics for whom his grandfather had stolen thousands of acres in Ulster, and the Cromwellian settlers, whose chief also had robbed the Irish to enrich their enemies. For the latter spoliation, the "merry monarch" made scarcely any reparation, preferring to act on Clarendon's infamous policy: Humor your enemies; you are always sure of your friends. Everything

---

*King James, while in Dublin, attended Mass in Christ Church. The Lord Deputies, or Viceroys, and the Lord Mayor of Dublin used to be sworn into office in Christ Church.

James could do to lessen his chances of success, which were good, he did. He went to Derry to protect his Protestant subjects, who were tolerably well able to take care of themselves and had powerful allies. His General, Hamilton, had almost succeeded in taking the city, but James thought his conditions too easy. Had this unlucky king remained in France and commissioned others to fight his battles, history would have a different tale to tell of the Jacobite wars in Ireland. The only ill treatment meted out to him on Irish soil was bestowed in sight of Derry ; he was refused admittance within its gates, and, to add injury to insult, one of his contumacious subjects fired on his sacred person. He returned to Dublin to meet his Parliament, in which, to the evident disgust of Macaulay, the *O's* and *Mac's* predominated. It was mainly a Catholic assembly, natural enough in a Catholic country, though this, too, failed to find favor with the Whig historian, or rather, romancist. Parliament was held in an old Dominican Priory occupying the site from which now arises the massive Four Courts. James appeared on a throne in the House of Lords in royal robes, wearing a crown.* He thanked the Irish for remaining true to him when his other kingdoms had deserted his cause. It was the last Parliament he opened, and though its proceedings

* James put a Catholic Irishman, Richard Talbot, Earl of Tyrconnel, at the head of affairs in Ireland ; this was one of his best appointments. Unhappily, future Viceroys were not selected with a view to the happiness of the people over whom they were placed. Queen Victoria and her advisers have not yet imitated the liberality, or rather justice, of the much maligned James II.

may not have been acceptable at Westminster, for which the Lords and Commons of Ireland were not legislating, yet some wise and honest measures were passed. Men, who for a century and a half had been persecuted for their religion established full liberty of conscience for all, and they repealed the Act of Settlement, by which Cromwell had legalized the robbery of the lawful proprietors of their estates. "Though papists," says Grattan, "they were not slaves; they wrung a Constitution from James before they accompanied him to the field."

Ireland had been nearly wiped out of existence by Cromwell. Goldwin Smith says, "The descendants of the Cromwellian land-owners became probably the very worst upper class with which a country was ever afflicted." The real owners were wandering about in misery, or had sought refuge in foreign lands; the Restoration brought no relief. "This country has been perpetually rent and torn since His Majesty's return," said Lord Deputy, Essex. "Men beaten with whips in Cromwell's time cry out they are now beaten with scorpions," wrote Bishop French, of Ferns. Since the accession of James, however, Ireland had enjoyed peace, and shown extraordinary recuperative power. To aid their King, the nobility equipped many military companies at their own expense; the country had been drained of its men by transportation and incessant warfare, but, "there was life in the old land yet," and had it been possible to save the Stuart King from himself, and put a greater soldier like Owen Roe O'Neill of an earlier era, or Patrick Sarsfield, who represented Dublin in James's Parliament, over the regiments hurriedly raised by McMahon, O'Reilly, Maguire, Nugent, and others, and let James do what his successors have generally done since, keep far from war's alarms, Ireland might have been saved to the Stuarts. In justice to James, it must be admitted he was not fighting on his own element; the qualifications of England's greatest admiral would not necessarily make him successful on land service; sailors fighting on land do no better than soldiers in a naval engagement.

IV

WILLIAM III. landed at Carrickfergus, under the walls of the castle, June 14, 1690. The stone on which he first set foot is still pointed out; from that memorial to the Boyne we have followed his trail. Between Newry and Dundalk two or three hundred of his men were routed by the Jacobites. Several skirmishes during the spring had resulted mostly in the discomfiture of the invaders. More than half of William's men were foreigners; he distrusted the English* and feared a reaction in favor of his uncle. Prince George of

* William thoroughly despised the English, and treated England somewhat like a conquered province. One of his medals bore a shattered oak and a blooming orange tree, with the legend: "Instead of acorns, golden oranges." Burnet's inaugural pastoral declared that William and Mary reigned by right of conquest. Bently published a book entitled *William and Mary, Conquerors*. These productions gave great offense; Parliament sentenced them to be burnt by the common hangman.

Denmark and other high personages he kept near him, rather as hostages than aids. His well-drilled strangers, representing nearly every European nationality, were not chivalrous warriors; their princes were wont to hire them out to the highest bidder. The whole invading force, including raw recruits from England, has been variously estimated at from forty to fifty-two thousand, double the number of the opposing army. Three provinces and part of Ulster kept their fealty to their old king. William was fighting on his own element; he never risked himself in a sea fight, yet he scarcely ever won a battle. Personal bravery he showed, and, however unfortunate in the field, he loved fighting, and was more at home in the carnage of battle than in his palaces. Though he was part of the dual head of the Protestant Church (1688–1694), and posed as a Protestant hero, he was a Dutch Calvinist by profession, and hated the English Establishment. His behavior in church scandalized many, even among his friends; he carried his irreverence so far as to keep his hat on during Divine service. He probably cared little about any religion; ambition and intense devotion to his worldly interest held religion's place in his soul. A great part of his life he spent as hired generalissimo of the ultra-Catholic power, Spain.

William was a man of mean presence, considerably below medium height. At the Revolution, his pictures represented him as a giant — a piece of flattery not without influence on his cause. His name is a synonym for bloodshed and religious intolerance. His "pious,

glorious, and immortal" memory is revered by Orangemen, of whom he is patron saint. Should you travel
in northern Ireland toward the great anniversary, you
will see that the cottagers take special care of the
orange lilies that set their gardens aflame — they must
be ready for "the walk" on the 12th. On that great
day, what commotion! gorgeous flags and fiery
streamers, purple banners fringed with orange or gold
— poor Catholics bar their doors, the Orangers are out.
The men wear orange sashes, the women ribbons of the
same bright color, edged with blue. High above the
crowd is borne a portrait of "the Oranger," of greatly
magnified proportions — there would be nothing imposing in a genuine likeness — on a white charger
crossing the Boyne. The procession moves on; the
horses are bedecked with orange flowers and streamers.
It passes under arches of evergreens and orange lilies.
On the other side of the Atlantic and below the Indian
Ocean, the same has been seen. The eyes are regaled
on these festive occasions, but the ears are not neglected. Band after band strike up Orange music.
Cheers for the small hero of Nassau are commingled
with groans and execrations for his hapless father-in-
law. No Jacobite now lives to squeeze oranges at the
wily stadtholder, or shout "Confusion to his hooked
nose," but the moving panorama rarely scatters without bloodshed.

Miss Strickland styles the foreign mercenaries of
William, "the wickedest and cruelest troops England
had ever seen"; by this it seems they surpassed the

bloody hordes of Cromwell. Schomberg's chaplain, Dr. Gorge, describes them as profligate, licentious, and wallowing in crimes too odious to mention. While in the marshy neighborhood of Dundalk, many of them were sick in the sand dunes. James might have annihilated his enemies with the help of the pestilence that was decimating them, but he could not be persuaded to attack the troops of " his son." This provoked Marshal Rosen * beyond endurance, and he exclaimed, in a burst of indignation : " Sire, if you had a hundred kingdoms, you would lose them all."

V

THE troops of James retreated to the Meath side of the Boyne, near Drogheda, from whose gate-towers floated his royal standard and the Flag of the Lilies. William had been only two weeks in Ireland, but had worked energetically from the moment of his landing. Still in the prime of life, in his fortieth year, he was everywhere, attending to everything. James was prematurely old for fifty-seven. William's marauders poured down "King William's Glen," and posed as "an army in battle array." From Donore Hill, James, surrounded by some French allies, viewed the unequal contest. " With admirable courage," says James, Duke of Berwick, " the Irish troops charged the English *ten times* after they had crossed the river." But James II. had no praise

* Lord Wharton boasted that he had sung James II. out of Ireland by a song called *Liliburlero*. This vile doggerel had a bold, catching air, which was sung everywhere and whistled in the hearing of James himself.

for these "very great scorners of death." "If love be-
gets love, the English should certainly love James II.
He would scarcely have been pleased had he vanquished
them. He would hardly have liked to see his English
defeated. They had persecuted him almost from his
birth. The Irish had shed torrents of blood for him
and his, and were still, at terrible odds, fighting his
battles. Yet he had no pity for them. When he saw
them bearing rather heavily on his countrymen, he cried
out, to the unspeakable disgust of his soldiers: "Spare,
oh spare! my English subjects!"

Over a thousand Irish corpses lay stark upon the
bloody field as the shades of evening fell on that bright
July day. The enemy deplored five hundred killed,
among them Schomberg,* and many wounded. The
defeat was due to the miserable King. The vanquished,
though they had fought seven hours under a burning
sun, were willing to continue the battle if they could

---

*William showed great grief for Schomberg, and a funeral at
Westminster was spoken of, but no further notice was taken by
him of the death of "the first captain in Europe." The dean and
chapter of St. Patrick's, Dublin, where his ashes lie, vainly urged
his relations to contribute towards a monument. A memorial was
at length put up by the church dignitaries. The inscription by
Dean Swift says that Duke Schomberg's reputation for valor
availed more with strangers than ties of blood did with his own
kindred. Walker, Bishop of Derry, fared worse. When the King
heard he was shot at the ford, he gruffly asked: "Why did the
fool go there?" Yet to this fighting parson he owed Derry, and
perhaps Ireland. From the effigy of Walker, on top of the Walker
monument, Derry, the sword is reported to have fallen the day the
Emancipation Act received the royal signature.

get rid of their unlucky leader. "Change Kings and we will fight it over again," was their pathetic cry.

The domestic miseries of this British Lear, added to the premature old age sometimes seen in persons who begin life too early, and the injury done him physically by severe attacks of sanguineous apoplexy, may have partially unbalanced the royal mind; the action of James after his expulsion, was often the action of a maniac. On this fatal day, he fled before the battle was over, gained Dublin in an incredibly short time, and, with base ingratitude (if he were in his senses), charged the Irish with cowardice. "The Irish, Madame, can run very fast," said the royal fugitive to Lady Tyrconnel, who came down the castle stair-case to meet him. "In this," she retorted, "your Majesty surpasses them, for you have won the race." It was the first battle ever James lost. He embarked for France at Waterford, leaving his faithful Irish to continue the war.*

When "Mary, the Daughter," heard of her husband's success, she wrote him a letter with the following passage, showing that, though she had violated the fourth commandment, she had some zeal for her own religion: "I have desired to beg that you be not too quick in parting with confiscated estates, but consider whether you will not keep some for public schools to instruct the poor Irish. I must need say I think you would do

---

* O'Halloran, almost a contemporary, says that it was by means of a barter trade with France, in which the Irish gave their wool, hides, tallow, and butter, for powder, ball, and arms, that the war was so long maintained against William.

very well if you would consider what care can be taken of the poor souls there; and, indeed, if you give me leave, I must tell you the wonderful deliverance and success you have had should oblige you to think upon doing what you can for the advancement of the true religion and promoting the gospel."

William never made the slightest reparation for the atrocities he inflicted on Ireland. The estates referred to he gave to the infamous Elizabeth Villiers, who had, even in the honeymoon of the Orange nuptials, supplanted the beautiful Mary in his affections. The Irish would not have accepted such "true religion" as "the daughter" proposed to give. But, strange to say, fifteen years after Mary's death, "the Villiers," who had meanwhile become Countess of Orkney, founded a school in Middletown, Cork (1709), for the education of the poor children in the Protestant religion, and endowed it with some of the above estates. They had been leased by King James at £200 a year to Sir Richard Mead and William North, Esq., being part of his private fortune, inherited from the earls of Clare and Ulster. The magnanimous William and Mary seized the property, as they did the very furniture and clothing of their desolate father and his saintly queen.

VI

IRELAND had been "brayed in a mortar." There were people living, in a country always famous for the number attaining longevity, who remembered the terrible bloodshed and planting of James I., the stand made for his son, when driven out by the English and sold for a groat by the Scotch, and the Cromwellian massacre of forty years previous. In the tragic and pathetic story of the century there was little to remember but wars and rumors of wars, and the perpetual warfare the people waged for religion and liberty. Of the space between 1641 and 1652, Sir William Petty says: " If Ireland had continued in peace for said eleven years, the 1,466,000 (population in 1641) had increased by generations in that time to 73,000, making in all 1,539,000, which were brought by wars (1652), to 850,000, so that 698,000 souls were lost, for whose blood somebody must answer to God and the King."

The recuperative powers of Ireland were literally enormous. In an account of Rinuccini's * sojourn in Ireland (1645–1649), preserved in the archives of the Irish College in Rome, the writer says : " Families are very large. Some have as many as thirty children, all living, and the number of those who have from fifteen to twenty is immense. All these children are handsome, tall and robust." The same unimpeachable authority mentions the extraordinary beauty of the women, their elegant manners, the superb entertainments given, the comeliness and strength of the men, the cheerfulness with which they bore every species of hardship. The description given in the Rinuccini papers of the fish, flesh, Spanish and French wines, excellent milk and butter,

* John Baptiste Rinuccini, Archbishop of Fermo, was sent to Ireland as nuncio-extraordinary by Pope Innocent X., with a supply of arms and money.

apples, pears, plums, and "all eatables" served to the Archbishop and his retinue,* is entirely at variance with Macaulay's words on the same subject. And both describe the state of things when the country was in her chronic condition—war. The papers mention with evident admiration, that the Irish, even in remote places, were thoroughly instructed in their religion, respectful to the clergy, and enthusiastically devoted to the Pope.

After the Boyne success, William III. repaired to Dublin, where he was cordially welcomed by the Protestants, now relieved from their agonizing fears that the Catholics might retaliate on them the cruelties they had remorselessly inflicted on the Catholics. Special thanksgiving was made for the victory which gave England a national debt and increased religious animosity a hundredfold. Sunday, July 6th, William rode

---

* The diet, housing, and clothes *is* much the same as in England; nor is French elegance unknown to many of them, nor the French and Latin tongues. *Political Anatomy of Ireland*—SIR WILLIAM PETTY. "What an answer to Lord Macaulay," is Maurice Lenihan's comment.

Mr. Lenihan quotes a curious letter of Captain Taylor, who sends to the camp near Limerick, August 20, 1690, "all this poor country can afford, and all that is left worth his Majesty's eating . . ." "one veale, 10 fat wethers, 12 chickinges, 2 dussen of frest butter, a thick cheese and a thin one, 10 loaves of bread, a dussen and a half of pidgeons; 12 bottles of ale, half a barrel of small ale, some kidnie beans." "We are strongly of opinion," comments Mr. Lenihan, "that no French *cuisinier* could provide a daintier feast for Royalty than did Captain Taylor, under the circumstances, provide for William III., while he lay before Limerick."

in state to St. Patrick's Cathedral. The spot in the choir is still shown on which he stood, with his uncle's crown on his head, to give thanks for the success of his ambitious schemes. From that day the Cathedrals of Dublin, Christ Church and St. Patrick's, two of the most beautiful churches in Christendom, and rich beyond the power of words to describe in religious and historic associations, have been in possession of the alien church. Catholics, within the memory of man, were obliged to worship, in peril of their lives, in a new form of catacombs. Schomberg's tablet is in the chancel of St. Patrick's. Swift reposes not far off. Near him is Stella's last resting-place. What a cloud of witnesses arises from the grave and surrounds one in this venerable spot. Stella came from the household of Sir William Temple, friend of William III., and the King knew Swift and offered him a post in the army. But what are the historical to the religious associations of a temple sanctified by the presence of saints? The French allies retreated westward, the Irish were gathering near the mouth of the Shannon. William turned his face towards Limerick, the Jacobite metropolis of Ireland. The eccentric little Lauzan, whose selection by James and his Queen for a high post in their army was a wretched mistake, was eager to return to France with the remnants of the Red, Blue, and White regiments, and they were easily spared. If Macaulay's accounts of them be true, they were some of the poorest warriors that ever cumbered Irish ground.

VII

FORTY days after the Battle of the Boyne, William appeared before Limerick, whose walls, Lauzan said, could be battered down with roasted apples. Limerick was a pretty town, and made a fine appearance from the river. Some forty years previous it had been the scene of many tragic and pathetic incidents, when besieged by Cromwellian warriors under Ireton,* son-in-law of the ferocious Protector. Pestilence was scourging the city; 8,000 died of the plague during the short siege of 1657. The heroic Bishop, Terence Albert O'Brien, lived among the stricken. Day and night he encouraged the people to be true to their God and their country. The besiegers offered him 43,000 gold crowns to leave the city, but he disdainfully rejected their treacherous advances. When the siege was raised no quarter was allowed to priests or bishops, and a price was set on O'Brien's head. It was in the pest-house, ministering to the sick and dying, that the enemy found this brave prelate. Brought before Ireton, he was tried by court-martial and condemned to the horrible death of a traitor, in which the gibbet preceded the block, and the quartering began before life was extinct. Undismayed by so dire a prospect, he upbraided Ireton for his cruel-

*Some sixty years before Ireton's attack, Spenser described " the most plentiful and populous country " of Munster as reduced to " a heap of ashes and carcasses " by the English soldiery. Later, the Puritans " swore to extirpate the whole Irish nation " (Clarendon). June 4, 1646, 5,000 Irish, under Owen Roe O'Neill, defeated 8,000 Puritans at Benburb. Napoleon said that, had this intrepid warrior lived, he would have proved a match for Cromwell.

ties, and, in stern words, which proved prophetic, summoned the unjust and sanguinary judge to meet him at the bar of eternal justice, to answer to God for his crimes. The noble head of the martyr was spiked on a tower in the middle of the bridge. The sacred spot on which he won his crown is proudly pointed out by his compatriots and reverenced by them with the piety characteristic of their race.

Eight days after this awfully dramatic scene, the dark and cruel Ireton was writhing in the agonies of the plague, which he had probably caught from the bishop's clothing. He raved wildly of the murdered prelate, and charged upon his council a crime committed by his own order. This fierce persecutor, who had spilt the blood of the saints like water, enjoyed no peace after the awful summons of his victim. In tortures no remedy could assuage, he died in despair. In an ancient street in Limerick is Ireton's house, a large, gloomy mansion, wearing a weird, or, rather, condemned look; it is let out in tenements, and gradually falling into decay. His corpse, which would scarcely be allowed to rest in consecrated ground in Ireland, was buried in Westminster Abbey, but not suffered to remain there. After an heroic defense of six months, two thousand five hundred of the garrison laid down their arms in St. Mary's Cathedral. As they marched sadly out of that venerable edifice, many of them dropped dead of the plague!

William III. came before Limerick (1690) thinking the city would at once surrender. The soldiers, relieved of the presence of their continental auxiliaries, guarded every post. William's twenty thousand men encamped on the crest of the hills of Singland, a few hundred yards from the city walls. In the previous century Limerick had been called the city of castles. Dinely, who made a tour of Ireland in the time of Charles II., mentions its houses as "tall, built of black or polished marble, with partitions five feet thick, and battlements on the top." Whitamore Castle, called also Sarsfield's Castle, as tradition says the great general lived there during the siege, was the Globe Tavern, and famed for its excellent claret. Ardent spirits were sold only in drug stores till William III. popularized their use legally and by example. The walls defending the Irish town were in better condition than those of the English town. William's friend, Herr Bentinck, and William himself, with Herr Overkirke and other officers, reconnoitred the premises. The dash and spirit of the besiegers, the heroic resistance of the besieged, and the peculiar circumstances of a bombardment in which fair matrons and modest maidens took part, are recorded by the aggressors and the defenders. The ruthless savagery of William's heterogeneous warriors is a tradition among the descendants of those who suffered from it. Their chief occupation was hanging all the unfortunate Irishmen who came in their way, on pretense that they were Rapparees, but really because they were true to their creed and country.

Among the objects of interest that rose above the walls was St. Mary's Cathedral, from whose battlements floated the standard of King James. This beautiful edifice, with its soaring towers and romantic bells, was seized by the Protestants, June 15, 1655, when all papists were commanded to leave the city.* It was restored by James II. to the owners, who held it during the sieges (1690–1691). After the Treaty it was retaken by the Protestants. Founded by Donald O'Brien in the twelfth century, it has resisted the ravages of time and escaped the iconoclastic rage of more ruthless destroyers. The poor of Limerick indulge the hope that it will yet come back to the rightful owners.

This venerable temple, though abounding in objects of interest to the historian and antiquarian, has a dark and gloomy aspect. A visitor lately remarked this to a poor woman selling apples in the shadow of its massive spire. "Ah, then," she replied, "why shouldn't it be dark and heavy? Didn't Cromwell's wretches and William's Orangers turn out the Blessed Sacrament and quench the lamp? *Sure it couldn't be bright or lightsome without Him!*"

VIII

SARSFIELD'S brilliant achievement, one of the grandest exploits of modern warfare, by which he led a chosen band out of Limerick and blew to atoms the siege-train of William, saved the city. The bravery of the besieged who flung back their assailants whenever they approached, extorted words of admiration from the phlegmatic prince, who was too enthusiastic a soldier not to appreciate the extraordinary heroism of the

* Cromwell's *State Papers.*

defenders, women and men. The official list puts his
loss at 500 killed and 1,100 wounded, but more truthful authorities rate it much higher, even over 2,000
killed. In the heaps of the slain were the uniforms of
almost every country in Europe. The lateness of the
season, constant rains, and other reasons are given for
raising the siege. But it was raised because William was
beaten, and for no other cause. The garrison, aided
by the heroic women, forced him to withdraw. Sarsfield's *coup* on the memorable night, August 11th–12th,
contributed immensely to the discomfiture of his battalions. To his dismay he learned that the walls which
the little knight-errant, Lauzan, considered incapable of
resisting roasted apples, stood firm against the scientific
engineering of the most famous artillerists in the world.
The maddened besiegers, in retaliation or revenge,
hacked and butchered every native they met. William
did not take his defeat philosophically. "Uneasy lies
the head that wears a crown," was especially true of
him the last night of the siege. He drank plentifully
of the strong liquor he loved, but this, instead of re-
storing the little good humor he had at his best, made
him more morose and gloomy. "He cursed the fate
that brought him to Limerick to witness a defeat un-
paralleled in the annals of warfare. None of his generals dare approach him. Tortured and maddened, he
cast the blame on all about him, and, as he weighed the
advantages of the Boyne with the losses and disgrace
of Limerick, he groaned in spirit.* A spirited ballad

* *Hist. Limerick* — LENIHAN.

by Thomas Davis, on the Battle of Limerick, August 27, 1690, concludes:

> "Out with a roar the Irish sprung,
> And back the beaten English flung,
> Till William fled, his lords among,
>   From the city of Luimneach lionnglas.*

> "'Twas thus was fought that glorious fight,
> By Irishmen for Ireland's right—
> May all such days have such night
>   As the battle of Luimneach lionnglas."

William raised the siege, August 31st, and turning his back forever on the "city of the Azure river," embarked for England September 5th, and reached Kensington September 16th. No doubt he was consoled by his adoring consort, whom he found in much better physical health than himself. After her return to England, Mary had grown enormously large.

William had lost his hold on "the country worth fighting for." Hundreds of regulars were dead in the trenches. Before starting for Waterford, he had left his well-drilled, but vicious, soldiers in command of his countrymen, Solmes and Ginckle.

IX

COLONEL RICHARD GRACE repulsed the Williamites at Athlone. "When provisions fail," said he, "I'll eat my boots, but never surrender." On June 18, 1691, Ginckle came before that devoted town with 25,000 men, and began a second siege. Grace, a gray-headed

* Limerick of the Azure river.

veteran, was removed to a subordinate position, and his place given to d'Usson. This was one of the numerous Jacobite blunders. Grace fell fighting at his post. Bad generalship caused most of the Jacobite disasters. However, prodigies of valor were performed by the besieged, and the enemy were retiring when, through a mistake of St. Ruth, Athlone was taken in a final assault. July 23, 1691, at Aughrim, was fought the greatest battle of the war. The enemy lost over 3,000, the vanquished over 2,000. The conqueror might have said with an ancient hero: "One such victory more and I am undone." The death of the impetuous St. Ruth* in the moment of triumph, caused the defeat. The reader will recall Moore's beautiful lines to the air of " The Lamentation of Aughrim," beginning:

> " Forget not the field where they perished
> The truest, the last of the brave,
> All gone, and the bright hope we cherished
> Gone with them, and quenched in their grave."

Aughrim is now a mere string of small houses, in a sweet pastoral country. The ruined castle from which the Stuart standard waved still frowns above it. The peasant will point out the field called in the Irish language: " The cry of the heart," where widows and orphans sought their loved husbands and fathers among the heaps of the slain. Hard by is " The Bridge of a

---

*St. Ruth showed his jealousy by ordering Sarsfield to the rear, and keeping him in ignorance of his plans. Yet, in ability and capacity, Sarsfield was infinitely superior to the other great soldiers of his time.

Thousand Heads," in defending which, tradition says, 1,000 Irish warriors fell; 7,000 are said to have perished at Aughrim, before the standard of St. George was flung out from the castle. Ginckle now tried his fortune at Limerick. What remained of the armies that had charged at the Boyne, and resisted unto death at Athlone, and shed their blood in torrents under the shadow of the ancient castle of Aughrim came down to the Shannon to defend the beleaguered city. It was said that Limerick looked somewhat like a spider, whose narrow waist was Ball's Bridge. Portions of the old walls flanked by towers are still standing. As late as 1760, seventeen gates stood around Limerick, whose sites may still be traced. The ramparts defended by women stretched from St. John's Gate to Clare street. Some of the walls thirty feet thick, were afterwards tunneled. In the next century, they were metamorphosed into Roche's beautiful Hanging Gardens, the wonder and delight of the people. The quarries of Garryowen supplied material for the citadel, the castle walls, and monuments; even the streets were paved with marble.*

For sixty days, the besieged, under Sarsfield, resisted the picked guards and legions of Ginckle, and the history of the late siege repeated itself. As the foreign mercenaries approached, Richard Talbot, Duke of Tyrconnel and Lord Deputy for James II., was struck with apoplexy, August 11th. He died August

---

* Limerick has always been famous for flowers and gardens; *Garryowen* is a corruption of *Owen's Garden*.

14th, and was buried in St Mary's Cathedral the following night.* The house in which he expired was long pointed out; only its site, near St. Munchin's Church, can now be traced.

The most disastrous incident of the siege was the massacre of the courageous men who held Thomond Gate against the enemy; 850 men were driven across the bridge when the French major in command ordered the drawbridge to be raised, lest, in a hand-to-hand fight, the grenadiers might enter the city. Into the river were pushed 150 men; 600 were cooped up on the narrow bridge, so closely wedged together that they were unable to defend themselves. The heaps of the slain rose higher than the parapets; over 600 perished of that gallant band that had for hours checked the advance of a whole army.

Want of food and ammunition made the defense of the city toward the close nearly impossible. The besiegers offered conditions with which no fault could be found; further resistance was useless, and on September 24th a three days' truce was begun. Sarsfield and the brave Scotchman, Wauchop, who ably seconded him, conferred with the Williamites, represented by their leaders. Near Thomond Bridge may be seen, raised by steps several feet from the ground, the large stone which tradition asserts was used as a table when the Treaty was signed, October 3, 1591, by which was

---

*Tyrconnel, an Irish noble, and a staunch friend of James II., was the first Catholic made Lord Deputy of Ireland since the Reformation — and, we may add, the last.

closed the war between James II.* and "his son,"
William of Orange. The treaty was quickly violated,†
hence Limerick is styled "The City of the Violated
Treaty."

Scarcely was this treaty signed when a French fleet
of eighteen ships and twenty transports, with three
thousand men, two hundred officers, ten thousand
stand of arms, with plenty of clothing and provisions,
appeared in the Shannon. Had this help come sooner,
Sarsfield would not have accepted the favorable terms
of the enemy; with this great force behind him he
might have taken back his word, and continued his
defense of Limerick. But the gallant soldier was too
honorable to commit a breach of faith — what he had
written he had written. He kept his troth, even
though Dopping, Protestant Bishop of Meath, was
teaching *ex cathedra* "the sinfulness of keeping your
oath or faith with Papists," — a sinfulness never committed in those days.

*James has been blamed for coining brass money and gun
money (*i.e.*, money made of old guns); also for raising the value
of English and foreign gold and silver coin. He promised to redeem all at the expiration of the "present necessity." Though
an able financier he did not think of issuing paper money, or
creating a national debt, like his successors.

 † When Sarsfield marched out of Limerick, colors flying,
drums beating, with all the honors of war, he fondly hoped that
he had secured liberty to his people. But, alas, he relied in vain
on the honor of a king. The "Treaty" was but "the perjured
preface" to the Penal Laws. Besides that of Limerick, there are
two violated treaties — Mellifont and Kilkenny.

X

THE Irish army, refusing to serve under William the Usurper, took service under the principal sovereigns of Europe; Ginckle strove hard to obtain these brave men for his master, but only about one thousand, mostly Englishmen or Ulster men, declined to go to the Continent. Twelve thousand two hundred entered the service of France,* increasing the Irish contingent there to nearly twenty thousand. This was the celebrated Irish Brigade, whose valor was gloriously displayed on almost every battlefield in Europe. When Maria Teresa instituted fifty crosses of the Legion of Honor, forty-six of them were won by Irish officers. Louis XIV. loved to welcome these exiles to his armies, and always spoke of them as "my brave Irish." Francis I. wrote: "The more Irish officers we have in the Austrian army the better." In several battles they turned the scale against the English; when defeated by their bravery and skill, the despicable George II. exclaimed: "Cursed be the laws that deprive me of such subjects." Yet this wretched creature added new and horrible enactments to the penal code already existing. In the English House of Commons it was said that more injury had been done to England and her allies by these exiles, than if all the Irish Catholics had been left in possession of their estates. To escape the penal laws, thousands of young men joined their friends in France, Spain, and Austria, and many emigrated to America. In Georgia and the Carolinas they

* Some, not choosing either service, returned to their homes.

soon formed the majority; in 1729 fifty-six hundred Irish landed in Philadelphia. The total emigration to France amounted to one million, and from 1691 to the Revolution, four hundred and eighty thousand Irishmen died in the service of France. After the defeat of the English at Fontenoy, May 11, 1745, the government decreed the penalty of death against any Irishman enlisting in France. Among the thousands who won distinction in foreign lands are Cooke, O'Shaughnessy, Lacy (Russia), Tyrconnel (Prussia), Nugent, O'Connor, O'Brien, Lally, O'Reilly, Captain-General of Cuba, Governor of Louisiana, Count McCarthy, and Marquis Casacalvo (O'Farrell), Louisiana.

Sarsfield,* " the Irish Bayard," *sans peur et sans reproche*, is commemorated in Limerick by a graceful bronze statue (Lawlor, sculptor). On the pedestal is the inscription :

" To commemorate the indomitable energy and stainless honor of General Patrick Sarsfield, Earl of Lucan, the heroic defender of Limerick during the sieges of 1690 and 1691, who died from the effects of wounds received at the battle of Landen, 1693."

---

*Sarsfield married Honora Burke, granddaughter of the Baron of Brittas, who suffered the horrible death of a traitor, in 1610, because he had harbored a priest. Sarsfield's widow, Countess Honora, married James Stuart, Duke of Berwick, and thus became daughter-in-law to James II., and sister-in-law to queens Mary and Anne, the so-called Pretender, and Princess Louisa Stuart. But these high connections could add no distinction to the widow of Sarsfield.

The site was presented by Most Rev. George Butler, bishop of Limerick. The writer had the pleasure of seeing this statue tastefully decorated with flowers and banners, on the second centenary of Sarsfield's defeat of William III.

Frightful statutes followed the violation of the Treaty. William, Anne, George I., and George II. enlarged the horrid code. A characteristic enactment of Anne gave a child who conformed to the Protestant religion, his father's estates, excluding other heirs. As the sister queens, Mary and Anne, had driven out their own father, it was supposed other children would not hesitate to grow rich in a similar way.* In these reigns Ireland touched the depths of her degradation ; yet contraband intercourse with the great world abroad kept hope alive in the hearts of many. The Pretender, "the son of a King," was to them a hero, because he would not renounce the true religion for a triple crown. When the saintly Mary Beatrice passed away, they bewailed her in their poetic language, and in their poor cabins sang a "Lament for the Queen" when the day's work was done.

Meanwhile the penal laws continued to debase those who executed them. "Where they were not bloody,"

*The heroes and heroines of the Revolution were mostly cursed with bad sons or had none. William and Mary had no issue. Queen Anne's eighteen children all died young. The heir of the Duke and Duchess of Marlborough, Lord Blandford, died a boy. Bishop Burnet's sons were daring reprobates. Thomas wrote a song on his father's death, beginning :

> "The fiends were brawling,
> When Burnet descending !"

says Edmund Burke, " they were worse; they were slow, cruel, and outrageous in their nature, and kept men alive only to insult in their persons every one of the rights and feelings of humanity.". Yet so slowly did the work of conversion proceed that it was computed it would take four thousand years to convert the Irish! Nay, they sometimes converted their masters. From the day that Strongbow married Eva, Englishmen and other foreigners in Ireland have shown a strong disposition to marry Irish wives.* Many of William's men,† and not a few Hessians of a later date, settled in the country and married Irish maidens. Ireton commanded his officers not to marry Irish women on pain of being cashiered. Yet many strict Catholics are descended from Cromwell's own soldiers.

Though ground to the dust, the Irish ‡ had comfort in hearing of the glorious career of their countrymen abroad. "Wherever the Irish served," says Fornman, "they had the good fortune to distinguish themselves; and it may be said, to their eternal honor, that, from the time they entered the service of France, they had never the least blot on their escutcheon." At home, though "doomed to death, they were fated not to die."

---

* The proudest Norman invaders of Ireland sought Irish wives, but the Normans in England would hold no social relations with the Saxons, whom they spoke of as little better than swine.

† This is how the late Bishop Hendricken of Providence, a native of Ireland, came by his name.

‡ Under no circumstances did the Irish ever give up their desire, their love, and their struggle for freedom. And this is, perhaps, the most remarkable feature of their history.

Far on in the next century they spoke their ultimatum :
"FREE TRADE, OR SPEEDY REVOLUTION." In the
Irish Parliament, April 16, 1782, Grattan's celebrated
resolution passed unanimously:

" That the kingdom of Ireland is a distinct kingdom,
with a Parliament of her own, the sole legislator thereof
— that there is no body of men competent to make laws
to bind the nation, but the King, Lords, and Commons
of Ireland,— nor any Parliament which has any authority or power of any sort whatsoever in this country, save
only the Parliament of Ireland."

Over two hundred years have passed since the
Treaty of Limerick was signed and violated. And to-
day, after a strange and wonderful history, the Irish
race is pre-eminently Catholic, at home and abroad, supplying the English-speaking Catholic world, to a great
extent, with clergy and teachers. Foreigners settling
in Ireland have mostly been absorbed into the race,
and are one with it in religion and love of the dear old
land. May the good God, who has upheld the ever-
faithful Isle in the past, be with her people in the future, to give them unity of sentiment and action, as
well as unity of faith.

" Here came the brown Phœnician, a man of trade and toil—
Here came the proud Milesian, a-hungering for spoil ;
And the Firbolg and the Cymri, and the hard enduring Dane,
And the iron lord of Normandy, with the Saxon in their train.

" And oh, it were a gallant deed to show before mankind,
How every race and every creed might be by love combined—
Might be combined, yet not forget the fountains whence they rose,
As filled by many a rivulet, the stately Shannon flows,"

ALABAMA

I—"HERE WE REST!"

ITTLE is known in Europe of the 50,722 square miles admitted to the Union, as the State of Alabama, in 1819; whose head is in the Appalachian mountain chain, and whose feet are laved by the bright waters of the Mexican Gulf. Of late years, its "coal, the source of power, and iron, the source of strength," have attracted the stranger within its boundaries; but its wonderful mineral resources, which have flashed into sudden prominence, have not been sufficiently utilized in developing its grand agricultural capabilities. Friends who assume to have its material prosperity at heart regret that the immigration directed towards this State is comparatively small. And this is surprising. For everything is here that attracts settlers to other centres, and more. The writer has often wondered why so many who make up their minds to leave the land of their birth for America should pitch their tents among the awful blizzards of the north and west, instead of seeking homes on the genial soil, in the balmy climate, of the beautiful South.

So vast a subject cannot be "touched with a needle," in a single magazine article. But we may at least give our readers some idea of the romantic history, the present possibilities, the social and religious condition of a semi-tropical region, which has an area 18,000 square miles larger than Ireland, and is as rich in natural wealth as any other tract of equal size on the American Continent. Besides, in its varied population, in which every country in Europe, and at least one in Asia, and every State and Territory of the Union, are represented, there has always been a fair sprinkling of Irish, who certainly have not been the least useful citizens of this commonwealth.

Here is how, according to a cherished tradition, Alabama received its sweet-sounding name. A band of Indians, who quitted Mexico during the upheavals consequent on the arrival of the famous ship-burner, Cortez, wandering eastwards in search of a new home, reached the noble river now known as the Alabama. Their chieftain, charmed with the gorgeous beauty of the forest scenery, gave the signal to halt, and, drawing up under the shade of a magnificent oak, struck his spear in the ground and exclaimed with enthusiasm: "Alabama!" which, being interpreted, means: "Here we rest!"

And it certainly cannot be denied that this State abounds in regions of wondrous natural loveliness. Parts of it dispute with New Hampshire the title, "Switzerland of America." It has sixty miles of sea-coast on the Gulf of Mexico; and its varieties of climate*—it lies between the 31st and the 35th parallels

---

* Mean annual temperature, 61 degrees. Land may be had at from $1 to $25 an acre.

of latitude — are said to be milder than the varieties of places of corresponding latitude elsewhere. Nor is beauty its only gift. Its rivers are channels of commerce, bearing its products of mine and field and forest to the southern seas. Its coal areas, and ridges of red and brown iron, are practically inexhaustible. Its cereal belt, mineral belt, cotton belt, timber belt, and prairie belt, are named from their respective staples. Fair villages nestle in the tortuous windings of its clear streams. Its fertile bosom is rich with the vegetation of high and low latitudes. Its trees bend beneath their golden, and purple, and yellow burdens, of orange, fig, and peach. Its fields are green with the rustling sugar cane, or white with the mimic snow of cotton, or covered with the soft verdure of higher regions, or the glory of primeval forests. Its cities are warmed and lit by its own coal, and its superabundant waters cool the dusty streets in the glow of summer. Its only port, Mobile, is circled by waters that never freeze. It has pleasuring spots, as Blount Springs, in a picturesque mountain region, and Point Clear, the "Long Branch of the South," which compare favorably with many more famous watering-places. Geographically, West Florida would seem to belong to Alabama, and Alabama has more than once tried to acquire it by purchase, offering for it, on one occasion, a million dollars. But the Floridians refused to part with any portion of their territory.

Alabama has Tennessee on the north, Georgia on the east, Florida and the Gulf on the south, and Mississippi on the west. Its population is but 29* to the square mile, though it is capable of supporting as many as Massachusetts, 286. As was the case with California, in the days of the gold fever, its agricultural possibilities are partially overlooked in estimating its undeveloped natural riches. For this State, as for the other Southern States, the Civil War was a social revolution. The slaves were freed, but no laborers were at hand to take their places. Immense plantations, once smiling gardens, were soon over-run with the riotous weed and the tangled vine. Farms have been reclaimed from these wildernesses, and the natural fertility of the soil increased by rotation of crops. It is not generally known on the other side of the Atlantic, that two, three, or even four crops in the year may be wrung from the plenteous bosom of Mother Earth, in the Sunny South. Louisiana's coat of arms, the Pelican, fabled as feeding her young from her breast, typifies the superabundant richness of the soil ; the same figure might be applied to much of the southern country. True, the chief use of this bird, common enough in the

---

* About half the population of Alabama is colored. Very few blacks outside Mobile are Catholics.ʳ Though the State has its share of intelligent citizens and has produced some eminent persons, yet in remote quarters there is not a little gross ignorance, especially as regards the Church. The vilest anti-Catholic literature is circulated among these people, and, through ignorance which seems invincible, believed as gospel truth. Isolation, and other causes — like isolation, daily disappearing — have produced some whites very low in the intellectual order, whom the negroes expressively call " white trash."

State which has adopted it, is to illustrate the goodness of Our Blessed Lord (whom St. Thomas addresses : *Pie Pelicane Jesu Domine !*) in feeding us with His adorable Body and Precious Blood in the Blessed Sacrament. And this brings us to the second part of our article.

II — RELIGION

RELIGIOUSLY, Alabama does not present the most brilliant aspect to the Catholic eye. It is, perhaps, the only territory once in possession of the French and Spaniards, that retains no Catholic Saint, or mystery of religion in the varied nomenclature of its cities, country, rivers, mountains — with the exception of some streets in Mobile. To a great extent it is in the hands of the sects. Methodists, Baptists, and other denominations, have large congregations everywhere. Catholics form but a small minority of the population. Of a French colony, planted here some generations ago, almost all the descendants have lost the Faith of their Fathers. The descendants of Irish immigrants, in many places, have done little better, and every "persuasion" has amongst its foremost adherents names decidedly Milesian. The immense size* of a country so sparsely peopled, the fewness of Catholic priests, the difficulty heretofore of going from Catholic centres to the interior, and the want of Catholic schools, are some of the causes of the sad decay of the true Religion. Often people lost that priceless boon without fault of theirs. Parents

* A missionary says that the district over which he travels *alone* is as large as Switzerland.

died, leaving children far from Catholic relations; naturally, such were brought up non-Catholics. Mixed marriages, which the Church has always " abhorred," played their evil part; the most eloquent and successful prelate among the non-Catholics of the South, was son of an Irish father, who died when he was a babe, and a Protestant mother. Unhappily, Irish and French names abound among the non-Catholic clergy of the South. And the doctrine, if any, which they preach, is not the whole " Faith once delivered to the Saints."

The diocese of Mobile includes Alabama and western Florida, and is about as large in territorial extent as England. Its muster-roll consists of one Bishop,* 18 secular priests, 4 of whom have been on the mission over 25 years — a proof of the healthfulness of the climate — 6 Jesuit Fathers doing missionary work, 8 Jesuit Fathers, with several Jesuit professors not yet ordained, at Spring Hill College ; 8 Benedictine priests ; houses of the Visitation, 1 ; Sisters of Charity, 3 ; Sisters of Loretto, 1 ; Sisters of Mercy, 3 ; Sisters of Notre Dame, 1 ; Sisters of St. Joseph, 1 ; Sisters of St. Benedict, 2 ; and Brothers of the Sacred Heart, 2. There are 35 Visitation Nuns ; 18 Sisters of Charity ; 13 Loretto Sisters ; 32 Sisters of Mercy ; 5 Sisters of St. Joseph ; 14 Sisters of St. Benedict ; and 14 Brothers of the Sacred Heart.† In the institutions of these re-

---

* Bishops of Mobile : Right Rev. Drs. Portier, 1829; Quinlan, 1859; Manucy, 1884; O'Sullivan, 1885; Allen, 1897.

† The above statistics are not correct now (1899). For instance, the Sisters of Mercy whose Mother house is in Mobile have six houses and seventy members.

ligious, about 1,900 children are educated. And the number of Catholics hardly exceeds 18,000, the entire population of the territory included in the Mobile diocese, being in the neighborhood of 1,600,-000. Considering its remoteness and its resources, the number of institutions is large, but, like the loaves of the gospel, " what are they among so many ? "

Of late years, religious prospects have brightened. Every part of the State has been explored by missionaries. Isolated Catholics in remote districts have been visited. Railroads, opened to subserve purposes of commerce, enable the Catholic priest to go about like the Good Shepherd, seeking that which was lost, and preaching the Sacred Name, whereby alone we can be saved. The harvest indeed is great, and the laborers are few — in many places none. But, within the borders of this fair and fertile region, prayer ascends without ceasing to the Lord of the harvest, that he may send laborers into His vineyard.

III — MONTGOMERY AND SELMA

THE reader will now be introduced to some Alabama towns known to the writer.

Montgomery, the capital, pleasantly situated on an amphitheatre of low hills, has some wide streets handsomely laid out and shaded with the native water oak. It is blessed with a Catholic Church, and a convent crowns one of its loftiest eminences. In history it lives as the first capital of the Confederate States, where the Confederate Constitution was adopted, and the Confederate President inaugurated. Here Jefferson Davis began his reign over a nation whose existence, if brief, was brilliant, and whose armies often recalled the finer qualities of the soldiers of Greece and Rome. A prehistoric race of Indians, known as Mound-Builders, left traces of their works about the locality, which have disappeared. The present city, once known as New Philadelphia, was incorporated in 1819, and chartered as a city in 1837. It is named after the dashing Irish soldier, General Montgomery, who fell at the attack on Quebec, December 31, 1775. The capitol is a handsome structure, and crowns a lofty and beautiful site.

Of Birmingham, the magic city, which has ·grown up as it were in a single night, like the gourd of the prophet, we cannot say much from personal observation, for we never beheld it save in rapid transit, and by moonlight. In the heart of the cotton belt is Selma, a city of 16,000 inhabitants. Its founder, Thomas Moore, a literary personage and a student of Ossian, took its name from that poet, who speaks of the songs of Selma, and Selma of the harps. In 1820, it was incorporated, its name being changed from Moore's Bluff. It was an important *dépôt* of the Confederates, and was stormed and captured by General Wilson, who burnt its arsenal and shot and shell foundries. Selma is a great cotton mart, being in a rich agricultural district, and close to the mineral regions. From its position it is called Central City. Several lines of railroad meet here, and it has some large factories. Its chief thoroughfare, Broad street, is beautifully shaded, save in the business portions, where it touches the river Alabama. Regular rows of trees line every street; this adds immensely to its beauty. It has over one hundred Artesian wells, and is well equipped against the dust, so disagreeable in long stretches of dry weather. Before the sprinkler and the hose became universal, the cities of the South were often Saharas of stifling dust, almost as bad as Salt Lake City or Ogden. Selma people are of many States and nations; there is a fair contingent of Irish, some of whom are pious Catholics, but some, alas, have lost their Faith for which their fathers bled for centuries. It has a neat stone church.* The pastors are Jesuit Fathers. It has also a Convent of Mercy and flourishing schools, attended by all the Catholics, and many non-Catholic children of the place. Selma is one of the handsomest cities in the South.

IV — MOBILE

MOBILE, the oldest and most historic of the Alabama towns, has a name which sounds strangely in European ears, and suggests a shifting city. It is not, however, derived from anything connected with mobility, but from a tribe of Indians who possessed lands stretching from its bay far into the interior. Their most important town, *Mauvila*, was strongly fortified.

* Built by Father John J. O'Leary Cork. A monument on its north wall "records his virtues and perpetuates his memory." R. I. P.

From their powerful cacique, Tuscaloosa, who made a brave stand against the Spanish invaders under De Soto (1539) and perished defending his ancestral domains, the former capital of Alabama is named. The historian, Garcilasso de las Vegas, says the Mauvileans lost nearly 11,000 warriors in this conflict. Their name is perpetuated in the Gulf City — a name suggestive of martial daring and heroic deeds. It became *Mobila* in the mouth of the Spaniards who sounded *v* as *b*, a pronunciation lately condemned by the Spanish Academy. The French have given us *Mobile*.

The bravery of De Soto and his followers became a fountain of poetry and legend for future generations. His chivalrous hosts were accompanied by priests, who, no doubt, converted many Indians. Some must have stayed behind when the hero swept, comet-like, through the western wilderness in search of other lands to conquer. Benign shades of gracious priests sometimes appear in Indian legend. Students of Southland legendary lore will recall the priest mentioned as going out in a frail barque, at twelve of the clock on Christmas night, lured by the mystic music of Pascagoula, in the vicinity of Mobile, and many another phantom priest.

A century and a half later the terrible palefaces, who lived in song and story, again appeared. This time they came to stay. In 1700, Bienville, who had made a settlement in Biloxi, came to the Mobile river, by order of his Government, to found the capital of Louisiana. This distinction, however, was transferred, in

1723, to New Orleans, founded by the same great Catholic colonizer, on the Mississippi.

Mobile progressed slowly. Famine often ravaged the new settlement, and now and then the Chickasaws and the Choctaws swooped down upon the colonists. Even when pacified by presents, they were a menace. Amid all this desolation, crowds were brought to the true faith. Many Frenchmen married Indian women, and the Church invariably sustained the lawfulness of such marriages. Bienville often sojourned at Mobile. From its shores, the gallant St. Denis started on his famous expedition to the City of Mexico, which seems to belong to the brilliant realm of romantic adventure, rather than the sober domain of history. Successive governors of Louisiana came hither from time to time, laden with presents for the aborigines. Often the settlers were on the point of withdrawing to New Orleans, but were dissuaded by Bienville, always ready to help them. In 1736 he arrived from New Orleans with nearly 600 white troops and a company of free negroes officered by men of their own race. They were joined by 600 Choctaws, and all proceeded to the Tombigbee, to fight the Chickasaws—a disastrous campaign to Bienville. The Chickasaws, incited to acts of hostility by the English, continued their depredations whenever they could do so unchecked. The great chief, Red Shoe, was in the English interest, though he accepted the liberal presents of the Louisiana governors. Hurricanes threatened the existence of the village of wattles. Beauchamp, the commander, tells of one,

September 11, 1740, that almost annihilated it. The storehouses containing the provisions of the garrison were swept away, and had he not sent his men "barrel fishing," they would have died of hunger. Another hurricane seized the boats, logs, and buoys in the bay, and scattered them in splinters about the streets, thus supplying the settlers with their winter fuel.

In 1746 Mobile had a population of 400. To this the Grand Marquis, Vaudrieul, Governor of Louisiana, added a garrison of 400 French and 75 Swiss. He also had every house defended by palisades, measures absolutely necessary for the protection of the embryo city. In 1763 the French surrendered Mobile to the English, and the "spotless banner" descended, never again to be raised over its fort. With malignant ingenuity the new masters tormented the colonists, and perfidiously violated the stipulations of the treaty, which placed them, against their will, under the British flag. But in 1780 the dashing young Governor of Louisiana, Bernardo de Galvez (for whom Galveston is named), wrested Mobile from the English, with an army of Spanish regulars, colonial militia (the splendid company formed by Governor O'Reilly), and free blacks, numbering in all 2,000. The English flag was taken from Fort Charlotte, and the flaming colors of Spain flung to the breeze.

When Mobile was 85 years old her population was but 746. Under the Spaniards it nearly doubled in three years. The census of 1788 gave the now flourishing settlement 1,468. In 1812 General Wilkinson took possession of it for the United States, and "the Stars and Stripes" have since floated over it, save for a short term ere the "Stars and Bars" of the Confederacy became the "Conquered Banner."

Mobile, situated at the mouth of the Mobile river, is one of the chief cities of the South in wealth, commerce, and population. · The entrance from the Gulf is three miles wide, and is defended by two forts. It is a handsome city, especially in the suburbs. For trees, flowers, fruits, and vegetables, it is the glory of the South. There is much culture and refinement, and no small share of literary ability, among its 60,000 inhabitants. The governors of Louisiana, under whom it fell for over a century previous to the American domination, were pious Christians and able men, and did not neglect the religious interests in the colonies over which they ruled. From Bienville to Aubrey under French sway, and from O'Reilly to O'Farrell (Casacalvo) under the Spanish *régime*, almost everything was done that could be done by zealous lay governors to promote religion.* Louisiana included a territory larger than Alexander conquered. But its early history was mostly enacted by the Mississippi, or on the sandy slopes of the Gulf of Mexico.

The religion of its founders flourishes in Mobile. It possesses a noble cathedral, which remotely suggests the Madeleine at Paris; and churches under the invocation of St. Patrick, St. Joseph, St. Mary, and St.

* In 1789 the King of Spain commanded, by a royal decree, that on every plantation there should be a chaplain.

Vincent. For over half a century the Visitation Convent has dispensed higher education to thousands. Sisters of Charity, Sisters of St. Joseph, Sisters of Mercy,
and Brothers of the Sacred Heart, also labor to fit the
young for earth without *un*fitting them .for heaven.
" The College," the best classical and commercial semi-
nary in the South, is conducted by the Jesuits, whose
qualifications as educators no one questions. There
are hospitals and orphanages, and many other institutions, on which space will not allow us to expatiate.
At one time a large share of Irish emigration was directed towards Mobile. Save St. Augustine, Mobile is,
with perhaps one exception, the oldest city in the South.
In spite of wars, foreign and domestic, floods and hurricanes that almost swept her from the earth, intrigues at
home and abroad, she still stands. Since her frail beginning, two centuries ago, dynasties have perished,
kingdoms have been overthrown, and Europe nearly
blotted off the American continent. When one looks
at Alabama's oldest and best paper, *The Mobile Register*, one sees a list of places of worship of various denominations, *headed by the Catholic cathedral.* This is
right and proper. The Catholic religion came hither
when the red men were offering human sacrifice. She
did her part towards encouraging the colonists and
humanizing the savages before the founders of most of
the sects were born. The city was begun by Catholic
enterprise, and sustained in the face of continual peril
by the great Catholic powers of Europe. Her founder,
the stately and reserved Bienville, of obscure Canadian

birth, but stainless integrity, a fervent Catholic, was the greatest of our colonizers. He suffered from the misunderstandings that wait upon all grand enterprises. And, like so many other benefactors of the human race, obloquy, exile, neglect, were the rewards meted out to him. The greatest of eleven brothers, every one of whom served his country by sea and land, he sought out new regions for France solely that new nations might be won for Christ.

Mobile, then, was established by Catholic genius and preserved by Catholic enterprise. May the disciples of the true religion increase and multiply in this exquisite region, so early consecrated to the true God. May they be thoroughly imbued with the best principles of morality, industry, and patriotism, and high in the order of merit as they are first in the order of time. True disciples of that holy Church which forbids all that is evil, commands everything good, and counsels whatever is perfect, may they abound in every grace, but, above all, in charity; that it may be said of them, as of their prototypes in the Gospel: "See how these Christians love one another."

MARY OF MODENA—HER DESCENDANTS —THE JACOBITES

PART I

I

THE traveler in Italy who loves to recall the days of Attila, and the poetry and romance of the Esté heroes, of whom Tasso, Ariosto, and Dante have sung, will linger with interest about the stately city of Modena, once the ducal seat of the Italian branch of the Estés. The Modenese territory, now absorbed into the kingdom of Italy, was about fifty-six miles long by thirty-six broad. It was our good fortune to traverse this land of song and story in bright August weather. The capital, on the ancient Via Emilia, north from Rome, set down among rich vineyards and waving corn fields, is indeed "a thing of beauty." The surrounding plain, watered by sparkling streams, is studded with fruit trees that bear no fruit, but serve as props for the luxuriant vines that drape them, and are festooned from one tree to another. There are no grand natural features, but one cannot imagine a more sweet and smiling landscape. The city is encompassed by ancient ramparts, now used as promenades, like the walls of Derry. From these the Appenines are visible in the blue distance, in fine contrast with the amber maize and green vineyards below.

Like most Italian cities, Modena has a wonderful cathedral. But the classic place absorbed our attention chiefly as the early home of the last Catholic Queen of England, Mary Beatrice, the fairest flower of the ducal house of Esté.

Compared with this Queen of Sorrows, sculptures, porcelains, and tapestries, awoke in us but little enthusiasm. In the glorious cathedral she received the great sacrament, whose sublime office it is to rouse and fortify the gift of Faith in the Christian soul. The fair princess often trod the colonnaded courtyard, and her languishing dark eyes rested admiringly on the gems scattered in bewildering abundance about the churches and museums. The noble Campanile, whose sweet bells summoned the faithful to prayer; the modest convent within whose blessed walls she had hoped to live and die; the palaces of patricians of lofty lineage; the cottages of the poor, in which squalor and splendor sometimes met — all were objects of interest to the princess who bloomed into loveliness in this soft and salubrious clime.

It is curious that the descendants of Forestus d'Esté, who distinguished himself against Attila and his formidable hordes in the fifth century, should be rival claimants for the crown of England 1300 years later — the elder branches Guelph (Wolf) being represented by the elector of Hanover, and the younger by the son and grandson of Mary of Modena, the titular King, James III., and Scotland's "Bonnie Prince Charlie."

II

THIS Queen was born in the ducal palace (now the Palazzo Reale), October 5, 1658. Her parents were Alfonso d'Esté, Duke of Modena, and Laura Martinozzi, a Roman lady, niece to Cardinal Mazarin. She was called Mary, after the Blessed Mother, and Beatrice in honor of her illustrious kinswoman, St. Beatrice, of the House of Esté. This royal saint was said to fulfill in regard to the reigning family an office analogous to that of the Irish banshee. She used to knock at the palace gate three days before the death of every member of the ducal family.

There is scarcely a grander sight in Modena than the vast and magnificent façade of the ducal palace. The ducal arms have given place to the white cross of Savoy. But, as in Florence one still sees in quiet places the arms of the Medici, so in Modena, one may easily discern here and there the crowned eagle of Esté.

Mary Beatrice had a brother to whom she was tenderly attached. The children had a very rigid training. The prince was compelled to study so closely that it was feared he would injure his frail constitution. But this had no weight with the Spartan mother. "Better have no son," said she, "than a son destitute of wit and merit." The future Queen of England sometimes had a box on the ear for a lapse of memory. Both were kept at an awful distance by their mother. But they sometimes eluded her vigilance. Sweetmeats were forbidden, lest they should engender gluttony. In after years Mary Beatrice said : " I advise my son and daughter not to eat sweetmeats, but I do not forbid them, knowing these things would be given them by stealth. . . . This would accustom them to habits of petty concealment, perhaps of falsehood." Wise words from a royal lady, who, throughout her whole life, was remarkable for truth and candor.

Her favorite governess became a Carmelite nun, and the princess grieved so much on losing her that her mother allowed her to go to the convent as a boarder. Here she found the discipline far less rigid than in her stately home, and was happier with the gentle nuns than with her severe mother. She resolved never to leave this venerable abode. Latin, French, music, and embroidery were among her studies, and she showed much taste for painting. But her future husband was surprised that she did not know there was such a place as York, or such a personage as the duke of that city. The fame of her beauty and intellect soon went abroad, and she was spoken of as the fairest and most gifted princess in Christendom.

The ambassador sent from England to find a wife for the sailor prince, James Stuart, declared that she was the only person who could make him happy. He told her that " the love of the prince, when she came to know him, would make amends for anything she now deemed a grievance." Unlike her predecessors, Henrietta Maria of France and Catharine of Braganza, she was not asked to marry a prince who differed from her in creed, but one who had sacrificed power, influence,

and the immense incomes of high offices for conscience
sake ; who might almost be styled a confessor in view
of the sacrifices he had made to join the persecuted
Church of Christ.

III

THE portraits of Mary Beatrice by Lely and Knel-
ler, to be seen in several British palaces, and those of a
later date in French collections, bear glowing testimony
to the wonderful beauty of this Mary Stuart. And,
from her letters and other sources, some idea may be
formed of her bright mind and the loveliness of her
soul. She appears to have been utterly devoid of vanity. When she heard that England's heir sought her
hand, she declared that his highness must seek another
bride, that she had given herself irrevocably to a spouse
who could neither change nor die. Never did woman
struggle so hard to continue " in maiden meditation
fancy free." She resisted her mother, her uncle, the
whole council.

> " Spotless without and innocent within ;
> She feared no danger, for she knew no sin."

The royal beauty gave everyone to understand
that it was useless to ask her consent. Her aversion to
marriage, and her grief at being taken from the convent,
so wrought upon her mother and uncle that they concluded to dismiss the English embassy. The proposals
of the Earl of Peterboro she received with lofty dis-
dain, and besought him " to avert further persecution
of a maid who had an invincible repugnance to marriage." Had the stout old cavalier been a man of less

determination, he would have given up in despair. He describes her as "tall, admirably shaped; her complexion of the last degree of fairness; her hair, brows, and eyes black as jet; the eyes so full of light and sweetness that they did dazzle and charm. There seemed given to them sovereign power to kill and to save . . . her face a most perfect oval . . . with all the beauty that could be in any human creature."

Indeed, it required the intervention of the highest personage in Christendom to induce the spirited girl even to listen to the advances made to her on behalf of England's heir. Her countryman, Muratori, writes:

"As the thoughts of this princess were directed to a higher object, she being resolved to consecrate herself to God in a monastery, it was almost impossible to obtain her consent. Nor would the difficulty have been overcome if the sovereign pontiff, considering that such a marriage would be for the good of Christendom, had not interposed his paternal exhortations."

James II., in his memoirs, confirms this testimony. "She had at that time a great inclination to be a nun, insomuch that the duchess, her mother, was obliged to get the Pope to write to her and persuade her to comply with her wish as most conducive to the service of God and the public good." It was then, in deference to the expressed wishes of his holiness, that the royal maiden of fourteen received the addresses of a prince twenty-five years her senior.

IV

LORD PETERBORO speaks of the order and magnificence of the Modenese court, its splendid ceremonies, its picturesque gardens, and expresses surprise at the grandeur of its appointments. September 30th the princess was married, by proxy, at a Nuptial Mass. During the balls, pageants, and rejoicing that followed, the bride wept constantly, dreading the hour that was to take her from her beloved home. A grand *Te Deum* was sung in the cathedral for the marriage that had all but broken her heart. Her dower was eighty thousand pounds, an enormous sum at that date. She was the last foreign princess that brought a dower to England. The kings who supplanted the Stuarts married into poor families, and brides and grooms have had to be paid to come to England to marry their relations, as the brides of George III. and George IV.; Leopold, who married the Princess Charlotte, and Albert, husband of Queen Victoria.

It would not be possible to imagine a more wretched bride than Mary Beatrice. For three days and nights she cried and screamed, so that her strength gave way, and she was kept in bed by force. She insisted that her mother should accompany her to England, and made her brother come two days' journey. On reaching England she was met by her husband, to whom she showed much dislike. Her swarthy brother-in-law found more favor in her eyes. "I loved King Charles very dearly," she said, "even before I became attached to my lord, the Duke of York." The fine manners and gracious ways of Charles II. captivated many a more experienced personage. The day came when she condemned as excessive her attachment to her husband, which she feared might come between her God and herself. Excessive in a bad sense it never was, for it never impeded her spiritual progress, or caused her to neglect the duties of her exalted station. To the close of her checkered career, she practised with ever increasing perfection the virtues she had learned in her early convent home.

Mary Beatrice was but little over sixteen when her first child was born. Although the duke had explained to her that the king, lords, and commons, had determined that her children, as the property of the State, should be reared Protestants, the young mother sent for her confessor and persuaded him to baptize her babe. Charles II. ignored this, and had the child rebaptized by a Protestant bishop, to the chagrin of the girl-mother, who feared she had been accessory to a sacrilege.

The youth, beauty, and edifying life of this princess, won her universal esteem. The court over which she presided at St. James was a contrast to the noisy, disorderly court of the king. The heirs that followed James were mostly at variance with the crown, as Anne with William and Mary, George I. with his son, George II., and Frederick, Prince of Wales. But no one ever questioned the fidelity of the Duke and Duchess of York to the king's interest. Charles II. used to say that "the most loyal and virtuous of his courtiers were to be found in his brother's circle at St. James's palace." The duchess wrote English far more correctly than her English stepdaughters, Mary and Anne. She loved the society of authors, artists, and musicians, always to be found about the Stuart princes. One of her maids, Anne Kingsmill, was celebrated by Pope as Ardelia. Another, Anne Killigrew, was immortalized by Dryden in the Ode beginning with that exquisite line:

"Thou youngest virgin daughter of the skies."

The aged Waller, who had written for Cromwell and Charles II., was encouraged by this cultured princess to continue to invoke the muse. Charles II., who was not devoid of literary taste, remarked that the "Ode to Cromwell" was better than the Ode to himself, and Waller aptly rejoined: "Does not your majesty know that we poets always succeed better in fiction than in fact?" Waller presented to Mary Beatrice his poems which celebrated the beauties of a former age, and addressed to her these elegant lines:

"Thus writ we then; your brighter eyes inspire
A nobler flame, and raise our genius higher;
While we your wit and early knowledge fear,
To our productions we become severe.
Your matchless beauty gives our fancy wing —
Your judgment makes us careful how we sing:
Lines not composed as heretofore in haste,
Polished like marble, shall like marble last;
And make you through as many ages shine,
As Tasso has the heroes of your line."

Dryden, in dedicating to her his "State of Innocence," compliments her on her descent from princes immortalized more by their patronage of Tasso and Ariosto than by their heroic deeds. He assures "the radiant d'Esté" that "she is never seen without being blessed, and blesses all who see her," that "although every one feels the power of her charms, she is adored with the deepest veneration, that of silence ; for she is placed above all mortal wishes by her virtues and exalted station." The mind was well fixed on heaven that was not inflated with pride by such praises from "Glorious John" and the greatest wits of the age.

V

ENGLAND was, for the Modenese princess, a land of persecution. Before the darts of envy and calumny were aimed at herself, she suffered in her husband. A powerful party had determined to exclude the Duke of York from the throne by arraying against him the prejudices of the nation, and conspiracies and "Popish plots" became the order of the day. The hideous ravings of Titus Oates are too well known to need repetition here. Twice was the duke banished to Scotland; once he was an exile in Belgium. His devoted wife shared all his wanderings. Her bitterest enemy has not dared to accuse her of the slightest impropriety of word or deed. When she was about eighteen, the celebrated Jesuit, Colombiere, came to England as her preacher (October 15, 1676), and was domesticated with her family at St. James. This venerable priest, who may yet be raised on our altars, wrote to his brethren in France: " I serve a princess who is good in every sense, of exemplary piety, and great sweetness." Though an honored guest at the palace, Colombiere led the life of a hermit. His bed was a mattress spread upon the ground, and his fare the coarsest. He was treated so shamefully by the anti-Catholic section that he styled England "the country of crosses." He was arrested, and, at the request of the lords, banished by the king. His office to the duchess, and the fact that he had been confided to the royal hospitality, doubtless saved him from martyrdom. He returned to France in 1679, quite broken in health. He taught the devotion to the Sacred Heart, which he had learned from his spiritual daughter, Blessed Margaret Mary, to many Catholics in London, including Mary of Modena, who became the first royal petitioner for a Mass and proper office in honor of the Sacred Heart of Jesus.

The enemies of the duke and duchess were preparing to force them into exile once more, when an unlooked-for event saved them from this indignity. Their chief enemy, the infamous Titus Oates, was a welcome guest at the court of their son and daughter, William and Mary, in Holland. When King of England, William allowed Titus Oates a considerable pension.

VI

ON THE morning of February 2d, Charles II. arose, after a restless night. His health had been failing, and he no longer took his morning rambles in the park, where his loving subjects used to watch him throwing grains to his pet birds, or playing with his small spaniels — (the species is still called King Charles). The manners of the king were as polished as his morals were reprehensible, and never was a sovereign of England more sincerely beloved. While dressing, his face became ghastly, and his courtiers were appalled to see him fall. As soon as possible, the queen and the duke and duchess were on the spot. Knowing that her brother-in-law was a Catholic at heart, Mary Beatrice besought her husband to have the royal patient reconciled to the Church. The king and his brother were devotedly attached to each other, and James declared that he would hazard every peril rather than fail in his duty to one he so tenderly loved. The dying man having declined the services of the Protestant prelates, James asked if he would accept those of the Catholic Church. "Ah," he replied, " I would give anything in the world to have a priest." James offered to bring one. " For God's sake, do, brother; but will it not expose you to danger?"

" If it costs me my life I will bring one," said James. It was a capital crime to admit a proselyte to the Catholic Church, nor was it easy to find a priest suited to the perilous service. Father Huddlestone, who had saved the king's life thirty-five years before, was brought to his bedside disguised as a minister. He heard his confession, made him partaker of the blessings the Church reserves for her departing children, and withdrew as quietly as he had entered.

The king's patience in extreme pain surprised every one. Mary Beatrice said it was impossible for anyone to face death with greater composure. He was most grateful for the least service, and regretted the fatigue which etiquette imposed on the courtiers that crowded his chamber. Perhaps he is the only man who ever apologized for the length of time it took him to die. "I ought to apologize, gentlemen," he struggled to say, "for the unconscionably long time I am taking to die, but it is the last time I shall trouble you." This exquisite graciousness won him the love of his people. Even the servant girls in London put on some emblem of mourning at the death of "the merry monarch."

Mary Beatrice was so grieved for the event that made her a queen (February 6, 1685) that she was afraid to show her sorrow lest she might be accused of hypocrisy. His kindness had won her heart, and she considered the crown dearly bought by the loss of such a brother. Evelyn says that she had comported herself so decently since her arrival in England that she was universally beloved. The royal couple ascended the throne peaceably, but she took no pleasure, she said, "in the envied name of queen."

And, indeed, how could she? Her three children were buried in Westminster Abbey; she was a childless mother. The audacious Catharine Sedley, who had neither grace nor beauty, appeared to have supplanted her in her husband's affections. James II. did honestly try to reform the court. He invited the Sedley to retire. Unfortunately, men who posed as his friends encouraged the vicious connection, hoping that the courtesan's strict Protestantism (?) might even wean him from the unpopular religion. Even Lady Rochester, the king's sister-in-law, ostentatiously patronized the Sedley "for the good of the church!" The injured wife was not afraid to reproach the king: "Sir," said she, "is it possible that for the sake of one passion you would lose the merit of all your sacrifices?" Again she threatened to leave him and enter a convent. "Give me my dower," she said, with righteous indignation, "make her queen, but let me never see her more."

Influenced by his queen, and some priests and Catholic peers, James soon shook off this degrading yoke. He commanded the Sedley to leave Whitehall, but the infamous creature declared that "she was a free-born Englishwoman and would live where she pleased." She affected to regard the king's resolution as an act of persecution, and styled herself a "Protestant victim." At last she was created Countess of Dorchester and was bribed by a present of a large estate in Ireland (whose?) to withdraw. It is a coincidence that the king's great enemy, his nephew and son-in-law, William of Orange, bribed, in a similar manner, the infamous Elizabeth Villiers. This glorious, pious, and immortal prince made Villiers Countess of Orkney, and gave her valuable estates in Ireland (again, whose?). The British aristocracy is largely descended from similar additions to its ranks made by infatuated vicious monarchs.

Despite his lamentable weakness, James revered his virtuous queen and was proud of her beauty, grace, and dignity. The medals he had struck in her honor are genuine works of art. Her coronation medal represents her in flowing drapery, seated on a rock, her hair negligently bound up in a Grecian fillet, her contour of classic beauty and simplicity. The inscription is most happily chosen from the address of Eneas to Venus: "O Dea Certe" (O assuredly a goddess). James bestowed immense pains on her coronation diadem. It has been used for all succeeding queen-consorts, and is by far the most graceful crown exhibited in the Tower of London, and the richest, save that of Queen Victoria. Her ivory sceptre is surmounted by a dove of white onyx. The coronation took place in Westminster Abbey, April 23, 1685.

James II. wished to inaugurate his reign by granting liberty of conscience, and he at once liberated several thousand Catholics and Dissenters, and 1,500 Quakers. The queen performed a gracious act of mercy by releasing all the prisoners in jail throughout the realm for small debts, taking on herself the payment of every debt not exceeding five pounds.

VII

THE Duke of Monmouth, reputed son of Charles II. and an abandoned Welsh woman, accused James II. of having poisoned the late king, and other high crimes, and proclaimed himself champion of the Protestant cause. Monmouth was defeated at Sedgmoor, July 6, 1685. He was tried, found guilty, and sentenced to death, as he richly deserved, on more counts than one. He wrote to the queen, and it may be owing to her influence that the king imprudently granted him an audience. His crimes, however, were of such a nature that James, though impelled to show the base creature mercy, could not pardon him.

Most of the plots against James were hatched at The Hague by his nephew, the Prince of Orange, whose wife, his dearly loved child, joined in the conspiracy. Documentary evidence proves that Mary and Anne, subsequently queens-regnant of England, are among the basest women of history — "the elder and the younger Tullia." They never made the slightest complaint of their stepmother, who was young enough to be their companion, even in extenuation of their vile conduct towards her. William and Mary were desirous of reigning in England. Anne did not choose to be set aside for a brother. It was agreed by these conspirators that if the queen should bear a son he must be represented as spurious. A daughter might rank as a real princess. On Trinity Sunday, June 10th, ever after called by the Jacobites "White-Rose Day," the unfortunate Prince of Wales was born. Later, his sister Anne coined for him a name which had more to do with his exclusion from the throne of his ancestors than any other circumstance, "The Pretender."

"The charge respecting a spurious heir," writes Sir James Mackintosh, "was one of the most flagrant wrongs ever done to a sovereign or father. The son of James II. was, perhaps, the only prince in Europe of whose blood there could be no rational doubt, considering the verification of his birth, and the unimpeachable life of his mother." Yet William of Orange gave, as one of his reasons for invading England, "to cause inquiry to be made by Parliament into the birth of a supposed Prince of Wales"—an inquiry never made. William III. afterwards offered to adopt the unfortunate prince as his heir!

The most friendly relations had always existed between the calumniators and the king and queen. The king announced the birth of "the child of prayers and vows" to William in a letter indorsed: "For my son, the Prince of Orange." The queen addressed Mary by her pet name, "My Dear Lemon." Neither the king nor queen seem to notice the coarse, vulgar libels and indecent lampoons that issued from the Dutch press, nor could they be taught to suspect treachery in their "Orange and Lemon" till it came on them as a fact. The birth of the poor child:

"The young blooming flower of the auld royal tree,"

regarded by James as the most auspicious event of his life, precipitated his ruin.

VIII

NO CHARACTER in history has been more reviled or misunderstood — not even his great-grandmother, Mary Stuart — than James II. Even in Catholic Ireland, the name of this unlucky prince, who renounced for the Catholic faith three crowns and an empire on which the sun sets not, is held in execration. As one stands to-day by the Boyne water, in a region of romantic beauty, beneath the shadow of the lying obelisk that marks the bloody field, the peasant will scornfully point to the hill of Donore, on which James II. stood, to watch the combat he did not share, and the road he took to flee from danger before the battle was over. Yet of this prince the great Turenne had said: " He knew not fear." He had to the full the courage of his convictions, and made heroic sacrifices to preserve the faith to his descendants.

We will not say "every school-boy knows," for school boys *à la Macaulay* we have not found to be common. But it is pretty well known that the early career of Charles II. was most stirring and romantic. It is not, however, equally well known that his unfortunate brother's early story is almost equally picturesque and dramatic. He was born at St. James Palace, 1633, and baptized by Archbishop Laud. He was the favorite son of his parents, Charles I. and Henrietta Maria, and was especially beloved by every member of his family. When a mere child he took part in the troubles of his parents, and at the age of nine marched to battle at his father's side, and beheld war's alarms with the cool demeanor of a veteran. Four years later he was imprisoned by the Parliamentarians, and Cromwell, who visited the brave and beautiful boy, knelt and kissed his hand. His escape from the enemies of his house and his adventures as a soldier of fortune would afford matter for a stirring drama.

Unless his early portraits belie him, James, like his parents, was remarkably handsome, and bore much resemblance to his great-grandmother, Mary Stuart. In this respect he was a marked contrast to his swarthy brother, Charles II. He was better educated than princes commonly are, spoke and wrote several languages, and had much talent as an engineer. He was one of the greatest naval warriors his country has produced, and the ablest financier of his age.

When about twenty-seven he married Anne Hyde, maid of honor to his sister Mary. This princess suborned false witnesses against the bride; her own father, Clarendon, proposed she should be sent to the Tower and beheaded (!) for her presumption in marrying the heir of Charles II. But James, when convinced of her innocence, treated her as his wife. It was of the children born of this impolitic marriage that he said in his deepest distress: "God help me! My own children forsake me!" Anne Hyde became a Catholic toward the close of her life. She gave her reasons in a long letter to her father, entitled: "Declaration of the Duchess of York to the Earl of Clarendon."

James followed her example, and this is the head and front of all his offending. As lord high admiral he showed proficiency in every branch of naval science. June 3, 1665, the fleet under his command gained the greatest naval victory ever gained by England. Nor was this the only time he conquered the Dutch, and caused the "meteor flag" to be respected. This year the plague broke out. On September 2, 1666, the great fire began; it lasted four days. Charles II. and his brother worked energetically to stop its ravages, and owing to their energy Westminster Abbey, the Tower, and other public buildings were saved.

James encouraged the people to keep up their ancient sports. The old May-pole, around which the Londoners had been accustomed to gambol in the days of his Tudor and Stuart ancestors, had been taken down by Cromwell's Parliament. James erected a new one, 134 feet high, in front of St. Mary's Church on the Strand, and watched with delight the dancers in motley attire frisking about the graceful column to the music of trumpet, pipe, and tabor, the crowds shouting themselves hoarse in frantic glee, to show their loyalty. He established colonies in America, India, and Africa. The Empire State, and the largest city in America are named from him — New York.

The Duke's success, so gratifying to national pride, made him the idol of the people. But when he became a Catholic his popularity vanished. The hosannas of to-day became "crucify him" to-morrow. On account of the extreme bigotry of the people, stirred up by evil men, this change of the right hand of the Most High, was as a sin unto death which his countrymen never forgave, and for the pardon of which they said in deed, if not in word, "Let not any man ask."

As heir-presumptive, it was necessary that he should marry. His choice fell on a private gentlewoman, but Charles II. would not hear of such a connection. "It would be intolerable," said he, "that you should make a fool of yourself a second time." James was still one of the most elegant gentlemen in Europe. Two years after the death of Anne Hyde, the Earl of Peterboro brought his royal highness the most beautiful princess of Europe, from the ducal court of Modena, and Mary Beatrice became the unwilling bride of a prince twenty-five years her senior.

PART II

IX

THE treachery of his own kith and kin was greater than James or his consort ever knew. Long after they had passed away, the letters of his daughter to her sister in Holland came to light. Of this precious pair and their husbands, Anne and George of Denmark were lowest in the intellectual scale. "I have tried him drunk and I have tried him sober," said Charles II., "and I never could find anything in him." When George heard a piece of news he used to say: "Est-il possible?" On his desertion to the Orange standard, King James exclaimed: "What? Est-il-possible, gone? In truth, a good trooper would be a greater loss." The king was mistaken. As husband of Anne, George had some importance at this crisis. James might have known that George would not have gone had it not been Anne's intention to follow.

Anne was but a tool in the hands of her favorite, Lady Churchill. Her letters to her sisters at this epoch are among the vilest that ever emanated from a female pen. That Mary and her husband encouraged her to write such letters is an indelible stain on their characters. They loathed the writer though they profited by her treachery, which was no worse than their own. A fierce Scotchman mercilessly satirized the base quartet:

"There's Mary the daughter and Willy the cheater,
There's Geordie the drinker and Annie the eater."

William did not enter Whitehall till his wife had first domesticated herself there. By this and in other ways he endeavored to throw the odium of the disgraceful doings he had encouraged, if not inspired, on the daughters of his uncle, Mary and Anne.

December 9, 1688, the last Catholic queen of England fled from its inhospitable shores, disguised as a washerwoman, and bearing in her trembling arms, as a bundle of clothes, her son, "the dearest gift of heaven." The agitated king confided mother and babe to Count Lauzan, to convey them to France. The party escaped through the gardens of Whitehall, and crossed the swollen Thames in a frail boat, at the peril of their lives. Their coach was at a neighboring inn and it took some time to fetch it. For about an hour the poor queen with her precious babe stood under the walls of the old church at Lambeth, in an agony of suspense. No other shelter was to be found in this bleak neighborhood from the fierce wind and the bitter cold. Quite recently we stood on the same spot, and thought of the beautiful mother and the babe sleeping peaceably in her arms, unconscious of his woes. Sixteen years before, she had come into England in regal splendor, the virgin-bride of York's great admiral. Now she was retracing her steps in misery and terror.

James had sent a yacht manned by three Irish captains, to bear his treasures to the French coast. Years after, she described this as a most doleful journey, and wondered how she had lived through it. They reached France December 11th. The unfortunate husband, whose action at this crisis was like the action of a maniac, speedily followed. Between the agony caused by the shameless desertion of him by his own children, and the hemorrhages that nearly terminated his existence, his intellect was undoubtedly disordered and the victory gained over him by " his son, the Prince of Orange," was the basest triumph ever won by a man.

On the historic spot on which the saintly queen, with streaming eyes and broken heart, looked her last upon the great city in which she had been crowned and anointed queen,

" Sad memory brings the light of other days around us."

All the actors in the mournful drama have long since moldered into dust. But the historian, albeit he possesses not the wand of a magician, can summon them, every one, from the misty past, and hear them speak, and see them act their respective parts, whether mean or dignified, or simply indifferent. And having weighed in a balance their words and deeds, who would not rather have been the lone queen, with pure hands and stainless conscience, fleeing in the dead of the night before her implacable enemies, than either of her triumphant stepdaughters who purchased exaltation at so awful a price?

393

X

BY ORDER of Louis XIV., the most courteous attentions were lavished on the exile queen. But nothing could comfort her while she was uncertain as to the safety of James. Her joy was perfect when he joined her, after many painful adventures. From the moment he uttered the sorrowful plaint, "God help me! My own children forsake me!" his actions were strange, and his speech rambling and incoherent. His greatest mistake was to leave his kingdom without striking a blow. Had he made such a stand as he would have made thirty years earlier, his descendants might still occupy the throne of England. But the period of action for him had begun when he was a child, and he was prematurely worn out, though but fifty-seven years old. Besides, the conduct of his nearest relatives had shattered his brain, and made him powerless to resist. Alluding to the pathetic circumstances of the unfortunate king, a modern poet says:

> " We thought of ancient Lear with tempest overhead:
> Discrowned, betrayed, abandoned — but nought could break his will,
> Not Mary, his false Regan — nor Anne, his Goneril."

But the will of the modern Lear was broken and his power to recuperate annihilated by the treachery of his Regan and Goneril. He was now no match for the foreign prince who withstood him with an army of deserters and foreigners.

The grand castle of St. Germain's was placed at the disposal of the royal exiles and here they lived in peace and happiness, always hoping to regain their rights. The news from England was not cheering. Catholic Churches were fired. The baby prince was burned in effigy. Into our own time, on days dedicated to the small hero of Nassau, the Pretender and the Pope have gone to the stake together. " Even political expediency," says Mazare, " should not be suffered to outrage nature." But nature was outraged in a hundred ways by the unnatural sisters of the baby prince.

The medals of the dual reign of William and Mary beneath criticism as works of art, caricature the child whose unwelcome appearance was to deprive his ambitious sisters and brother of the reversion of a triple diadem : nor is his helpless father spared. In the numismatic collection of this period is a medal which represents James II. moving with giant strides, flinging aside his crown and sceptre, a Jesuit pushing onward with him ; the king carries his babe — another proof that the designer knew the child was his — the motto, profanely taken from the liturgy, is " Ite, Missa Est."

James made many efforts to recover his crown. In 1690 his lieutenant in Ireland reminded him that Ireland still held out for him. To-day the peasants will show the routes of the armies that battled on his account. Only for the Boyne combat, James would have retained the sympathy and esteem of his Irish subjects. But cowardice is a vice which Hibernians will not condone. And to those who knew not his inner story, and the difficulties of a seaman fighting on land, the conduct of England's greatest admiral on that occasion seems inexcusable. In modern warfare one does not see the head of the navy leading an army to victory, nor would the general of an army be selected to command a fleet.

Close to the famous battlefield is " King William's Glen," a wild region covered with the largest and most beautiful ferns we ever saw. An ancient peasant pointed out to us the plan of the battle. He said that the plough and the spade had often turned up ghastly memorials of the ill-fated day, as skulls and bones, and that when he was a boy spurs and broken weapons gathered here were preserved as curiosities by some neighboring families. Of poor James the Unlucky, he spoke with loathing, and repeated the story of the Irish crying out: "Change kings and we'll fight the battle over again." Another old man said that James checked the ardor of his soldiers by exclaiming: "O do not make my daughter a widow!" Had James remained in France, or even in Dublin, his men would have won the day.

(Near Aughrim is the "Bridge of a Thousand Heads," and the field called, in the expressive Irish tongue, "The Cry of the Heart." The peasants still speak of the Jacobite wars, and say that a thousand heads fell defending the bridge, and when the armies had moved on, and the women came to look for the bodies of their kin, their shrieks were such as to give that sad name to the historic field. Aughrim Castle is to-day little better than a huge moss-grown ruin. Aughrim is now an inconsiderable village on the carriage road between

Ballinasloe and Loughrea. Many curious details are preserved in contemporary ballad, " The Lass of Augh-rim.")

The king died the death of a saint in 1701. His youngest and fairest child, Princess Louisa Stuart, born 1691, cheered his declining years. The conjugal tenderness of his devoted wife never abated. She was still one of the loveliest women in Europe, and retained to the last the graceful, sylph-like form, which made her a contrast to the portly Anne Hyde. Her wit and regnal talents were acknowledged in France, where she became immensely popular. Madame de Sevigné, granddaughter of St. Jane Frances de Chantal, who was, next to the great Louis himself, the acutest observer at the French court, has not words to describe the beauty, dignity, and grace of the English queen. " Every one," she writes, " is much pleased with this queen, she has so much wit. On seeing Louis XIV. caressing the Prince of Wales, who is very beautiful, she said : ' I had envied the happiness of my son in being unconscious of his misfortunes, but now I regret the unconsciousness which prevents him from being sensible of your majesty's goodness.' Everything she says is full of good sense." The fastidious Louis XIV. regarded her as a model of regal grace, praised her beauty, her manner, her wit, her perfect devotion to her husband, and pointing her out to his German daughter-in-law, La Grande Dauphine, significantly said : "See what a queen ought to be." He envied James the treasure he possessed in her. Her virtue made him revere her. " She was a queen in her prosperity," he said, "but in her adversity she is an angel." No woman of history has been more traduced, but she never uttered an evil word of her husband's daughters and nephew. When their crimes were mentioned in her presence she would say: "As we cannot praise them, we will not speak of them, since it only excites irritation, and gives rise to feelings that cannot be pleasing to God." Those who knew her intimately described her conduct and deportment as saintly.

XI

MEANWHILE, how fared the triumphant faction? William and Mary did not live happily together. Like many another wife, the more shamefully her husband treated her, the more devoted she was to his interests, which were, indeed, her own. Her letters to him are love letters, but whether she felt genuine affection for so coarse and rude a prince may be doubted. She yielded to him her place in the succession, but without him she could not have been queen. The slights he put upon her through at least two of the Villiers's sisters were such as no woman could easily forget or forgive. That her intellect was above the average her letters and her administration in her husband's absence show. The possibility, and sometimes probability that her father would be restored disturbed her peace. The people were fearfully taxed. Trade and commerce declined. The military sovereign seemed to regard his people merely as " food for powder." He was always fighting, but scarcely ever gained a victory.

In the absence of this unlucky warrior Mary conducted the affairs of state with marked ability, but she
was severe rather than merciful.   Authors, artists, and
musicians became very scarce at court.   Dryden, the
greatest literary man of the age, was dismissed from the
laureateship, which she bestowed on the wretched
rhymster, Shadwell.   The revolutionary sovereigns
showed much enmity towards Dryden, which "Glorious John" cordially reciprocated.   When his publisher,
Jacob Tronson, put the head of William in the character of the pious Eneas, for a frontispiece to the transla-
tion of Virgil, the irate poet wrote:

> "Old Jacob, in his wondrous mood,
>   To please the wise beholders,
> Has placed old Nassau's hook-nosed head
>   On wise Eneas's shoulders.

> "To make the parallel hold tack,
>   Methinks there's something lacking,
> One took his father pick-a-back;
>   The other sent his a-packing."

Day after day Queen Mary sat among her courtiers
knitting thread fringes — a curious occupation for the
majesty of England, which the London wits did not
overlook.   Sir Charles Sedley wrote:

> "O happy people, ye must thrive,
> While thus the royal pair do strive,
>   Both to advance your glory;
> While he, by valor, conquers France,
> She manufactures does advance,
>   And makes thread fringes for ye.

"Blest we who from such queens are freed,
　Who by vain superstition led,
　　Are always telling beads;
But here's a queen, now thanks to God,
Who when she rides in coach abroad,
　　Is always knitting threads.

"Then haste, victorious Nassau, haste,
　And when thy summer show is past,
　　Let all thy trumpets sound.
The fringe which this campaign has wrought,
Though it cost the nation but a groat,
　　Thy conquests will surround."

Sedley's infamous daughter said to Queen Mary: "I have not sinned more grievously against the seventh commandment than you have against your father in breaking the fifth." Archbishop Sancroft refused to crown her, and when she asked his blessing said: "Get your father's blessing first; without that mine would be of no avail."

Mary spent her life as queen at enmity with her sister, Anne. She died of smallpox, December 28, 1696, in the thirty-third year of her age, and the sixth of her reign. From over-indulgence in eating—her enemies add, in drinking—she had grown to an immense size, and the contrast was ludicrous when she appeared abroad with her short, lean, shriveled husband. Their wax figures, preserved in a glazed case at Westminster Abbey, show the queen as very tall; William, though perched on a stool, is a dwarf in comparison. Mary left a letter reproaching him with the iniquity of his conduct toward her during their whole married life, and asked the Archbishop of Canterbury to reprove him. He took the reproof well, and saw Elizabeth Villiers no more — in England. Holland was their future rendezvous.

Like Mary, William died at enmity with all his relatives. Full of plans against the peace of Europe, he sent his favorite Keppel to bring him news as to how matters stood for new campaigns. He was almost dead when Keppel returned, and, for the first time, martial tidings awoke no interest in him. "Je tire vers ma fin" (I draw towards my end), said he. Neither Anne nor her husband was allowed to approach him. A black ribbon which bound his wrist was found to contain Queen Mary's hair.

Though head of the church and defender of the faith, it is doubtful if William was even baptized. The same is said of Archbishop Tillotson. A squib of the day says:

> " That schismatical primate and Hollander king
> Are still in the want of a christening."

The actions of this prince should consign him to the Gehenna of history. The burning of the sick soldiers at Waterford, the violation of the Treaty of Limerick, the massacre of Glencoe, flogging in the army, the pocketing of the revenues of Anne and her son, the creating of informers by awards of blood money — these are but a few. Perhaps the greatest evil he did was to encourage the distillation of ardent spirits. Had he possessed the virtues of St. Louis, they would have been neutralized by his love for whisky and his efforts to promote the same among his unfortunate people. It was against the law to change malt into spirits, save a small quantity for medical purposes. William had this beneficent law repealed. By word and example, he encouraged the use of fire water. He went frequently to the House of Lords to recommend its manufacture, as may be seen by the journals of that house. Gin palaces were opened for the sale of ardent spirits, heretofore sold only in drug stores. Miss Strickland writes truly: " Most of the crime and sorrow of the present day, and, indeed, the greatest national misfortune that ever befell this country (England) originated from the example of William III. and his Dutch courtiers, as imbibers of ardent spirits." Unfortunately, this vice exists more or less wherever the English language is spoken, and is the curse, the disgrace of our boasted civilization. "William's personal tastes and his desire to induce the consumption of a taxable article, were the causes of his conduct." Macaulay's hero is one of the most unfortunate characters in history. Drunkenness, murders, bribes are connected with him. Even the " Peep-o'-Day Boys " of the last century who swore to wade knee-deep in Papist blood, who defiled themselves by every crime the divine law forbids, and whose evil deeds are a blot upon our own day, could find no more appropriate patron than the peevish warrior of Nassau, and no better name to express the frightful objects of their confederacy than — Orangemen.

XII

IF GOD allowed James II. to be deprived of his kingdoms, He gave him better gifts. Henceforth he led the life of a saint. Often did he thank God for the loss of his triple crowns — he had only to change his religion to recover them — but his heart was set on a heavenly kingdom.

March 4, 1701, while in the chapel of St. Germain's, the aged king was deeply affected by the anthem: "Remember, O Lord! what has come upon us. Consider and behold our reproach ; our inheritance is turned to strangers, our houses to aliens." These touching words overcame him. He was attacked by sanguineous apoplexy, and carried from the church. "I suffer more than he does," wrote his faithful wife, "in anticipation of greater sufferings for him." He was no longer able to walk without the support of her arm. In September he passed away, with so high a reputation for sanctity that his canonization was spoken of, and it was said that miracles were wrought at his bier.

To his son he gave excellent advice. His words to his lovely daughter whom he called "La Consolatrice," are singularly beautiful:

"Adieu, child. Serve your Creator in the days of your youth. Consider virtue as the great ornament of your sex. Follow closely after that great pattern of it, your mother, who has been, no less than myself, overclouded with calumnies ; but Time, the mother of Truth, will, I hope, at last make her virtues shine as bright as the sun " — a hope splendidly verified.

James desired to be buried in Westminster, at the restoration of his family, but the sceptre had passed away from the royal Stuarts. His body remained unburied at the Benedictine Church, Paris, and was reverenced at the height of the Revolution, when the ashes of the French monarchs were scattered to the wind. In 1813, he was buried in the Parish Church of Germain's. Quite recently, the writer sought the spot where the remains of the last Catholic king of England repose. A modest monument of black and white marble records his name and rank, in Latin.

An Irish gentleman, Mr. Fitzsimmons, who was imprisoned in the Benedictine Convent in the Reign of Terror, writes, in *Notes and Queries:* "In 1794 the embalmed body of James II. was in one of the chapels awaiting interment in Westminster Abbey. It was in a wooden coffin enclosed in a leaden one, and that again in one covered with black velvet. The corpse was very beautiful and perfect; the hair and nails were very fine. I never saw so fine a set of teeth in my life. A young lady, a fellow prisoner, wished much to have a tooth. I tried to get one for her, but could not, they were so firmly fixed. The feet also were beautiful. The face and cheeks were just as if he were alive. I rolled his eyes and the eyeballs were perfectly firm under my fingers. Around the chapel were several wax molds, made probably at the time of the king's death; the corpse was very like them."

To this bier poor Mary Beatrice made many a pilgrimage during the 16 years she survived her "sainted king."

Anne succeeded William in 1702, but not for her own happiness. On the death of her son, in 1700, she had promised her father to do justice to her brother, but justice was never done the unfortunate prince. Though mother of eighteen children, she was childless, and her exaltation only made her, as she pathetically said, "a crowned slave." Her last hours were disturbed by visions of that hapless brother whom she had irreparably injured, and she continually moaned: "O, my brother, my poor brother, what will become of you now?" These were her last words.

Mary Beatrice, who but for her children would have taken the veil at the Visitation Convent, Chaillot, closed her life by a holy death, May 7, 1718. Her beautiful daughter, Louise Stuart, preceded her to the tomb. The Stuart cause was never more prosperous than when managed by the royal widow—a regent without a realm. Her eloquence brought the French princes and Madame de Maintenon to her side. Through reverent love for her, the Grand Monarch, whose generosity and delicate courtesy to the fallen Stuarts half redeem him, allowed her son to be proclaimed James III., King of Great Britain, Ireland, and even France, at the gates of the Chateau of St. Germains.

XIII

THE STUART dynasty was singularly gifted and singularly unfortunate. Its graceful princes, liberal patrons of art, literature, and music, were frank, courteous, and gay with their loving lieges, and their charming manners covered many faults. They were peace-loving sovereigns, and never needlessly embroiled their subjects in foreign wars. History, which records their ill deeds with merciless fidelity, has too little to say of their generosity and kindness. The fallen Stuarts evoked the last genuine loyalty the world has seen. Whole families accompanied them into exile. Nobles from Great Britain and Ireland surrounded the car of the vanquished. The personal attendants of the queen followed her, though their fidelity meant outlawry and the confiscation of their estates. The cause, always a losing or a lost one, inspired poets, and Jacobite songs inferior only to Moore's Melodies are still sung with enthusiasm. Under foreign military sovereigns who had no sympathy with the people, many fondly turned to "the king over the water." Under various types and figures they besought him to "come hame." The ill-favored king, who, unlike the Stuarts, " hated boetry and bainting," was satirized as " The wee, wee German Lairdie." Rhymsters bewailed in bold doggerel the evil consequences of James Stuart's act when he "gave his daughter to an Oranger." Charles Edward succeeded his father in the love of the Jacobites, and many a song that now obsolete deity, " the muse," inspired for him : " What's a' the steer, Kimmer?" " Come over the stream, Charlie, dear Charlie, brave Charlie," " O gin I were a Bonnie Bird," " Welcome, Royal Charlie," " Wha wadna fecht for Charlie?"

When the butchery of Culloden extinguished the Stuart hopes, the poet mourns over the dashing hero, Charles Edward, in many an exquisite strain :

> "A wee bird cam' to our ha' door,
> He warbled sweet and clearly,
> And aye the out-come o' his song,
> Was ' Wae's me for Prince Charlie!'"

These poets sang as the wild bird sings. The success and misfortunes of the Stuarts inspired more ballads than those of any other dynasty the world ever saw. Words touched by the alchemy of genius trilled in ravishing notes, and awaken enthusiasm to-day by their impassioned love pleadings.

The contempt of the Irish peasantry for James II. was not transferred to his son or grandson. By the hillside and by the streams, "the king" was invited home in pathetic verse. The genuine merit of some of these effusions has won lasting fame. " The Royal Blackbird" is still warbled by the Irish peasant to a tune rich and wild as the native wood-notes of the king of song-birds. "Adieu Forevermore," and many kindred songs make us regret that the song-writers of our day lack the inspiration of the Carolans, the Connellans, and the other " Wandering Willies" of the Jacobite era.

The exiled Stuart race, which renounced so much for the Catholic religion, ended, appropriately, in a priest, Cardinal York,* the titular Henry IX., who died

---

* George III. bestowed a pension of £5,000 a year on Cardinal York, which was badly needed, as the Cardinal's bishopric, Frascati, had been ravaged by the wars early in the present century.

in 1808. After 1688, the Stuart titular kings nominated the Catholic bishops of Ireland, though this was not generally known. In St. Peter's, Rome, near the great entrance, is the Stuart monument, by Canova, on which the elder and younger pretenders (?) and Cardinal York, are commemorated respectively as James III., Charles Edward, and Henry IX., Kings of England, Ireland, Scotland, and France. Opposite is the tomb of Mary Clementine, of Poland, granddaughter of the great Sobieski, wife of the Pretender (?) James III., and mother of "Bonnie Prince Charlie" and Henry IX. Her monument, surmounted by a half length portrait of Her Majesty, commemorates her as Queen of Great Britain, Ireland, and France. Except James I. and Charles I., all the Stuart sovereigns were Catholics. Henry Stuart, Cardinal York, grandson of Mary Beatrice and James II., a kind and gentle prince, died Bishop of Frascati. And so the most picturesque and romantic of dynasties passed away forever and became only a sad and touching memory.

An enormous sum, counting principal and interest, was due the Cardinal from the money voted by Parliament for his grandmother, Queen Mary Beatrice, most of which was never paid, though he made many efforts to recover it. Cardinal York returned to the English king some of the crown jewels which he inherited from James II., through his father, James III., the so-called Pretender.